"Simp ... nestly addressing the brutal hardships of the western migration."

—*Publishers Weekly* (starred review)

"Carson is known for her world-building and strong female characters and she handles everything with carefully constructed, well-researched aplomb. . . . Illuminates an important segment of American history . . . sustaining YA interest through adventure, fantasy, and romance."

—*Booklist* (starred review)

"Heartfelt and exciting, grueling and wise, *Walk on Earth a Stranger* is an invigorating addition to the fantasy genre."

—*Hypable*

"Pure storytelling gold."

—*The Daily Summit*

"An empowering and powerful read perfect for one who enjoys history and adventure."

—*Romantic Times Bookclub*

"A celebration of great courage, the ability of people to come together as family, and the healing power of love. . . . Exciting, sweet, and satisfying."

—*Booklist*

"An *Oceans 11*-esque climax that . . . sees romantic satisfaction for many of the trilogy's long-suffering characters leads to a well-earned, if rosy-hued, conclusion."

—*The Horn Book*

# INTO the BRIGHT UNKNOWN

RAE CARSON

*Greenwillow Books*
*An Imprint of* HarperCollins*Publishers*

This book is a work of fiction. References to real people, events, establishments, organizations, or locales are intended only to provide a sense of authenticity, and are used to advance the fictional narrative. All other characters, and all incidents and dialogue, are drawn from the author's imagination and are not to be construed as real.


First published in hardcover in 2017 by Greenwillow Books;
first paperback publication, 2018.

 For information address HarperCollins Children's Books, a division of HarperCollins Publishers, 195 Broadway, New York, NY 10007.
www.epicreads.com

The text of this book is set in 11-point Hoefler.
Book design by Paul Zakris

Library of Congress Control Number: 2017951925

ISBN 978-0-06-224297-6 (trade ed.)—ISBN 978-0-06-224298-3 (pbk.)

18 19 20 21 22 PC/LSCH 10 9 8 7 6 5 4 3 2 1

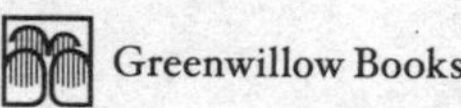

*For my husband,*
*who came with me on this long journey*

# *Dramatis Personae*

Leah "Lee" Westfall, a sixteen-year-old girl

Jefferson Kingfisher, Lee's fiancé

The Joyners

Rebekah "Becky" Joyner, a widow from Tennessee

Olive Joyner, her seven-year-old daughter

Andrew Joyner Jr., her five-year-old son

Baby Girl Joyner, an infant

The Glory, California Crew

"Major" Wally Craven, former wagon train leader

Hampton Freeman, formerly Bledsoe

Mary, Lee's friend

Old Tug and the Buckeyes, miners from Ohio

Wilhelm, a hired thug turned blacksmith

The Illinois College Men

Jasper Clapp, a doctor

Thomas Bigler, a lawyer

Henry Meek, currently seeking employment

Others, in San Francisco

James Henry Hardwick, a wealthy businessman

Miss Helena Russell, an associate of Hardwick's

Jim Boisclair, a former store owner from Dahlonega, Georgia

"Mr. Keys," Hardwick's accountant

Frank Dilley, a hired gun

Sheriff Purcell

Sonia, a pickpocket

Billy, a young orphan and thief

Melancthon Jones, a ship's carpenter and cook

# Late January 1850

# Chapter One

The log cabin I share with the Joyner family is murky and dank, with a packed dirt floor that moistens to near mud at the base of the walls. But it has a solid roof, a cozy box stove, and—best of all—a single bright east-facing window with a real glass pane. Real glass! It's such a rarity since coming west to California, but our claims have proved out so well that we can afford a few luxuries.

I work hard each day and fall into my bedroll exhausted but happy. Usually, I'm awakened by Zeus, Becky Joyner's proud rooster, who trumpets every single dawn like it's going to be the best day of his life. Sometimes I don't wake until the first light of morning shines through that window, warming my cheeks and eyelids.

And every great once in a while, I'm so late abed that Becky or one of the children must intervene.

"Miss Leah Westfall, you get up right this minute, or I'm going to pour the wash bucket onto your face."

A skirted shape looms over me, backlit by the light of the window. Her hands are on her hips, her head cocked to the side. I groan and rub my eyes. "Becky?"

"Pull on your boots and a coat and come help me. Quick."

Obeying Becky is such a habit that I'm sitting up and reaching for my boots before her words sink in. "Something wrong?" I ask.

"Just got news the peddler is coming. Any miner within fifty miles square is showing up this morning, and a few Indians besides. Every seat is full. We'll probably run out of food, but we can keep everyone full up on coffee."

Becky is a terrible cook, but that hasn't stopped her tavern business from booming. People come from all over to experience the "bad food, bad service" of the Worst Tavern in California. Or so they say. I expect the real reason they travel so far and spend so much gold is that our town of Glory now boasts a few female residents. Becky suffers at least one marriage proposal per day. Mary, her hired waitress, gets several per week. Even I get my fair share, in spite of the fact that I'm already affianced to the best fellow in all of California.

Thinking of Mary puts a puts a nervous hitch in my breath. I've been meaning to talk to her about something important—about the *real* reason for Glory's prosperity—but I keep finding excuses to delay: Knowing the truth might put Mary in danger. Knowing the truth might chase her away. Knowing the truth might make her stay, but for all the wrong reasons.

I've been putting if off for weeks, ever since we escaped

Uncle Hiram's mine together. I just need to gather my gumption and get it done.

"I'll see you outside," Becky says, and she leaves.

I lace up my boots, splash icy water on my face, and wrap a scarf around my neck. I'm still wearing yesterday's skirt of soft yellow calico, a parting gift from a friend who left for Oregon territory. If Mama were alive, she'd box my ears to see me wearing my everyday skirt to bed.

My hand goes to the golden locket dangling at my throat, like it does every morning. It's my last keepsake from Mama; I took it from her still-warm body right after she was murdered, and it traveled all the way across the continent with me.

And as I clutch the locket in my palm, letting the precious metal invade *all* my senses, I realize that Mama would have been fine about the skirt. She was smart and practical, and she would have understood that things are different in California.

I pull on my coat, push open the door, and step into the brisk morning.

It's a clear, bright day, perfect for prospecting. Frost surrounds the stoop, covers the canvas roofs of the nearby shanties, even edges our big muddy pond at the end of town. The sun is just now peeking over the oak and pines, turning all that frost into glittering diamonds. Shanties and lean-tos and tents hug the slope of our hill, all the way down to the muddy field and paddock. The structures don't look like much from the outside, but one tent houses Jasper, a doctor; another has Wilhelm, a blacksmith; and still another a leather worker.

Glory is a right and proper town now, as fine a town as any I've lived in, with even finer people.

To my left is the Worst Tavern, full up on folks sitting at long tables beneath an enormous, thrice-patched awning. Mostly miners, a few Indians. Two woodstoves keep everyone in steady biscuits and provide extra warmth—the seats nearest the stoves are always first to fill. Becky works a griddle, flipping flapjacks and bacon. Her daughter, seven-year-old Olive, is at the other stove, using tongs to lift biscuits into a basket. Mary, Glory's only current Chinese resident, is scurrying back and forth between the stoves and the tables, delivering food, filling coffee cups, growling at customers.

When she sees me, she gives me a relieved smile.

"What can I do?" I ask.

"Coffee. Here, take this." She shoves the pot into my hands. "Olive's got a second pot brewing on the stove for when that's empty. Sure hope that peddler brings another one. We'll need three pots going at once by the end of the month."

I start at the nearest table and fill all the cups to three quarters full. Mary grabs dirty plates and heads toward the wash station. One of the miners, a grizzled fellow with a big bald spot dead center on his scalp, reaches up with grasping fingers for Mary's backside.

Mary whirls and—quick as a viper—whips out a handkerchief and snaps it at him.

The grizzled man snatches his hand back. "I was just being friendly!"

"Be friendly without using your hands," Mary says.

The man frowns. "You ask me, this tavern ought to be called Uppity Women."

Mary grins. "Thank you for the compliment, sir."

He squints. Before he can suss it out, I step forward with my pot. "Hot coffee, sir?"

"Don't mind if I do!" he says, Mary forgotten.

This is how it is most days at the Worst Tavern. Becky and Olive and Mary work themselves ragged to feed hungry miners, making mountains of biscuits, flapjacks, scrambled eggs, and bacon, cleaning dish after dish, all while avoiding the wandering hands of fellows who think coming to California means they no longer have to act like gentlemen. Sometimes I help out, but most days I'm out in the goldfields, working my own claim or helping my friends with theirs.

I return to the stove for more coffee, just as Mary comes back for more biscuits. "I need to talk to you," I whisper to her. "Just as soon as the morning rush is over."

She hefts the plate of biscuits with one hand and wipes her brow with the other. "Sure, Lee," she says, and she's off.

Becky leans over. "You're going to tell her?" she whispers.

"Yep."

Becky's brow furrows. "You sure you can trust the girl? She's young and . . ." Her voice trails off.

And Chinese? And foreign? I'm not sure what it is Becky won't say, and I keep my face smooth with some effort.

"She deserves the truth, Becky," I say firmly.

Becky turns away, scrambling her eggs a little too violently.

"She helped me destroy Hiram's Gulch, remember? We

wouldn't have escaped without her. I can't begin to guess how many lives she saved. Besides, she's been working here for a month. In all that time, she's earned for you three times what you pay her, without once complaining. I trust her, and so should you."

I'm preaching to myself as much as Becky, I suppose. I trust Mary. I do. It's just that my secret is such a big one, and so many people have been hurt because of it.

"What does Jefferson say?" Becky says. "He's going to be your husband; it's only proper you consult him."

"Jeff trusts her. He says it's up to me whether I tell her or not."

She shovels eggs onto a plate just in time for Mary to dash by and sweep it up. "If you think it's best," Becky says.

The morning passes quickly. Miners only linger if they had too much to drink the night before; otherwise, they're up and away to their claims as soon as possible. Everyone knows the easy diggings will be gone soon, and there's no time to spare.

A final wave of hungry miners heads our way, and I look up, hoping to see Jefferson, but it's just Old Tug and his Buckeyes from Ohio. Jefferson must be at his claim already. With our wedding coming up, he's keen to build his stake.

"Morning, gentlemen," I call out as Tug and his men find seats. "Coffee?"

Tug wipes at bleary eyes. "Please, Miss Leah."

"Hard night, huh?" I ask, filling his cup.

He grins through wiry whiskers, showing all two of his teeth. "Won two gold eagles playing cards," he says.

"Congratulations."

"Two gold eagles makes me mighty eligible, don't you think? High time I found a Mrs. Tuggle."

*Not this again.*

"It's a pity I'm already affianced," I tell him solemnly.

"Oh, not you," he says with a wave of his hand. "Got my eye on that little China girl." And sure enough, his gaze follows Mary as she heaps bacon onto plates and wipes up spills with her handkerchief.

I sigh. Poor Mary.

"You think she'll have me?" he asks.

"I doubt it," I say.

His eye widen with affront. "Ain't nothing wrong with me!"

"Course not. But Mary is one of the handsomest girls I ever saw. Also, she's a woman of intelligence and learning. Did you know she speaks three languages?"

He shakes his head.

"So, I suggest that instead of proposing straight out, you court her. Woo her. Show her what a fine gentleman you are."

"You think so?"

"I do." That will give me time to warn my friend. Old Tug has asked every woman he's met to marry him, starting with Becky Joyner and then me.

"I reckon you might be right," he concedes. "I don't want to mess this one up."

I give his shoulder a pat and move on to the next table.

The Buckeyes eat quickly, but unlike most customers, they scoot their chairs and benches in and take their dishes to the wash station themselves. They tip their hats at Mary, who is elbow deep in the washtub. Old Tug lingers. "Have a fine day, Miss Mary," he says, with the most earnest, hopeful gaze I ever saw on a fellow.

She looks up from her dishwashing and smiles. "Thank you, Mr. Tuggle. You too."

After they leave, Mary turns to Becky. "All right if I steal away with Lee for a spell? She needs me. I'll be back to finish the dishes; I won't shirk."

Becky stops scraping the griddle just long enough to give a wave of permission.

Mary grabs my hand and pulls me away from the stoves and the giant awning and into the sunshine. "I'm so glad you wanted to talk," she says. "I needed a break."

"Is it awful, working for Becky?"

"No, not exactly," Mary says. We head toward the creek and then turn upstream. The path is rocky and steep, but well traveled now that so many Glory residents have claims in this direction. "But after the miners leave, it's just me and Becky and Olive, working in silence. Olive is a sweet thing, but I don't think Becky cares for me much."

I'm not sure she's wrong. "Becky is distrustful of all things unfamiliar," I tell her. "But she'll come around."

Mary shrugs like it's no big deal, but Mary is not one to share her thoughts easily, and the fact that she did is a sure sign that she is vexed.

"Becky hasn't been unkind to you, has she?" I ask.

"No. But she hasn't been kind either. Anyway, what did you want to talk about?"

"Not yet. Once we're out of earshot of town."

Mary raises her eyebrows but doesn't protest.

We continue uphill until we reach a spot where the creek stairsteps down a series of boulders, creating frothing rapids. The sound of the rushing water ought to mask our voices.

I glance around to make sure no stray miners are passing by. "So," I say. "I have a secret."

"I'm listening," Mary says, and she has that unreadable look again, the one I used to find so daunting.

I take a deep breath. Why does this never get easier? "You see . . . I . . . You know Old Tug?" Silently I curse myself for cowardice.

"Yes."

"He's sweet on you. He might ask you to marry him. Didn't want you to be caught by surprise."

Her face brightens. "Maybe I ought to encourage him."

Not the answer I expected. "Mary! He's vile!"

She nods. "Yes. All men are vile."

"No, they're—"

"Lee, I know a lot more about men than you do, and trust me, they're all gross, disgusting creatures. But Tug is nice. Maybe the nicest man in Glory. He never grabs me or threatens me or treats me like I'm not a person. He could stand to bathe more, but he always picks up his dishes, and he leaves me generous tips."

"Huh." I consider defending Jefferson, who is the opposite of vile, but I decide I'd rather not argue. "I hadn't pegged you for the marrying kind."

She gives me a look that would curdle cream. "Because of my previous occupation?"

"No! You're just . . . I guess I don't know."

"Well, I haven't decided if I want to marry or not. But if I do, it will be to a kindhearted fellow like Tug. Is that what you needed all this secrecy for? To tell me about him?"

"No."

Mary crosses her arms. "Out with it, Lee."

I sigh. A breeze sends a gust of waterfall spray, and as I wipe my wet face with the end of my scarf, I say, "So . . . remember my uncle? How he kidnapped me? Forced me to help with his mining operation?"

"I was there, remember?"

"Right. Of course." The end of the scarf twists in my hands. *Twist, twist, twist.* "Before that, he killed my parents. Took over the homestead. And after I escaped, he chased me across the continent."

Mary peers into my face. "I always thought his obsession with you was mighty peculiar. I mean, you're his niece, but still."

"It was more than that. And Mary, you have to swear up and down and sideways that you won't tell another soul what I'm about to tell you."

"I'll swear no such thing. You either trust me or you don't."

I glare at her. She is determined to make this difficult. "Fine. Here it is. I can find gold. Not like a miner. Like a witch. I have a . . . power."

Her black eyes fly wide as she blurts something in Chinese.

"What? I don't know what you just said—"

"Something my mother would have whipped me for saying. Are you serious, Lee? You *are* serious, aren't you. You're not funning me at all."

"I'm not funning you."

Her sudden smile could light up all of California. "Show me!"

"Wait. You believe me?"

"Of course. You may be daft sometimes, naive in the ways of men, but you're not a liar. And it makes sense. All those rumors about the Golden Goddess . . ."

"Yeah. Those."

"Show me," she says again.

I've had to prove myself before, so I know just what to do. I reach behind my neck and unclasp my locket. I hand it to her, chain and all.

"I'm going to turn around and close my eyes. Hide the locket somewhere, and I'll tell you where it is."

"All right."

I turn my back to her, extending my gold sense. The locket shines like a beacon in my mind, a spot of warmth and light. Only a few seconds pass before I say, "Don't put in your pocket, Mary. That's too easy." Mary gasps. "Hide it somewhere more interesting."

A moment later, I hear scuffling, scraping of rocks, a bootheel digging into the ground.

"Okay, find it," Mary says breathlessly.

My back is still to her, but I can sense the locket just fine. I roll my eyes. "It was clever of you to make all that racket, but the locket is still in your pocket."

"No, it's not," she lies.

In answer, I imagine invisible fingers wrapping themselves around the locket. I picture them clenching into a fist, lifting the trinket into the air.

Mary blurts something in Chinese again. I turn around to find her gaping at the locket, a shiny bit of gold floating in the air before her, chain dangling.

But this is a new trick for me, and I can't keep hold of it for long. My mental grip weakens fast, and the locket plummets to the ground. Slowly, almost reverently, Mary crouches to retrieve it, brushes off dirt and pine needles, and offers it to me.

I put it back around my neck, where it belongs.

"Who else knows?" she asks.

"Jefferson, of course. The Major. Becky and the children. The college men. Hampton."

"Even the children?"

"They've seen some hard things since leaving Tennessee. They understand consequences, and they know to keep quiet."

"Well." Mary gazes into the distance. The damp air is chilly here by the rapids, making me shiver. A raptor screeches from far away, and I look up, expecting to see one of California's giant condors, but the sky is a bright blue bowl of emptiness.

"Thank you for telling me," Mary says finally. "For trusting me."

"You should understand, Mary, that being my friend is

dangerous. My uncle murdered to get his hands on me, to control what I can do. You have a right to know what you're in for."

Mary waves it off. "California is nothing but danger. I expect being your friend might also be . . . useful . . ." Her mouth forms a little *O*. "That's why Hampton's claim is doing so well! And Jefferson's. And *yours*. Lee, you're going to be rich. If you're not already . . ."

I know that gleam in her eye. I've seen the fever take people a thousand times.

"Don't worry," she adds, as if reading my thoughts. "I won't tell anyone. And you don't have to help me get rich. Though . . ." She waggles her eyebrows. "It wouldn't hurt if you put in a good word for me with Becky. She should pay me more."

I laugh. "I'll see what I can do."

"I'd better get back to the dishes before Becky—"

"Lee! Mary!" comes a high little-girl voice. It's Olive, running toward us, skirts in her hands to keep them out of the mud. "Ma needs you again."

"What's wrong?" I ask, just as Mary says, "Everything all right?"

"It's the peddler," Olive says, gasping for breath. "He's here. And Ma got a letter."

"From the Robichauds?" I say excitedly. "The Hoffmans?"

Olive shakes her head. "From a stranger. In San Francisco."

I have no idea what that means, and my excitement slips away like water through a sieve. Letters ought to be exciting. Joyful, even. But as Mary and I follow Olive back to town at a jog, an uneasy feeling tingles the back of my neck.

By the time we reach the Worst Tavern, several of our friends have already gathered. The Major is there, bouncing the unnamed Joyner baby on his knee. The college men—Jasper, Tom, and Henry—have their heads together at the other end of the table, reading Becky's letter. Jefferson and Hampton arrive just as Mary and I do, little towheaded Andy at their heels, followed by the dogs, Nugget and Coney.

Everyone else must be out perusing the peddler's wares, because we have the tavern all to ourselves.

Jefferson grins when he sees me. Already, a smudge of mud sweeps across his brow, and his temples are slick with the sweat of hard work. The sight makes me happier than a lark in a meadow. I grin right back.

"We'll have to move fast," Tom tells Becky from his place at the table. "Seems as though the letter took a while to find you, and your cargo won't be stored much longer."

"What do you mean?" I say. "What's going on?"

"It's my house," Becky says. "The one my late husband had disassembled and shipped across the Panama Isthmus. It arrived in San Francisco some time ago, and a letter to Andrew asking him to claim the cargo just now reached us."

Jefferson sidles over so he can put an arm around my shoulders. I lean into him. My head barely reaches his jaw now, and I decide I like that just fine.

"So what are you going to do?" Mary asks.

Becky raises her chin. "I'm going to get what's mine, of course."

"You sure it's worth the trouble?" the Major asks gently. "You earn so much each day with your restaurant, and you have a sound cabin already."

Becky's eyes soften. "I do. And I'm grateful for all of it. But that house has sentimental value. And it comes with other items of worth—some furniture, a few heirlooms. It would be a final courtesy to Mr. Joyner to lay hold of it all and pass it along to his children someday."

"Well, that's good enough reason for me," the Major says.

"Ba!" says the baby girl in his lap.

"I would dearly love to see San Francisco," Henry says. "My claim has done fine. I could take my stake to the city. Get a job as a tutor."

"Maybe this is a good time to set up my law practice," Tom says.

Jasper says, "I'd love the opportunity to study with a city doctor for a while."

I stare at the college men, my heart sinking. "So . . . you want to leave Glory?" We traveled across a whole continent together, and I can't imagine the place without them.

"Maybe," Henry says.

"Just temporarily," Jasper says, with a pointed look at his friends. "I'm not giving up *my* claim."

But Tom grasps Henry's hand with his own, and some kind of understanding passes between them.

Hampton reaches down to scritch Coney behind his long ears. "I wouldn't mind heading to San Francisco, see if there's any word of my wife, Adelaide." With Tom's help, Hampton arranged to buy his wife's freedom. We're hoping to hear the sale has gone through and she's on her way. It's probably way too soon—it takes months for letters to find their way back east—but you can't blame a fellow for being optimistic.

Becky turns to Jefferson and me. "What about you two? Any interest in a trip to San Francisco?"

"I don't want to give up my claim," Jefferson says. "I'm about to be a married man!"

"Tug and the Buckeyes could work your claims while you're gone," Tom suggests. "In exchange for keeping a percentage of what they find. They've proven themselves hardworking and trustworthy. I could even draw up some quick contracts."

"I suppose that would work," Jeff says. "Lee, what do you think?"

"I think . . ." I take a deep breath. Mama and Daddy were originally from Boston. They used to tell me about the sea, about water that stretched farther than a body could gander, a color that's the most perfect deep blue in the world. "I think I want to see the ocean."

"Then it's settled," Jasper says.

"Wait, Becky, what about your restaurant?" I ask. "You have so many customers that—"

"I'll do it," Mary says, and we all look at her. "I can do it," she insists.

Becky taps a finger to her lips, considering, sizing up the girl.

"I might need to hire a little help," Mary adds, "but I can keep the place running."

"Very well," Becky says at last, and Mary grins from ear to ear.

"We should leave soon," Tom says. "Maybe even tomorrow. I don't know what they do with unclaimed property, but if Becky doesn't act fast, it could get dumped into the bay. Or even stolen."

We work out a few more details, but it's settled in no time. The Joyners, the college men, Hampton, the Major, and Jefferson and I are all headed to San Francisco. The Buckeyes and Mary will stay behind to keep things running smoothly.

When our meeting comes to an end, Jefferson and I head out toward our adjacent claims, walking hand in hand, the dogs at our heels. I'm already rich. My stash of gold pieces and nuggets and dust is fit for a king. Still, I want to find as much gold as I can today, because who knows what our journey will bring?

"There's another reason I want to go to San Francisco," Jefferson says after a stretch of silence.

"Oh? Something you didn't want to say in front of everyone else?"

"That James Henry Hardwick fellow. Doesn't he have holdings there?"

We had some business with him over Christmas. We paid him a tidy sum for his services, and while he made good on his word to get rid of my uncle once and for all, he still hasn't fulfilled *all* the terms of our agreement. "You're thinking of the town charter he owes us."

"Yep. If we don't get that straightened out soon, the people of Glory have no protection. The town could just . . . go away."

Together we leap over a small rivulet, onto a rocky embankment that marks the boundary of Jeff's claim. "I thought you didn't care about owning land and all that fuss."

"I don't. But Glory is bigger than me. It's a safe place for a lot of folks now."

"A sanctuary."

"Exactly. A sanctuary. So maybe we can find Hardwick, remind him he still owes us that charter."

I frown. "He gives me a bad feeling."

"Oh? Why?"

"He uses tricky words and fancy deals and shiftiness. Like my uncle. I prefer a straight-up fight."

Jefferson laughs. "Well, maybe we'll learn to fight differently. Anyway, going is the right thing. It's fitting."

"What do you mean?"

"Once we get to San Francisco, once we see the ocean, we'll have really gone all the way across the continent. I mean, it'd be a pity to come all this way and not finish the journey."

I squeeze his hand. "Then let's do it. Let's finish the journey."

## Chapter Two

On a cold, cloudless morning, after weeks of hard travel, we reach the busy San Francisco docks. The Major and the college men depart right after breakfast to pursue their own errands, so it's just me, Jefferson, Hampton, and the Joyners.

The huge bay is a wonder, so crowded with ships it looks like another city spread out across the water. Masts rise like steeples of a hundred churches, each one a temple to the love of gold. Seagulls dive between ships, or settle on abandoned masts, or swirl in the air. Beyond the ships, choppy gray-green waves froth into white peaks.

The air is breezy and wet, and it smells of salt and fish. To our left, out of sight beyond the golden hills of the peninsula, the Pacific Ocean supposedly stretches as far as the eye can see. We caught glimpses of it on our way here—smudges of blue shining through the creases of the hills—but I've never seen an ocean up close, and there's no way I'll allow us to do our business and be on our way without setting eyes on such a marvel.

I turn to say as much to Jefferson. He's riding Sorry, the sulky sorrel mare that carried him all the way from Dahlonega, Georgia, to the goldfields of California, the same way my palomino girl, Peony, carried me.

Jefferson's hat is tipped back, his dark hair spilling out around the edges. His eyes are alight beneath raised brows. An odd thing happens every time I look at his face, ever since I asked him to marry me and he said yes: my heart beats faster and everything else in the world—the crowds, the noise, even the smell of fish gone sour—disappears like a puff in the wind.

A grin plays at the corner of his mouth.

"What?" I wipe the back of my hand across my cheek, thinking of the crumbly sweet bread we had for breakfast at Mission Dolores.

"That look!" he says. "Miss Leah Westfall has seen all the wonders of the continent, and she still turns into a slack jaw at something new."

I clamp my mouth shut and glare at him.

"It's one of the things I like most about you," he admits.

"Well, can you blame me?" The wide sweep of my arm encompasses the city, the ships, and the bay. "They say it's one of the most perfect harbors in the world. Canyon deep all the way through the Golden Gate, but shallow in the shelter of the bay."

He turns his head toward the water, which is fine by me, because I like his profile as much as any other part of his face.

Peony shifts beneath me. We've all stopped to take in the view, but the folks around us are starting to glare, like we're taking up too much space.

The muddy street overflows with people bustling by foot and cart and horse, with faces and fabrics from all over the world. A brand-new warehouse goes up before our eyes as workmen scamper up and down the scaffolds. Beyond the warehouse rise the hills of the San Francisco peninsula, the slopes covered with every manner of building, house, and tent. The air resounds with voices shouting in a hundred languages, hammers pounding, wagons creaking.

Jefferson says in a soft voice, as if we're all alone, "Those ships look like the woods after a wildfire. No leaves, no branches, nothing left but barren trunks standing up against the sky."

I see it through his eyes. A forest of abandonment. "What will happen to them all, do you think?"

"They'll get scavenged. Used for building up on land. Some might be turned into prisons, like the one we saw on the Sacramento River."

The one holding my uncle Hiram, is what he doesn't say. We've been through a lot together, Jeff and me. I reach out and clasp his fingers with mine.

"Will the two of you stop mooning over each other?" Becky Joyner asks, from the wagon behind us. "You'd think nobody in the world ever fell in love before the two of you invented it."

"Becky!" Heat fills my cheeks, and I drop Jefferson's hand.

She grins at me.

Becky sits with Hampton on the wagon bench, holding the reins of a team of cart horses we bought at Mormon Island. The one on the right, a chestnut with a wide white blaze, tosses his head in impatience.

"I don't care if the two of you make eyes at each other all day like lovebirds in a cage," she says, "but can you carry on with it *after* we get my house? If we don't run into any snags, we can shop for your wedding dress and then head home as early as tomorrow."

I frown. This is not the first time we've had this discussion. "Jeff and I don't need a fancy wedding, and I don't need a fancy dress."

"Nonsense. We're family now, and your family wants to see this done right."

"Jefferson?" I plead.

The traitor holds up his hands in mute surrender.

Hampton quickly schools his grin. "We might even have time to get a proper suit for thc groom," he suggests with a perfectly straight face.

Jefferson and I glare at him.

"All right, folks," Becky says. "Let's go get my house."

I urge Peony toward the docks, and the wagon rattles behind. We carefully make our way down the slippery, muddy slope until we reach the dock described in the letter.

"That's it!" Becky calls out.

I swing a leg over Peony's back to dismount, but as soon as my feet touch the ground, my legs turn to jelly, and I stumble.

Becky jumps down from the wagon, and Jefferson leaps off

Sorry, so that within seconds I have someone at each elbow, steadying me.

"You all right?" Jefferson asks.

"Just need get my bearings," I say, suddenly breathless. There's no need to explain the problem—they all know my secret.

Gold has been singing a muted song for our entire journey here, sometimes from far away, sometimes buzzing in my throat. But this, when my feet touch ground here . . . *this* is like hearing a chorus of a thousand voices.

Softly, so only Jefferson and Becky can hear, I say, "I think it's all the practice I've been doing, learning how to control the gold when I call it to me. It's made things . . . sensitive."

"How bad?" Jeff asks.

"It's everywhere—like trying to sip water from a flood."

"What do you mean, everywhere?" says Becky, looking around in consternation. "I don't see—"

*"Everywhere,"* I whisper.

My gold sense is always strongest when I touch the earth. Men are digging a hole in the street outside the warehouse to sift gold flakes from the dirt—there are two ounces to be found if they've half an eye. A block farther, a couple of children sit outside a tavern, where they lick the heads of pins and use the wet tips to pick gold dust out of the sweepings, speck by speck. They won't get much for their labor, but each mote of gold burns like a tiny ember. Buttons and watches and brooches and hairpins flare all around me. Gold is in almost every purse and pocket. My own significant store of gold, in Peony's saddlebag, brought along for an emergency. The locket dangling at my throat. A half-dozen nuggets in Jefferson's right trouser pocket—he's been carrying them for months, ever since we escaped from my uncle's camp. And, in a little velvet clutch tied to her waist, Becky has more than a dozen gold coins—

A group of laughing, dirty-faced children plows into us, setting the horses to bellyaching. They are no older than Olive or Andy. A few apologize with "Sorry, ma'am!" and "Sorry, sir!" while others shout "Tag!" and "You're it!" before dashing away.

Becky brushes dirt off her skirt, as if the children's behavior might be contagious. "So rude. I have to wonder where their mothers are."

"Becky, where is your—?"

I sense her purse, or rather the particularly shaped pile of gold coins in her purse, moving away. I scan the crowded street ahead.

There—a towheaded little scamp, rapidly disappearing among taller bodies. Without taking my eyes off him, I hand Peony's reins to Jeff. "Hold this," I say, and I start running.

The boy is small and quick as a rodent, disappearing behind people and barrels and wagons. I'm not really pursuing him, only what he carries, and all the other gold around me is a distraction, like trying to follow the buzz of a single bee in a hive. But my practice pays off. With focus, I hear the unique melody of Becky's gold, not quite overwhelmed by a cacophony of overlapping songs.

I have him in my sights. "Hey! Stop!"

He glances over his shoulder, sees me gaining, and pumps his legs even faster, dodging carts and barrels. His head is cranked around, eyes wide with fear, when he careens into a young woman, maybe even younger than me. Her hair is dirty blond, her skin is darkened by the sun, and her secondhand calico dress—too loose on her by half—is dimmed by dust and wear. She clutches a small cloth bag to her waist like it contains all her possessions in the world. The boy bounces away and falls down.

She snatches him by the collar, smacks him on the back of his head, and scolds him. He's almost in my grasp when he tears free and darts around the corner into a warren of smaller streets and shanties. The young woman continues calmly toward the docks as if nothing has happened, clutching that bag tight.

I tear after the boy. I'm around the corner and halfway down the street when I catch myself.

The melody of Becky's gold is moving in the other direction now. Away from me.

The bump was a handoff.

It was done so smoothly that I didn't suspect a thing. Without my witchy powers, I'd have missed it, for sure and certain.

I dust myself off and turn around as if I've reluctantly given up pursuit. My performance is wasted. The boy is long gone, and the young woman is headed away, oblivious to me.

She walks at a normal pace, like a woman with nothing to fear, so it's easy to extend my stride and catch up. Seeing as how she's leading me right back to Becky and Jefferson and Hampton, I'm in no rush.

I steadily close the distance and listen for the gold. The shape of it tells a story. She has a secret pocket sewn in the waist of her dress, which she hides by clutching the mostly empty bag in front of her. The pocket holds Becky's purse and two others, plus several large nuggets of varying shapes and a few loose coins, including a half coin with a sheared edge.

That last one's call feels sad, like a song in minor key. The shape of it is so distinct and specific that it's easy to single out from the rest. It becomes my beacon.

As I approach her from behind, I focus all on my attention on that broken coin.

When I first learned to call the gold to me, it was all or nothing. Every nugget, every flake, every piece of dust in range came flying and left me standing there like a statue covered in gold leaf. The first time, it happened when a few folks happened to be watching.

It was dark and rainy, and no one knows for sure what they saw. Still, in the months since, the story spread faster than a summer wildfire. Even some of the miners in Glory have been telling tall tales of a Golden Goddess. They say she's lucky. That if you catch a glimpse of her in the hills, you'll be blessed by a straight week of pure color.

There's no stopping tall tales from spreading, but letting those stories get connected to me will draw a deadly kind of attention. So with Jefferson's help, I've been figuring out how to control my power.

Only a few steps behind the young woman now. The waist of her dress is cinched as tight as it can go, and it still hangs loose. In spite of the cool air, sweat curls the dirty blond strands at the nape of her neck.

I think hard about that broken coin. Then I hold my hand out in front of me and close my fist.

The jagged edge surges toward me, straining against the pocket seams.

I unfold my hand and push the broken coin away.

The gesture is unnecessary—I can control the gold just fine without it—but I've found it makes things a little easier, acting like a focus for my thoughts. So my fist clenches and releases, clenches and releases, as we walk down the street. I probably seem daft to anyone looking, but San Francisco is a busy place, and no one pays me any mind.

My friends are waiting just ahcad. Hampton has climbed down from the wagon. Jefferson stares at me with a worried frown. Becky seems distressed.

I ignore my friends for the moment and work harder, pulling and pushing the rough edge of that coin like a saw against the seam of the hidden pocket. The young woman's steps quicken; surely she has noticed something odd by now.

She's making her way around our wagon, and my friends are stepping toward me, when the seam breaks and the coin comes flying out of the dress.

I mentally grab everything else in the pocket—the other purses, the nuggets, the coins—and imagine a sharp tug downward, just like milking a cow.

A small fortune in gold tumbles from her dress and plops into the mud. She gasps, falling to her knees, ruining her skirt.

"Ma'am," I say, rushing forward before she can gather it all up herself. "Ma'am, you dropped something."

She faces me. Up close, she's even younger than I expected. In spite of her light hair, her eyes are as brown and hard as acorns. An awful lot of thinking is going on in those hard brown eyes.

"I reckon this is yours." I pick up the broken coin and put it in her hand. It gleams like a half moon. Her palms are calloused, her fingernails ragged as if trimmed by teeth. She did hard labor before turning to thievery.

Her fingers close around the coin, and she slips it quickly into the cheap cloth bag she carries. I squat beside her.

"I don't know what happened," she says, quickly gathering nuggets and loose coins into her bag. "I must have tipped my bag when I wasn't paying attention."

"Just an accident, I'm sure," I tell her. "My name's Lee."

"Thank you, Lee. I'm Sonia. I can't tell you how much your kindness means to me."

She reaches for Becky's coin purse. I pin her wrist with one hand and snatch up the purse with the other.

"Sonia, I'm afraid this one belongs to my friend. There's an engraving on the inside of the clasp that says R.J., and I can tell you exactly how many coins are in it and what their weight comes to."

Her brows knit, and she stares at me with those hard eyes. She tries to jerk her hand free, but I'm not about to let go—I've spent my life doing hard labor too, on the farm at home, on the wagon train west, in the goldfields.

Becky, Jefferson, and Hampton surround us. "What's going on here?" Jefferson asks, genuinely mystified.

"My new friend Sonia here dropped some things, and I'm helping her pick up," I explain. I hand Becky's purse to her. There's a firm set to Becky's mouth, and unlike Jeff, she knows exactly what we're about.

Sonia jerks her hand away, and this time I let go. Her face shows relief as she shoves the remaining items into her bag and stands. No one will be turning her in today.

"Thank you for your help, Lee. Not everyone in this town would've been so kindly."

"That little blond-haired boy—is he your brother?" I ask.

"Billy? No, ain't many left as still got family. Just a few friends."

Maybe I'd be in her place, if I didn't have Jefferson and Becky and Hampton and everyone else. "It's important to have friends."

She holds my gaze. "Thanks again. Be careful here in San Francisco—this city is full of thieves." She pauses, her stare unwavering. Then, carefully: "The biggest thieves, the *real* ones, will take everything you have, even the clothes off your back."

She rushes off before I can respond. Jefferson removes his hat and scratches his head. "What just happened here?"

Hampton laughs, a deep rumbly sound. "That little slip of a girl just tried to rob Mrs. Joyner. Thought she had a sunfish on the line, but it turned out to be a shark."

I glare. "*I'm* the shark?"

"Meant it as a flattery."

I turn to Jefferson, the question in my eyes, and yes, I'm not ashamed to admit I'm fishing for a compliment.

"Well, you do have a dangerous smile." Before I can follow up, he says, "But seriously, what just happened here?"

I say, "She's working with that group of children who bumped into us. I bet she walks down the street and identifies the targets—"

"Marks," says Becky. "Mr. Joyner always called them marks. Gullible gamblers. Different situation, same principle."

"So she walks down the street and identifies the *marks*—"

"Probably while the two of you were staring all googly-eyed at one another," Becky interrupts again. She's clutching her purse tight in both hands, knuckles white as she comes to grips with the fact that she nearly got robbed.

"And then she sends the little urchins out to play in the street and pick pockets. They bump into her coming back the other direction, but it's really a handoff. That way, if anyone catches the children, they don't have any evidence."

"Anything *incriminating*," suggests Becky, who never heard a fancy word she didn't want to flaunt. "There was a pack of orphan children back in Chattanooga that functioned much the same."

Maybe that's what my life would have been like if my uncle Hiram had murdered Mama and Daddy and left me an orphan when I was five instead of when I was fifteen.

"She almost got away with it," Jefferson says.

"Well, she didn't," Hampton says, climbing back onto the wagon bench. "Let's get on with it. I want to check the post office when we're done, see if there's any word of my Adelaide."

Hampton started out his journey on the California Trail as a slave. When his master died, he followed the wagon train west, secretly aided by the Illinois college men. Once we got to California and found gold, he bought his own freedom, with Tom's help.

"What ship are we looking for?" Jefferson asks.

"It's supposed to be right here at Washington Pier," Becky says. "It's called the *Charlotte*."

"Then let's have a look around."

# Chapter Three

Calling it Washington *Pier* is being optimistic. A long, muddy street winds down the marshy hill until it meets the bay. Toward the end, where the mud gets so bad it's almost impossible to walk, a boardwalk begins, jutting well into the water. To either side of the boardwalk are abandoned ships run hard aground. People dump wheelbarrows of dirt into the soupy muck, turning it into land and trapping the ships right where they sit. On our right, a crew swarms over one of the hulks, stripping the wood like a pack of termites devouring a pine shack. On our left, a lonely twin seems to await a similar fate.

At the end of the dock, men swing precariously over the water, hammering boards into an empty framework. An anchored ship waits to tie alongside, just as soon as the dock is ready. A foreman hollers at us to step aside as a group of workmen rumble past, carrying a huge log smeared with pitch on their shoulders—another pile to drive into the water and extend the dock even farther. The whole structure sways precariously from side to side as they go.

"I think I'd rather stay here," Hampton says, eyeing the dock with distrust.

"Sure," I reply.

"I'm not sure those fellows know a single lick about building piers."

The workmen drop the new pile, and the dock shakes so hard one of the boards pops loose and falls into the water. "We need someone to watch that wagon and the horses anyway," I assure him.

Jefferson and Becky and I step onto the rickety dock, which feels more solid under my feet than I expect. I can't help gawking at the ships as we go. Jefferson, never one for shyness, cups his hands to his mouth. "The *Charlotte*!" he hollers. "We're looking for the *Charlotte*!"

Sailors shake their heads. One rakish fellow leans over the side of his ship and shouts in an Australian accent. "Oi! If you find Charlotte, tell her I'm looking for her, too!"

"Rude humor is a mark of low character," Becky shouts back.

"Of course I've got low character," the sailor responds. "I come from down under!"

His crewmates laugh. Jefferson looks to me as if to share a grin, but I shake my head. Becky Joyner is on a mission, and this is no time to cross her.

The sailor wisely returns to work. We pass another ship and reach the end of the dock. Still no *Charlotte*.

"Maybe this is the wrong place," Jefferson says.

"I'm sure this is it," Becky says. "I reread the letter and checked the directions with people at the mission before we came down to the waterfront."

If Becky says she's sure, she's sure. "Maybe they left already?"

"I made inquiries," Becky says. "The *Charlotte* was expected to remain in port."

Her knowledge doesn't surprise me one bit. Thanks to her restaurant regulars, Becky now has more connections and better information than anyone I know.

"We must have missed it," I say. "We just need to head back and start over."

We return to Hampton and the wagon. "Things got mighty precarious," Jefferson tells him solemnly. "But the dock didn't fall into the bay."

"But you didn't find anything either, so I was better off waiting here, wasn't I?" Hampton says.

"I think this is the ship right here," Becky says.

"What?"

She's staring up at the abandoned hulk, the one that's never setting sail again because the bay's been filled in right around it. The faint outline of weathered letters appears on the bow, obscured by soot and mud. They *might* have once read the *Charlotte*. I'm almost certain of the A and the R.

There's no way to climb aboard, so I pound on the side, which I recognize for the long-shot hope it is. The hull echoes back at me like a giant kettledrum. "Hey! Anyone aboard?"

A thump, like a body falling out of a hammock, then an

apple-shaped face pops up over the side, surrounded by a rat's nest of gray-black hair.

"Whaddayawant?" he says.

It comes out as one angry, messy word, but I reckon that's a natural state of things, rather than any specific anger being directed at us. I've heard the same New York accent from other miners we've met.

"We're looking for the *Charlotte*," Becky says. "It sailed out of Panama, carrying cargo that came across the isthmus, including my disassembled house."

As the stylish Southern lady addresses him, the New Yorker stands straighter and combs fingers through his hair, though without noticeable effect. "I have some good news and some bad news," he says.

He bends, and with a grunt and heave, he slides a gangplank down to the dock. It lands hard and sets the dock to swaying. The man puts hands to hips and says, "Well, come aboard. I'm not gonna shout at you from way up here."

I look to Hampton. "I volunteer to watch the horses," he says.

The gangplank is sturdier than it looks. Becky, Jefferson, and I make the steep climb single file and step onto the deck. It's an old ship, and because of the faded paint and soot marks on the hull, I expect it to be in disrepair, perhaps even in the process of being scavenged. But everything is tidy and well stowed, the deck clean of debris and dirt.

"Name's Melancthon Jones," the sailor says. "What can I do for you?"

We introduce ourselves. "I have to ask," I say. "What happened to . . . ?" I glance over the side at the faded lettering.

He shrugs. "We made port, and the captain and the rest of the crew jumped ship to go find themselves a fortune."

"But not you?" I say.

He shrugs. "I dug ditches to help build the Erie Canal. So much digging. A *lifetime* of digging. If I never touch another shovel in my life, it'll be too soon."

"So you're just . . ." Jefferson glances around the deck. "Here?"

"I'm no sluggard, if that's your implication," Melancthon says with a glare. "Hoping for a chance to catch passage back east, but no one's hiring. The ships keep coming in, but most never leave. The few that do leave don't need crew."

Becky steps forward. "You said there was good news and bad news?"

He slips his thumbs beneath his suspenders. "Good news first. This ship here is—or was—the *Charlotte*, and we had your cargo aboard. Loaded it myself down in Panama. I was the ship's carpenter, and I admired the way everything had been taken apart, labeled, and stored. A fine bit of work."

Becky nods. "My husband supervised everything himself. He was very particular. What's the bad news?"

"Because the ship has been abandoned, the Custom House holds claim to any cargo left behind. You'll have to get permission from them to collect it, and you'll need to hurry before they auction it off."

"They can't do that!" Becky says.

"Oh, they can and they will," Melancthon says. "They're going to auction off the ship, too—sell it right out from under me."

"Will they let you stay?" Jefferson asks.

"Seems unlikely. Too much money to be had. If you have the means, you can buy a piece of property here for ten thousand dollars, then turn around two months later and sell it for twenty." Jeff and I exchange a look of consternation. Back east, a body can just about buy a whole town for ten thousand dollars.

"Where will you go?" I ask Jones.

"Don't know," he says. "Been nice having a free roof over my head. Better quality than any boarding house in the city, too. Good thing, because the captain took off without paying my wages. I might have to look for work ashore soon."

Becky smoothes the front of her dress, adjusting the pleats. "So my cargo can be found at the Custom House?"

"No, ma'am, I'm sure it's stored in one of the warehouses. The folks at the Custom House are just the ones in charge." A seagull lands on the railing, but Melancthon shoos it away.

Jefferson is stiff in the space beside me, and I can practically sense his frown.

"What's wrong?"

"This whole state," he grumbles, "no, this whole *country*—is based on stealing things from people, starting with their land. And if you don't have land, they'll take whatever you do have."

"I reckon you're right."

He's been dwelling on this a long time. Jefferson is the son of a poor white man and a Cherokee woman. His whole family on his mama's side was forced to march west after their land was stolen out from under them. Jefferson was left behind with his good-for-nothing daddy; legally, his mama didn't have options on that account. He hasn't seen her since she left, and he doesn't even know if she's alive. Now the same thing is happening to the Indians here in California. We've watched their land get taken, watched them forced into slavery, even watched them die.

"And where will I find the Custom House?" Becky persists.

"A block up the street, at Portsmouth Square," Melanchthon says, pointing. "Follow the sound of hammers. The city burned near to the ground on Christmas Eve."

"That was barely two months ago!" I say. No wonder there's soot on the hull.

"That why they're in such a hurry to rebuild."

We were headed toward Portsmouth Square anyway, since the best hotels are found there. We thank Melancthon for his help and wish him well, then make our way back to Hampton and the wagon.

"Was the good news good enough, or was the bad news worse?" he asks, giving Peony a pat on her nose.

"Not sure yet," I say.

"Our next stop is the Custom House," Becky adds. "We have to clear some things up."

Jefferson says, "Hampton, if you want to go check the post office, I'll lead the horses and the wagon. Meet up at Portsmouth Square?"

Hampton brightens. "I'd be obliged."

As he hands the reins over and takes off, Becky says, "Don't you worry, Lee. We still have plenty of time to get this straightened out *and* shop for the wedding."

I look to Jefferson for rescue, but he is wholly focused on tying up the horses to the back of the wagon. "Please, let's not hurry," I say. "All I need is Jefferson at my side, and my friends there to witness."

She waves this off with a flutter of her hand. "Yours is going to be the first wedding in Glory, California. Ever. Not only will it set a precedent for a proper wedding to everyone that follows, but it'll become part of the town's history, and that will make it part of the history of the new state. Your betrothal was a bit . . . unconventional." That's a kind way to put it—I was the one who did the proposing, during the Christmas ball in Sacramento. "I wish I could have been there to guide you. But as your friend and bridesmaid, I have a responsibility to make sure everything *else* is done properly."

I definitely consider Becky my friend. But she used to be my employer, and I will always remember the Mrs. Joyner who, on the wagon-train journey, served her husband's every meal on a fancy table set with a perfect tablecloth and fine, fragile china. I sigh. "Yes, ma'am."

It's a short walk to Portsmouth Square, just as Melancthon promised. The Custom House is a long, low adobe building stretching the full length of the square. An American flag whips from a high pole out front—thirteen red and white stripes, and thirty stars in a block of five by six. They'll have to figure out how to add another star once California officially becomes a state.

Along a wide veranda are three evenly spaced doors. The nearest is marked OWEN AND SON, BANKERS, the door in the middle has a sign for law offices with a much longer list of names, and the entrance at the far end is the Custom House. Jefferson offers to watch the wagon, and Becky and I line up behind a dozen others waiting to get inside.

The orderly, colorful crowd represents every corner of the globe—Peruvians and Chinese and a whole family of Kanakas from the Hawaiian Islands. It makes me feel like I'm part of something bigger than myself, something that involves the whole world.

The door opens onto a room with a long counter made from ship planking. Facing us from the other side is a small line of white men in starched shirts and perfectly barbered hair. Becky and I listen as, one after another, the people ahead of us receive answers to their problems.

The men in starched shirts are very sorry.

It isn't their fault.

The claimant will have to take it up with the original ship owner.

No, they can't help find the original ship owner.

The claimant might wish to go to a bank to solve that problem. They can recommend the one two doors down, the oldest and finest bank in San Francisco.

Unfortunately, the claimant will need to acquire legal advice to solve that particular problem. There are law offices all over the city, but perhaps they might care to try the services of the office next door.

Tears do not bring different answers.

Becky and I exchange a dark look. I'm starting to get a bad feeling.

Outrage doesn't help the Chinese man in line ahead of us, although it does tend to quickly mobilize a couple of rough-looking men who stand at the ready in case of trouble.

The cheerful and helpful-sounding men in starched white shirts have an answer to every question, but no one leaves satisfied.

The line moves efficiently, and soon Becky and I reach the front. My view has darkened, as though I'm in a state of about-to-be-angry, but Becky stands patiently and confidently, with all the assurance of a person who is used to having things work out for her.

"Next!"

We step up to a clerk with a face as angular as a wedge of cheese, framed by a pair of bushy sideburns. Small wire spectacles sit on the end of his nose. When he looks up from his ledger and sees us—or, rather, sees Becky, who is a fine lady in California, and therefore dearer than gold—a delighted grin spreads across his face. He reaches up and straightens his collar.

"How can I help you, ma'am?" He eyes me over the top of his glasses and amends: "Ma'ams." I'm still wearing my travel trousers, sure, but my hair has grown long enough to put up in a proper bun, and I'm no longer binding my chest with

Mama's old shawl, so the fact that I'm of the feminine persuasion is obvious to anyone paying attention.

Becky smiles at the clerk like he's a perfect piece of cake. "I believe that a house, disassembled for shipping, was delivered aboard the *Charlotte* out of Panama, and before that from New Orleans, and originally Chattanooga. Mr. Melancthon Jones, formerly the ship's carpenter aboard the *Charlotte*, reports that unfortunately, due to the irresponsible behavior of the captain, who, I understand, also neglected his duty to compensate his crew, the cargo of the ship has now been entrusted to your authority for rightful delivery to its proper owners. Here is the letter we received stating that the cargo was ready for collection."

She hands the letter over, and I want to whistle my appreciation. That was a mouthful to be sure, but Becky made it flow like fresh cream over strawberries.

The clerk appreciates it also, to judge from his childlike grin. "That's an excellent summary, Miss . . ."

"Mrs. Joyner."

His face falls a little. "Of course, *Mrs.* Joyner. You have to understand that very few people come prepared with all the appropriate information." He reads the letter and hands it back to her. "So the house is in the name of . . ."

"My husband, Mr. Andrew Joyner Senior."

She doesn't mention that he's dead. She may be scrupulously honest, but I notice that doesn't extend to volunteering information that hasn't been requested.

"Of course," the clerk replies. He rises from his seat and

goes to a stack of record books on another table behind the counter.

"I'll be so glad when this is resolved," Becky says.

"I thought we'd have more trouble."

"I did, too. But these are clearly very capable, competent men doing their best in difficult circumstances."

I gape at her. Becky sees men with authority as associates. I see them as adversaries. It might be the biggest difference between us. Rather than explain, I say, "You must have really missed that house, sleeping in the wagon for months."

The corners of her eyes crinkle. "It was our honeymoon cottage, on Andrew's father's plantation. I was seventeen when we got married—just a little older than you and Jefferson."

"You must have a lot of happy memories of it."

"Oh, goodness, no. We were far too young to marry, even Andrew, who was eight years older. It's one thing to be in love at that age, but it's another entirely to go live with someone."

I stare at her. Becky has never been forthcoming about her marriage.

"Don't act so surprised. Men are difficult and uncouth. And it didn't help that Andrew's father didn't approve of me, and he didn't want us living in the big house with them. Andrew was wild then—always a gambler. I suppose I was a bit wild, too."

I'm not sure what Becky considers "wild." Daring to go without a hat or bonnet on occasion? Using the dessert fork first? Before I can ask, she says, "I had several miscarriages before I became pregnant with Olive. That's when I finally began to settle, I think. After she was born, Andrew's mother put her foot down, and we moved into the mansion. And finally, after I bore a male child, we were set up with an inheritance and a place of our—"

She doesn't finish because the clerk returns, his thumb marking the spot in an open ledger.

"Found it," he says. "So many people have unsolvable problems. It's a pleasure to help somebody with an easy solution."

Becky smiles at me as if to say "I told you so."

"Now if you'll just have Mr. Joyner come in and sign this release form . . ."

Becky reaches for the pen on the counter. "I'll sign on his behalf."

The clerk jerks the ledger away, and his smile falters. "I'm sorry, but I can't allow that."

"But I'm his *wife*."

The clerk's smile fades a little more. "Have you heard of coverture, ma'am?"

Becky's answer has a strong streak of vinegar. "Are you a lawyer, sir? Do you presume to lecture me on the law?"

"If you know the law, you know that a wife has no legal standing. All her rights are covered by, and thus represented by, the rights of her husband. Thus, coverture. It's the law everywhere in the United States, and California will soon be confirmed as part of the United States." He slams the ledger shut. "Mr. Joyner's signature is absolutely required."

"But—" Becky says.

I squeeze her hand, hard, and she falls silent. "But what if her husband is up in the hills protecting their gold claim and working the land?" I say. "He can't be in two places at once."

I'm careful to phrase it as a possibility, because I don't want to lie direct and offend Becky's sense of propriety. She squeezes my hand in response.

"He'll just have to make the trip down here," he says.

"When is the auction scheduled?" Becky asks.

The clerk peers at the calendar on the wall and says, "A week from Tuesday, at the Hardwick Warehouse on Montgomery Street."

A little chill goes through me at the mention of the name Hardwick—most likely the very same fellow Jefferson is hoping we'll run into. James Henry Hardwick funded my uncle Hiram when Hiram kidnapped me. Then Hardwick took every penny we could raise in Glory in exchange for a promise to charter our town . . . a promise that hasn't yet been delivered. It seemed like a good idea at the time, but I've worried ever since that Hardwick may be no better than my uncle.

"There's no way we can retrieve Mr. Joyner in Glory and return by then, not with this weather," Becky says. "The winter roads are terrible—you know this to be true." I clear my throat, hoping she'll understand my message: "Stop talking." Becky is smart, but she's accustomed to getting her way. She has no idea how, as a woman with no husband and no property, the world is not on her side anymore.

The clerk rubs his cheese-wedge chin thoughtfully. "You could always buy the house at auction."

I was already thinking the same thing. It would attract more attention than we want, but I can afford it. Thanks to my gold-witching ways, I can afford to do a lot of things for my friends right now. "That's a good idea," I say.

"Where will we get the money to do that?" she asks tightly.

He says, "If you need a loan, you might go to a bank to solve that problem. I can recommend the one two doors down."

"And how am I supposed to get a loan without my husband's signature?" Her voice is sharp enough to shave with, and I imagine it taking the fellow's whiskers clean off.

"I see the problem," he says. "But the law's the law. Perhaps you might wish to consult with an attorney. I can recommend you to the gentlemen in the office next door."

"But—"

"I'm sorry. I've done everything I can here to help you." He looks past us to the next group in line, a Chinese family trying to speak through an interpreter who's dressed in black like a missionary. "Next!"

I'm willing to stand our ground and keep arguing, but Becky, ever conscious of protocol, turns and leaves. I follow her outside to the cold shade of the veranda, where Jefferson waits.

"So, how did it go?" he asks.

Becky's glare is so withering that he takes a step back.

"Not well," I say. "They'll accept Mr. Joyner's signature only, and no substitutes."

"Coverture is a barbaric doctrine," Becky says. "What am I, a piece of property to be handed around from one man to the next like a gambling chit? Now that Andrew's passed on, I suppose I'm covered by my father-in-law, a man who still despises me. Given half a chance, he'll take Andrew Junior to raise as his heir and send me off to a convent or something."

Jefferson and I exchange a surprised glance. We've heard more and more of Becky's opinions since the death of her husband, enough to know she's been thinking them in the quiet privacy of her own mind for a long time, maybe years. But this is one of the strongest we've heard pass her lips.

"We could always buy the house at auction," I suggest.

"Or have a man buy it for me, you mean," Becky says.

"Or that."

"No. I won't pay again for something that's rightfully mine."

"If the law's involved, we should talk to Tom about it," Jefferson suggests, and I could kiss him, because that's the perfect next step. Actually, I could kiss him anyway. "You should have let him come with you."

"He had his own worries," Becky says.

"Not sure it matters now," I say. "He's out looking for space to rent, which means he could be anywhere."

"Just saw him," Jefferson says. "Went next door. Said he was having trouble finding a place in his price range. He's rethinking his plan to go independent."

"Fine," Becky fumes, stomping away. "Let's go see Tom."

# Chapter Four

If anyone can help us, it's Tom, and Becky holds her head high and marches into the law office, me following behind.

It's the same size as the Custom House, with comparable furniture and decor, but that's where the similarities end.

Instead of orderly lines, calm voices, and every nationality, I see only well-dressed white men, smoking cigars while talking over one another. The song of gold is loud—the main chorus comes from the bank next door, but notes of it sing from fine pockets around the room. Voices suddenly crescendo to threatening shouts, and I tense, ready to grab Becky and run, but laughter follows a split second later, accompanied by hearty slaps on shoulders.

"There's Tom," Becky says. He's been tromping around the city half the day, but I don't see a speck of mud on him. Though he dresses plain, it always seems he rolls out of bed in the morning with his hair and clothes as neat and ordered as his arguments.

We walk over to join him, and he acknowledges us with a slight, perfectly controlled nod.

He's one of the college men, three confirmed bachelors who left Illinois College to join our wagon train west. Compared to the other two, Tom Bigler is a bit of a closed book—one of those big books with tiny print you use as a doorstop or for smashing bugs. And he's been closing up tighter and tighter since we blew up Uncle Hiram's gold mine, when Tom negotiated with James Henry Hardwick to get us out of that mess.

"How goes the hunt for an office?" I ask.

"Not good," Tom says. "I found one place—only one place—and it's a cellar halfway up the side of one those mountains." Being from Illinois, which I gather is flat as a griddle, Tom still thinks anything taller than a tree is a mountain. "Maybe eight foot square, no windows and a dirt floor, and they want a thousand dollars a month for it."

"Is it the cost or the lack of windows that bothers you?"

He pauses. Sighs. "Believe it or not, that's a reasonable price. Everything else I've found is worse—five thousand a month for the basement of the Ward Hotel, ten thousand a month for a whole house. The land here is more valuable than anything on it, even gold. I've never seen so many people trying to cram themselves into such a small area."

"So it's the lack of windows."

He gives me a side-eyed glance. "I came to California to make a fortune, but it appears a fortune is required just to get started. I may have to take up employment with an existing firm, like this one." Peering at us more closely, he says, "I thought you were going acquire the Joyner house? I mean, I'm glad to see you, but it seems things have gone poorly?"

"They've gone terribly," Becky says.

"They haven't gone at all," I add.

"They'll only release it to Mr. Joyner," Becky says.

Tom's eyebrows rise slightly. "I did mention that this could be a problem, remember?"

"Only a slight one," I say with more hope than conviction.

"Without Mr. Joyner's signature," Becky explains, "they'll sell my wedding cottage at auction. Our options are to buy back what's ours, which I don't want to do, or sue to recover it, which is why I've come to find you."

If I didn't know Tom so well, I might miss the slight frown turning his lips. He says, "There's no legal standing to sue. Andrew Junior is of insufficient age, and both his and Mr. Joyner's closest male relative would be the family patriarch back in Tennessee. You see, it's a matter of cov—"

"Coverture!" says Becky fiercely. "I know. So what can I do?"

"There's always robbery."

I'm glad I'm not drinking anything, because I'm pretty sure I'd spit it over everyone in range.

"Tom!" Becky says. "Are you seriously suggesting—?"

"I'm merely outlining your full range of options. You don't want to buy it back. You have no legal standing to sue for it. That leaves stealing it or letting it go."

This is the Tom we've started to see recently. A little angry, maybe a little dangerous. I haven't made up my mind if I like the change or not.

"I'm not letting it go," Becky says. "Just because a bunch of men pass laws so other men who look just like them can legally steal? Doesn't mean they should get away with it."

We've been noticed; some of the men in the office are eyeing us curiously. "How would *you* go about stealing it back, Tom?" I ask in a low voice, partly to needle him and partly to find out what he really thinks.

He glances around, brows knitting. "I suppose I would get a bunch of men who look like me to pass some laws in my favor and then take it back through legal means."

I laugh in spite of myself.

"You're no help at all," Becky says.

He holds up his hands as if in surrender. "I'll give it some thought, make some inquiries. There may be options I haven't considered."

The front door bangs open; conversations stop.

"Miss Leah Westfall!"

My hackles go up as a tall man strides into the room. His white hair and bushy sideburns frame ax-sharp cheekbones and a wide, smug mouth. He's dressed immaculately, with gold buttons on his dark jacket, a gold pocket-watch chain, and a gold-knobbed cane in his left hand. His right hand clutches a cigar, which he puffs with obvious pleasure.

James Henry Hardwick. Though he's only a councilman in Sacramento, some say he's the richest man in California at the moment, and the power behind the powers.

An entourage follows him into the room. The first is a small, mousy fellow with the tiniest nub of a chin, who stands so close to Hardwick you'd think they were tied together. A ring heavy with keys hangs from his belt loop, tugging down his pants. He carries a large leather bag, which he shifts from arm to arm. A fortune in gold is piled inside that bag; it knocks on my skull like an undeterred suitor.

A beautiful auburn-haired woman follows. She steps around the fellow with the keys, and slips her hand through Hardwick's elbow. She wears a green dress—a full crinoline skirt with flounces, a bodice that makes her waist look unbreathably narrow, and a low-cut neckline that makes you forget about her waist. She smiles on the room like a queen bestowing graces, and I can tell from the gazes of most of the men in the law office that Becky and I have all but disappeared.

Hardwick's two bodyguards follow last, and that's when I discover my stomach can sink even further, right through the floor.

Frank Dilley.

My uncle's right-hand man. Former right-hand man. The no-good snake who kidnapped me last fall. I'd heard that Frank had died during the insurrection at the mining camp a couple months past. In fact, it was Hardwick himself who told me as much, that lying Cain.

The right side of Frank Dilley's face looks like melted wax—likely he'll never grow hair there again. When he sees me, his left hand drifts to the revolver at his waist.

"Frank," I say, trying not to let my voice quaver. "I heard you died."

"Still alive and kicking," he says. "No thanks to you."

And because sometimes I can't control the meanness in my heart, I say, "You're looking better than ever."

Hardwick laughs. "Well, isn't this almost a family reunion?"

I glance around, half afraid I'll see Uncle Hiram. If Hardwick lied about Dilley, maybe he lied about my uncle being gone, too. Maybe I ought to run like blazes.

Hardwick steps toward me, and his associates trail in his wake like a school of fish. "I was on my way to the bank when I recognized Mr. Kingfisher outside, and I knew you wouldn't be far away. Of course I had to divert my path to join yours. It's not everyone who gets the better of me in a deal!"

He says it condescendingly, like me dealing with him was adorable and sweet . . . but there's a fire in his eyes that makes my belly squirm. A moment ago, I had been invisible to the men in this office. Now every eye is turned toward me. A few are merely curious, but not one of them is kindly.

Hardwick takes a puff on his cigar and blows a huge cloud of smoke in our direction. His breath is wet and sickly sweet with tobacco.

"Mr. Hardwick," I say, more as an acknowledgment, and falling just short of a greeting. "I didn't expect to see you with Dilley. You told me he died."

"Well, we thought he had! His men hauled him to the mission, where, with care and prayers, he made a miraculous recovery."

"Praise the Lord," Frank Dilley says.

"You still working for my uncle?" I ask Dilley flat out.

"You didn't know?" he says. "Westfall is halfway to Australia by now."

No reason for him to lie about that, and the relief almost buckles my knees.

Becky is bristling beside me. "We were about to be on our way."

"No need to hurry," Hardwick says. "What brings you all the way down from—what was the name of that little camp of yours—Charity?"

"Glory," I answer, and I regret it as soon as the word slips my mouth.

"Glory be!" Hardwick chuckles. "That's right, Glory. What brings you all the way down from Glory?"

The beautiful auburn-haired woman leans over and whispers in Hardwick's ear.

"Excuse me, I don't believe I've had the pleasure," Becky says, and I know she cannot bear to have anything whispered around her. "I'm Mrs. Andrew Joyner, lately from Glory, but before that from Chattanooga, Tennessee."

"Mr. James Henry Hardwick, at your service, Mrs. Joyner. Allow me to introduce my newest associate, Miss Helena Russell."

He makes "associate" sound like a fancy word for something I don't quite understand.

"At your service," Miss Helena Russell says, with a tinge of the mountains in her voice. Nothing about her is the least bit servile, but up close, I can see how the makeup and fine clothes cover a life of labor. Her skin is weathered and freckled. The wide sleeves of her dress fail to conceal forearms corded with the kind of muscle that comes from carrying milk pails and swinging axes. She may be dressed as stylishly as Becky Joyner, but she has more in common with me.

We pass introductions all around, and I'm still looking for a convenient way out that doesn't include fighting past Frank Dilley when Hardwick doggedly returns to his original question. "You never did say what brings you to San Francisco, Miss Westfall."

"No, I didn't," I reply. "What brings you?"

He laughs, and I wonder what puts a man like him in a good mood. Maybe it's the lady standing at his elbow. "I'm here for the same reason you are," he answers.

"You lost your home and family and had nowhere else to go?"

"I came to make my fortune."

He's already taken thousands from us, which seemed like a fortune at the time, but now, sensing all the gold of San Francisco—even just in this room—I know he has bigger ambitions. "And how are you going to do that?"

"Any and every way I can," he says, nodding to himself. "Any and every way I can."

"And that includes taking advantage of men like my uncle."

Another puff on his cigar, while he considers this. "I didn't know you cared about him. In fact, our agreement led me to believe that all you cared about was being free of him."

"I care about the people he robbed to pay you. I care about the people he hurt trying to get rich, in order to make you richer."

"You didn't come out of the affair too badly. You somehow ended up with enough money to pay all his debts."

My hands start to tremble, and tears well up in my eyes. I was kidnapped and force-fed laudanum. Dressed up like a doll for my uncle's amusement. The Indians had it worse; I watched them beaten, starved, murdered. "We still haven't received the charter for the town of Glory," I blurt, just to get the images out of my head.

That was the key part of my agreement with Hardwick at Christmas. We'd pay off my uncle's debts, and Hardwick would use his influence to get us a town charter so we could govern ourselves.

"California isn't a state yet, my dear, and the wheels of politics grind slowly." His grin is slow and satisfied. "And sometimes those wheels require additional amounts of grease to keep turning."

*Additional grease?* "You're saying you'll need more gold."

He scowls, and he glances around the room at the assemblage of lawyers. "This isn't something we should haggle over in public."

My whole body is tense, like a bent spring. "That's not fair."

He puffs himself up like a cock ready to cry doodle-do. "Sweet girl, you'll learn. Life's not fair."

"Then we're honor bound to make it fair," I snap.

He laughs at that, a genuine belly laugh, and it's like a slap in my face. My cheeks flush hot, and I look toward the door, hoping for a swift, easy exit, but the doorway is blocked. It's Hampton, striding inside.

I gasp. Because right behind Hampton is someone I thought to never see again: Jim Boisclair.

He made it to California after all. He's really here.

Jim was a good friend of my daddy's back in Dahlonega, a free Negro and store owner who helped me run away from my uncle the first time. I'm so happy and relieved to see him that I barely keep myself from giving him the hug of his life. In fact, I'm so overcome that it takes a moment to realize the whole room is as silent as the grave, and every single person in it is now staring at Hampton and Jim.

"I didn't know you were in San Francisco," I say cautiously.

He gives me an unsmiling nod, and there's an awful lot in that nod I'm not sure I understand. His eyes sweep the room warily, like he just stepped into a snake pit. "Glad to see you safe and hale, Miss Leah," he says, but his eyes are on everyone but me.

Jim had been a free man in Georgia, and he found enough gold in the rush there to set up a general store. There's a lot more to his story than I know, but I trust him with my life, and if he's wary in this place, then I am, too.

"Found him at the post office," Hampton says, waving an envelope. "Needed someone to read my letter to me."

"Good news?" I ask with false cheer.

"My freedom papers!" Hampton says, with another flourish of the envelope. "It's all official, but still no word on Adelaide." His voice is tight, and I know exactly why. It's tempting fate for two Negroes to walk into an office like this, even free ones. We need to leave, and fast.

"I don't want to intrude on another happy reunion," Hardwick interrupts, sounding bored. "So I'll take my leave. It was a pleasure to see you again, Miss Westfall."

The pleasure is all his. "Until we meet again, Mr. Hardwick." And as soon as I say it, I know I'll be seeing him again as surely as water fills the Pacific Ocean.

The conversation officially over, I take Becky's arm and start walking toward the door, herding Hampton and Jim before me. The air in the room feels like a clothesline about to snap.

Tom follows behind me. As we pass Hardwick, Miss Russell leans over to whisper in his ear again. He replies, "Are you certain?"

We're only a few feet from the door and escape when Hardwick calls out. "Mr. Bigler—a moment of your time."

We freeze. "Tom," I whisper, meaning to follow it up with a *don't*.

Tom turns, his face expressionless. "Mr. Hardwick?" he says.

"My lawyers tell me that they've never seen a tighter, cleverer contract than the one you wrote for Miss Westfall at Christmas. I would like to discuss the temporary application of your considerable talents to a venture of my own."

I don't want Tom to do it. I'm shaking. Surely he can tell? As surely as I sense his stature swelling huge with pride? All the attorneys in the room are now evaluating Tom, trying to determine if he is a potential ally or a new rival. Strange how all that scrutiny directed at me moments ago made *me* feel small.

At least no one is staring at Hampton and Jim anymore. Becky leans in and whispers. "Go on, Tom. It can't hurt to listen. Maybe you can find a way to do something about my house."

"Perhaps I can," he says quietly. "I'll rejoin you later at the hotel." And then, louder, "I'm delighted to see what I can do, Mr. Hardwick. Perhaps some of the gentlemen here can lend us some chairs to talk."

Chairs scrape across the wood floor, and a dozen voices compete to invite the conversation into their own space.

Hampton, Jim, Becky, and I go to leave, but Frank steps in our way and blocks the door. "I would have saved myself a heap of hurt if I just let you die in the desert," he says.

"The way I recall," I say, "you did leave us to die in the desert, and Therese Hoffman paid the price."

Becky adds, "And then one of your men killed Martin." Her voice quakes with the effort to hold back tears. "You know what would have saved you a heap of hurt? Not fighting against us every time. Choosing to join us even once."

He doesn't have an answer for that, and the rest of Hardwick's school of fish is moving toward a desk at the far corner of the office. Frank sneers at me. Or maybe he smiles. The burn on his face makes his expressions hard to parse. Finally he lets us be and hurries off after his new boss.

We flee out the door and out into the cold winter light, and it feels like emerging from my uncle Hiram's mine all over again. I breathe deep, as if the sea salt air can cleanse my soul, but I can't stop shaking.

## Chapter Five

"Lee! Are you all right?" Jefferson is blocked by two men with revolvers. Panic surges in my throat, and I bolt toward him, hands balled into fists.

The men step out of the way at once, guns lowered. Up close, I recognize their faces. I don't remember their names, but I'm certain they used to work for my uncle. "We were just trying to keep him out of trouble, Miss Westfall," says one. "He tried to follow Frank inside, and I thought someone might come to harm. Thought it might be the fellow without a gun."

"Don't do us any favors," I say. I throw my arms around Jeff, not caring that everyone is watching, and he wraps me up in his. After a moment, I stop trembling.

When I step away, the men with guns are gone. Jefferson says, "There were two of them, or I would have forced my way inside."

"I know. Are you all right?"

"They didn't give me trouble, really. That one fellow was

just trying to calm things down; he didn't want anyone getting hurt. Did Frank—?"

"Frank Dilley is still a bully and a coward, but I'm fine." As I say it, I know it to be true. Trouble is brewing, for sure and certain. But I'm breathing easier, more clearheaded. Jeff and I have been through so many troubles together, and I know we'll find a way through the next one, even if haven't quite put my finger on what it is yet.

"It was Jim's idea to go in and check on you," Jefferson says, with a nod toward Jim and Hampton. "When those fellows trained their pistols on me, he thought you might be in a pickle."

So that's why they dared the lion's den. I turn and clasp Jim's hand. It's large and rough, warm and steady, like the man himself. "Thanks, Jim. I'm real glad to see you."

Finally, he smiles, and thc genuine warmth and welcome in that smile go straight to my heart. "Goes both ways, Miss Leah. It's good for the soul to see you and Jefferson arrived safe. Also . . ." Jim clamps Hampton's shoulder. "I enjoyed meeting your friend here. He told me a bit about his situation, coming west."

"He's done well for himself," I say. "We're still hoping to bring his wife out, though."

"We can't wait to meet Adelaide," Becky adds.

"I have to know," Jim says, eyes full of concern. "Your uncle Hiram . . . did he . . . is he—"

"He's no longer a problem," I say firmly.

"Well, that's a blessing."

"Where's Tom?" says Jefferson, indicating the law office. "Did he help you with the house?"

"Not yet." Becky says. "Nothing's gone quite as expected."

I glance toward the door we just exited, feeling an overwhelming urge to flee. Next time I encounter Dilley or Hardwick, I plan to be armed. All our guns are stashed in the wagon, unloaded for the journey. "Let's discuss it elsewhere," I say.

Becky nods. "My mother always said it's not wise to go shopping after such an upsetting encounter, especially not for something important like a wedding dress. We'll catch up with the others for now."

I don't know how that woman can think of shopping at a time like this.

"Miss Leah," Jim says, suddenly formal. "I have a little surprise for you. I was planning to track you down in the spring, but since I've found you, I'll fetch it and bring it around tomorrow."

I'm not one for surprises, but I say, "We'd surely love to see more of you. Call on us at the Parker House hotel."

We take our leave of Jim, promising to chat more soon.

"Can you believe it?" Jefferson says, staring after our friend. "Seeing Jim is like having a little piece of home."

"Sure is." If Mama and Daddy are looking down on me now, they're smiling to see that Jim and I found each other.

We climb into the wagon for a short ride across the plaza to the Parker House. It's the largest hotel I've ever seen, so wide it fills the street front from corner to corner, with a row of dormer windows all the way across the second floor. It is also, the proprietor informs us, completely full.

Becky's big blue eyes somehow grow bigger and bluer as she tells the innkeeper about her "sweet children who are desperate for a roof over their heads after a harrowing journey through the wilderness." He is helpless under her gaze, and he suddenly recalls that our friends stopped by earlier. He gestures through the window toward the City Hotel, a smaller structure with a garret, where he assures us we will find rooms and our friends.

The innkeep at the City Hotel is gambling in the smoky parlor with some of his customers. When we ask after our friends, he grunts in the direction of the stairway. Jefferson is taking care of the horses and wagon, so Becky, Hampton, and I tromp up the narrow staircase to the garret, following after the sound of laughing children.

Becky dashes down the hall to an open door. There's little space in the tiny room, so Hampton and I hover in the doorway. Olive, seven years old and a hundred years curious, peppers her mother with questions, while Andy plays on the floor with clever wooden animals carved by the Major. Major Wally Craven sits on one of two canvas cots in the room, feeding something mushy and unidentifiable to Becky's baby girl.

We met the Major on the wagon train west, and he's been a good friend ever since Jasper amputated his leg to save his life. He's a large, strong fellow, clever with his hands, who wears a wooden leg of his own design. Becky won't travel anywhere without her children, and she doesn't trust anyone but the Major to watch over them.

"The room's barely larger than a wardrobe," Becky says, hunching over to avoid the bare rafters. "But the children have endured worse."

The Major shifts the baby to his shoulder and pats her on the back to burp her. "There were only two rooms available. Twenty-five dollars each per week, rent paid in advance. I took them both. Apparently a fire took out a lot of buildings last month." He points up to the bare rafters. "They barely finished this place before they moved on to the next. We'll have to sleep in shifts."

"Oh, dear," says Becky, in a tone that I'm pretty sure means *This won't do*. "San Francisco has not been kind to us so far. At least Hampton got his freedom papers!"

Hampton waves them triumphantly.

I sense someone approach and turn to see Henry, clean-shaven and hair slicked neat as you please. A silk cravat hangs around his neck, a brighter blue than fashionable.

I say, "I thought you'd be out looking for a teaching job."

"The new state constitution requires public schools," Henry says, "but it seems no one has gotten around to building them. I was told the first school will be built in Monterey."

"So what are you going to do?" I ask.

"Some wealthy white and Mexican families hire tutors, so I've set up a few meetings."

"Poor Henry," I say. "Sounds like you'll have to get up early for a change."

"No. I'll meet them tonight." His eyes sparkle. "In gambling dens."

"Oh, dear," Becky says again.

"You're a terrible gambler," I point out. "Even I can tell when you have a good hand."

Henry blinks. "I'm only doing it to make connections, of course."

Jefferson, having stabled the horses and wagon, makes his way down the hall with our bags. He drops my saddlebag on the floor with a heavy thump. "What did you pack, Lee, a bunch of rocks? Oh, hello, Henry."

"Have you seen Tom?" Henry asks. "I hope he had better luck than I did."

I say, "He's interviewing for a post with Hardwick. And I have a bad feeling." I explain everything that happened.

"You don't have to worry about Tom," Henry assures me.

"I wish I could be sure. He's . . . different."

"Working in your uncle's mine was hard for him. He . . ." Henry hesitates, considering. "Well, he gets wound up at night and can't sleep because of it."

"I can understand that," I admit.

"Tom has been hard to read lately, it's true," Jefferson says.

"He's the one who should be a gambler," the Major points out. "He has such a poker face."

"*No one* should be a gambler," Becky says.

Henry squeezes my arm. "Give Tom some time. I know he's intently focused right now. He thinks we've got a better chance to practice our professions here, and the sooner we get to work, the more of a head start we'll have on everyone else."

I can't help the little sigh that escapes. "Sometimes I just wish things could go back to the way they were, when it was just us, relying on each other. Looking to stake our claims and make a better life for ourselves."

"That's exactly what we're doing," Henry says. "We're just staking a different set of claims now."

"But if the three of you stay in San Francisco, I'm going to miss you."

"Me too," says little Andy from the floor. I should have realized he was listening carefully to every word. "I'll miss you the most."

"Then you must continue to work on your letters," Henry says. "So we can write to each other every week."

The stairs creak, and Jefferson says, "Hey, Tom. We were just talking about you."

"Speculating on my prospects of future employment?" Tom asks as he strides toward us.

"Praising your immaculate presentation and good looks," Henry says.

"Don't let me interrupt you then," he says dryly.

"Did Hardwick offer you a job?" I ask.

"He did."

"Did you take it?" My voice is a lot louder than I intend.

Tom pauses. "I asked for time to consider his generous offer."

I want to follow up, demand to know why he didn't reject it outright, but a door to another room slams open. A large man reeking of booze and wearing only an undershirt, thrusts his bald head into the hall. "If you all want to have a confab, that's why God invented parlors. Get yourselves downstairs and use one—some of us are trying to sleep!"

He slams the door shut again.

After a brief pause, Henry whispers. "Anyone else tempted to start a rousing chorus of 'Used Up Man'?"

Becky can't hide her grin as she waves us all into the tiny room, then closes the door behind us. We take seats on the cots, the two small chairs, the floor. I grab a spot beneath the single window. The rough wood of the unfinished wall makes my back itch. Jefferson squeezes in beside me, and Andrew comes over to show off his wooden animals. Jeff agrees that they are very fine animals and makes an appropriate variety of barnyard and woodland sounds, which somehow makes me want to kiss him even more than usual.

Becky drags one of the room's two chairs to the center of the floor and sits like a queen on her throne, hands folded in her lap. "Our original plan to come to the city, get the house, and depart directly isn't going to work," she begins.

"I've got my freedom papers, but I don't have any word on Adelaide," Hampton adds. "The postmaster says it could be a few days or a few months until the mail comes next. It all depends on when the ships arrive. So I might have to stick around."

"Hardwick's going to break our agreement and cheat Glory out of its charter if he can," I add.

This is news to some, including the Major, who frowns. "People could lose their homes," he says.

"Once word gets out that our charter's not coming," Becky points out, "we'll start having trouble with claim jumpers again. The promise of a proper town has given us a lot of protection."

"Once California is declared a state," Tom says, "we'll have legal recourse. Until then, the contract gives him a loophole."

"By then it might be too late," I say.

Becky says, "But one thing at a time. Right now the problem I care about is my house. Tom, did you think of something?"

He shakes his head. "Hardwick wants my help with his auctions—many involving properties of dubious provenance—and he needs legal assistance managing the contracts and bills of sale to alleviate questions of legal ownership. Your house is currently stored in one of his warehouses. Working for him might give us another option for recovering it."

Maybe that's why Tom was so eager to hear Hardwick out—so he could help us. Henry was right; Tom would never betray us.

"What if we buy it?" I suggest. I reach out with my gold sense, assuring myself that all the money we need is right there. In my mind, my saddlebag shines brighter than a full moon.

"The auction is a week from Tuesday," Becky says. "Staying almost two weeks in this city will cost a mother lode. And there's no guarantee we'll be the highest bidder."

"Almost every item has a 'buy now' price," Tom says. "I could find out the price for your house. It's likely to cost twice as much as you'd pay for it at auction."

"Let's do it," I say. "I'll chip in. Let's just buy it and get out of town." And away from Hardwick and Frank Dilley and everything else that's making me feel as tangled up as a squirrel's nest. The wind blows outside, shaking the roof tiles. "There's something bad here," I say. "It's like . . . it's like a snake's rattle, warning us to back off. Let's buy the house, however much it costs, and get on our way."

It's a reasonable request. Everyone can see that, I'm sure.

But Becky's frown deepens, and she raises one finger in the air.

"So let me get this straight," she says. "My dear late husband, Mr. Joyner, already paid once in full to ship this house to California for me. Now the petty self-appointed bureaucrats of this territory want me to pay a second time to reacquire my property. And if I want it in a hurry, without the disadvantage of bidding against strangers after a costly stay away from home, then I have to pay for it a third time."

"That's about the size of it," the Major grumbles.

"No!" She jabs her finger at him. "It's wrong, and it won't stand."

"So what are we going to do about it?" he asks. The baby is nearly asleep on his shoulder. She has recently discovered the wonder that is her thumb, and her tiny cheek pulses with drowsy sucking.

"Have you decided to steal it back?" Tom asks, brightening.

"I can't steal back what's already mine," she says. Olive, sensing the tension in the room, scoots over to lean against her mother. Becky strokes her daughter's bright blond hair and says, "But I have a plan."

"Sounds intriguing," Henry says.

"Henry Meek," she says. "How would you like to be my husband?"

"What?" Henry gulps.

*"What?"* the Major adds.

"She just wants someone to pose as her husband," I say gently. "Remember? We discussed the possibility last fall in Glory."

"*I* can do that," the Major says, a little too eagerly.

Becky shakes her head. "The Joyner family is well known back in Tennessee, and it's possible there are a few folks right here in San Francisco who are familiar with my late husband, at least distantly. Henry can pass for Andrew at a glance. But you, Wally, you're . . ." A little smile plays at the corners of her mouth. "You're as different as can be."

Henry straightens. "I was quite the thespian in college," he says. "And I would be honored to pose as your fine gentleman spouse."

The Major does not seem convinced, but Becky brightens, saying, "Then this is what we're going to do."

# Chapter Six

Noon the following day finds me and Jefferson sitting on the wagon bench in front of our hotel, keeping an eye on the Custom House across the plaza. Jeff's arm is settled across my shoulders, and I lean into him, loving how easy it is now that we're affianced. When I want to hold his hand, all I have to do is reach for it. When he wants to press his lips to the top of my head, he doesn't hesitate.

Hampton has gone off in search of his supper. Wisps of fog still dally with the hilltops, and the air is thick with chilled wetness. I wear a floppy straw hat, in part against the cold, in part to cover my face.

The clerk who helped Becky and me yesterday entered the office right when it opened this morning, and he hasn't yet emerged. For Becky's plan to work, he needs to take a break. Then, we'll approach one of the other clerks, who won't remember our failed attempt to acquire the house once already.

Becky strides toward us from across the square, accompanied by a tall gentleman in a fine suit. For a split second, I wonder where Henry is, even though he was supposed to accompany her, preparing for today's adventure.

Of course, the finely dressed gentleman *is* Henry, and I let out an appreciative whistle. "Hello, Mr. Joyner."

He preens, but Becky scowls, and Henry slips into a dour expression that reminds me so much of the late Andrew Joyner that's it's almost a punch in the gut.

"What do you think?" Becky asks.

The resemblance is uncanny. "How?"

"We visited a variety of shops," Henry says in a perfect Southern drawl, turning so I can see him from every angle. "Until I found the perfect suit. You'd be surprised at the items that have made their way out here. Why, I could dress myself like anyone—from a Japanese samurai to a French countess."

He extends his arms so we can admire the flashy cufflinks on his shirt. They're exactly the sort of thing Mr. Joyner would have bought.

"You even sound like him!"

"He used to imitate my husband," Becky says. "To amuse the other bachelors when he thought no one else was listening." She scowls up at him. "But *I* was listening."

"The lesson is that someone's always listening," Henry says without breaking character, though he does manage a small amount of shame. Mr. Joyner was an uppity ne'er-do-well and few cared for him at all. But he *was* Becky's husband, and I hope Henry's imitations haven't pained her.

Jefferson says, "I swear you've aged a decade since yesterday."

"Sleeping on the hard floor of a garret, with six people in a room meant for two, will do that to a soul," Henry says.

"Stop bellyaching," Becky tells him. "We all slept in much worse conditions while crossing the continent."

"But if you recall, *I* always slept on a feather mattress!" Henry says, fully into his character.

It's the worst thing he could say. Mr. Joyner packed a whole household's worth of fine furniture for their journey west, including a full-sized bed that filled most of their wagon. It was the furniture that killed him, in an accident high in the Rocky Mountains. He sacrificed his life trying to save a huge oak dresser, and I can still picture him smashed and bloody in the dust, broken pieces of wood scattered all around him.

Henry sees the expression on my face and says, "I'm . . . I'm sorry."

"No, that's good," Becky says, and maybe I've overestimated her heartache. "That's exactly the kind of thoughtless thing he'd say. You stay in character until we have my house."

Henry gives her a small bow. "Your wish is my dearest desire." He turns to Jefferson. "We stopped at a ladies' store to sample some of the maquillage. It makes a lady look younger, but a gentleman much older."

"It's astonishing," I tell him, because it is.

Becky nods toward the shaded veranda of the Custom House. "Has our helpful friend from yesterday taken a break from his duties yet?"

"Not yet," I say.

"And we're sure no one is using the back door?" she asks.

Jefferson shrugs. "I circled the whole building. Nothing back there but trash."

"A flaw in our plan, perhaps," Henry says.

"I'm optimistic he'll leave through the front, just like the others," Becky says firmly.

As I settle back into the crook of Jefferson's arm, our friend Jim appears around the corner and heads for the front of the hotel. He carries a large rolled blanket. I shout hello to him, and he changes course, waving to us.

Jefferson tips his hat. "Free Jim," he acknowledges.

"Just Jim now," Jim and I say in unison.

"Well, all right then," Jefferson says, with a hint of a smile. "Jim it is."

"Glad I caught you," Jim says to me. "Was afraid you'd be out and about, and I'd miss seeing the look on your face when you opened this."

He hands the long package up to me, and I lay it across my lap. It's a heavy weight. A familiar weight. I know what it is; I'm sure of it. My hands shake as I peel the blanket away, because now I've gotten my hopes up, and what if I'm wrong?

Polished wood and steel glint up at me.

"Lee?" Jefferson says. "That's a dead ringer for your daddy's Hawken rifle."

"It *is* my daddy's Hawken." I examine the stock and find familiar scratches, plus a few more. I hold it up and sight along the barrel. "Jim—where . . . ? How . . . ?"

He smiles like the cat that ate the canary. "Remember

when we saw each other last? In Independence? It was on a rack in that general store, and I recognized it right away. I figure somebody carried it west, and then traded it for a pan and shovel. That, or you were so desperate for money you had to pawn it yourself. I snapped it up right before I left, but then I couldn't find you again."

A laugh bursts out of my chest, a pure clean feeling of delight. I jump down from the bench and throw my arms around him and give him the tightest hug, and I don't care what anybody thinks.

Jefferson climbs down and shakes his hand. "We appreciate this a great deal, Jim," he says as I take a step back and admire the rifle all over again.

"Reuben Westfall bought that gun in my store when you were barely toddling around," Jim says.

I can't stop staring at the rifle. Three brothers robbed me of it last year, when I was barely out of Georgia. I never thought I'd see it again. "This is the last thing I have to remember Daddy by," I tell Jim.

"Aren't those his boots you're wearing?"

I look down at the boots and scuff them in the dirt. They aren't the same, no matter how much they look like Daddy's boots, but I'm grateful to have them. "Nah. The Major made these for me. They fit me a lot better. I'd have had fewer blisters had I hiked west in these." I hold up the rifle again, just to admire it. "But Jim! This gift—it's . . . it's . . ."

"Too much?" suggests Jefferson.

"A surprise?" asks Jim, suppressing his grin.

It's the best thing to happen to me since Jefferson agreed to marry me. "You have to let me pay you for—"

"There he is!" shouts Becky. She's pointing at the Custom House. "There he goes!"

Sure enough, yesterday's clerk is strolling along the veranda with one of his fellows. I grab the blanket, rewrap the rifle, and stuff it under the bench. "Let's go," I say.

While Jefferson catches Jim up on what's going on, Becky, Henry, and I set off across the plaza at a brisk pace. "So, you'll stand watch?" Becky asks me.

She must be nervous, because we've been over it a thousand times. "If I see the clerk coming back, I'll come inside and signal so you can slip out," I assure her.

Henry jumps in with, "Then I'll take the letter and continue to wait in line by myself. If you still have concerns, I can go in alone."

"No, no," Becky says. "I'll feel better if I see it through myself. And though we've done our best to anticipate questions, the situation might still require a woman's touch."

*Because that worked so well for us yesterday.* But I refrain from saying as much.

Becky and her false husband step into line. Across the plaza, Hampton has returned to the wagon, and my stomach rumbles when he offers something to Jefferson and Jim.

Everyone is in place now, so I lean against the wall between the Custom House and the law offices, like I'm waiting impatiently for someone inside, which will be my excuse should anyone bother me. I pull the brim of my hat down over my face so I don't have to make eye contact with anyone. I pull my sweater down over my hands because I'm cold. I cross my arms with what I hope is a strong signal to leave me alone.

From the corner of my eye, I catch sight of a woman approaching, and for a split second, I think it's Helena Russell, the woman who was keeping company with Hardwick. I'm like a deer about to bolt, until a closer look reveals the truth: it's the pickpocket from the previous morning.

"Hello, Sonia," I say without warmth. She must frequent Portsmouth Square often. A lot of miners here with gold to spend. After they've had a few drinks, it's probably easy to part them from their fortunes.

"Oh. Miss Lee," she says, eyes widening, feet faltering. She turns and dashes away.

I'm almost sad to see her go, because two generously whiskered fellows come along and lean against the wall beside me. They pretend like they're talking to each other—about the empty lot one just purchased, and the lucky card streak the other is on—but I'd bet my boots they're bragging to get my attention. I pretend they don't exist. It's a damp, chilly day, and my attitude is even chillier. Eventually they move on.

Becky and Henry make it inside. The line isn't long compared to yesterday. After about twenty minutes, I notice that everything has gone peculiarly silent, and people are leaving the Custom House—folks who made it inside *after* Becky and Henry. They all seem anxious and hurried.

I start to worry a little.

Then our helpful clerk from yesterday saunters back with

one of his fellows, and I start to worry a lot.

I peel off from the wall and stick my head in the door, about to wave the signal for Becky to cover her face and slip away.

I freeze.

Frank Dilley stands just inside, Colt revolver trained on Becky and Henry. They are seated in chairs, guarded by two impeccably groomed men in suits. One of the guards is very large, and the other is larger. Frank grins when he sees me. He motions with the gun for me to stand beside the chairs.

Henry is hunched over on himself, looking defeated. Becky is like a stray cat cornered in the barn—I can't tell if she's about to bolt or attack with her claws.

"This won't take but a minute," Frank says. The burn on his face is smeared with glycerin, giving it a red shine. The scar pulls the corner of his mouth back into a joyless smile. It looks painful. I hope it's painful.

"Just play by the rules and nobody will get hurt," Frank says. "I know that goes against your nature, but do it this once, for the sake of your friends. Then we'll all be on our way."

I walk slowly to Becky's side, hands up, eyes on that gun. The clerk comes through the door and skids to a stop. "Oh," he says. "Oh, my."

The other clerks peer at us from across the counter, like this is a show they've been waiting to see.

"Mr. Brumble," Frank says.

Yesterday's clerk bobs his head. "Yes, sir. Present, sir."

"Are these two . . . well, I don't know what to call the two of them together, but for the sake of argument, we'll say *ladies*.

Are these two ladies the ones who came in yesterday and tried to collect property belonging to one Mr. Andrew Joyner?"

"Yes, sir. Yes, sir, they are."

"And this gentleman here presented himself today as Mr. Andrew Joyner. You can confirm this, correct?" Frank waves his hand in the direction of another man in a starched white shirt, who immediately provides assent.

"This time last year," Frank says, drawing the words out with obvious pleasure, "I was wagon master on the train that brought this sorry group of deceivers and reprobates west to California. Mr. Andrew Joyner was a member of our party, but he got himself killed crossing the Rocky Mountains. That boy there with the fancy suit is Henry Meeks, fresh out of college and completely ignorant of honest work. He is not Andrew Joyner. Do all of you recognize their faces now?"

The line of clerks nods, solemn as a jury.

"If any of these troublemakers makes another attempt to claim property belonging to the late Mr. Joyner—or anyone else, for that matter—you are authorized to seize them for fraud, and hold them until they can be arrested by the sheriff or his deputies."

"Does that come from the sheriff?" asks a small, balding clerk. It's not much defiance, but it's *some* defiance, and I appreciate him for it.

But Frank says, "That comes from *Mr. Hardwick*," and the clerks nod, even the balding one. We have no champions here.

Frank twirls his gun and slips it into his holster—a fancy trick I'll have to teach myself if I get the chance. He pulls out a pocket watch and checks the time, then nods to the large gentleman guards. "I've got an appointment with Mr. Hardwick. Hold these folks for a couple minutes and then send them packing. Catch up to us later."

He slips out the door, and the clerks try their best to look busy. The two guards continue to hold guns on us. Maybe we should just walk out. Would they really shoot us if we did? The fact that Dilley wants us to stay put for a spell is interesting. It means he's a little afraid of us, of what we might do, and he wants to get away clean.

Becky is furious, but she makes no motion as if to leave. Henry is pale under his maquillage.

"You didn't see Dilley come in this morning?" Becky asks me.

"No," I admit. "I'm sorry."

"Wouldn't have made a difference," says Large.

"We were all here before sunup, since we weren't sure when you'd show," adds Larger.

"Was about ready to give up, myself," says Large.

"Frank was too, but the boss told him to wait."

"So we waited."

A hard knot settles in my gut. "You *knew* we were coming," I say as Becky and Henry exchange an alarmed glance. "How?"

The only people who knew of our plan were in that room last night. I'll go out on a limb and assume that neither the Major, nor any of Becky's three children gave us away. And either Becky and Henry are the finest actors in the whole wide west, or they're just as shocked as I am. Jefferson would never do it. That leaves only Hampton and Tom, and I can't imagine either of them would be betray us either. Maybe the drunk in the other room eavesdropped through the walls, but we kept our voices low after his outburst.

"I never know how the boss knows what he knows," says Large.

"He's Mr. Hardwick," says Larger with a shrug. "You just assume he knows everybody and everything."

Large holsters his gun and waves toward the door. "Shoo. Get out of here. Don't misbehave."

Larger follows suit. "Go, and sin no more."

Becky rises slowly and primly. Henry bolts out the door before I can say boo. We catch up to him outside beneath the veranda, where he paces in a tight circle with his hands deep in his pockets.

"Frank wasn't going to hurt us," Becky assures him. "He just wanted to scare us."

"Well, he sure did *that* like an expert," Henry says.

"He's an expert bully," I tell him. "He has loads of practice. He knows that house belongs to Becky morally, if not legally. Sometimes people are inclined to do the moral thing regardless, and a different clerk might have let us sign those papers." I'm pretty sure the small balding fellow would have helped us if we'd been lucky enough to get him yesterday instead. "This was meant to scare all the clerks too."

That changes Henry's perspective a bit, and he stops circling like an anxious dog on a short leash. "So what do we do next?"

"We can still go buy the house," I say.

Becky shakes her head. "Now that they know how much I want it, they'll charge five times the price."

"Or ten," I say. "But it might be worth it just to be done with all this."

"No," she says firmly. "We'll wait until the auction and take our chances then. New houses go up so fast here, there's no reason for someone to overpay for one tiny, disassembled cottage shipped from Tennessee."

Which is an excellent point. "But I can afford it. Even at ten times the price."

My words ring hollow, even to myself. Spending that much money at a public auction will attract attention we don't want. Besides, it feels like giving in. Hardwick has already hinted at shaking us down for more money. The last thing we need is to let him get started at it.

Becky looks offended that I would even suggest such a thing. Her mouth is shaping a reply, but a commotion reaches us from across the plaza—shouts, the sound of a hammer smacking wood, the whinny of a frightened horse. San Francisco is a boisterous place, and I've already grown accustomed to ignoring its daily clamor, but Henry says, "That's Jefferson and Hampton. Looks like they're in trouble."

# Chapter Seven

I spot Jim first. He sits in the mud in front of the wagon. Blood flows down his scalp and fills one eye. I sprint across the plaza, dodging delivery wagons and shoving my way through clusters of people as Jim tries to stand, slips, falls again.

Beside him, Jefferson is trying to manage the horses, who dance nervously from side to side. A fierce-looking man in a bearskin coat swings a bully club at Jefferson. He dodges in the nick of time, but the man winds up for another swing.

"Hey!" I yell, and the man hesitates.

Three other thugs have Hampton pinned facedown on the ground. Hampton thrashes as one tries to pull a burlap sack over his head. A second straddles his waist as he binds Hampton's hands with rope, and the third struggles to pin his legs. Mud flies everywhere.

I lower my shoulder and ram the man pinning Hampton's legs. We both sprawl in the muck.

Hampton kicks out, knocking loose the second man, but

not soon enough to keep his hands from being tied. He rolls over onto his knees and tries to rise just as the first man cinches the bag around his neck.

I lunge forward, intending to yank the sack away, but one of the men swings a fist. I dodge left. My feet slip out from under me, and my backside splats into the muck again.

"Lee! Duck!"

Jefferson's voice. I cover my head and roll. A club glances off my shoulder, scraping a chunk of skin with it.

I come up with a handful of mud and fling it blindly in the direction of my attacker. A splat sound tells me I've hit something, so I grab and fling again while struggling to my feet.

A hand grabs my elbow and pulls at me, so I lash out. My fist connects with something solid and I hear an *oof* from Jefferson.

"Sorry!" I wipe the mud from my face with the back of my forearm. Jefferson grabs my waist and yanks me back just in time to avoid a swing from Bearcoat's club.

"Let's go!" someone yells to Bearcoat before he can try again.

Hampton is now in the back of an empty dung cart, ropes binding his wrists and ankles. The man in the cart seat gestures at Bearcoat to follow.

But Bearcoat and his friends won't be budged. They're frontiersmen. Bullies for hire. I recognize the type from the hills back home.

"That one's a girl," says one, like it's the worst thing a person can be.

"She rung my bell," says another, picking up a coonskin cap

from the mud. He's the one I knocked off Hampton. "She should pay, girl or not."

Bearcoat still holds the club out in front of him, daring Jefferson or me to take a step. "That's up to them."

Becky and Henry arrive at that moment. "I demand to know what's going on here," Becky says. "Why have you attacked my companions?"

"This ain't no business of yours," Bearcoat says, jabbing the club in her direction.

"The hell it isn't," I say, taking a step forward. Jefferson grabs at me, but I shrug him off. "You're kidnapping our friend."

"Ain't no kidnapping," says Bearcoat. "Got a notice from an Arkansas paper saying he's a runaway slave. Perfectly legal for us to catch him, return him to his proper owner."

"He's a free man," Jim says, and I cast a glace over my shoulder to see him rising to his feet and wicking mud from his trousers. His gaze is unfocused, and he teeters when he moves.

"The Bledsoe family says otherwise. Says he ran away last summer."

Hampton's cart is rolling out of sight, beyond the Parker House.

"You are mistaken," Becky tells the three roughnecks. "He has his freedom papers. In any case, California is going to be a free state. There's no slavery here."

Buckskin snarls at her. "Where you from?"

"Tennessee, but—"

"I thought I could hear God's country in your voice, ma'am, but you are on the wrong side here."

"I'm on the side of my friends. I'm on the side of doing the right thing. Where are you taking Hampton?"

"Don't answer that," Bearcoat says. He checks over his shoulder and confirms that the cart is long gone. "Let's collect our bounty and be done. It's already been more trouble than it's worth."

The three men back away slowly, then turn and hurry.

I spin around. "Jim! Are you all right?"

He's standing, leaning against the wagon, hand pressed against his temple, while Henry calms the horses.

"I'll be fine as soon as my head clears," he says.

I reach under the seat and peel the blanket off my daddy's Hawken rifle.

"What are you doing?" asks Jefferson.

"I'm going to find out where they're taking Hampton. He might be hurt."

"I'm not sure that's a smart—"

I don't hear the rest, because I'm already off and running.

A mood's taken hold of me, the same way fire takes hold of grease. First came all the reminders of my uncle and the horrible things done in his mine. Then Frank Dilley and his bullies held guns to our heads to scare Becky and keep her from what's rightfully hers. Now this. It's gone too far. I'm not sure what I aim to do about it yet, but it's not fair. And I can't lose another friend like I lost Martin and Therese.

*Girl, you'll learn. Life's not fair,* Hardwick said.

Well, maybe I aim to make it fairer.

I turn the corner onto Clay Street and head downslope

toward the bay. The coonskin cap bobs up and down a block or so ahead. Beside him is Bearcoat. They're walking fast, but by the time they turn right on Battery Street, I'm less than half a block behind.

Slave catchers look the same whether they're in the woods of Georgia or the hills of San Francisco—covered in fur, well armed, mean as snakes. To them, a person is just another animal to hunt. Well, I can hunt too.

Battery Street is one of those waterfronts being filled in. To my left, a ship has been grounded and transformed into a saloon. An awning flaps at the entrance, and above it, the ship's masts have been replaced by a second story, built right on top of the deck. Across from the saloon to my right is an old brig still moored in water, but who knows for how long.

A sign hangs on the side of the brig: SAN FRANCISCO JAIL.

The empty cart is parked at the water's edge. Hampton kneels on the ground beside it, the driver looming over him. A small cluster of familiar figures surrounds them, and my steps falter.

Hardwick and Frank Dilley are conferring with the slave catchers. Miss Russell, Hardwick's "associate" from the law offices, presides over them all, wearing a dress of deep violet and fine lace.

Dilley searches Hampton's pockets and removes his precious letter, while Hardwick counts out gold coins to the roughnecks.

The driver shoves Hampton into a waiting boat and starts rowing him out to the brig.

I'm all alone with no plan. But somehow I have to get that letter. It's the only proof we have that Hampton is a free man.

I take a deep breath and stride forward, hefting my rifle, trying to appear more certain of myself than I feel. My gun isn't loaded, but no one needs to know that.

Helena Russell is the first to notice me. She leans over and whispers to Hardwick, who pulls out his pocket watch and checks the time. He nods, raising an eyebrow as if impressed. Somewhere in the city, church bells ring out the hour. Frank Dilley gives me a side-eye, then sticks a cheap cigar in his mouth and strikes a match to light it.

I stop about twenty feet away. Jefferson runs up behind me, out of breath. Part of me wishes he hadn't followed, because I have no idea what I'm about to get myself into, but I'm glad to have him at my side just the same.

"What do you think you're doing, Mr. Hardwick?" I shout.

"I might ask you the same thing, Miss Westfall."

"I'm checking on the welfare of a friend."

"That's very gentlewomanly of you. I'm upholding the laws of the land by paying professionals with a specific set of skills to locate and apprehend a runaway slave. I'll arrange for his transportation back to Arkansas and collect a hefty fee. The law and profit go hand in hand."

"He's no runaway, and you know it. You were there when he showed us his freedom papers."

"These papers?" says Frank Dilley. He waves the envelope he just took from Hampton, lifts it toward the glowing end of his cigar.

I whip up my rifle and aim it at his head. Dilley's free hand reaches for the gun at his holster.

"I don't miss," I tell him. "Especially not at this range, which you well know. You want to bet your life that you can draw faster than I can pull a trigger, you just go ahead."

Dilley's face goes white, but he doesn't draw.

"Do you want us to take care of this?" Bearcoat offers, tapping Hardwick on the arm. The other two roughnecks look like they're itching for a fight as well.

"There's no need for violence," Hardwick tells them. "You've been paid. The Apollo saloon is just across the street. I suggest you repair to that location, acquire something refreshing, and enjoy the show."

Bearskin shrugs, and the three men peel off to the saloon. They join the crowd of drinkers who have come outside to watch the commotion.

"It's wrong to make a show out of someone's freedom," I say. "You still there, Jefferson?"

"Yeah," he says behind me. His voice is quiet and very controlled.

"Would you please walk over to Mr. Dilley and take that letter from him? And make sure it's Hampton's letter."

"Glad to," he says.

"Frank?"

Frank glares. His gun hand twitches at his side.

"You hold that letter way out to your side—the other side. Away from everybody else. I want to see your gun hand the whole time. Jeff?"

"Lee?"

"Best stay well out of my line of fire. I don't want anything coming between this rifle and that varmint."

Jefferson closes the distance like a man approaching a nest of angry hornets. Hardwick whispers something to Miss Russell, and she moves behind him. I get the impression he's protecting her, using his own body as a shield. What makes a man like him do something so selfless?

Jefferson snatches the envelope from Dilley's outstretched hand and pauses just long enough to glance inside. "This is it."

"Good. Get back behind me."

He returns a whole lot faster than he went, keeping his eye on Dilley the whole way.

"Mr. Hardwick," I say, enunciating carefully. "Release Hampton."

"Can't do that. It would be breaking the law. But someone going through the proper channels could arrange to purchase his bounty from me before I sell it to the owner in Arkansas. Arkansas is an awful distance."

"This letter proves he's a free man."

"And I have a bounty that proves he's a runaway. Who is the law going to believe? A runaway Negro and a runaway girl? Or an upstanding man of industry?"

I think I might hate Hardwick. "Release him anyway."

"Ah, no," Hardwick says, smiling. "You'll have to take that up with the sheriff, since the runaway has been remanded to the authority of the jail."

"So, let's talk to the sheriff."

Hardwick just grins.

"Let me guess—the sheriff isn't here right now."

"He's a man with many duties."

Part of me wants to storm over and free Hampton by force. But there's just me and Jefferson with two unloaded guns between us. "This isn't over," I say fiercely.

Hardwick's smile widens. "I would be disappointed if it was."

I back away slowly without lowering the gun. Before I've taken a dozen steps, Hardwick puts his arms around Dilley and Helena Russell, herding them toward the Apollo saloon. The last thing I hear him say is, "A round of drinks for everyone, on me."

I lower the rifle. My arms are shaking.

"Let's go," Jefferson says. "Before they change their minds."

We hurry around the corner and trudge up the hill, toward Portsmouth Square. The first block passes in silence. Partway up the second block, he says, "You know that rifle isn't loaded, right?"

"Frank didn't know that," I say.

"What were you going to do if he called your bluff and drew on you?"

"My plan didn't account for him making that choice."

"Lee!"

"What?"

"Sometimes you need a better plan."

"But Hampton's letter was as stake! What if Dilley burned it or threw it into the bay before we could get it back?"

"I don't know if the letter mattered one whit. Like Hardwick said, who's the law going to side with? The white man, of course."

I'm silent a long while. We've reached the square before I can admit it. "You have a point."

"Thank you. I don't mind going along with whatever you want to do, but I'd appreciate it if you didn't put me in the line of fire without a better way of backing me up. And running off half-cocked isn't the kind of thing that hurts you and me; it's usually the people we're trying to help who get themselves killed. We learned that at your uncle's mine."

"I'm sorry. It was the heat of the moment." He's right. It's always the most vulnerable who suffer most. I'm lucky Hardwick didn't take it out on Hampton. Yet.

"Well, give me a warning if there's more heat coming."

"I . . . I'll be more careful."

Jefferson leans over and plants a kiss on the top of my head.

When we get back to the wagon, Becky, Henry, and Jim are waiting for us. Jim sits on the bench, looking shaken but much better than he did before I ran off. Henry tends to Jim's wound, wiping the blood from his face. Becky paces on the boardwalk. When she sees me and Jefferson, she demands, "Where's Hampton? Is he safe?"

"For the moment, but maybe not for long," I say. I offer a quick accounting of what happened, leaving out the bit about me threatening to shoot Frank Dilley with an empty gun. "At least we got his freedom papers back before Frank burned them."

"Let me see those," Jim says, hopping down from the wagon.

Jefferson hands them over, and Jim opens the envelope, checks the letter, then folds it right back up. He slips it into the pocket of his trousers.

"Maybe we should give the freedom papers to Tom?" Becky says. "He's a lawyer, and he—"

"We have more than a hundred years' experience with this sort of thing," Jim says. "But Tom is welcome to take a gander at them anytime."

"We *have* to get Hampton back," Henry asks. "And we have to do it soon. There's not a prison in the world that keeps a man hale."

"We'll find the sheriff and pay Hampton's bounty," Jefferson says.

"I've got some money—" I begin.

"Hold on to it," Jim says.

"Why?"

"You're acting like this is the first time a free Negro has been kidnapped and locked up until he pays a fine," Jim says. "When the law can't take our freedom, it takes all our money instead. Takes both when it gets the chance."

"We can't leave Hampton in jail," Becky says.

"We won't. But it's important for us to solve this, because it affects all of us."

"We *are* trying to solve it," I say.

"Don't get me wrong; we can definitely use your help. But freeing Hampton is taking the easy way out. We can do that part just fine ourselves. And when I say *us,* I mean free

Negroes. This is our problem. It was our problem before Hampton got arrested. It's gonna be our problem long after he gets free again. "

My heart aches. The fire that was burning inside me just a little while ago has about gone out, leaving me cold.

"What do you want us to do?" I say.

"We want to help," Becky adds.

"Hampton is our friend," Henry insists.

Jefferson stands beside Jim. He doesn't say a thing, but he doesn't need to.

"You can't barge in and try to fix Hampton's situation like it's something unusual, like it's a one-of-a-kind circumstance," Jim says. "That's what white people do. They fix one tiny thing and think they're heroes."

He stares right at me as he says it, and my gut churns in response. When I met Jim in Independence, I mouthed off to the store clerk for treating Jim poorly. I thought I was doing the right thing then, but maybe I was just making things worse.

"What happened to Hampton happens to free men all the time, all over this country," he continues. "*We* will take care of him, but then you gotta take care of Hardwick. It ain't enough to rescue a man in trouble, if you don't stop the man who put him there. Hardwick'll just do it again to someone else."

*Life isn't fair.*

*Then it's our job to make it fairer.*

*Oh,* I realize. *This* is what that means.

"Jim's right," I say. "My uncle took everything from me.

Then . . . remember how Dilley treated the Indians we met crossing the continent? Hardwick funded my uncle's mine, and we know what happened to the Indians and the Chinese there."

Henry adds, "Then Hardwick took all the money we raised in Glory and promised us a town charter, only now he's holding the charter ransom for even more money."

I nod. "He's stealing Becky's house, and he's going to sell it to somebody else. Now he's stealing Hampton's freedom. Over the last year, we've been treating all these things like separate problems, but they're not. They're all one problem."

"What's the one problem?" Jefferson asks. "Hardwick's an evil cur?"

"No, there are lots of bad men. I mean, yes, he is, but the real problem is the way he's got the law all tied up with money. He uses the law to rob people. Then he uses his money to change the laws and to buy lawmakers so he can rob even more people. It's a vicious circle, and it won't stop until he's not able to do whatever he wants to anyone."

"So what are we going to do?" Becky asks.

"We're going to stop him."

Jefferson steps forward, puts his hands on my shoulders, and looks at me dead-on. "You know I'm with you, right, Lee? Always, no matter what. But this time, we need a plan. No more going off half-cocked."

"A plan," Becky agrees.

"Something foolproof," Henry adds.

"Easy," I say. "Right?"

## Chapter Eight

Two mornings later, we take leave of the City Hotel, long before our full week is up—paid in advance, both rooms, all four cots—and form a small parade with all our possessions to walk down to the docks.

The Major has the baby tucked in one arm and holds Andy's hand with the other. I'm afraid he's going to topple over on his wooden leg, but he stomps along like a man who's been doing it his whole life and not just a few months.

Olive flits like a hummingbird. She runs ahead half a dozen steps, notices something new, and then immediately dashes back to tell us about it. "Ma, the sign on that big house says it's an oh-per-uh. Ma, what's an oh-per-uh?"

"An opera is a form of musical entertainment—"

"Jasper, is that man sick? He's sitting against the wall and his skin is *blanched*. You said that when a man's skin is—"

"Hush, dear," says Becky. "It's not polite to point out such things."

The three bachelors walk together. It's the first time they've all seen each other in days, because Jasper has been volunteering at doctors' offices throughout the city.

"I'm trying to find someone I can learn from," Jasper tells his friends, "but when a man with a crushed hand needed two fingers amputated, I was the one teaching the doctor how to do it instead of him teaching me."

"That's still better than my search," Tom says. "Plenty of law offices, but none willing to give me a job unless I bring in my own clients. If I had my own clients, I could afford rent, and I wouldn't need a job."

Henry rubs his eyes. I suspect he was up all night again. I don't think he gambles as much as he says, else he'd be broke by now, but he sure loves dressing fine and being sociable.

Jefferson and I bring up the rear, leading the wagon, which is loaded with our bags, and Peony and Sorry, who seem relieved to be let out of the stable. It's our first private moment together since the walk back to Portsmouth Square the other day.

"I think Becky's forgotten about the wedding dress," I tell him. Softly, so there's no chance of Becky overhearing.

"Not a chance," he says.

"How can you be sure?"

"Well, this is Becky we're talking about."

"Good point."

"Also, she asked Henry if he'd be willing to help me find a proper suit."

"Really?"

"I tried to dissuade him, but without luck. He knows just the place. And he's certain he knows just the color for me."

"What color is that?"

"I'm pretty sure he said plum."

*"Plum?"*

"Plum. Which, until that moment, I could have sworn was a fruit."

I want to ask if any other colors were mentioned, but it's a very short parade route and we have arrived at our destination, which is the *Charlotte*. I don't see Melancthon anywhere about the deck, so I bang on the side.

"Whaddyawant?" comes from somewhere inside the cabin.

I hammer the side of the ship again. "Prepare to be boarded!"

His rat's nest of hair bobs to the surface of the ship, and Melancthon Jones squints over the side at us. "Oh, it's you," he says, frowning. "I already told you, the house we loaded in Panama isn't here anymore. You'll have to go up to the customs office in Portsmouth Square."

"We've been and gone," I say. "That situation isn't resolving as quickly as we would prefer. In the meantime, we've bought this ship."

Major Craven reaches into my saddlebags, which are a lot lighter than they were a couple days ago, much to Peony's delight. And much to mine. Carrying around all that gold was worrisome.

The Major holds up a deed for the ship and the land underneath, and waves it at the sailor.

Melancthon straightens like a man called to attention. After a moment's pause, he hurries to the side of the ship and drops the gangplank.

"Come aboard," he says, but he eyes us with mistrust. As far as he knows, we've just bought his house out from under him.

The children are the first to rush aboard. Andrew jumps up and down, cheering. "We have a ship! We have a ship!"

"A *land* ship," Olive clarifies.

The Major pauses at the top of the gangplank and allows Melancthon to inspect the bill of sale.

"This is unexpected," Melancthon says, combing his hair with his fingers, once again with no noticeable effect. "I didn't plan to vacate until next Tuesday, but it'll only be a few minutes' work to gather my things."

"Don't be in such a hurry," I tell him. "You said you were a carpenter?"

"That's correct, ma'am. Started out as a carpenter's mate nigh on twenty years ago. Been ship's carpenter for seven years, the last three aboard the *Charlotte*."

I like the way he squares his shoulders when he speaks, like a man who takes pride in his work.

"I need a carpenter," I tell him. "Are you familiar with the Apollo saloon?"

"Formerly the *Apollo*? Now sadly run aground, down on Battery Street. I may have had a nip or two there on occasion."

"I noticed they added a door at street level, along with an awning, and a second story above the deck."

"Yes, ma'am. And they've got a very nice saloon inside—a

long bar running the length of the lower deck, with booths and tables beside. Do you mean to turn the *Charlotte* into a saloon, ma'am?"

"Would that be a problem?" I ask.

"It's just you don't look . . . old enough to be the proprietor of a saloon. No offense intended."

"None taken," I assure him. "What can you tell me about this ship?"

"She's one hundred fifteen feet in length, with a beam of twenty-eight, and a depth of sixteen—"

"I meant, more generally, what can you tell me about the ship?"

"We were a whaler, came sailing around Cape Horn, where we put in at Paita in Peru. The captain received an urgent letter from the American consulate there, enjoining him to pick up passengers and cargo at Panama and bring them to San Francisco. We sold off or unloaded all our stores right there, and converted the ship as well as we might en route to Panama. Once we got here, the captain decided to run the ship aground at high tide. . . ."

Again, not exactly what I need to know. "Maybe it would just be better to take us on a tour."

"I can do that," he says.

"Olive! Andrew!" calls out Becky. "Gather around. We're going to take a tour of the ship."

Our group, which had been wandering and inspecting independently, converges at the center of the deck. Melancthon points to the front of the ship. "That's the foaksul . . ."

"Pardon me, the what?" asks Tom. "Could you spell that please?"

"F-O-R-E-C-A-S-T-L-E."

"Ah," says Tom, as if this makes perfect sense.

"Forecastle?" I ask.

"That's what I said!" Melancthon points in the other direction. "And that's the quarter deck, and there in the rear, that's the poop deck."

Olive turns to her mother. "Ma, did he just say *poop* deck?"

"I'm certain you misheard," Becky says.

"It's from *la poupe*, the French word for the stern of the ship," Henry explains. "Which, in turn, is derived from the Latin word *puppis*."

"La poop, la poop, la poop," Andrew says. His mother turns scarlet.

This is all going terribly off track. "Maybe I can just tell you what I want, and you can tell me if it can be done, and, if so, how fast you can do it."

"Yes, ma'am," Melancthon says.

"I'd like separate rooms for us to sleep in, and a larger room where we can meet."

"We already did the first part, turning the crew deck into cabins, before we picked up the passengers in Panama. I can take you down the main hatchway and show you. And the galley, where we serve meals, that's already as good a room as any to meet in."

This may turn out easier than I'd hoped. "What about storage? Is there room enough to stable our horses and store our wagon?"

He points to a hatchway at the center of the ship, currently covered by a tarp. "For certain. We transported some cattle in the hold, at least until it was time to eat them."

Even better. "What about putting a door in the side of the ship, so we can take the horses in and out just like a stable?"

Melancthon goes pale and takes a step backward. "You want to put a . . . *hole* in the side of the *Charlotte*?"

"Two holes," I clarify. "One that would lead to the cargo hold, where we could stable the horses and store the wagon, but move them in and out easily. And then another one right here at the front of the ship, so we can walk in and out without climbing up the gangplank."

"But . . . my ship . . ."

"Is never going to sail again. I'll pay you to do the work, daily wages, whatever a carpenter makes in San Francisco right now. So if you can't find a ship to hire you, by the time you're done working for us, you can buy passage on one. This is your way out of California. In the meantime, you can stay aboard for as long as we're on the ship. Rent free."

The light comes back into his eyes. "So you're going to settle here in San Francisco?" he asks.

It's a reasonable deduction, but I'm not eager to explain our plans to a stranger. "That remains to be seen. But look, no hard feelings if you don't want to do the work. I'll just hire a different carpenter, and you can find somewhere else to stay."

He shrugs. "I guess I'll get started."

"Stable for the horses is the highest priority," I tell him. I'm nervous about leaving them tied up outside, especially Peony, who's been stolen once already.

"That's smart, ma'am," Melancthon says. "Every horse thief in San Francisco will take notice of that pretty palomino of yours."

"It's settled, then. Can you show us to the cabins below? And the meeting room?"

"Cabins and galley. Yes, ma'am. If you'll all follow me this way."

As we crowd together toward a ladder, Becky leans over and whispers, "You handled that *very* well."

"I did?"

"Once you started giving orders, he never once looked to any of the men for confirmation." She squeezes my arm.

Jefferson comes up on the other side. "Don't let it go to your head."

"Huh?"

He nods at my right hand. "You're the only one holding a gun, which kinda demands attention. And you tend to jab with it emphatically whenever you're making a point."

"I do not jab."

"You jab."

He points again. My arm is tensed and I'm thrusting the barrel of the gun at his feet while I talk.

"Huh. I never noticed that before."

Melancthon has been a good caretaker, and the area below decks is spick-and-span. Our steps have a hollow sound that will take some getting used to. Thin wooden walls divide the lower deck into eight smaller cabins, most outfitted with cots or beds. It's not the same as private rooms, but they're semiprivate. Tom and Henry take one together. Becky takes a larger one for herself and the children. She invites me to join them, but there's plenty of room, and Jasper, Jefferson, the Major, and I each take cabins for ourselves. Four empty cots make mine feel a little lonely, especially after we've all been piled on top of each other for days.

Henry sticks his head in the door. "This was a really good idea," he says. "A perfect base of operations for going after Hardwick."

I grin. "We are going to destroy him. Get everyone together in the galley—I'll be there in a minute."

I pick one of the cots and shove the saddlebags underneath it. The blanket from another cot becomes a wrap for Daddy's rifle. I slide it underneath, beside the saddlebags. It's not much in terms of worldly possessions.

But I have friends. And a purpose. And now a ship.

I find all the adults gathered in the galley, seated around a large wooden table that's nailed to the floor. An oil lamp hangs from the ceiling, casting a warm glow. The seat at the head of the table is empty, so that's the one I take.

Becky rocks the sleeping baby in her arms. "Where are Olive and Andrew?" I ask.

"They're amusing themselves in the cabin for now. They're glad to have a larger space."

I waste no time. "It should be clear to everyone now that James Henry Hardwick is coming after us. He provided the money for my uncle's scheme last fall." I nod to Tom and Jefferson, who experienced worse in that ordeal than I did. "Since then, Hardwick has failed to live up to the terms of the contract we signed with him at Christmas."

"But we can take that to court and make him enforce it," Jasper says.

"Is that true, Tom?"

Tom shakes his head. "Right now, California barely has courts worthy of the name. Influence counts for more than the law. The courts do what Hardwick tells them, not the other way around."

"And there's the matter of Becky's house," I say.

Becky stops stroking the baby's cheek and looks up.

"And the fact that Frank Dilley and those roughnecks held you and Henry at gunpoint in the Custom House," I add.

The Major frowns at Becky. "I'm sorry I wasn't there for that."

Becky absently puts a hand on his arm, even as she bounces the baby on one knee. "It turned out fine," she says. The Major stares down at the hand covering his arm, color rising in his cheeks.

"And then we come to the matter of Hampton," I say.

I'm met with nods and murmurs of agreement from around the table.

"There's one more thing," Tom says, his face grave.

"Oh?"

"I can't be the only one who has noticed," he says, glancing around the table. "But Hardwick seems to have taken a peculiar interest in Lee."

"It's true," Becky says.

"Lee, I don't like the way he looks at you," Jefferson adds.

I don't like it much either. He gives my belly the same wormy feeling I always got around my uncle Hiram.

"What makes you all say that?" Jasper says.

"Well, he keeps showing up everywhere we go," Jefferson says.

"He's going to ask for more money for Glory's charter, remember?" Henry says.

"He called Lee 'intriguing,'" Becky says. "Which gave me a shiver, I don't mind saying.

"He knows we've all got more gold than we ought, although . . ." She lowers her voice to a whisper. "I don't think he knows about your particular . . . blessing."

"In any case, his fascination with Lee is . . . unnatural," Tom says.

They're all looking at each other, more than they're looking at me. Finally, Jefferson clears his throat. "The thing is, Lee, there's always going to be men like that in the world."

"And your point is?"

"We can't make that problem go away forever."

"When you're hungry, and you eat, do you expect your hunger to go away forever? When you're sick, and you go to a doctor"—I point to Jasper—"do you expect to stay well forever? Of course not. Hardwick is the problem in front of us right now. We can't solve the problem forever, but we can solve *him*. That's what we're going to do."

"You aren't planning to shoot Hardwick, are you?" Tom asks. "With your daddy's rifle?"

"No!"

"Because that would be wrong—"

"Because that would be ineffective."

"And also wrong," says Jefferson.

"Yes, but it wouldn't get the job done," I clarify. "Jeff, you remember our teacher back in Dahlonega? Mr. Anders?"

Jefferson is leaning forward, fingers steepled. "Yeah."

"What was that monster he told us about? The one where you cut off its head and it grows two more?"

"The hydra?" he answers, as all three of the college men blurt out, "The hydra!"

"That's the one," I say. "Hardwick is the head of the monster, but the body that feeds him is the money and the businesses that are making him rich right now. If he died tomorrow, a bunch of other men would just divvy up his businesses and his money, and they'd all go on doing the same thing. It's not enough to cut the head off the monster. We have to destroy the body too. We're not just going to bring down James Henry Hardwick, we're going to ruin his empire and take every penny he owns. Who's in?"

Silence. Faintly, a burst of distant laughter filters through the hull; probably from one of the nearby saloons.

Jasper spreads his large, capable hands on the table. "I hear what you're saying, and I admire your intent. But I came to San Francisco to learn. And there's so much to learn. Malnourishment, diseases, every kind of wound and injury. But my time is limited. A year from now, when this is a more settled place, those problems won't be here, not in the same degree. I can get a lifetime of experience in the next year if I want it, and that's what I want."

"You're already the best doctor I've ever known," I tell him.

He grins. "And I'm going to get even better."

"That makes perfect sense," I say, even though I'm disappointed. "I wish you well. You're welcome to stay aboard the ship, even if you're not part of our plan."

Jasper stands. "I'd like to maintain a cabin here, if you don't mind, Lee."

"Of course I don't mind!"

"It's just the doctor I'm working with has invited me to board with him on weekdays, because there's no telling what hour of the day an emergency will come knocking. He calls it 'a residency.' My home will always be here, with you." He glances toward Henry and Tom, his face a little apologetic. "But I think I'll take him up on that. Spend most of my nights there, come back to the *Charlotte* on weekends."

Henry and Tom exchange a glance, part resignation, part relief, and suddenly I understand. Henry and Tom have always been especially attached to each other, and Jasper is leaving them be, giving them space of their own.

I swallow hard and force myself to say, "That doctor is lucky to have you."

"Now, this doesn't mean I won't help. Hampton is my friend, and we've been through a lot together, and I'll do just about anything to get him back. So, if you think of something I can do, you let me know, understand?"

"Count on it."

He rises from the table. Becky says, "You'll come around often, won't you, Jasper?"

"Of course!"

The Major shakes Jasper's hand. Jefferson puts a hand on his shoulder and squeezes.

Henry crosses his arms and says emphatically, "See you *soon*."

"See you soon," Jasper echoes.

"See you soon," Tom whispers.

With a final nod, Jasper leaves the room. I stare around the rest of the table. "Anybody else want to go? Now's the time to do it."

Nobody moves. The Major reaches down to rub the stump of his leg. "Just promise me there's a chance to take down Frank Dilley too."

"That's definitely part of the plan," I promise him.

"Then I'm in."

Tom pushes his chair back from the table and rises. Before speaking, he straightens his collar and cuffs. "I think I need to go see a man about a job," he says in a tight voice. "I'll catch up with all of you later."

I nod to him, not trusting my words enough to say anything.

"Tom . . . ," Henry says.

Tom smiles the tiniest bit. "I'll be back."

When he's gone, I lean forward. "All right then. Let's get to work."

Just below us, deep inside the ship, a hammer pounds on thick wood. A moment later comes the rasp of a saw.

# Chapter Nine

The first thing we decide to do is find out how much money Hardwick has and where he keeps it.

The day we ran into Hardwick, his entourage included the fellow whom Henry has taken to calling "Mr. Keys," real name unknown. All we do know about Mr. Keys is that he's a small man with a narrow face and no chin, and—most importantly—he sticks close to Hardwick, carrying a large ring of keys and a heavy leather bag full of gold.

It's a sure bet some of Hardwick's money is at that bank. But it's a surer bet that not all of it is. And if anyone is in charge of Hardwick's money, it's Mr. Keys.

Jefferson took off before dawn to make inquiries about Hardwick's main business office and hopefully put an eye on the little fellow.

In the meantime, before the bank opens, Becky and I camp out in the parlor of a hotel kitty-corner to the Custom House building. We find two large armchairs and drag them from the fireplace to one of the windows. The window is dirty but large, and it gives us an unobstructed view of the bank. This is one of the establishments where miners, flush with gold, stay up all night to gamble, and are then late abed, so we have the downstairs mostly to ourselves.

Their gold sings to me, though. Several coin purses' worth, mostly upstairs, but a larger stash hides away in the downstairs office.

The air is especially chilly. Nothing close to a frost, but still the kind of cold that seeps into your bones and makes you ache for a warm kitchen and bread right out the oven; even a chunk of half-burned, half-doughy bread from Becky's restaurant would be just the thing. A light rain falls, so the plaza feels sleepier than usual. The men who come to open the bank have hunched shoulders and dripping hats. They pause beneath the veranda to kick mud off their boots before unlocking the doors.

For the next hour or so, a handful of brave but unfamiliar souls, similarly inured to the cold and wet, are the only ones to enter and leave.

"Excuse me, ladies?"

I'd been so intent on watching the bank that I hadn't noticed anyone approach. The proprietor of the hotel, wearing a green velvet vest and an air of self-importance, looks down his blunt nose at us.

I'm not sure what to say, but Becky doesn't hesitate.

"My dear sir," she says smoothly. The baby kept her up half the night, and it's a wonder she's not dozing in her chair. "How may we be of service?"

"That's just it," he says, hooking his thumbs into his vest pockets. "You can't."

"I'm afraid we don't understand your implication," Becky says.

"That is, what I'm trying to say is, this is not the sort of establishment where we welcome women who provide services."

My head whips back around. *"What?"*

Becky reaches out and taps her fingers on his hand. "Oh, sir, that's such a relief to hear. You've put my heart at ease."

"I have?" he says, thrown off-balance.

I'm torn. I need to watch the bank, but I'm equally captivated by Becky—I have no idea what she plans to say next. It never occurred to me that we'd be a problem sitting in a public parlor on a cold day.

"You have," she says. "You see . . ." She whispers the last phrase conspiratorially, leaning forward. The proprietor bends down to listen closely.

"My dear, beloved husband," she says, "brought our gold into San Francisco to invest it, but I'm very much afraid he's been spending it instead. It's one thing if he gambles a bit of it. Why, that's natural, and any man might do the same, whether for entertainment or in hopes of increasing his stake. But if he's been spending it elsewise . . ."

She lets the last sentence trail off like an unspoken threat. Taking notice of my attention, she jerks her head to the window, and I oblige by turning my head around again to watch the bank, trusting her to take care of the proprietor.

"And you're certain he's a resident of our establishment?" he says.

"Not at all," Becky says. "But he didn't come home last night, and one of his usual companions said he was last seen in your gambling parlor, around midnight. So I've come to check. You say there are no women here who might keep the gentlemen company?"

"Ah," the proprietor says.

In his silence, I hear a different story: that any such women here are discreet enough to avoid being seen in the front parlor in the morning.

"Perhaps he had a bit too much to drink and decided to sleep it off before coming home," Becky suggests.

"That's entirely possible," admits the proprietor. "If you would like to give me a name, I could check our guest ledger."

"Absolutely not!" Becky says. "If my suspicions are unfounded, I would certainly not wish to sully the reputation of our good name."

A short man carrying something heavy walks toward the bank. I rub a circle clean on the window with my sleeve, then realize that Becky and the proprietor are both staring. I suppose that using my sleeve to clean a window is probably ill-mannered. "I apologize," I say, hiding my sleeve under my arm. "I thought I saw . . . him." *Him* being Mr. Keys, not Becky's imaginary husband. "But I was mistaken."

"Have all of your guests come downstairs yet this morning?" Becky asks the proprietor.

"No, ma'am," he says. "No, they haven't."

"Then we'll just wait here until they do. Thank you for allowing us to do that. Your thoughtfulness means everything."

I take another glimpse, just to see his jaw working, trying to figure out how he ended up giving us permission. Finally he snaps it shut and takes a moment to gather himself. "I guess that will be satisfactory," he says thoughtfully, perhaps considering how he can sneak upstairs and warn his customers that someone's angry wife is lying in ambush in the parlor. He turns to go, saying, "If there will be nothing else, then?"

"Oh, thank you kindly for offering," Becky says. "It's so dreadfully cold out. A cup of tea would be perfect. Do you want a cup of tea, dear?"

I realize she's talking to me. "Coffee, please."

"And sugar," Becky says. "Lots of sugar."

We pass the morning supplied with a side table, and restored at regular intervals with fresh tea and coffee. Becky pretends to watch the lobby, deflecting conversations with the proprietor and anyone else who comes along. I keep an eye on the bank.

Gold from last night's winnings pokes at my mind from the rooms above our head. After the proprietor leaves to make his rounds, I feel some of it moving out of the rooms and away, disappearing without coming down the front staircase.

By early afternoon, the rain has let up. We enjoy fresh sandwiches from the kitchen, while Becky pretends to enjoy the company of the hotel's cook. Across the street, the bank's clerks leave in small groups for lunch, and then return. It takes hours, but eventually even Becky's mighty composure crumbles into fidgeting as she becomes bored and restless, ready to call it quits.

But my daddy taught me how to hunt with that Hawken rifle Jim returned to me. He showed me how to hole up in a blind and wait for my quarry to come along, even if it meant staying for hours in the cold and snow. Days, if we were desperate enough.

Sitting in the parlor of a hotel, even a low establishment like this one, is so much easier than sitting in a deer blind. Nobody ever brought me fresh coffee or sandwiches in a blind.

Becky is deflecting a fresh round of questions from the afternoon manager when I finally see our target. "There he is," I announce, rising.

Becky nearly spills her cup of tea.

"You've spotted the lady's husband?" the manager asks.

"Sometimes if you can't catch them going, you get them coming," Becky tells him, and we rush out the door. At the corner, we pause to catch our breath.

"You're sure it's him?" Becky asks.

"Absolutely." I drop my voice to a whisper. "I sense his bag of gold. Also, he has two armed guards." I point to the two men leaning against the wall beneath the veranda. One is pushing a wad of chewing tobacco into his mouth, while the other blows on his hands to warm them. "They were with Frank Dilley the other day. Which means they might recognize us. Are you ready to do this?"

"As long as my constitution holds," Becky says. "I should

have taken the opportunity to relieve myself when I had the chance."

"If I'm right, we won't be in there long."

"We weren't counting on guards. How do we get past them?"

"We've as much right to go to the bank as anyone. We'll just lower our heads and—"

A cry of "Tag! You're it!" rings out at the far end of the building, and Sonia's group of urchins tears around the corner, bumping into everyone below the veranda before scattering in all directions. The guards give chase, patting down their pockets even as they tear after the children.

Sonia's group must be well practiced at pickpocketing to bump and grab so quickly and easily. It couldn't have happened at a better time. While the guards are distracted, Becky and I dash across the street and into the bank.

The moment we pass through the door, a clerk rises to assist us. I pause to catch my breath, because the gold in this room is overwhelming. Here, it's less like a choir singing and more like a giant crowd shouting at the top of its lungs.

"How may I help you ladies?" the clerk inquires.

I blink rapidly, trying to focus. As planned, I pull a handful of large gold nuggets from the plain leather purse I carry, then screw up my face like it's hard for me to think, which is not entirely an act. "Found this. Prospecting."

He's seen larger amounts of gold, but his eyes widen appreciatively.

Becky steps in and covers the gold with one hand, placing her other on my shoulder. "My friend's a hard worker, but a little . . . unsophisticated," she says. "I've tried to tell her not to carry nuggets like these around—that's just asking for trouble. I've told her that she should have it converted to coinage. And she ought to keep it in a bank, where it can be safe."

I take stock of the bank while she's talking, trying to ignore all the gold weighing down my senses. A long counter divides the space. Behind the counter are a few desks, and behind the desks is an iron cage bolted to both floor and ceiling. The cage contains both a small strongbox and a larger safe.

Mr. Keys sits at one of the desks. Across from him is a gray-haired man with heavy jowls, who appears to frown even when he smiles. Likely Mr. Owen, the owner of the bank.

"I don't see many prospectors of the female persuasion," the clerk notes. "It's too hard a life for the weaker sex."

Becky bristles. "I'll hear no more from you about the weaker sex until you've birthed three babes."

"I . . . of course. Apologies." He wisely changes the subject. "Is that all the gold that your friend has?"

"Oh, no, sir, I got lots more," I say, and I flip my purse, like I'm going to dump it on the floor. I can tell the clerk is trying to gauge its weight with his eyes. Becky grabs my hands and stops me again.

"You have to forgive her," Becky says. "She works day and night. I think the mercury has affected her some. She uses so much of it, refining the gold she finds."

"Some people have a knack," the clerk says with a shrug.

He doesn't know the half of it.

"Let's retire to the privacy of my desk," he offers, signaling to the far end of the room.

"I like that desk over there," I whine. "It's by the pretty window." Which is just about the daftest thing to say, but I can't think up another excuse.

Becky shrugs, as if to say, "What can you do?" The clerk accommodates my request by taking us to the desk beside the window. Becky proceeds to ask him a number of pertinent questions about turning gold into coinage and the protection of this bank compared to others.

From here, I have a perfect view of everything behind the counter, everything inside the cage. Which is where the bank's owner is leading Mr. Keys.

Mr. Owen inserts the key into the cage's lock. The iron door creaks open, and everyone stops work for a moment. You'd think the bank would oil the hinges.

"We have one of the strongest cages in the city," the clerk is saying. Then he recites a flurry of details about its manufacture, installation, and maintenance.

The owner steps aside, and Mr. Keys pulls out his namesake ring and sorts through a dozen options, looking for the correct key. I reckon he knows them all by sight, because he slides one into the small safe, and it opens correctly the first time.

Mr. Owen removes himself from the cage and looks discreetly in the other direction. I have no such compunctions and gawk like a child at a carnival.

Before we came, I warned Becky that I wouldn't be at my

level best, not surrounded by so much gold, and we decided I would act a bit touched to cover any lapses. Good thing we did, because there there's enough gold in that safe to ransom a kingdom. Stacks of coins and ingots. Hundreds of pounds. More than I have ever seen—or sensed—in one place at one time.

Mr. Keys removes even more gold coins from his little bag and stacks them carefully inside. When finished, he makes a notation on a ledger inside the safe; then he pulls a small notebook from his bag and writes what is certainly a matching entry. He locks up the safe and exits the cage. Mr. Owen latches the cage behind him. They shake hands, and Mr. Keys passes us on his way out. Becky has her back to him. I lean against my hand to hide my face. If he recognizes either one of us, he gives no indication.

"So you're saying you can turn these nuggets into gold coins for a small percentage of the weight?" Becky says, pulling me back into the conversation.

"A nominal fee. The Pacific Company is known to charge up to twenty percent, and many other banks in town will require a similar amount. Our fee is only ten percent."

"What about impurities?"

He smiles. "Yes, our assayer determines the level of impurities in the gold, and that amount is also charged against the weight."

I imagine that it amounts to at least another ten percent.

"But everyone does the same," he assures us. "Did you know that forty million dollars in gold was collected by miners last year?"

It boggles the mind. "How many gold coins is that?" I ask.

"Let's use the fifty-dollar eagle as the standard. In that case, the total number of coins would be . . ." He pauses to think.

"Eight hundred thousand gold coins," Becky says.

"No, it's . . ." The clerk counts his fingers. "Oh, yes, it's about eight hundred thousand gold coins. You guessed right." He smiles at her like she's a performing dog.

"That seems impossible. Where would people keep it?" she says.

"We estimate that half of it went out of the country, back to Mexico, or Peru, or Australia, maybe Sweden or China—wherever the miners came from. They struck it rich, packed up their money, and took it home. Once California is a state, we'll pass more laws to keep foreigners out in the first place. We want as much of that gold as possible to stay right here in the United States where it belongs."

"We're all foreigners here," I point out, forgetting for a moment that I'm supposed to be a bit addled by mercury.

Becky shoots me a warning look. "If my friend wants to keep her money safe until she needs it, she can store some of it here?"

"Absolutely." He twists in his seat and indicates the cage. "Our strongbox is the most secure in the whole city."

The strongbox is little more than a traveling trunk, with breakable hinges and a flimsy padlock. It doesn't contain a quarter of the amount in the safe that sits beside it. There's so much gold in the safe that I feel slightly sick, like I would after eating a whole pie, when all I needed was a single piece.

"But the safe," I say. "The safe looks safe. I want my money safe. In a safe."

"My friend likes the safe," Becky says. "The big black one. Is it available to customers?"

"That's a Wilder Salamander safe, one of only a few in the entire state of California," the clerk says. "It's got double walls, insulated, to protect the items inside in case of fire. State of the art. But that's the personal safe of one of our most elite customers."

"But I just saw somebody put something in there?" I say.

The clerk smiles at me. "As I said."

Becky says, "He must be a very good customer."

"He's very nearly a bank unto himself," the clerk exclaims, and then, glancing at the gray-haired owner, decides that circumspection is called for. "But let me assure you that your friend's money will be triply protected here. First by the strongbox itself, which only the manager has keys to. Then by the cage, which is similarly locked. And finally by the guard who patrols our building at night."

"That's a lot of protection," Becky says.

"It's not safe if it's not in the safe," I say, failing to sound angry.

Becky puts a hand on my arm. "Why don't you go outside and get some air? I'll join you shortly."

"Yes, ma'am." She knows I want to lay eyes on Mr. Keys if I can. I give her a grateful look and exit the bank without another word. Beneath the veranda, I scan the square for Mr. Keys and his guards, but they are already gone.

Becky joins me outside a few minutes later. "You've upset the poor gentleman. He's very concerned that if you take your business to another bank, they'll take advantage of you. On the positive side, young Mr. Owen—he's the son of that other fellow—is impressed by my mathematical abilities, considering that I'm a woman, and he asked me to tea, which I reluctantly declined."

I grin, in spite of the churning in my belly. "I'm getting sick from being near so much gold," I whisper. "Let's walk."

We stroll into the plaza, and I feel a little steadier with each step. Halfway across the square, Jefferson slides in beside us.

"Hello, Lee, Becky. How'd you like the distraction? I ran into Sonia's little gang and paid them to make a ruckus so you could slip past Mr. Key's guards."

"That was clever," Becky says.

"We saw where Hardwick keeps his gold," I say, and I describe everything we observed in the bank. "It's more gold than I ever imagined. More than one man could ever spend or need."

"Then I have some bad news for you," Jefferson says.

"Worse news than 'He has more money than we could ever steal'?"

"Yes, worse than that." We cross the street and head downhill toward the *Charlotte*. The scent of saltwater marsh rises to greet us. "I found Hardwick's main business office, which is at his house. His mansion, I mean. Takes up half a block. And I started following our pal, Mr. Keys, first thing this morning.

This bank wasn't his first stop. It wasn't even his second."

"Where was he going?" I ask.

"To other banks," he says. "He took a large bag from Hardwick's office, went to a couple of banks, made deposits, and then went back to Hardwick's house to collect another bag."

"I counted forty-seven gold coins in his deposit," Becky says. When I look at her in astonishment, she says simply, "Well, something like that. It was hard to count and talk at the same time, so I might be off a coin or two. Assuming they were all fifty-dollar coins, which seems to be the most common denomination, that's a deposit of two thousand three hundred fifty dollars. Three of those comes to more than seven thousand dollars! Just this morning."

"More than three banks," Jefferson says.

"Exactly how many banks?" I ask, my voice rising to a near-panic register.

"Eleven," Jefferson says.

Becky and I stop in the middle of the street to stare at him.

"This was his eleventh bank visit of the day," he assures us. "In and out within a few minutes at each stop. Like it's something he does every day. But that's not possible, right? There's not that much gold in all the world."

"Maybe there is," Becky says. "According to Mr. Owens Junior—who seems a reliable compendium of details, even if he's a bit slow at multiplication—California is home to at least twenty million dollars in gold."

"No wonder I was so distracted when our boots first

touched this territory," I say. "It was like a constant ringing in my ears."

Jefferson nods. "And Hardwick is trying to get it *all*."

Becky resumes her journey toward the *Charlotte* and gestures for us to keep pace. "This job just got a lot more complicated," she says.

"Yep," I say. "We need to think bigger."

"And smarter," Jefferson adds.

# Chapter Ten

When we paid Hardwick four thousand dollars to settle my uncle's debt, we thought it was a lot of money. But it was nothing.

Four thousand to settle a debt.

A few thousand to auction off the pieces of someone's house.

A few thousand more for a man's freedom.

These little bits and pieces add up. No doubt this is how Hardwick's fortune started. But it's clear that the big money in San Francisco is now being made in property, through land sales and rents. If Hardwick is filling safes in eleven banks, then this is how he's doing it.

Jim Boisclair has been in San Francisco for months, and I figure if anyone can help me suss it all out, it's him. So I arrange to meet Jim early the following morning at Portsmouth Square.

I spring out of bed and scarf down a quick breakfast, eager to see my friend. Even though it's not raining, the air is so damp with fog, it might as well be. I don a wool coat over a flannel shirt and sturdy trousers, and I'm still cold.

Jim is already waiting for me, leaning against a lamppost. He tips his hat and grins.

After we exchange greetings, I say, "Are you *sure* we can't ride? Peony could use the exercise." She's taken well to being stabled in the hull of a ship; it's the not smallest or worst place I've had to keep her. But I know she likes to stretch her legs.

"You don't see as much when you're riding," Jim says, pausing to blow on his fingers and rub them together for warmth. "You rush by, in too much of a hurry. Might as well hire a carriage with curtains on the window—that way you don't have to see the truth or talk to anyone at all."

I sigh, but I don't disagree.

"But I'm real glad to hear that pretty mare of yours is all right," he adds. "I remember the day she was foaled."

"I couldn't have made it here without her," I say. "Which way are we going?"

"Up," he says. "We're going to tour some of the city's most profitable areas, where Hardwick makes most of his money." He leads the way west, up the city's hills. The steep climb warms me quickly. "Pay attention as we go, and tell me what you see."

"And what are you going to do?" I ask.

"I'm going to point out the things you're not seeing." It's exactly the kind of thing my daddy would say, and it puts a lightness in my heart.

Everywhere we go, people are already up and working.

Clearing land and roads. Loading wagons full of dirt, unloading wagons full of supplies.

"I see a lot of people working hard," I tell Jim.

He smiles. "That's a good start."

Jim has always been one of the most sociable people I've ever known, and traveling across a whole continent has not changed him one bit. He stops and talks to everyone who will speak to us, and he isn't shy with his questions. Do they own the land or rent it? Some rent it. More say they own it, but when Jim asks about prices, it sure seems like they're paying installment plans at rates that sound a lot like rent. Why are they working so hard to improve it? So they can sell it for a profit once they've paid off the loan. A handful of the laborers are Negro, and they take plenty of time to answer Jim's questions and give specific answers. We spend almost half an hour talking with an enthusiastic fellow named Isaac who hails from Cincinnati.

Before we take our leave of Isaac, Jim says, "You hear the news about Hampton Freeman?"

"Sure did," Isaac says. "We're praying for him."

"We'll be taking up a collection."

"I've already told the fellows down at the foundry."

"That's good, that's good."

When we near the peak, Jim turns north. Outside a two-room shanty is a family of five—husband, wife, and three young children—just sitting there with a pile of belongings. Must be moving day.

But as we walk past, two white men carry a bed frame

through the doorway and drop it carelessly to the ground.

The family is not moving by choice. They're being evicted.

I glance up at Jim, who nods. "If we'd been on horses, you might've missed that," he says.

After crossing a muddy street, we find ourselves in a whole new neighborhood. It's similar to the first one we passed through—rows of shanties interspersed with the occasional house, lots of men and only a few families—but the faces here are mostly Chinese. They regard Jim and me with suspicion. No one wants to answer our questions.

We head farther north toward Goat Hill, where the semaphore tower raises flags to signal ships coming into harbor. Hammers sound in the quarry, breaking rock to use as ship ballast. Neighborhoods are forming here as well—mostly shacks and tents, though they're laid out along regular streets. We stop and talk to a few people, and nearly all the accents are Irish.

We head downhill toward the bay. Jim pauses at the corner of Sansome and Vallejo. It's a whole block of open land, without a single house or structure.

"It's a cemetery," I say. Crosses and gravestones stretch before us.

"They call it the Sailor's Cemetery," he says. "It's where all the sailors used to be buried. Now it's where all the outsiders are buried. People like me. Foreigners. Are you hungry?"

It's past lunchtime. "Starved. And you're not a foreigner." But as soon as the words leave my lips, I know they're not true. We're all foreigners, everyone but the Indians, that is, who have made themselves scarce in this city, or more likely been forced to leave. Very few Indians remain in San Francisco, and almost all who stayed are at Mission Dolores.

"Anyway, I know a place," Jim says. "Just found it a couple days ago."

Thinking about how we treat the Indians is chasing away my appetite, but I say, "All right, sure."

He leads me past the cemetery and down toward the choppy gray bay.

"Have I seen what you want me to see?" I say as we walk.

He shrugs. "Maybe." Jim wants me to put the pieces together myself, but so far I can't solve the puzzle. I see a lot of people working hard, improving the land, making something for themselves.

We duck into a building without any signs or special markings on it. Conversation trickles off the instant we come through the door.

The room is low ceilinged with exposed rafters, and it's filled with the darkest-skinned men I've ever seen, all clustered around a series of small tables. Most wear something between a robe and a blanket, thrown over one shoulder, all in bright colors. The air bursts with the scents of coffee and spices.

I'm sure it's a mistake to be here, but Jim takes a seat at an empty table and motions for me to join him. When I do, Jim looks to the proprietor and holds up two fingers.

After a moment's hesitation, the proprietor nods. The men stop staring and resume their conversations. The room buzzes with unfamiliar words.

I glance around nervously. "Why'd you want to meet here?" I'm whispering.

"Makes you feel a bit uncomfortable being around faces that don't look anything like yours," Jim says. It's not a question.

"No," I say. A bit too quick and sharp, which gives life to the lie. "Maybe."

"That's right," Jim says. "And it makes Hardwick and all the fellows who work for him uncomfortable, too. Hardwick has spies, maybe even spies close to you. Remember? He *knew* you were going to the bank that day to get that southern lady's house back."

"You're thinking it was Tom," I say darkly. "Tom wouldn't do that."

"If you say so." He waves his hand around the room. "In any case, these fellows came all the way from Ethiopia to dig gold. They're just waiting for spring to get sprung. I figure this is the one place in town we can talk privately, because a spy would stick out like a snowball in summer."

The shop's owner brings us two bowls of food, which is a stew with flatbread. The spices are unfamiliar, and I'm a little afraid to eat it. But I don't want Jim to know that.

I wave at the proprietor. "Some silverware, please?"

Jim shakes his head. "Like this," he says. "You break off bread to scoop up the stew. No, use your right hand only. You don't want to be rude."

I follow his example. The bread is spongy, like a pancake, but it has a sour tang.

Jim laughs at my expression. "You get used to it." He scoops more stew and pushes the bread into his mouth. After he swallows, he says, "Tell me what you saw this morning."

So I tell him what I've been thinking: the people of San Francisco work hard, improve property, build better lives for themselves.

"What I saw," Jim says, "are a whole bunch of folks not protected by the law."

I open my mouth to argue. Close it. Take another bite of food.

"You saw how Hampton's not protected by the law, right? Well, neither am I, nor any other Negro man or woman," he says. "Same goes for the Chinese, the Indians, and all the other immigrants. The Mexicans did all right at first, but that's changing, and it will change even more when California's statehood becomes official."

"I see your point," I say, thinking of the family being forced out of their home by Hardwick's men.

"So Hardwick owns land in every neighborhood we walked through today. He doesn't sell it outright. People jump at the opportunity to *rent* from him when they first arrive, expecting to pick up gold on every corner. They make outrageous payments, figuring the next month, the month after, they'll be rich beyond their wildest dreams. Instead, they go broke, and Hardwick rents the land to some other newcomer with a nest egg."

"And that's how Hardwick made his fortune?"

Jim shakes his head. "We're just getting started. Sometimes he sells property on an installment plan. A fellow with a lot of optimism buys a house lot for twelve thousand dollars. Only he doesn't have twelve thousand dollars, so Hardwick promises to sell it to him for just a thousand dollars a month, plus interest and some handling fees. The man signs the contract, but the interest and fees bring the payment closer to fifteen hundred a month, and meanwhile he's not getting rich like he planned. After a few months of hard work, during which he's been improving the property, he's broke. He can't make payments. So Hardwick's men kick him out."

"That family sitting in the street . . . they'd been evicted."

He nods approval. "Hardwick's men reclaim the property—now worth more—and he resells it for a higher rate as improved land."

"And not everyone lives long enough to go broke," I say, thinking of that huge cemetery. "California is a dangerous place."

"Exactly. Most people left their loved ones behind. They come alone, and they die alone. There's no effort made to contact a family back in France or Australia or China."

"Or even back east."

"Or even back east. The property goes into probate, which means it goes to the court. Hardwick owns the court, so the property reverts to the previous owner, which is him, and he starts the process all over again."

I take a bite, chew thoughtfully. This sour bread isn't so bad. "So Hardwick is selling the same land over and over again."

"Exactly."

"You know, a while back I met a pickpocket. Sonia. She

told me San Francisco was full of thieves. Real thieves. The kind who take everything from you, even the clothes off your back."

Jim nods. "A lot of folks are on the streets these days because Hardwick put them there. It's gotten worse in the past month or so, since that Frank Dilley showed up. When I found you and Jefferson at the law offices that day, it sounded like you all knew each other."

"Wish we didn't. He was master of our wagon train on the way out, once the Major got hurt. Left us to die in the desert, seemed disappointed when we didn't. Ended up working for my uncle Hiram."

Jim pauses midchew. "So Hiram did make it out to California," he says around a mouthful of food.

"Yes, and I need to talk to you about Uncle Hiram when we're done here. But Jim—be careful of Dilley. He's . . . an unsavory fellow."

"The world's got plenty of those," Jim says.

"Yeah, but Frank Dilley's a special sort. He *likes* to hurt people, especially anyone different from him."

"The world's got plenty of those, too. There was an overseer who . . ." Something awful flits across his face, but it's gone before I can put a name to it. "Well, I was lucky to buy my way out when I did."

The proprietor brings two cups of the strongest coffee I've ever smelled. I look up to thank him, but he won't make eye contact with me.

Jim continues, "Anyway, most of the land we saw today has

been sold, and resold, four or five or six times, just in the past year."

I give a low whistle. "Why do people keep doing business with Hardwick?"

Jim shrugs. "What other choice do they have? A couple years ago this was a town with a few hundred people. Now there are thirty thousand. Most of them spent everything they had to get here. They can't exactly turn around and leave."

The Hoffman family gave up and went back home after arriving in California. But they had a golden candlestick and a witchy friend to help them pay for return passage. If not for that, they would have been stuck here like everyone else.

"And the whole city almost burned to the ground just two months ago," Jim continues. "Hardwick profited from that too—folks lost everything and couldn't afford to rebuild, so he bought their land out from under them and then rented it back at twice the price."

I've lost most of my appetite, but I force myself to sip the coffee. It's sharp and bitter enough to penetrate the constant buzz of gold, which I appreciate. I take another sip and say, "If he's investing all this money, how come he has so much of it locked up in banks?"

"You remember my general store, back home in Dahlonega?"

"I'll never forget it."

"When I wanted to buy supplies, I had to buy them with cash up front. Nobody would extend credit to a Negro. That's not the deal Hardwick has."

"Huh?" I clutch the coffee mug close; maybe I'm seeking comfort.

"Hardwick owns everything on paper, but that doesn't mean he paid for it all. The banks extend him credit. So he takes the title on the property, and collects rents, and he gives everyone else their cut. He pays his gang more than they could make doing carpentry work or prospecting. He pays the sheriff to look the other way, and I guess the politicians and judges, too. Maybe even the bank. In the end, he has a nice chunk of money left over. And he never had to buy anything up front in order to get it."

I think back, trying to remember if I saw Mr. Keys count out a portion of coins to the bank manager, but I wasn't paying close enough attention.

"Don't like the food?"

I glance down at my bowl. Most of it is uneaten. I'm pushing the remaining stew around with a piece of bread. "It's just . . . you've given me a lot to think about."

Chairs scrape as a handful of customers rises to leave. When they exit, light pours in through the door, and I have a brief but perfect view of the street. Two tall fellows stand there, peering inside and not even trying to be subtle about it. I recognize them as the polite gunmen in nice wool suits we met at the Custom House: Large and Larger.

"We were followed," I tell Jim.

He nods. "As long as they don't come inside. Just keep your voice low."

I'm not sure Large and Larger can see me from where they

stand, but just in case, I take a defiant sip of coffee and stare over the edge of the mug at them as if I'm not afraid at all.

"Anyway, I came to San Francisco planning to set up a new general store," Jim says. "It's like Dahlonega all over again. In two or three years, once the rush settles and regular business gets established, that'll be the way to make a living. But every piece of property I look at costs too much. And your best business is regular customers, folks that come in month after month, year after year. There can be no regulars if your neighborhood changes every time the moon wanes. All because of the problems I've been describing to you."

"So what are you going to do?"

"I'm not going back to Georgia, that's for damn sure. I hear parts of Canada are pretty nice." He pushes back from the table.

I put a hand on his arm. "Wait."

He sits back down, eyeing me warily. Gray hair grows at his temples now, which is new since I last saw him. The trip west was hard on us all. "That's right. You wanted to ask me something about your uncle."

If Jim thinks it's safe to talk freely here, then I have to get my questions out now. "Well, him and Mama, actually. After I got to California, Uncle Hiram found me. He . . . kidnapped me."

"Oh, Miss Leah, I'm so sorry." He leans toward me, forearms on the table. "But you got away? You said Hiram wasn't a problem anymore."

"He held me captive. Dressed me up in clothes my mama

used to wear. He had this mine going, worked by local Indians. It was awful. They were sick and starving and there was an uprising and . . ." My heart beats too fast, my breath comes in gasps, as memories pour in. I'm not over what happened yet. Not by a long shot.

"Take your time," Jim says.

It's a long moment before I trust my voice to obey. "Before I got away, he told me something. I thought maybe you'd know if it was true or not."

"Oh?"

"He said I was his very own daughter. Not Reuben's girl, but his. That he and Mama . . ."

"Ah," Jim says. "I see." He regards me with frank honesty. "I always suspected."

"You did?"

"Your mama, Elizabeth, was all set to marry Hiram. They were sweethearts. But then one day she suddenly got herself hitched to his brother, Reuben, instead. No one was more surprised than Hiram. He carried a grudge ever since."

I'm frowning. "But that was years before I came along."

Jim nods. "Hiram carried a torch for Elizabeth for a long time. It was plain as day to anyone with eyes. But a man like that can't truly love another person. He can only love selfishly, his heart full of his own needs. I think . . . I think maybe he . . ."

"You think he raped her."

His lips press together into a firm line.

My next words are a whisper. "Did Daddy know?"

"I reckon so." Jim's gaze turns fierce. "Your daddy loved you more than life itself, don't think he didn't. You were his very own daughter in every way that mattered."

"I know."

"But you might have noticed that Hiram left Dahlonega. He wasn't much welcome after that."

"I hardly saw him or heard tell of him, growing up."

"And when your parents were murdered, and you came to my store all forlorn but with the fire of determination in your eyes, I had a pretty good idea who had done it. I knew you had to get out of town as quick as possible."

I reach for his hand and give it a squeeze. "I wouldn't have made it without you."

Another group stands and clears out. The proprietor is giving us the side-eye. Maybe we've overstayed our welcome. Maybe he's a spy for Hardwick after all, no matter what Jim thinks.

But there's one more thing.

"Jim, I have to ask." My voice is a deadly whisper now. I trust Jim, I do, but I can't risk being overheard. "Did Daddy ever tell you anything about me? I mean . . . anything special that . . . I can do?"

His eyes sparkle. "You mean the way you can recite the presidents backward and forward?" he whispers back.

"Um, no. I mean—"

"Oh, I know. It's the way you can hammer together a sluice in under twenty minutes."

"Well, that too, but—"

"I've got it! Reuben once told me you could blow a spit wad through a piece of straw and hit something at four paces."

"Six paces!" I glare at him, realizing he's funning me. "So you do know."

"Yep. Since before you could walk. It's an amazing thing, Leah. An amazing thing."

"It's one reason Hiram chased me all the way across the continent."

"I figured. He was the only person besides me who knew. If your mama had had her way, even *I* wouldn't have known."

"But the thing is . . ." I glance around. Lots of customers remain, and no doubt plenty of them understand English just fine. "Jim, do you have any idea where it came from? I mean, I know Mama left Boston in a hurry. She hated it whenever I said the word 'witch' or even just mentioned what I could do. She had a mighty fear. And I was wondering . . . did she have a gift too? Something special *she* could do?"

He doesn't hesitate. "She did."

*"What?"*

The proprietor turns, startled. My face flushes.

"What was it?" I repeat, back to a whisper.

"She could find lost things."

I shake my head in disbelief. "I don't remember anything like that. Not one single instance of . . ."

"She only used it once that I know of," he says. "It was a few weeks after the Cherokee were forced out of Dahlonega by President Jackson. Old Man McCauley came bursting into the store, saying he couldn't find his five-year-old boy."

"You mean Jefferson!"

He nods. "Your daddy was with me that day. McCauley told us Jefferson had been missing for hours. He was afraid the boy had gone after his mama, who was halfway to Oklahoma Territory by then."

I know this story. Well, part of it. Jefferson told me my daddy found him in a ditch by the road, several hours out of town.

"Daddy found him," I said. "But you're saying it was really Mama?"

Jim nods. "We looked for half a day. Finally Reuben went home to your mother, carrying Jefferson's favorite blanket, and begged her to use her gift, *just this once*. And forgive me, Leah, I don't know the details of how it all worked; your mama and daddy didn't like to talk about that sort of thing, even with me. All I know is that blanket helped her somehow, and she sent Reuben off with specific directions on how to find the boy."

"Well, I'll be." I knew. Somehow I had always known there was more to my mother than met the eye. Her final words make a lot more sense now. *Trust someone. Not good to be alone as we've been. Your daddy and I were wrong. . . .*

She wasn't just talking about my gift; she was talking about hers, too. About feeling so alone with a certain bright, screaming knowledge you think you might die of it. About being so full of fear that you never dared trust anyone with that knowledge, not even your own daughter.

But I've dared. I've dared a lot. Even in my darkest days,

hemmed in on all sides by awful people like Hiram and Hardwick, I'm surrounded by people I can trust.

That was Mama's final wish for me.

I put my hand to her locket, dangling at my throat. *I did it, Mama. Just like you hoped.*

The proprietor clears his throat. It's definitely time to go. I pull out some coins to pay for our meal, and Jim tells me when I've counted out enough. "Let's go," he says, rising from the table.

I squint at the light when we step from the building. The sky has cleared, and the air has warmed. Large and Larger are still keeping watch from across the street.

"It appears your caution in choosing our establishment for lunch was well founded," I say.

"Friends of yours?" he asks.

"Friends of Hardwick. Or maybe just employees. I don't think Hardwick has friends."

"That's as sure as heaven. Most of his friends would turn on him in a second if he couldn't pay them. Let's head to the waterfront."

Eyes bore into my back as we amble along the shore. I know this part of the city better than any other. Ships on one side. Warehouses on the other. Streets turning into docks as they stretch out into the bay. We stroll down Battery as far as California Street, Large and Larger continuing to trail casually behind.

"Sorry to bring my troubles your way," I say.

"What? Oh, you mean them. Negroes are followed all the

time, everywhere we go. White folks just assume we're up to no good."

*How have I never noticed that before?*

"You all right, Miss Leah?" he says. "That was an awful lot to take in back there."

"I . . ." I reckon it *was* an awful lot. "I'm fine. Better than fine." And it's true. It almost feels like a weight has lifted from my shoulders. I make sure Large and Larger remain a safe distance behind us before adding, "I'm eager to get back to the business of figuring out Hardwick."

He shrugs. "In that case, what are we standing on?"

I glance at my feet. "I don't know. Land that used to be water?"

"Exactly. We're standing on the most valuable property in all of San Francisco. This is where all the business happens. It's flat and easy to build on. If I could open a store anywhere, I'd do it here." A sweep of his arm indicates the water. "And all of that?"

"Future land."

"Yep. And here's the thing—Hardwick doesn't have to wait for it to be land in order to sell it. The whole thing is marked out in a grid several blocks into the bay. There's an auction every month—"

"Let me guess. Next Tuesday."

"That's right. A sheriff's auction."

We had made inquiries about the auctions when we were thinking about buying Becky's house. "Cash only, paid in full up front."

"In the morning, right before the auction starts, one of Hardwick's men passes out maps showing available lots. Prices vary widely month to month, depending on how much cash he thinks people have."

"How do you know all this?"

"I thought future land might be cheaper than real property, so I went to a couple auctions thinking maybe I'd buy a lot to build my general store. I had my eye on a particular corner at Market Street and Drumm." He points to a spot on the water, which is, I'm guessing, the future intersection of Market and Drumm.

A man is rowing a small boat out in the bay. Jim waves at him, and the man waves back. Jim beckons him in our direction.

"That's going to be the heart of the business district someday," Jim says. "Now, if you were Hardwick, and you didn't plan to stick around long, what might you do?"

It takes a few seconds for my mind to put the pieces together and find the answer. "Sell the same piece of future property to a bunch of different buyers."

"Last two months, I watched the corner of Market Street and Drumm get auctioned off twice."

"Cash in full, up front, both times."

"You got it."

I rub my forehead. "So Hardwick is planning to leave. He's not going to wait around for the courts to settle this."

"That's my guess. You want to go visit Hampton?"

The man in the rowboat has pulled up to the edge of the

dock. "Whoa. We can do that?" I say.

Jim grins, saying, "Sometimes it's better to ask forgiveness than permission." He helps me into the boat, which wobbles precariously as I settle onto the bench. The sailor pulls away from the shore, and I wave merrily to Large and Larger, who stand on the dock with their hands on their hips, watching us go.

Wind whips my hair, and salt spray stings my face and chills my fingers. Fortunately, it's only a short paddle across choppy water to the sheriff's floating jail. I assume we'll climb up and go inside, but the sailor rows us around to the far side of the brig, out of sight of shore. The water is rougher out here, and our little rowboat rocks unsteadily as Jim raps hard on the side of the jail ship. A small round porthole opens just above, and a dirty white face peers down.

Jim calls out, "We're looking for a fellow by the name of Hampton!" A moment later, Hampton's face appears in the porthole, and I think, *Surely this is the strangest visitor calling I've ever done.*

I cup my hands to my mouth. "How're you doing?"

His forced smile doesn't fool me even a little bit. "The quarters are small and the meals are smaller, but at least nobody's working me to death."

"Hang in there," Jim says. "We're working on your situation."

"Does my friend Tom know about this?" Hampton asks. "He could set it to rights."

I hesitate, and the waves bump our rowboat against the side of the brig. I start to grab the edge of the boat, but think better of it. If we hit the side of the ship again, I could lose those fingers.

Finally I shout, "Tom had to a take a job in one of the law offices."

"I trust Tom," Hampton says. "He'll help, regardless of where he's working."

"You need anything?" Jim calls up.

There's shouting inside, and Hampton glances away from the porthole. "Gotta run," he says. The porthole slams shut.

"Well, that visit didn't last long," I say.

"I'm not sure the prisoners are technically allowed to receive," Jim says.

The sailor says nothing, just picks up the oars and rows us back to shore, taking us close to the *Charlotte*.

"Thank you, Jim," I say as we reach our familiar dock. "For today. For everything."

"Anything for Reuben's girl," he says. Then something in my face makes his eyes narrow. "What are you thinking, Leah?"

"I'm thinking I have one big advantage over Hardwick, but only if he never, ever learns what it is."

# Chapter Eleven

My uncle Hiram wanted to be rich because he thought it would make him important. He thought money would make people show him the respect he wanted. He had a picture in his head: politicians and businessmen asking for his opinion. A big chunk of land. A wife, servants, maybe even a daughter like me.

And everything he did, from speculating down in Georgia, to murdering my mama and daddy, to following me out to California and making me dress up and parade around his gold mine—it was all about building that picture in his head.

We all have something like that. I've got one, too. The picture in my head includes me and Jefferson together, neither of us hungry, in a nice cabin with a woodstove and a big bed with a pretty quilt like my parents had. It makes me blush a little to think about that bed.

Hardwick has something he wants, too. Some picture in his head that requires all this money. Something he does with the gold coins besides pile them up in banks.

So that's why, come nightfall, Henry and I are waiting in a hired carriage outside Hardwick's San Francisco mansion. I'm wearing a nice dress Becky picked out for me—she spent part of the day searching the best shops for wedding dresses—and the bodice makes me itch. Henry is wearing yet another new suit. I had to pay for it, but he insisted it was necessary.

Hardwick is the last fellow I care to get to know or spend any time with, but for our plan to succeed, I have to learn more about him. I have to figure out what picture he sees in his head.

I pull aside the curtain in the carriage window and take another look: adobe walls, tile roof, several sprawling wings and outbuildings, nested in a garden property, all surrounded by a wall. The only entrance is a wide iron gate. Guards shadow the gate, the orange glows of their cigars and cigarillos like stars against the night. This was once the villa of some Mexican official, and it survived the recent fire without any damage.

"I wonder how much a place like this costs to buy," I say, not really expecting an answer.

But Henry says, "He didn't buy it. He rents it from one of the local dons, a man who prefers to live on his ranchero than in the city."

I can't imagine renting a place so huge. "So he's not putting down roots." Just like Jim suggested.

"Maybe," Henry says. "He's been here less than a year. He was living in Sacramento, but when the weather turned cold last year, or maybe when they had the convention for statehood, he sold off a chunk of his interests in Sacramento and elsewhere. Shifted his operations to San Francisco."

"How do you know so much?"

"I always come home from a night of cards poorer in cash," he says solemnly, "but richer in knowledge."

"I'm glad that's . . . paying off for us. For some reason, I thought Hardwick had been here a while."

"His interests are spread out all across the territory," Henry says. "But his activities here have increased noticeably. Seems like he's old friends with the new sheriff, and they figured out some deal with the auctions."

"I keep hearing about this sheriff," I say.

"He and his deputies used to be part of a notorious gang of steamboat robbers."

"Really?"

"Really."

I peek out the curtain again. Hardwick will leave his compound eventually, and we aim to follow him. Surely the guards have noticed our carriage by now, skulking here in the dark. "Do you know how Hardwick came to be here in the first place?" I ask, to pass the time and keep my mind off what might happen if the guards grow suspicious.

"He probably landed in San Francisco with the navy in 1846. He was a war profiteer, buying supplies on the cheap and selling them at marked-up prices to the army. His nickname was John Mealy Hardtack."

"Hardtack? Like the biscuits?" We ate an awful lot of it on

the trail to California. If I never do battle with those molar breakers again, it will be too soon.

Henry nods. "He bought old hardtack biscuits, usually filled with mealworms, and sold them to the army, who didn't have a lot of other options."

"And the sheriff—wait, something's happening." Beyond the wall, lanterns bob across the property. A team of horses noses toward the gate, ready to leave.

"Seems like the army is how Hardwick met Sheriff Purcell," Henry says, dropping his voice, though I'm sure no one can hear us from all the way across the street.

"How much do you know about Purcell?"

"Not much. After the war with Mexico, he and his gang left the army and returned to their old ways, only this time they robbed and terrorized Mexicans and California Indians. Apparently that qualified him to be elected sheriff. That's why you don't see too many Indians here in the city, outside of the mission anyway, and the ones you do see are most likely to be Sioux or Cherokee, come west like the rest of us."

"You found out all of this by gambling?"

"Of course," he says. "There's no more popular topic of conversation in all of San Francisco right now than Hardwick. Every man of money either wants to work with him, copy what he does, or avoid him like the measles. But he has an advantage, something no one can quite put their finger on."

"What do you mean by that?"

Henry lifts the curtain and points. "I think it's her. Most

folks think he's courting her, but no one is sure. I'd bet my first edition of the *Coquette* there's more to it than that."

Guards pull open the iron gate to let out the carriage. Hardwick, dressed in a suit and top hat, offers his newest associate, Miss Helena Russell, a hand as she climbs inside and takes a seat.

"Henry, what's an associate?" I whisper.

He looks puzzled. "Someone who associates?"

"No, I mean, is it a polite way of saying something else? Does it mean something like . . ."

"Business partner?" he suggests helpfully.

"Prostitute? Mistress?"

"Not as far as I know. Why?"

"When Hardwick introduced Helena Russell to me, he described her as his newest associate. I've been struggling ever since to figure out what that means."

"You're not the only one."

Hardwick's carriage pulls out of the gate and clatters down the street. Henry sticks his head out the door and tells our driver to follow, not too closely, and to stop when it does. Our carriage lurches forward. The road is not as smooth as I'd like, and I find myself grateful for the seat cushions.

"From what I can gather," Henry says, "Hardwick has never been married, and never been publicly involved with any woman. It's a common problem here, seeing as men have outnumbered women ever since the war. So a month or two ago, when Miss Russell showed up, everyone assumed that Hardwick had finally found himself a lady."

I think of her strong arms and calloused hands. "I don't think she's a lady."

"Lee! Are you being catty?"

"No! I didn't mean it like that. I mean she's not . . . refined. She's . . . like me, I guess."

"Nothing wrong with that," he says sternly.

"I wasn't fishing for reassurances."

"Well, Miss Russell is an odd one, that's for sure. She doesn't accept lunch invitations from the wives of the other rich men and politicians. She's not engaged in charitable work for the improvement of the city. She hasn't hosted any parties."

"What does she do?"

"She accompanies Hardwick to all his business meetings. She's met every one of his partners and major clients and political allies. Some find her unnerving."

It *is* unnerving, the way she always whispers in his ear.

The carriage rattles to a stop. Henry peers out the window. "Ah, the Eldorado. Miss Helena Russell is accompanying him to a gaming house."

"Is that unusual?"

"Not lately. But before she arrived, Hardwick never gambled. Now he plays high stakes every night. Apparently he's as lucky in cards as he is in business."

The door opens, and Henry tips the driver as we step down.

The world shifts beneath my feet, and I grab Henry's arm for balance. "Henry, there's an awful lot of gold in there," I whisper.

He gives me a sympathetic look. "You're sure you want to do this?"

I take a deep breath, letting the gold sense surround me, pass through me. Things have been a whole lot easier since I learned not to fight it. "I'm sure," I say, already steadier on my feet.

A huge crowd is gathered outside, and we start to push past elbows and cigars to reach the entrance. But the dress I'm wearing is like magic; men part for me and tip their hats like I'm a one-woman Fourth of July parade. And maybe I am. All the gold here is setting off fireworks right behind my eyes.

Inside is a high-ceilinged, smoky parlor. Eight gambling tables take up most of the space, and an excited mob surrounds each one. Lots of Mexicans here, in dusty serapes and more elaborate boots than I'm used to. White men in shirtsleeves and suspenders shout in a variety of accents, announcing their origins from the Yankee north, the cotton south, the Irish isle, and faraway Australia.

A long bar runs the length of the parlor. On the wall behind it are shelves with row after row of bottles. Lots of men and a very few women crowd against the bar, drinking and laughing. In a little balcony above, a pretty Negro woman plays the fiddle.

The room smells of sweat and booze and cheap tobacco, which I'd normally find distasteful, but this time I inhale deep, letting the scents ground me. Because otherwise I'd be overwhelmed by gold, not just by the amount of coins in play, but by their constant movement. It's like a whirlpool of stars.

For a brief, fool-headed moment, I imagine calling all of that gold toward me. Part of me *wants* to do it. But this time, it wouldn't be a cloud of soft dust, coating me, turning me into the Golden Goddess of miners' tall tales. It would be a deadly hail of coins. Enough to bury me.

Or I could push it all away. It would be a relief.

I close my eyes. Sweat rolls down my forehead. My hands shake.

Maybe, with one burst of power, I could send every gold coin, every lucky nugget and pin and button in this room flying.

"Lee," Henry whispers. "Lee? Are you all right?"

"I'm . . . not sure."

"People are staring. Let's keep moving."

The size of the crowd makes it hard to see the players at each table, so we circle the room once, and then twice, looking for Hardwick and Russell. Henry pauses to talk to a number of people he recognizes, and then gets distracted by one of the games. A cherub-faced miner is on a winning streak, and the crowd cheers as he keeps doubling his bet and winning.

"He started the night with a fifty-dollar coin," explains a redheaded man standing beside us. "And now he has more than three thousand dollars."

"Maybe he should quit while he's ahead," I say.

"He should keep going while he's lucky!" Henry says, exchanging a grin with the redheaded man.

Two hands later, the miner has doubled his money again. On the third hand, the cards fall against him, and he loses everything. A collective groan of disappointment sweeps around the table on his behalf. Several bystanders offer to buy him drinks.

But he looks crushed. He's a boy barely old enough grow a beard, not even Jefferson's age. Tears roll down his sunburned cheeks.

Under the nearest table, trapped beneath the shoe of a man who's doubling down on a losing streak, I sense a small coin, dropped and lost. I bend down to pretend to adjust my boot, focus my energy very carefully, and call the coin.

The coin skitters across the floor and into my hand. But my control isn't as focused as I would like; on the table, the loser's stack of gold coins topples over.

I rise and turn to the young boy being consoled by his friends. I press the coin into his hand and say, "So you won't leave broke tonight. Here's a second chance."

His jaw hangs open. I expect, sooner or later, a thank you will emerge.

Instead he spins around and shoulders his way back to the table. "I'm in the game," he says. "I'm back in the game!"

"That was very kind of you," says Henry.

The boy sits down and scrubs away the tears with the sleeve of his shirt. "I'm not so sure," I say. "Where's Hardwick? I don't see him anywhere."

"Oh, he's almost certainly in the private rooms in the back."

"Why didn't you say so?"

"Because we won't be able to get in, at least not until much later in the night, when they start to relax the rules. In the meantime, we should just enjoy the entertainment, and if Hardwick leaves, we'll follow him to the next place."

"Why can't we get into the private rooms?" I ask.

"It's high stakes. You need at least a thousand dollars just to walk through the door."

When we came into San Francisco, with my saddlebags full of gold, I had thought I was the richest woman in the world. Now my resources are rapidly dwindling before we've even put a dent in Hardwick's enterprises.

But I came here to see him in action. I need to know who he associates with, how he spends his leisure time, figure out what he cares about.

"What if I happened to have twenty gold pieces with me? The fifty-dollar gold pieces."

He grabs my arm, then promptly lets it go again. "Are you teasing me?"

"Henry, am I a person who teases?"

"But you have a thousand dollars in gold on you?"

Slightly more than a thousand. The weight of it tugs at me, both physically and mentally, from the small purse hung over my shoulder and tucked inside my sweater. "I always carry gold with me now. Jefferson keeps some of my stake. A fair bit is with Peony. Even Mary has some, back in Glory. Never keep all your money in one place, right?"

"True enough."

"So, where do we go?"

He stares at me, as if torn. I don't get to ask him what he's torn between, because he grabs my hand and leads me through the parlor and down a long hallway.

Two men in wool suits stand outside a door: my old friends, Large and Larger.

"There's a thousand-dollar minimum," Large says.

"Do I need to count out the coins for you, or will you take my word for it?" I ask.

The two behemoths glance at each other. Finally Large shrugs.

"We can take your word for it," Larger says.

"Mr. Hardwick thought you might be coming tonight," Large explains. "Told us to look for you."

Unease fills me. We didn't go to huge pains to keep our presence a secret, but even if he had noticed the carriage, how could he have known it was us inside? Maybe someone had spotted me peeking from the window.

Henry and I move to enter, and Larger places one of his huge, meaty hands on Henry's chest. "But *your* thousand dollars, we'll need to see."

"Mr. Hardwick didn't say anything about *you* visiting tonight," says Large.

Henry's eyes plead with me for a moment. I'm not carrying enough for both of us, and I doubt Henry has more than one or two coins left. "He doesn't intend to gamble," I say. "He's my *associate*."

Larger rolls his eyes. "Nice try."

My heart sinks. It's one thing to be brave when you're with a friend; it's another thing entirely to do something brave all by yourself. "I'm sorry, Henry."

He squeezes my hand. "I'll wait for you in the main parlor."

My gold sense flutters my stomach as I enter the room. This parlor is much smaller. In one corner is a short bar manned by a single bartender. Even so, there's a lot more gold in this room. Four tables play host to a number of distinguished-looking gentlemen who are sipping from glass tumblers, smoking fragrant cigars, laughing. Each one has a stack of gold coins at hand.

I feel like a fish in a tree, and everything in me wants to escape. But then I spot Hardwick, sitting at the farthest table from the door. He's as impeccably dressed as ever, with a gold watch chain swooping across his left breast. His stark-white sideburns are combed flat over gaunt cheeks, and a cigar dangles from thin lips. Helena Russell stands beside him.

She notices me first and whispers in his ear. My heart rocks in my chest as Hardwick says something to everyone at the table. In response, the other gamblers gather their coins and stand. Staring quietly at me, they disperse to other tables.

One fellow pauses to smile. "A pleasure to see you again," he says. "Still golden, I hope."

It's the governor of California, and the pleasure is all his. I met him once before, at the Christmas ball in Sacramento, when all the tall tales about the Golden Goddess were spinning around. If they're still spinning, I'm in a heap of trouble.

But the governor tips his hat and moves on without another word. I breathe relief.

Hardwick beckons, and I stride over and sit like it's the most natural, normal thing in the world. I open my purse and set my coins on the table while the dealer shuffles the cards.

Miss Russell seats herself on his left, slightly behind him, with one gloved hand slipped through his arm. Perfect for leaning forward to whisper in his ear.

Hardwick watches me the way a cat watches a bird's nest in an apple tree. "How would you like to come work for me, Miss Westfall?"

My heart hammers in my throat, and the air suddenly seems a bit thin because all I can think is *He knows. He knows what I can do.*

After too long a pause, I manage to say, "Doing what?"

He takes a sip of whiskey, then wipes his mustache with a handkerchief. "I'm not sure. I admit, I don't quite have you figured out."

*Well, that's a mercy.*

"But you keep showing up in the most interesting places," he continues, "and it's clear that you have some ability for accumulating resources."

So maybe he doesn't know after all. I try to keep the relief from my face. "In other words, you've determined that I have some gold, and you'd like to take a portion of it."

His sudden laugh is surprising for how genuine it seems. "No one acquires gold by accident," he says, eyes twinkling. "I have gold, you have gold. There's a chance that both of us could acquire a lot more gold by working together. How do you want to bet?"

The dealer has turned up a pair of cards. "I'm sorry, but I don't know how to play. You'll have to teach me."

Hardwick makes a small circular motion with his finger, and the dealer reshuffles the cards. "This game is called Spanish monte," Hardwick says. "The rules are simple, and it's almost impossible to cheat."

I only half listen to Hardwick's instructions, because Miss Russell is peering at me in the most peculiar way, like she's seeing through me, or beyond me, and—most disconcerting of all—her irises are saturated with a deep shade of violet.

I could have sworn her eyes were blue.

The dealer lays down two cards, a two of hearts to his right and a jack of diamonds to his left. He places the remaining stack of cards between them.

"And now we bet," Hardwick says, tossing a fifty-dollar coin onto the jack.

I toss a coin onto the deuce, determined to ignore Miss Russell's violet gaze.

Hardwick makes the go-ahead motion again. The dealer turns over a seven of hearts. "The young lady wins," he says.

"The odds change as he works his way through the deck," Hardwick says. "Someone who pays close attention can increase their chances of winning after a few hands."

The dealer deals, and again I choose the card that Hardwick doesn't. This time I lose, but so does Hardwick, and both our coins get taken. "I should have quit while I was ahead."

"That's the trick, isn't it?" Hardwick says. "To exit the game when you're at your peak? But you're young. You're just learning how the game's played, and you've barely started."

I'm not sure we're still talking about gambling. "What about all the people who never get ahead enough to quit?"

"That's their problem, isn't it?" he says. From behind him, Helena Russell reaches for his whiskey, takes a sip, sets the glass back on the table. Hardwick doesn't seem to notice or care. "But that doesn't apply to you or me. Your friend Tom is a very good lawyer."

If he's trying to throw me by changing the subject abruptly, it might be working, because I lose on the next hand, and Hardwick wins. "I'm not sure I would recommend him," I say. "He only negotiated the one contract for me, and I thought it was airtight, but it turns out there's no way to enforce it."

"Sometimes that's a temporary problem, with the system, not with the contract. I was just talking with the governor and with California's new senator. They seem to think that when statehood becomes official—in a few more months, maybe a year at most—we'll have the rule of law here, as strict as any state in the nation, with honest judges, and checks and balances, and all the other trappings of civilization."

I can't tell if he finds the prospect appealing or not. "I didn't realize you had so much respect for the law."

This draws another belly laugh. "I respect the laws so much I want to make them," he says. "Your bet."

Hearts come up again, and it's been several deals since I saw them, so I toss two coins down, and this time I win. One hundred dollars, just like that.

Helena's eyes widen. They've returned to their normal blue, which doesn't make me feel the least bit better. She hasn't said a word since I sat down, not to Hardwick or to me, but my skin prickles under her gaze.

Maybe it's nothing. A trick of the light. But maybe it's quite a bit of something. I know one other person whose eyes change color—me. And only when I'm sensing gold.

In the next round, I lose everything I'd won. I say, "One thing I can't figure out is why you started gambling. Everything you do is so careful and planned, but this is a game of chance. You can't help losing."

He finishes his glass of whiskey and smiles. "Who owns this parlor?"

I think about Large and Larger watching the door. "You do."

"So when I win, I win. And when I lose, I still win. Excuse me, I need to refill my glass. Would you like something to drink?"

"No, thank you."

He rises and heads toward the bar in the corner. As the dealer gathers up all the cards and starts shuffling, Helena scoots her chair closer to mine.

Something tingles at the back of my neck, and I freeze, like a ladybug caught in a spider's web. Helena leans forward, avidly, hungrily, and places a hand on my knee. I open my mouth to ask her what in tarnation she's doing, but a small bolt of lightning shoots through me. Her eyes are so dark now, the color of ripe plums.

"You have to tell me," she says breathlessly. "Quick, before he comes back. How do you do it? How do you do that thing with the gold?"

My heart starts racing.

Her gaze is awful. Like she's looking right through my skin and into my heart. Her nose is a tad too long, her skin a bit too world-weary, her lips pressed thin. But there's a compelling wild energy about her that makes me shiver just as much as that violet glare.

"I don't know what you're talking about," I manage.

Her eyes narrow. "You're up to something, and I'm going to figure you out. You're not going to get his money."

I shoot to my feet and start gathering my coins.

Hardwick returns. "Quitting so soon?" he asks. "Sweet girl, the first rule of the game is you can't quit before you're ahead even once."

I sway dizzily. There's too much gold in this room for me to risk making abrupt moves, but I can't help scrambling backward, away from the table and Helena's horrible eyes. The backs of my knees knock the chair as I push it back. "Sometimes it's better to know when to cut your losses," I say, and I rush out the door before he can respond.

# Chapter Twelve

I find Henry sharing drinks at the bar with the cherub-faced gambler. Henry babbles and sways, noticeably in his cups.

"We have to go, Henry. Now."

Drunk or not, Henry doesn't hesitate. He tosses a coin at the bartender and follows me out the front door.

Once inside the relative safety of the carriage, he asks, "You talked to Hardwick, yes? Did something go wrong?"

My heart still feels like a drumbeat in my throat. "I'm not sure what happened. I . . . I'm not quite ready to talk about it."

He doesn't press, but he says, "I got some good information tonight. Let me know when you're ready to hear it."

"All right. Thanks." I'm grateful to be left with my own thoughts as we ride back to the *Charlotte*.

We pull up, and the sight of the ship ought to give me great comfort, because Melancthon's handiwork is beautiful. A new door greets us, framed by a small porch and two lanterns that cast warm, buttery light onto the stoop. But all the hominess just reminds me that I'm *not* home, that my real home was taken from me, and all our efforts to establish a new one depend on making sure Hardwick is no longer a threat.

Melancthon and a man I've never seen before are sitting on their heels, huddled in front of the door. As we exit the carriage, Melancthon rises and greets us with a wave.

"Just putting the final touches on this great big hole. How many keys do you want?"

The fellow with him stands, wiping his hands on something that looks a lot like Wilhelm's blacksmith's apron, but with a lot more pockets. "Name's Adams," he says. "Locksmith." He's tall and angular with a long, narrow nose and a meticulous black mustache.

"Nice to meet you Mr. Adams," I reply. "How many keys can you make?"

"As many as you need, ma'am."

"In that case . . ." I count companions in my head. "I need eight keys."

His eyes widen slightly, but he says, "No trouble at all."

Adams pulls a flat tray the size of a writing slate from a bag. From his pocket, he withdraws a large iron key. He presses the key into the tray; I peer closer and see it's filled with milky wax.

When he lifts the key out, a perfect impression remains in the wax. Adams wipes the key on his apron and hands it to me. "This will have to do for now. I'll deliver seven copies tomorrow."

I look back and forth between the key in my hand and the wax tray in his.

Melancthon hands a few coins to the locksmith, who takes his leave. I stand back, admiring my new porch.

"Nice work, Jones," Henry says, admiration in his voice.

"It's beautiful," I agree. "Thank you."

Melancthon beams.

We step through the doorway, and voices echo up from the galley. Henry goes off to join them, but I'm not ready to be around anyone yet. I've learned too much today—about Mama, about Hardwick's *associate*—and I need time for things to settle. So I head up to the deck and climb the stairs to the stern—the poop deck, as Olive and Andy inform me every single time.

My intention is to sit and gaze at the stars over the hilltops and pretend I'm someplace far away. But someone else has gotten there first, and I recognize his lanky, perfect shape even in the dark.

Suddenly, having company doesn't seem so bad. I sit beside him, my back against the railing. The sky is covered with clouds, not a star to be seen.

After a while I reach over and squeeze his hand. He squeezes back. We sit in darkness holding hands, not saying a word. I find I don't miss the stars at all; the hills of the city are covered with lights.

"I'm scared I'm doing the wrong thing," I say finally.

"We could leave. Go anywhere."

"Is that what you want?"

"No." I'm relieved to hear him say it. He adds, "But as long as I'm with you, I'll be right as rain, no matter where we go."

"We can't leave. You promised Becky you'd wear a plum-colored suit for our wedding in Glory," I say.

Both of his warm hands fold around mine, and he pleads. "Please, please, let's get out of here and run away before we have to do a big wedding. I already feel sick every time I look at a plum."

I flash back to Helena Russell's plum-colored eyes.

"Lee?"

I blink to clear the memory. "Becky will be so disappointed in us."

"Becky lives to be disappointed in people. If we get out of her way, she'll expand her horizons. She'll find all sorts of new people to be disappointed in."

I chuckle while Jefferson leans back against the railing. "You know, I think that baby girl is going to be full-grown before she gets a name," I say.

"The Major's been calling her Rosy, 'cause of her rosy cheeks. Becky caught him doing it the other day, and I thought she was going to rip off his other leg before she was done."

"Jeff!" I say, but I'm laughing.

"I'm serious. She wants to control everything, so nothing can go wrong. She won't even give that baby a name because she's afraid it'll be the wrong name." He takes a deep breath, like he's carefully considering his next words. "You can't get so scared of doing the wrong thing that you don't do anything at all."

I let that sink in for a moment. Jefferson's voice has changed.

It's deeper than it used to be. Warmer. A voice a girl can trust. "That's not why I'm scared," I tell him.

"Then what are you worried about?"

"Something happened tonight. When Henry and I followed Hardwick."

"Tell me."

And just like that, my heart starts pounding all over again.

"Lee?" His fingertip traces my left eyebrow.

I wanted to keep this to myself a little, hold tight to it, let it stew. It feels so monumental. So personal. But this is Jefferson. I can tell him anything. "It's about Helena Russell, Hardwick's associate. I think she knows what I can do."

Jefferson sits straight up, his fingers leaving my face. "You mean, your witchy powers?"

"I don't know. Maybe." I explain what happened at the gambling parlor.

He rubs his chin with a hand, pondering my words, and it turns out it's a *relief* to tell someone I trust, to share the burden of thinking with him. At last he says, "That thing about the eyes. More than a little bothersome."

"Yeah." I scoot closer so our thighs touch. He's like my own personal woodstove, a shield against the cold night.

"You think she can find gold? The way you do?"

"No. Not exactly. I mean, she asked me how I did 'that thing with the gold.' If she could do it herself, she wouldn't ask, right?"

"That makes sense."

"But I do think she has . . . magic. Something miraculous

and amazing that she can do. And Jeff, I have to tell you. I talked to Jim today." It pours out of me, everything about Hiram and Mama and her ability to find lost things and how, one time, the lost thing she found was Jefferson.

Jeff is silent a long time. "So this kind of thing is passed down, generation to generation."

"Maybe."

"And Helena Russell can recognize it in someone else."

"It's possible." A bit of wonder tinges my voice.

"Does that mean Hardwick knows about you?"

I force myself to consider this sensibly, without panicking. "He noticed my particular affinity for gathering wealth, for sure and certain," I say. "But he always seems baffled by it. Maybe Helena knows but hasn't told him for some reason."

His arm drapes my shoulders again, and I lean into him. "So that's why you're so scared," he says.

"We need to tell everyone. If Helena knows . . . things . . . it will be very hard to make a good plan."

He's silent a long time. "But maybe, also, it's a little bit wonderful? It must be hard to hold those two things in your heart at the same time. Fear. Delight. All about the same darn thing."

I can't help it; I turn my face and kiss him hard on the lips. Because he understands without me having to say. I'm not the only girl with witchy powers. I'm not alone.

## Chapter Thirteen

The next morning I wander to the galley, drawn by the smell of coffee and the sizzle of bacon. That alone would leave me more than satisfied, but the big table also contains platters of scrambled eggs and fried potatoes. My mouth waters. Before I take the first bite, I know that Becky didn't cook this meal. I pour some coffee, cup it in my hands, and hold it to my face, just breathing in the aroma.

The lanterns are lit, and a candle brightens the table. If we're here for any length of time, maybe I should commission some windows. And it's as though I summoned him with a thought, because Melancthon enters with a huge platter of flapjacks and thumps it down on the table.

"I hired you to be a carpenter, not a cook," I tell him. "You're under no obligation to feed us."

"Who's feeding you? All of this is *my* breakfast." We both grin. "No, seriously, I just wanted to show my appreciation."

"It's no problem for you to stay here. There's more space than we need."

"It's not just the room and board, and giving me honest work for honest pay, although I appreciate that. It's my thanks for saving the *Charlotte*. This was my home for three years, and I've worked on every part of her—I know every beam and strake, every inch of timber. Thought I'd see her torn apart and used for lumber. But you saved her."

"So you've forgiven me for wanting holes in her."

"Let's not get carried away."

I sip the coffee. "Have you given any more thought to your long-term plans?"

He sits beside me and pours a cup of coffee for himself. "It's been on my mind. This meal is a bit of a thank-you, yes, but it's also a bid-thee-well. Word has it the *Argos* is setting sail for New York next week."

The thought of losing Melancthon saddens me. I barely know him, but he's already proved himself a decent fellow, and pleasant company besides. "Do you have enough to purchase passage?" We've paid him fairly for his work, but I have no idea how much it costs to sail from San Francisco to New York by way of the Panama Isthmus.

"That's just it; I wouldn't have to buy passage. The captain and I sailed together before, on a whaling ship out of Newport. He says the ship is privately chartered. Won't say for who, but he did say that the customer is paying very well for his privacy. He wants to hire me as a carpenter—his last one caught gold fever."

I am now fully awake and alert, and it has nothing to do with coffee. Well, maybe not everything to do with the coffee. "That's . . . interesting."

Melancthon stares into his cup. "He also says they have valuable cargo that might create some problems, and they'll need a steady hand moving all of it once they get to Panama."

This definitely sounds like Hardwick. "When exactly are they sailing?" I'm willing to bet the rest of my savings it's not before Tuesday's auctions.

"End of the week," Melancthon says. "After the auctions."

Time enough to collect all the money first. *Sometimes you have to quit when you're well and truly ahead,* he told me.

"Do me a favor, Mr. Jones," I say. My mind is churning, churning, churning. Hardwick leaving so soon could present an obstacle. Or maybe . . . an opportunity. "Wait a day or two before you accept that offer."

He opens his mouth to ask why, but Jefferson wanders into the galley, whistling like a yellow warbler with a mouthful of spring. He pulls up a chair and sits beside me.

"You're in a good mood this morning," I say glumly. "Like every morning." This is what I have to look forward to for the rest of my life: Jefferson's morning cheer assaulting me like a bag of bricks.

"Yep." He grabs a plate and helps himself to a large serving of everything.

Becky enters carrying the baby, who is most certainly not named Rosy. The Major follows behind, guiding Andy and Olive toward the table. He and the children eye the flapjacks with distrust. I reckon they're not used to seeing such a fine, evenly cooked repast. Henry stumbles in a moment later.

"I'll make myself scarce," Melancthon says, gathering up his plate and coffee.

"You can stay," I tell him, but I don't enthuse too hard.

"I expect you all have things to talk about," he says. "And I like to sit on deck in the morning."

He leaves, and everyone starts eating. Once we all have a bit of food and coffee in us, I spring the bad news. "We have to move up our timetable."

"We had a timetable?" the Major says around a mouth of flapjacks. He's chewing them uncertainly, like a cat with a feather stuck in its mouth, and I get the strangest notion that he might prefer Becky's.

"But we've barely started gathering information," Becky says.

Jefferson nods. "I'm still trying to find an angle on Mr. Keys. I've never seen him alone, without at least two guards. And he doesn't gamble or have any bad habits, as far as I can tell."

"It doesn't matter. It's not *our* timetable; it's Hardwick's." I tell them everything I've learned over the past few days. Hardwick selling off his other properties in the state, wringing every dollar out of his San Francisco interests, bragging to me about getting out while he was ahead. "And then there's this news: according to Melancthon, someone's chartered a ship called the *Argos* to take valuable cargo out of San Francisco to New York. It has to be Hardwick, leaving town with all his gold."

"Why would he do that?" Jefferson asks.

"People sometimes make rash choices when they're in love," Becky says. "He's got that new lady friend, right? We met her at the law offices. What's her name?"

"Helena Russell," I say. My voice squeaks a little.

"So maybe he's ready to get married and settle down. Maybe they want to start a family."

I shake my head. "They have a closeness, an . . . intimacy, I suppose," I say, thinking of the way she hung on his arm, drank from his whiskey glass. "But I don't think they have marriage in mind."

"Why not?" Becky asks.

"He calls her his associate, and she goes with him to all his business meetings."

"Like a secretary?" Becky says.

"Not exactly like," I say. "She watches everything. She . . ." I hesitate. I should tell them about her eyes, about my suspicions, but the words lodge in my throat.

"Last night I learned that she used to be a fortune-teller," Henry offers. "A few months ago she was running a scam, mostly on miners, pretending to tell their futures, if they'd find gold, that sort of thing."

I give him a sharp look. "Who told you that?"

"That girl Sonia."

"The pickpocket?"

"She and Billy and their mob of runaways were hanging around the Eldorado last night. Looking for easy takes, I suspect. She didn't have any information about Mr. Keys. But she and Helena Russell targeted some of the same people."

"Marks," Becky says.

"Yes, they targeted some of the same marks. So she knew all about Russell's scam."

The air around me is suddenly hot and tight. I'm not sure I'd discount Russell's fortune-telling as a scam.

"I asked about Hardwick," Henry continues, "but Sonia said they avoid him—his guards kill anyone who crosses them. Or *worse*. When I told her he was back in the private room she and her crew made themselves scarce."

"That explains what Helena wants with Hardwick," the Major says. "She's trying to run some kind of scam on him and take his money. But what does he want with her?"

Silence around the table. Beneath it, Jefferson grabs my hand and squeezes, as if to say, "Go ahead. Tell them."

Before I can change my mind, I blurt the previous evening's events, leaving nothing out.

Another silence follows.

"The second sight," the Major says at last.

"Huh?" I ask.

He wipes his mouth with a napkin; before keeping company with Becky, he would have wiped it with his sleeve. "I mean, what if Hardwick keeps her around because her fortune-telling powers are real?"

*That's exactly what I was thinking.*

"I knew some women like that, not on the Craven side of my family, but the O'Malleys. Something passed down from the old country. We called it the second sight. They could find lost items, tell a person's future just by looking at him, dream about things far away. I've seen it with my own eyes."

I lean forward. "Seen *what*?"

He takes a sip of coffee and considers his next words. "When we were small, my little brother fell out of a tree and broke his right arm. The same day it happened, my mother got a letter from Aunt Lizzy, her sister, warning that she had had a dream about my brother breaking his arm, and telling my mother to be careful. It'd been written days before."

"That's not exactly proof," I say.

He shrugs. "No, but there were other things, too. Even now, for example, there's this girl . . ." He gives me a knowing look. "Who can sniff out gold better than a bloodhound on the trail. When she does, her brown eyes turn the most mesmerizing shade of gold."

"Really?" Becky says. "I never noticed that!"

Everyone is suddenly staring at me, as if expecting my eyes to shoot daggers. Like I'm *dangerous*.

Something inside me breaks just a tiny bit. Sniffing out gold is the most valuable, wondrous thing I can do. But even the people closest to me, the people I love with all my heart, sometimes view my power with suspicion. And maybe they're right to do so.

Mama was the same way. She loved me, for sure and certain, but she never wanted to talk about what I could do, even when it was just me and her and Daddy all alone by the box stove. *Magic makes mischief,* she always said, and left it at that. If she'd had her way, I never would have used my powers, even if it meant holes in the roof and a bare cellar.

She changed her mind at the very end, but it was too late. She was murdered for my gift. So I don't blame my friends one bit for being a little bit scared sometimes.

"It's one of the prettiest things I ever saw," Jefferson says, breaking the silence.

"A marvel, truly," the Major agrees.

"Well, I've never noticed Lee's eyes," Becky says, "but her particular abilities have been an incredible blessing, and I'm grateful to be among the lucky few who benefit."

Henry raises his coffee mug. "To Lee and her . . . second sight."

Everyone grins, raising their own mugs, and I look around at them all, tears filling my eyes as it slowly dawns on me: I misread their stares. They're not afraid of what I can do. They're not like Mama at all.

"In any case," the Major says, "I'm concerned about Miss Russell, but I'm even more concerned with how Hardwick is using her. Her fortune-telling is giving him an edge in all his dealings."

Becky shakes her head. "I bet she can't do anything at all. Not like our Lee. It's a confidence game." She's feeding bits of scrambled egg to the baby, who tries to grab them from the spoon with her chubby hands. "She's fishing for information," she explains. "'That thing with the gold?' That's just her way of getting you to reveal how you attained so much. I mean, you were in a gambling parlor owned by Hardwick, and she said that you aren't going to get any of his money." She waves the spoon in the air. "*I* could make that prediction."

The Major says, "But the things my aunt Lizzy knew . . . of course, with her, it was only family members. Or people she was well acquainted with. I don't think her sight ever worked on strangers."

Becky reaches over and pats the Major's hand. "Now, Wally, I'm sorry. I didn't mean to impugn the memory of your beloved aunt Lizzy. I just think there are good reasons to be skeptical."

He covers her hand and smiles at her, and she smiles back. Maybe Jefferson and I aren't the only ones who think they invented falling in love.

I grab the napkin and wipe my mouth to cover my smile.

Henry taps the table like he's forming a message in Morse code. "I think we're missing the point here. What is Hardwick's goal?"

This is exactly my question. What's the picture in his head? The perfect life he envisions for himself?

Henry's eyes light up like a city on fire. "What if . . . ?" And then his mouth stops, to make room for his spinning brain.

"What if *what*?" I ask.

"What if he's going back to New York to get into politics?"

"Then good riddance to him," I say. "But why would he have to go to New York to get into politics? He already controls every politician in California."

"No, think about it," Henry says. "California isn't even a state yet, not officially. And it's way out on the far edge of the country. It takes weeks or months for news to reach us.

Being governor here is like being a bullfrog in a washtub. It makes a big noise, but it's still just a washtub. But New York is different! Just think about who ran for president in the last election."

We all shake our heads until the Major says, "Well, Zachary Taylor ran—that's how he ended up being our president."

"But why did the Whigs put Millard Fillmore on the ballot with him? Because he's from New York. Why did the Free Soil Party pick up ten percent of the vote with Martin Van Buren on their ticket? Because he's from New York."

This is the most passionate I've ever seen Henry on a topic. But I'm pretty sure everyone else is staring at him just as blankly as I am, because I don't know what he's getting at.

Seeing our confused expressions, he opens his hands, like he's begging for understanding. "New York has thirty-six votes in the electoral college—no other state is even close. Didn't any of you vote in the election of 1848?"

Becky folds her hands on the table and sits up primly. "Henry, dear, I'm not allowed to own my own property, much less vote."

"I'm not old enough, but if I was, I've got the same problem," I say.

"Well, of course," Henry says, looking from us to Jefferson. "But . . ."

"Don't look at me," Jefferson says. "My mother was Cherokee. Government says I can't be trusted to vote."

Henry's mouth drops open. Then he turns toward the Major. "What about you, Wally?"

The Major shrugs. "I never worried too much about politics—as long as the system works for me I'm happy. The system always seems to work for me."

Henry throws up his hands in disgust.

"You're awful worked up about this," I observe.

"Think about it," Henry says. "A self-made millionaire returns from California to New York—a man who is now rich beyond imagination. People will love that story. He decides to get into politics on his claims of being a successful businessman—because it was the frontier, it's like being a war hero, only more glamorous. Meanwhile, nobody in New York knows his character, what he's really like. Someone like that could get nominated to run for president. It doesn't even matter which party."

Jefferson leans forward. "You think that's Hardwick's plan? He's going to take the millions of dollars he's made and go back to New York to get elected president?"

"I'm not sure," Henry says. "The timing is good. It's three years to the next election. He goes back now, invests his money in a bunch of legitimate businesses, spends the rest to establish himself. He'd be in prime position."

"I don't know," Becky says. "It seems far-fetched."

"He mentioned something last night," I say. All the faces turn toward me. "I accused him of not respecting the law. He told me he respected laws so much, he wanted to make them."

Henry leans back in his chair and folds his arms, as if putting a period on his argument.

"This is a good thing, right?" the Major says. "He'll be out of California and out of our hair. We can go back to living our normal life."

"How can you think that?" I snap.

The Major looks at me, genuinely confused.

"He paid to exterminate Indians—whole tribes of them, all of their families, destroyed. Muskrat is probably dead, and it's because of ***him***. He ignores the rights of free men, and profits off buying and selling people's lives. He takes advantage of the poor and people without legal protection, and gets rich by using the law to rob people of their hard-earned wages." I point across the table at Becky and the kids. "He steals from widows and children. It's bad enough that he does it out here, but what if he's in charge of the whole country? Think about everyone he'll hurt."

By the end, I'm shouting. My face is hot with anger. The longest silence yet follows, broken only by the uncomfortable shifting of Becky's children in their chairs.

"Ma, may I be excused?" Andy whispers.

"Olive, take your brother, and the two of you go play in our room for now," Becky says.

Olive quickly gathers up her brother and flees.

"You're right, Lee," the Major says softly. "It was a thoughtless thing for me to say."

I overreacted, and I'm fixing to apologize, but Jefferson says, "Once Hardwick leaves California, we can't touch him. The minute he sets sail on the *Argos*, our chance to stop him is gone."

"The auction is Tuesday," the Major says. "How can we stop him before then?"

"I wish I knew." I stand abruptly, gather my dirty dishes, and carry them to the washtub, where I stack them loudly.

Jefferson brings his dishes over. "Do you want to talk about it?" he whispers.

Guilt twinges in my chest. I'm being rude. "No, I want to think. But thank you." I should scrape and wash my own dishes, but I leave them and flee down to the hold to see Peony.

It's neat and tidy, with four separate stalls and space to store the wagon. The stalls have fresh straw, and somebody has mucked them out recently, so it smells familiar—like the clean barn my family always kept. The last time I set foot in that barn, I was hiding from Hiram, waiting for my chance to escape.

And once again, it only serves to remind me that this is *not* home. Not really. Not yet. No place can be home until we're safe from Hardwick and people like him.

Peony snorts when she sees me, shuffling eagerly. I imagine she's tired of being cooped up in here. I find a brush and groom her.

"Sorry I'm not taking you out for fresh air," I say. "You deserve better. We all deserve better." She nuzzles my hand for the treat I didn't bring, so I spend extra time cleaning her coat, especially the little swirl of hair on her withers she likes brushed just so.

Thumps on the ramp signal someone stepping down into

the hold, and I have the urge to hide, but within a split second I realize that hiding will not stop Hardwick or solve any of my problems.

Melancthon approaches with that peculiar rolling gait of his, like he's compensating for waves that aren't there anymore. He pauses when he sees me.

"You did a good job down here," I tell him. "The horses seem as comfortable as can be expected."

He nods. "Thank you. It's been a long time since I was around any kind of creature that couldn't swim."

"Peony swims just fine. Most horses do."

"Huh. Haven't worked with horses since my canal-digging days. Would rather be on the water, though."

"Weren't you ever afraid?" I ask.

"Of horses?"

"No, of sinking, when you were sailing the ocean." I touch the smooth, curved hull with my fingertips, thinking of the ship Hardwick will sail to New York. Maybe we'll get lucky and he won't make it that far. Which I recognize for a bit of meanness, considering all the other people aboard. "This doesn't look like much to keep between you and the bottom of the sea."

He grins, pounding the hull with his fist. "Those are three-inch planks, and the hull is double planked, so that's six inches of solid oak between us and the water. We needed it, the one time we took her around Cape Horn."

"So it's hard to break the hull of a ship like this."

He rubs the back of his neck thoughtfully. "Not if you drive it onto rocks, or get rammed by another ship, I suppose. But that takes a particular kind of bad luck. Although I once had the misfortune to be aboard a ship that capsized, so I figure I've used up my bad luck for a spell."

*"Capsized?"*

"Another whaling ship, the *Salem*—got caught in swells in the North Atlantic. It shouldn't have been a problem, but we only had half a hold full of cargo, and a new cargo master who didn't know better, and the barrels broke loose in the waves. Shifted from one side to the other, before we could stop them, making the ship roll more with every wave until it rolled right over."

I stare at him in horror. "I hope all your crewmates survived."

"We got safely into the ship's boats, not a soul lost. But the ship and all the cargo sank to the bottom of the ocean. Lost everything except the clothes on our backs."

I rub Peony's nose, and she nuzzles my face. I lost everything once, everything except this horse and Mama's locket. "That sounds awful. I'm so glad you—"

"Lee?" A familiar female voice shouts down into the hold. Peony's ears flick with recognition. "Lee?"

I drop the brush and run to answer. "Mary?"

# Chapter Fourteen

My friend stands at the stable door, and even though she's supposed to be back in Glory, taking care of the Worst Tavern, I'm so glad to see her. She's wearing a printed wool challis dress, with beautiful patterns in swirling red and purple. I throw my arms around her and hug tight, before remembering she doesn't much like to be hugged.

I step away sheepishly. "Sorry. I'm just really glad to see you."

"I forgive you."

"What are you doing here?"

"About a week after you left Glory, I missed you and decided to come to San Francisco to find you."

I study her face. "That sounds like a bunch of hogwash."

She frowns.

"Mary? What happened?"

She becomes fascinated by the bridle hanging beside Peony's stall. "Nothing. I mean, I left before something could happen."

"Mary! Tell me!"

Her frown deepens. "It wasn't safe for me, all right? Once my friends left, everyone expected me to . . . be like I was before. Some of the men were . . . demanding. They just assumed that because I'm a girl from China, I'm in a certain line of work. So I left."

"Oh. I see." And I do. Mary was a prostitute before she joined up with us in Glory. At barely seventeen years old.

"This town is even bigger than when I was here last," she says, but I won't let her change the subject just yet.

"What about the Worst Tavern? Becky left you in charge." She glares, and I hold up my hands in protest. "Not judging. Just asking."

She sighs. "Old Tug and some of his Buckeyes are working the place in shifts—when they're not working claims. They're terrible cooks, but no worse than Becky."

"And how is Tug? Wait . . . is he one of the fellows who—"

"No! He's the best man in Glory, if you ask me. Kept an eye on me as best he could, but he couldn't be there every waking moment. Even Wilhelm could only loom so much. But you and Becky and the Major—you're the leaders in our town. And once you left . . . one of the Buckeyes' claims was jumped. And a group came down from Rough and Ready trying to make trouble. Almost had our very own gunfight, but Tug talked them down. It's just not the same without you all there."

"So you set off for San Francisco. All on your own. Mary, that was dangerous! You could have—"

"Hey! I stowed away on a ship and traveled across an ocean

all by myself. And if I recall correctly, you covered half a continent with nothing but your mare and a saddlebag. So don't be lecturing me about it now!" Her eyes are bright and fierce, made more so by the meager lantern light.

"You're right. I'm sorry. And I'm sorry we left you there all alone." It doesn't set well, that Glory could turn out as lawless and frightening as any other frontier town. As if Glory's residents are a parcel of naughty children who play dangerously when their mama and daddy are away. That could be Glory's future, instead of the "sanctuary" Jefferson imagines.

"Wasn't your fault," Mary says. "I was the addle head who said she wanted to stay." The fight melts out of her, and she leans against the stall, looking a little defeated. "If I go back there, it has to be with friends. And when I do, I think maybe I should find someone who will marry me. A single girl from China . . . it's just not safe. You know, California isn't a very good place, if you're not white."

She'll get no argument from me.

"But now I've found you—which, by the way, was easy as pie. Everyone knew you from your description. Not many white women in San Francisco."

This does not sit well at all.

She says, "I can stay here, right? You don't mind?"

"Of course. Actually, we might be able to use your help with something."

I fill her in on everything that has happened with Hardwick. By the time I'm finished, she's grinning like a kid at Christmas. "This will be *fun*," she says.

◆ ◆ ◆

After Mary leaves to claim a cabin of her own, I go to my room and grab my saddlebag. It's easier to heft than I'd like. I spent so much money buying the *Charlotte*. Doing something about Hardwick is proving more complicated and expensive than I expected.

I sit on the floor at the end of my cot, saddlebag between my feet. Inside is a small pile of gold. A few eagle coins remain, along with a handful of gold nuggets I could get assayed if I need more money—though plenty of folks here take raw gold in payment. Still, there's more saddlebag than gold by weight.

Back in Glory, I practiced working with gold every day, and although I've had a few opportunities here in San Francisco to use my witchy powers, I need to be more disciplined about it. No one becomes a dab at something by laying about, Daddy always said.

I close my eyes and reach out with my gold sense. The shape of it eludes me at first; there are so many individual pieces. The coins ring loudest at first, at 90 percent gold. Nuggets are sometimes purer than that, but not these. One is so muddled up with quartz ore it's barely fifty percent. For my idea to work, I need this pile of gold to hum a single, familiar song, but this seems more like church ladies at a picnic all vying for attention.

I concentrate harder, trying to imagine all the little bits of gold as a single entity. It doesn't work. There are too many tiny pieces to keep track of, and they insist on singing their own tunes.

So instead of focusing on the whole mess as one, I wrap my thoughts around as many individual pieces as I can, holding their shapes in my mind. A twenty-dollar piece, a half eagle, the largest nugget.

I stretch out my hand, and I close my fist as if grasping that sound-shape in my mind. Then I open my palm and fling it across the room.

The saddlebag slithers along the floor and thumps into the far wall. I gasp, my eyes popping open.

I did it.

I've called gold to me before, and pushed it away, but it's another thing entirely to move something else with it. My shoulders ache, like I've been lifting hay bales. A throb is forming at the base of my neck.

I clench my fist and summon the gold back to me, but the saddlebag doesn't move, just gives a little hiccup on the floor and stays stubbornly still. I stretch out again with my gold sense. What did I do wrong? I used the same . . . aha. All the bits of gold settled into new places when it slid across the floor. I have to wrap my focus around the mess all over again if I'm to move it.

I take my time about it, going slow and careful. It's several heartbeats before I've latched on well enough to give it another try. My patience is rewarded; the saddlebag slides—faster this time—back across the floor, and I stretch out my boots to stop it. The impact shivers through my knees.

Eyes closed, thoughts swaddled tight around the gold, I open my fist and fling it away again. The saddlebag rips across the floor and slams into the wall. My fist closes tight, and it returns; this time I open my hand and stop it just before it hits me.

Over and over again, I practice: slide *thump*, slide stop, slide *thump*, slide stop.

The muscles in my neck and shoulders burn, and my head feels like there's a tiny miner inside, jabbing with a tiny pickax. But in a way it's also calming. It takes so much concentration, leaving no room to think about anything else.

Slide *thump*, slide stop.

A soft tap at the door interrupts me.

"Come in," I say.

The door creaks open, and Jefferson pokes in his head tentatively. "I cleaned up your dishes," he says, as though it was a monumental feat of heroism.

"Thanks."

His gaze goes from me, to the saddlebag against the wall, and back to me, sitting cross-legged on the wood plank floor. "Practicing again?"

"Yep."

He frowns. "Lee, are you feeling all right?"

"Why? Don't tell me I'm covered in gold again."

"Your face is flushed," he says, plunking down beside me at the end of the cot. He stretches his legs out. "Like you've gotten too much sun. And your eyes are as bright gold as I've ever seen."

"Huh. Well, I've been trying something new."

"How's it going?"

"It's going."

"Show me."

"All right." I'm suddenly nervous, like I'm performing for the most important person in the world, but I concentrate a moment, and sure enough, the saddlebag goes scooting across the floor.

"Isn't that something!" Jefferson says. His gaze turns thoughtful. "We can use this. Somehow . . ."

"I'm trying to figure out how to direct it better. Stop and start, change direction, that sort of thing. But it's hard. It . . . makes my head hurt a little."

He's staring at my face now, in a peculiar way that sets my heart to thumping. "Your eyes. They're almost glowing."

"Oh?"

Jefferson's fingers reach up to gently touch my cheek. "They're beautiful."

"Oh."

His gaze drops to my chest, and his eyes narrow.

"What?"

"That locket," he says, indicating the charm with his chin. "Have you tried working with it?"

Of its own accord, my hand goes to the golden heart shape hanging from my neck. Inside is a lock of hair, taken from my baby brother, who only lived a few days. "No, not really. Why?"

"You wear it every day. Remember how you found little Andy with it? When he was lost on the prairie?"

I nod, seeing what he's getting at. When I told Mary about

my gold sense, I was able to make it float in the air a little.

"You once told me that you feel the shape of things. You know the shape of that locket like your own hand."

I reach behind my neck and undo the clasp. I lift the tiny chain so the locket slips off into my palm. Though I see it clear with my eyes, feel it cool and firm against my skin, my magic perceives it as a sparkling ember, ready to do my bidding.

Just like with the gold inside the saddlebag, I wrap my mind around its shape, then I push the locket away. It flies forward until, with a thought, I command it to stop. It hovers in mid-air for the space of a breath before dropping to the floor.

"Well, I'll be," Jefferson breathes. "You saw that, right? It . . . floated."

"Yep." I blink to clear vision that's gone a little fuzzy. "I've done that before. It's easy compared to moving a mess of gold in my bag."

Jefferson's eyes dance. "This is going to be useful."

His excitement is catching. "I don't know how yet, but we'll think of something. Maybe you could help me practice?"

"Sure," he says. "What do you need me to do?"

"I'd like to test my range. Can you take the saddlebag to one of the other decks and leave it in an open space?"

"Which deck?" He stands, tossing the bag over his shoulder.

"Don't tell me. That's the whole point. I want to see if I can figure out where it is."

"If I took the locket, you'd find it, no trouble at all."

"Well, yes, but I want to get better at this."

"Then let's give it a try," he says. He bends down, kisses me quick on the lips, then closes the door on his way out. My cabin is suddenly empty and quiet without him.

His footsteps fade down the hall, toward the hatch that leads to the lower deck with the horses. Listening to his footsteps feels like cheating, so I close my eyes and focus on the gold instead of Jefferson's boots. It's like a torch in my mind, descending to the lower deck, growing gradually fainter, then brighter again as it passes directly beneath me and up the other stairs. Clever Jefferson.

The saddlebag finally comes to rest on the poop deck, where Jefferson and I watched the stars last night.

It's at the end of the ship farthest from me now, but the torch in my mind is still bright. I reach out my hand, close my fist, and try to pull the gold.

It slips through my fingers like water.

I squeeze my fist and try again.

My arm shakes. Fingernails dig into my palm hard enough to hurt. My head pounds like a steam engine about to explode. I yank my fist toward my stomach.

The gold moves.

It slides across the deck, thumps down the wooden steps to the quarterdeck, and slams against a railing.

I fall backward, panting, dizzy, partly because the use of power is heady and strange. But partly because I think I've figured out what we're going to do with it.

Jefferson's boots pound down the steps and through the hallway. "Lee! Lee!"

The baby starts crying, and Becky shouts, "Jefferson Kingfisher, I just got this child to sleep!"

"Sorry, ma'am! Won't happen again."

I stand up and fling open the door. Jefferson is wide-eyed and grinning as he comes down the hall, saddlebag over his shoulder. He fights hard to keep his voice a whisper: "Did you do that?"

I grin back at him. "You know I did. I need to rest, then I need to practice again. I might have an idea."

He plants a quick kiss on my lips. "You are a wonder," he says, with that almost smile I love so much.

I want more than a little kiss. "All this practice. My shoulders hurt—do you want to come rub them for a bit?" As soon as the words leave my mouth, I know I'm the daftest girl who ever tried to flirt. My cheeks flame.

But Jefferson grins. He slips the saddlebag off his shoulder and quietly shuts the door. "That's a good idea."

He lifts my hair and kisses the back of my neck, sending tingles up and down my spine. "Jeff," I say. Like it's a warning. Or maybe an invitation.

"Just a little kissing, right?" he says.

"Right."

His strong fingers sink into my muscles, hurting and relieving hurt at the same time. The throbbing in my head starts to subside. I let myself sink down into the cot like it's the most comfortable featherbed that ever existed. Doing something about Hardwick can wait for a while.

## *Chapter Fifteen*

I allow myself one more day of thinking and practicing with my gold and plotting with my friends. It takes all of us together to figure out how to take Hardwick down. And it will take all of us together to do it, even Jim Boisclair and Melancthon, though the sailor will never know the particulars. By evening, after several meetings and a few errands, we have the skeleton of a plan. Tonight, we begin putting it into place.

To blend into the night, I'm wearing dark trousers and an old black sweater that Henry found at a general store. A miner's hat made of dark brown leather will hide my hair. For the first time in months, I've bound my breasts with a shawl.

The goal is to go unnoticed. But if I am noticed, it's best I be seen as a boy, which makes me a dime a dozen in this city, not unusual at all.

"You sure you're ready?" Jefferson says, as we walk together toward the galley. Like me, he's dressed in dark trousers and a dark woolen shirt. "You're about to take an awful risk."

He's right. We could use several more days of planning. Weeks, even. "The auction is in two more days, and after that, Hardwick's going to take his money and run. We have to do this now."

"We have to steal his money, his reputation, and his allies—that's what you keep saying."

"I like how it sounds when you say it. We have to steal justice."

He grins. "Let's start with his money. I asked Mary to—"

"Stop right there," I say. "I can't know the details of your part of the plan."

"Why not?"

"Because of Helena Russell!"

"You don't believe in her *second sight*, do you?"

"If someone told you about a poor orphan girl from Georgia who knew how to witch up gold, what would you say?"

He rubs his chin. "That's different."

"Only because you know me." I grab his hand to steal some of his strength. "Did you know that I'm Irish, too? On my mother's side? What if Miss Russell can tell the future? Or read my mind? Maybe the fact that I have powers of my own makes it easier for her to scry my footsteps. Or even my thoughts. So, I can't know too many details, or maybe Hardwick will know them. And you have to stay away from her. We all do."

He squeezes my hand in reassurance. "I'm not sure about seeing futures or thoughts or whatever, but better safe than sorry, right?"

"Right."

We've reached the galley. A cast-iron stove now rests on a tile platform in the corner, with a stovepipe running up and out the side of the ship. Poor Melancthon—another hole. A small fire inside has made the room toasty warm.

Melancthon and the Major are at work on their own part of our plan—though Melancthon has no idea what he's laboring on; he's simply following the Major's orders. They're cleaning a hose that looks like it's been salvaged from one of the ship's pumps. An empty rain barrel stands nearby, and their tools are spread out over most of the table. I turn my gaze away. I don't want a picture of it in my mind, lest Helena Russell susses it out.

At the table's corner, Olive sits beside Henry. She clutches her new rag doll while he reads to her quietly from Washington Irving's *Sketch Book*, pointing to the words and sounding them out. Andy plays on the floor with his menagerie. Becky sits in a rocking chair with the sleeping baby. The chair rocks back and forth. Becky's lids are half closed.

"Where did you get a rocking chair?" I ask.

"Wally and Melancthon put it together for me," she says, smiling. "They're exceedingly clever."

The Major looks up from his current work just long enough to wave off the compliment, but I can tell he's proud of his work.

"Becky," I say, "Now that Mary's here . . ."

Becky pauses midrock, and then continues, rockers creaking on the floor. She pulls the baby's blanket tighter, as though she'd been fussing. "I saw her this morning at breakfast. She left to run errands in town."

I bet she did. Where Becky is concerned, Mary prefers to make herself scarce. "I understand if you need to pack up and head back to Glory right away."

She sits up straighter. "Not until we're done here and I've gotten my cottage back. No low-down, mean-spirited, pusillanimous, thieving scoundrel is going to keep me from collecting what's mine." There's so much vehemence in her voice that the baby startles and fusses for real. "Now see what you did?"

"Sorry," I say in a lower voice. "So you're not mad? About Mary?"

Becky lifts her nose into the air. "I let her know she's welcome here, and she always has a place to stay with us." As if she's a queen bestowing favors on the unworthy.

"Well, I, for one, am awful glad to see her," I say.

"Are you and Jefferson going out soon?"

"We are," I say.

"Please be careful. If something happened to you . . . well, the children would miss you a lot."

I glance over at Jefferson, who hides a small smile.

"Will do, ma'am," I tell her.

Jefferson and I exit the *Charlotte* and step out into the street. It's a quick walk to Portsmouth Square, which is busier at night than most places are during the day.

One side of the square is formed by the long building that contains the Custom House, the law offices, and the bank.

The other three sides are filled with hotels and gambling dens. The square is crowded with people, drunk, joyful, weeping, fighting people, alone and in groups, stumbling from one hotel to the next, abandoning one gambling parlor for another, climbing in and out of carriages as they arrive from private parties or prepare to return home. Light fills the square, thanks to lanterns hanging beside almost every stoop, even a few torches. It's no wonder this place burned almost to the ground.

It's a perfect environment for Jefferson and me to blend in while we watch the Custom House building. Arm in arm, like two chums out for a stroll, we pretend we aren't in the least bit nervous as we go from one hotel to the next, fall in or out of one group or another, and skirt the square as we watch the bank. A guard paces the veranda, or sits on a cane chair outside the door and smokes. From time to time, some of his friends come by to chat, but nobody draws him away.

"That seems like hard duty," I say to Jefferson as we stroll past.

"I bet it gets harder a few hours after midnight, when the gambling dens close their doors and everyone goes home or finds a bed. That's when we'll have our chance."

"I've never broken the law before," I say, speaking in a low whisper.

"Me neither," he says. "And I'm man enough to admit I'm a bit anxious."

A large, cold drop of water lands on the tip of my nose. When I look up, a few more patter on my face. Rain might make tonight's task especially difficult and dangerous.

The rain does us one favor, which is bring an earlier end to the evening's festivities. By the time the ships' bells in the harbor are ringing midnight, the streets are already clearing, and some of the parlors close their doors. Jefferson and I find a bench and sit. It's chilly, and I'd love to burrow into his chest, let his warm arm wrap me tight. Instead, we sit shoulder to shoulder, barely touching.

We're in the dark, in the shade of an awning, unmoving, so I don't *think* the guard can see us. But we can see him just fine in the light of his lantern. He sits alone for a long time, smoking, rolling one cigarette after another. I start to doze off.

"There he goes," whispers Jefferson.

I snap to and sit up straight. The rain is still falling, a dismal curtain of cold droplets. The guard is standing, shaking out his empty tobacco pouch. He peers into the dark for a long minute. He paces to one end of thc veranda and looks around, then heads back to the other. Having assured himself that no one is about, he runs across the street for the parlor of the hotel where Becky and I stood lookout a few days earlier.

"What time is it?" I ask Jefferson.

"The ships just rang five bells," he says. "So, two thirty in the morning,"

I stand from the bench. "Then I had better get moving. I might not have much time."

"He'll probably want something hot to eat, something hard to drink, and take time to relieve himself. But if he comes back early, I'll distract him."

"All right. Here I go—"

A sharp whistle cuts through the night, slicing from one end of the square to another. A dark shadow slips around the far corner of the veranda, carrying a pry bar. The shadow sprints down the length of it, staying close to the wall, pausing only long enough to blow out the lantern.

The rain muffles the sound, but there's a soft, woody snap. The pry bar forcing the door open.

"Whoa," I whisper, my heart sinking. "I think the bank is getting robbed."

"Seems like we're not the only ones up to no good tonight," Jefferson says.

"This is bad for us," I say. "We can't do this if they get there first."

"They won't be successful," he says. "Not going through the front door like that. We'll just come back tomorrow night."

"Hardwick will double his security. We won't be able to touch his gold."

"Do you want to go across the street and tell the guard?"

I stand up and start moving toward the Custom House building. Jefferson follows me. Then I pause. "Won't matter," I say. "Whether the robbery is successful or not, Hardwick will double the guard. Let's see how far they get." I'm not sure it's the right decision, but it's my best guess.

A metallic clang rings through the rain. The cage lock is broken.

The clomp of hooves and the creak of wheels freeze me against the wall. A mule plods into view from a side street.

Jefferson leans over, like he's a drunkard and I'm helping him keep his feet, but both of us watch the mule cart.

The driver glances our way, but he chooses to ignore us. He pulls the cart up to the front of the bank.

Jefferson and I ease closer, all the way to the corner of the veranda.

The first man pushes Hardwick's safe through the bank door.

"They put it on wheels," Jefferson whispers.

"That's one way to do it," I whisper back. But now I'm worried the robbers will get away with their theft, which could make our task impossible. Hardwick needs to feel confident. Overconfident, even.

The driver stretches a plank from the back of the cart to the hard porch. The safe is heavy, but together the two of them muscle it up the ramp into the cart. The wheels sink several inches into the mud, and the mule snorts and fights against his traces.

No movement from the hotel. The guard shows no sign of returning.

They're going to do it. The robbers are going to get away with Hardwick's money.

"What do we do?" Jefferson whispers.

The thieves toss the plank on the back of the wagon and leap onto the seat. The driver lashes the mule, which lurches forward, straining against its harness. The traces rattle, and the shafts snap tight. The wagon doesn't move, and for a second I think we might be saved by the mud.

The driver lashes the mule again, harder, and the other

man jumps down to push from behind. With a huge sucking sound, the wheels break free of the mud, and the wagon begins to slowly roll forward.

"That poor mule," I say.

Jefferson says, "I'll follow them, see where they go."

"Wait a second," I say, grabbing his wrist.

I can sense the gold in the safe, and for once, we've had a bit of luck. Because inside that safe are several gold bars, which have as large and regular a shape as a military marching song. All I have to do is beckon it.

I concentrate hard, reaching with my mind.

The driver whips the mule again, and the wagon starts to surge forward. The thief jumps onto the bench seat.

I pull the gold harder than I've ever pulled.

The safe slides backward off the cart and lands in the mud. It's so heavy it sinks half a foot deep, maybe more.

I drop to my knees, light-headed, gasping for air, like I just sprinted up a hill.

"Lee," Jefferson says, kneeling beside me. "Lee, are you all right? Did you just—"

"I just," I say.

The thief leaps down from the wagon bench and tries to shove the safe, but it won't budge. The door of the hotel slams open. The guard runs out, followed by several others. The driver whips the mule, and the cart clatters into the night. The other thief starts to chase after, shouting "Wait!" The mud trips him up. The guard and his friends fall on him, punching and kicking.

Jefferson pulls me to my feet, but my knees are wobbly. "We have to get out of here, Lee, before someone sees us," he whispers.

"I can't," I tell him. If I try, I might lose my supper. Hearing the wet *thunk* of feet and fists against flesh isn't helping. I should have let the poor man get away.

"I'll carry you," Jeff says.

Which he does. He puts an arm around me and lifts me like I'm passed-out drunk. We make our way back to the hotel awning. Carefully he lowers me to the bench to rest.

"Lee! I can't believe you moved that whole safe."

"Good thing I've been practicing," I say. My head won't stop spinning. I topple sideways, falling slowly, like the drizzle.

# Chapter Sixteen

I wake up in my cabin in the *Charlotte*. Jefferson sits across from me, a worried look on his face. Dark hollows circle his eyes. Olive, bless her heart, sits on the floor beside my cot, holding my hand.

"Ma," she cries, with all the piercing volume of a child with important news. "Lee's awake!"

"What time is it?" I ask.

"Around noon," Jefferson says.

I start to rise, but Becky bursts through the door, sees me, and pushes me firmly back into the blankets. "Don't even think about getting up, young lady."

"But—"

"I'll have absolutely no buts from you."

"No butts," says Andy, following her into the room. "No butts on the poop deck!"

"Andrew Junior," Olive says, with all the imperiousness of her mother. "Lee's sick. Be quiet."

"La poop, la poop, la poop," he says, dissolving into giggles.

"We have to *be quiet*," Olive says, in the loudest whisper I've ever heard. "Lee, are you ready to drink some water? Jasper says sick people need to drink a lot of water. I brought a pitcher, just in case you woke up." She indicates an old spouted bucket on the floor beside my cot.

Before I can answer, Becky puts her hands on her hips, looks down her nose at me, and says, "What exactly did you think you were doing?"

"I was trying to—"

"That was a rhetorical question, Miss Westfall." She wags her finger at me, and that's when I know I'm in real trouble. "I once saw a man try to lift a fallen tree. It was after a June thunderstorm, and it was blocking the way of several carriages, including ours. Some of the men were hitching up a team of horses to drag it out of the way, but this fellow couldn't wait and he wouldn't ask for help. He strained and groaned and then, with a prodigious heave, much like Samson, he flung it aside. And do you know what happened then?"

"Is that another rhetorical question?" I ask. Meekly, I hope.

She glares. "It's a story, and it's a story I think you should attend to."

"What happened?"

"The tree dropped on one side of the road, and he dropped on the other." She imitates by flopping her hands to either side. "The strain was so great that his heart burst, and he died right there on the spot."

I swallow. My throat feels drier than the Humboldt Sink

we crossed last summer, and my head pounds fiercely. "Could I get that drink of water, Olive?"

Olive leaps for the "pitcher," but Becky doesn't slow down. "So what do you think would happen if a little slip of a girl like you tried to move a safe full of hundreds of pounds of gold all by yourself?"

I am most certainly not a little slip of anything, but she's on a roll, and I can tell she's genuinely worried about me. Olive hands me a cup of water. I drink greedily.

"I had to do something," I say. "I didn't know what would happen."

"Well, now you do," she scolds. "And I don't want you doing anything foolish like that again."

"I'm pretty sure she'll find something else foolish to do," Jefferson mumbles under his breath.

Jefferson and I exchange a knowing look. I have way bigger plans for my gold sense than simply moving one little safe.

But Becky doesn't know that part, and it's best we keep it that way. Because if everything goes as intended, Becky will be close in Helena Russell's company at least once before our work is done here.

We are saved by a slight tap at the door. Melancthon stands there with a tray containing a tureen of chicken soup, along with a bowl, spoon, and napkin. The soup smells like sunshine to me, and if my mouth wasn't so dry, I'm sure it'd water.

"There's lunch in the galley for them that want it," he says. "I brought this for Lee, so she wouldn't have to get up."

"I can make it to the galley," I protest.

"You most certainly will do nothing of the sort," Becky says. "Come, children, it's time for lunch."

Olive takes Andy by the hand and leads him away. She pauses at the door to look sternly over her shoulder. "I'll be back to check on you soon, Lee."

"Thank you," I say.

Becky follows her children from the room, and Melancthon sets the tray down on an empty cot. Beside the soup are bread and butter and a variety of cold meats. "For Mr. Kingfisher," he says. "If he's hungry, too. Holler if either of you need something more. Can I do anything else for you?"

I glance over at the wall. "Well, there is one thing."

"Just name it," he says.

"Is there any chance I could have a window in my room?"

His mouth drops open and he pauses. Then he tosses up his hands. "What's another hole? You're the captain of this vessel now, more or less. Windows for everyone, I suppose."

"I think the fresh air would be good, and I'd love to have some daylight in here."

He stops at the doorway on his way out. "I don't know precisely the nature of your . . . accident. But I'm glad to see you up and well."

"Thank you. And Melancthon?"

"Yes?"

"Have you made up your mind yet about the *Argos*?"

"I haven't."

"Is the captain a close friend of yours?"

"He's not the kind of man you can be close friends with. If

you help him with something he needs, he'll help you with yours. A matter of expediency."

"I see."

When he shuts the door behind him, Jefferson slides closer. He brushes the hair from my face and looks me right in the eyes. "You scared me half to death," he says.

"How bad was it?"

"Bad enough that you scared me half to death." He grabs a hunk of bread and gnaws off a huge bite. I ladle some soup into the bowl and spoon a sample into my mouth.

"I meant specifically," I say, between sips.

"You keeled over on the bench, and I didn't know anything was wrong for a moment, except that you were weak, because your eyes were still open and you were saying words. But the words didn't make any sense. Then you just collapsed, and nothing I could do would rouse you. So I picked you up and carried you back here, and then I woke Henry and made him run and fetch Jasper."

"You didn't need to do that!"

"Oh, yes, I did. You were really pale, and your eyes were half open—and uncanny bright, like tigereye gemstones—but you wouldn't respond to anything. Jasper came and tested your reflexes and listened to your heart and your breathing, and said he thought you'd be fine with some rest."

"Jasper was here and I missed him?"

"He was here until after sunrise, when he said he needed to get back to his office and take care of his other patients. He plans to come by and check on you again this evening."

My bowl of soup is already empty, so I ladle out some more. "So what did he say was wrong?"

"He was worried that maybe you'd had a stroke."

"A stroke?"

"Like an apoplexy. But he said your reflexes were equally responsive on both sides of your body, and you were talking in your sleep. Your words were clear, so he decided that was a good sign, too."

I pause with the spoon halfway to my mouth. "What was I saying?"

"Stuff about gold. Becky kept Melancthon away, in case you started babbling about your power. You were just shining and smiling like you'd done something amazing."

"To be fair, it *was* pretty amazing."

He grins, which lights up his whole face. "Yes, it was."

"I moved a whole safe full of gold."

"From almost a hundred feet away!"

"It's like, the bigger the gold is, the more it magnifies what I can do." I shake my head, half in disbelief. "Do we know what happened to the gold and to the robber?"

All the light in his face is extinguished.

"Tell me."

"Way I heard it, the guard spun a tale. Said he noticed the robbers hanging around earlier in the night, and he set a trap to catch them in the act. Had to let them get the safe out the door, so there was no question of their guilt."

"And Hardwick believed that?"

"The boys from the hotel backed it up, said he came to them

for help. Hardwick rewarded them all. But the safe was well sunk into the mud by the morning. They couldn't budge it, so Hardwick hired some Chinese laborers to do the work."

None of that explains his dour expression. "What aren't you telling me?"

He takes another huge bite of bread, and follows it with a cut of sausage, and I can tell he's playing for time to think about his answer. There's still soup in my bowl, but I've lost my appetite, so I put it down.

"Jeff?"

"The guy in the wagon got away. They didn't catch him, and he's probably halfway to Mexico by now. His friend refused to tell them who he was."

"And the one they caught?"

"The guard called the sheriff, and the sheriff came and arrested him."

Trying to get the story out of him is like trying to weed dandelions from the garden. I might get a handful of truth, but every yank leaves just as much behind in the ground as I clear away.

"Did they take him to the jail with Hampton?" I ask.

"No," he says, staring off at the floor. Then he turns to look at me. "They hanged him. Right there in the square."

"Without a trial?"

"Sheriff said he was caught in the act, so he didn't need a trial. There's no tolerance for theft around here. They put up a gallows and hanged him just after sunrise."

I cover my face with my hands, and then grab my pillow and

pull it over my head. "It's my fault," I mumble through the pillow. "I got that poor man killed."

"You did nothing of the sort," Jefferson said. "That's on the men doing the killing."

"But I made sure he got caught!"

"You didn't know what was going to happen. His friend got away, and he might have gotten away, too, if he hadn't run back for—"

"Don't! I don't want to hear any excuses."

My eyes are closed and my face is covered, but all I can see is that day back in the Hiram's mine when I tried to give one of the Indians a drink of water, and Frank Dilley shot him dead. I tried to do a good thing, for selfish reasons, and it got a man killed. Now it's happened again.

Jefferson's hand rests on my shoulder, and I flinch away.

"Lee," he says.

I fling the pillow at him, which he catches neatly. "You know, that could be you! Our plan to rob Hardwick could get you killed."

He sets the pillow aside and comes over to sit beside me.

"Maybe," he says. "But it's still the right thing."

"Not if you get hanged."

"That won't happen. My father's name is McCauley, right? Maybe I have a second sight of my own."

He wraps an arm around me, and I've never been the clinging type, but I can't help clutching fistfuls of his shirt and holding him tight against me, absorbing his warmth, taking him in. He smells of wood shavings and clean hay. "That's not funny."

"We're going to be fine. Besides, this is proof that you've been right all along."

I lift my head. "Huh?"

"Hardwick has no respect for laws and the process of justice," Jefferson says. "If he's not stopped, more people are going to get hurt. More people are going to die."

"At least it won't be you."

"But it'll be someone," he says. "I've been thinking a lot about what Henry said. It's all the people who don't have a say in the government who get hurt by it. Indians, Negroes, Chinese, women, children. Poor folk. We don't mean anything to Hardwick and men like him. We can't stop all of them, but we can stop him."

"This robbery put a hiccup in our scheme."

Jefferson reaches around me for another bite of bread. "Tomorrow is the auction. We'll stick to that part of the plan and steal his reputation. We'll figure out the rest too."

"I guess." I pick up the spoon and force myself to eat another bite. "Nobody ever got hanged for stealing a reputation, did they?"

## Chapter Seventeen

Tuesday morning comes, cold and plodding. Five of us attend the auction under a grim gray sky—me, Jefferson, Becky, Henry, and Mary. An auctioneer's platform has been set up in Portsmouth Square, near the Custom House. A body hangs from a hastily constructed gallows, swaying in the wind. A group of dirty children makes a game of throwing pebbles at it.

It casts a pall over me, a long shadow that seems to follow me no matter where I stand or the angle of the shrouded sun. There's no way to look at the auctioneer's platform and not notice the limp body out of the corner of my eye. I can't help staring at it, feeling that the dead man is staring right back, accusing.

"It's not your fault," Jefferson says as we wander through the milling multitude. "It's Hardwick's."

"Are you sure you should be up and around?" Becky asks. She's wearing a beautiful dress of soft green calico, which she gleefully chose in spite of it being an inappropriate color for this time of year. Her own minor mutiny, I suppose. "Jasper says you should rest and take it easy for a couple days."

"I'm fine," I say. It's true. I do feel fine. Maybe I feel better than fine, the way you do after you run a mile to the neighbor's house, chop an extra cord of wood, carry two full buckets from the spring instead of one. At first, the day after, you're tired and sore. But then you get busy again, feeling stronger than ever.

Henry slipped away for a moment, but now he returns, handing out sheets of paper to all of us. "These are the preliminary auction items," he says. "The map shows plots of land for sale, along with their estimated values. The other list is marked with opening bids."

Mary skims the list and glances over the map. "Why did you say preliminary?"

Henry and I exchange a glance. The preliminary lists circulate first, and that is part of our plan. But I shut the thought down as soon as it forms. I don't see Helena Russell anywhere, but she's sure to be near.

"At these auctions, they often circulate one list early to see what people's reactions are, then print another, final list, with prices higher or lower, based on what they think they can get," Henry says.

"They'll hand out the final list right before the auction starts," Jefferson adds.

"Well, that's clever," Mary says.

"There's my house!" Becky says. "They have no right to sell my house." She turns toward the crowd and shouts it again.

"They have no right to auction off my house!"

"Right doesn't come into it," I say.

"It's whatever they think they can get away with," Jefferson says. "Speaking of getting away with things . . ."

He tenses, like his hackles are going up, and I follow his gaze.

Two workmen in muddy coats stomp up the platform steps, hauling an auctioneer's podium. They're followed by a thin man in a blue-striped shirt and a pair of round spectacles. He wields a gavel, like a judge.

Following the auctioneer is Frank Dilley. The burned half of Dilley's face shimmers with glycerin, making his sneer gleam like the edge of a knife. His jacket is pulled back to reveal the guns in his holster, one on each hip.

Dilley is the last fellow I care to see, but I'm a little relieved at the same time. If he's here as Hardwick's representative, then maybe Hardwick won't be coming at all. Which means we might be clear of Helena's second sight for a spell.

The workmen deposit the podium in the center of the stage. Frank Dilley drops a lockbox beside it; it thumps hollowly. It won't be hollow by the end of the auction. And from here, it's just a short walk to the bank, where he'll add it to the rest of Hardwick's money.

Watching it all makes me wish our practice run had gone a whole heap better. There's still so much we don't know, and tonight will be for real.

Dilley twirls the key to the lockbox on his finger, bored as he surveys the crowd. He gaze lands on me. He snaps his fist closed on the key and shoves it into his pocket.

"We've been spotted," I say, remembering that we have as much right to be here as anyone, that of course Hardwick and his people knew we'd come. I shuffle my feet and fight the urge to run.

"At least Miss Russell isn't here," Jefferson says, softly, soothingly. His calmness is an anchor as my emotions roil like a storm. "After our failed practice run, we deserve a spot of luck."

I glance around for Helena one last time, but as far as I can tell, Becky, Mary, and I are the only women here. Still, I discipline my mind, just in case. I will think only of my tiny role today. Concentrate on my outrage. Nothing else.

"Final prices! Final prices!"

A towheaded little boy, not much bigger than Andy, scampers into the crowd from the direction of the printer's office. He lugs a huge stack of papers and hands them out to everyone he sees. The crowd murmurs at the updated sheets.

Henry grabs a handful. "Well, this is it, then," he says, distributing them to us. "We should probably split up for better effect."

Jefferson grins and heads off to the far edge of the crowd, in the opposite direction of Henry.

"This should be interesting," Mary says, then weaves nearer to the podium.

Becky reaches out to squeeze my hand. "Good luck," I tell her.

"We don't need luck."

The little boy hands the remaining copies to the auctioneer. I watch for his reaction. He stares at the price list, then takes his glasses off, wipes them clean, and stares at the sheets again.

A voice whispers at my side. "Are you ready?"

I look up and find Jim Boisclair. "Ready, willing, and able. You?"

"Always," he says. "Might even pick up a lot for my general store."

"Better be careful—I hear they'll sell the same lot right out from under you."

"You don't say?"

The auctioneer places the list on the podium before him. He stares at it one last time. Then he picks up the gavel and bangs. "We'll begin with the sale of future lots!"

Jim steps forward, lifting his sheet high. "Hold on! They're auctioning off a lot I already bought and paid for!"

I give it a few seconds to sink in, listening to the growing unease around me. Then I wave my sheet in the air like a battle flag. "They're trying to rob us! Selling the same property twice!"

From across the crowd, I hear Becky's voice. "They're selling my house! Which I own free and clear!"

From another direction, Mary, with a strong Spanish accent: "They're robbing us! *Ladrones!*"

The voices of women in peril have gotten everyone's attention. People in the crowd bow over their lists, studying them with a critical eye.

Henry yells, "Is that my trunk you're selling?"

Jefferson: "You can't sell my land without my say-so!"

The auctioneer bangs his gavel, but the crowd is provoked now. The murmur swells to a roar of angry voices. Frank Dilley's right hand moves to his gun belt.

"I already own this lot on Front Street! I paid for it last week!"

"Lot twenty-two on Fremont belongs to me!"

"What's going on here?"

"Crooks!"

Jim leads a surge toward the podium, and I follow in his wake. "I demand an explanation," he says. "What's going on here!"

"We have a right to know," I shout. "Why is Hardwick trying to rob us?"

Someone, a stranger, hollers, "Hardwick's trying to rob all of us!"

The crowd is riled up, turning into a mob. The auctioneer bangs his gavel and shouts, but nobody listens. Frank Dilley hollers, "Pipe down! Pipe down! Hardwick ain't robbing nobody! Shut up or clear out of the square! We've got an auction to run!"

Jim and I push all the way to the front of the crowd. "Hardwick is selling the same property three and four times!" I shout.

Frank Dilley sees us. Smiles.

"I demand an explanation," Jim shouts.

"I got your explanation right here," Frank Dilley says. And he draws his gun and aims.

I don't know if Dilley is aiming at me or at Jim. All I know is Dilley is capable of killing in cold blood as easily as you can say boo.

I yank on Jim's sleeve. "Jim, get d—"

The crack of gunfire. A puff of smoke. The sharp scent of gunpowder.

Jim drops to the ground like a sack of flour.

The crowd goes dead silent.

Everyone steps back, and I'm kneeling in a semicircle of aloneness while a scarlet flower blooms on Jim's side. We lock gazes, and God help me, but I'll remember this look on his face for the rest of my life. "Damn fool, he shot me," he mumbles. "This . . . not part of our plan. . . ."

Frank Dilley holsters his Colt, yelling, "We've got an auction to run here! If you don't want to buy anything, then clear out. If you got a problem with the items for sale, then go talk to the sheriff!"

Everyone stares, cowed. After a moment, the crowd begins to thin as several slip away, quiet but fast.

The auctioneer picks up his gavel and bangs it again. "Our first lot up for sale is . . ."

Why is no one helping us? A man lies bleeding on the ground and no one cares. It dawns on me: because he's a Negro.

Jefferson and Mary appear at my side. Jefferson says, "Jim, are you . . . is he . . . ?"

"Alive," Jim murmurs. Flecks of blood land on his lips. "Stings a fair bit."

"We have to get him to Jasper," I say. "Now."

"I could fetch the wagon," Jefferson says.

"No time," Mary says.

"He didn't shoot my legs," Jim says. "Help me up."

I'm terrified that letting Jim walk is an awful idea, but I'm not sure what else to do. Jefferson squats to put Jim's arm around his shoulder. "Jasper's office is in Happy Valley," he says, lugging Jim to his feet. "Nearly ten blocks away."

"Then we better get going," Jim says, and he starts toward Kearney Street.

"Walking will just make him lose blood faster," Mary says.

Becky and Henry rush over. "We're coming with you," Becky says.

"Here, let me help," Henry offers, reaching for Jim's other arm, but Jim shrugs him off.

"Someone needs to stay," Jim says. "If we can't shout the truth, we can still whisper it where people will hear. Stay here and finish what we started."

"We can do that," Becky says.

"You're a born performer," I tell Henry. "You stay with Becky and help her."

He nods solemnly. Behind us, the first tentative bidders are shouting offers for a scrap of land that's still ten feet underwater.

We move fast for the first four or five blocks, with me and Jefferson helping Jim along while Mary presses a handkerchief to his side. Maybe that bullet just grazed Jim, I tell myself, but there's a hole in the front of his shirt and nothing in back. More worrisome is the way he's coughing up blood.

By block six, Jim is flagging. Mary bolsters his armpit and grabs his belt in her fist. "Run and get Jasper," she says to me. "As fast as you can."

I sprint down the final blocks as fast as I've ever run in my life, through the courtyard and into the parlor of the house, where a variety of sick people are waiting to be seen. A clerk or secretary of some kind sees me. "The doctors are busy, but if you'll have a seat—"

"Jasper!" I shout, running from room to room. In the second room, an older doctor with remarkable whiskers looks up from his examination of a red-faced businessman. I find Jasper in the third room, wrapping plaster around the arm of a little Mexican boy. He's standing there in shirtsleeves, with his cuffs rolled to his elbows. "Jasper!"

"Lee?"

The clerk appears behind me. "I told her to wait!" he says.

"It's Jim. Frank Dilley shot him," I pant out.

Jasper beckons the clerk over and orders him to finish wrapping the boy's arm. Jasper wipes his hands on a towel while he says, "Where is he?"

"In the street outside, a block or two away." The words come out in tiny desperate gasps. "We couldn't get him all the way here."

He grabs his stethoscope and puts a hand on my shoulder, as calm as I am terrified. "Show me."

As we dash through the parlor, Jasper calls out in broken Spanish to a couple of men, who grab a stretcher and follow. Together, we sprint up the block.

Jim has collapsed to the ground. A small group of neighbors has gathered around Jefferson, who is kneeling with Jim's head propped up on his lap. Mary is still doggedly pressing her handkerchief to his wound, but it is now soaked with crimson.

Jasper bends down to check Jim's pulse and listen through the stethoscope.

"You did a good job getting him this far," he said. "He has a chance."

Jasper beckons the workmen over with a wave of his hand, and they put the stretcher down and gently lift Jim onto it. "We'll take him through the side door and directly to the operating room in the back of the house," Jasper says. "Mary, keep pressure on that wound as we go. Lee, walk with me and fill me in on the details."

Blood covers Mary's hands. There's even a bit of it matting her black hair, just above her ear.

The workmen rush Jim back to the office, the rest of us following behind. I babble the whole way, telling Jasper everything. I end with, "I think Dilley wanted him dead because he figured out Hardwick's scam to rob people."

The older doctor with remarkable whiskers meets us at the side door. He's taken off his suit coat and is now wearing a clean white apron.

"I suppose this is another one of your charity cases, Clapp," he says, not unkindly.

"No, sir," I tell him. "We'll pay whatever it costs." Even if it's the last of my gold.

Jasper blocks the door. "You can't come in. You'll have to wait in the parlor."

"I . . ." I hate feeling so helpless. "You'll do everything you can for him, right?"

"I always do everything I can for my patients," he says, turning away.

The door closes. We stare at it a moment.

At last Mary says, "I know you're worried about Mr. Boisclair, but this may have presented us with an opportunity."

"What do you mean?" I say, still staring at that door. My oldest friend in the world besides Jefferson is behind that door, his life hanging in the balance.

"I mean, it depends on how things turn out, but—"

"What do you mean, Mary?" Jefferson repeats, more sternly.

Quickly she sketches out the beginnings of a plan. A plan within a plan. Another thing we can't dwell too hard on, lest Helena Russell pluck it from our thoughts.

"So, what do you think?" she says.

"It's a good idea," Jefferson says.

"Better than what we had already come up with," I concede. "It solves one of our remaining problems."

Mary wipes her hands on her skirt, leaving bloody smears. "I guess I'll go find the others. Let them know what we're about."

She turns to go, but I grab her arm. "Thank you, Mary," I say.

"Of course." She yanks her arm away and heads off at a jog, as if our recent exertions have not winded her even a little.

Jefferson takes my hand and leads me back to the parlor, where we find seats. The red-faced businessman is leaving. The clerk escorts the little boy with the broken arm to his mother, and a short while later, he brings Jefferson and me some tea.

Jim is in surgery forever. People come and go while we wait. Gold changes hands, small amounts, unlike in the hotels and gambling dens. It's a relief of sorts, not to have so much of it around.

The sun is low, shining through the parlor window, when the older doctor with remarkable whiskers appears at the end of the hall, wiping his bloody hands on a white towel. He glares at us and glances away, saying nothing.

"If Jim dies," I whisper to Jefferson, "is it my fault?"

"Don't be daft."

I give him a sharp look.

"You're scared," he says. "You're sad and you're angry. Dilley shooting Jim is a reason to stay to the course, not doubt it."

I feel numb, maybe too numb to take in what he's saying, but a distant part of me knows he's speaking the truth.

Jasper appears at the end of the hallway, blood on his shirt and pants, beads of sweat on his upper lip.

I jump up, and Jefferson follows. "Can we see him now? Is he going to be all right?"

Jasper's expression conveys a world of bad news. "Come this way," he says, gesturing. "We have some things to talk about."

# Chapter Eighteen

We spend a long time with Jasper, talking things through, making all the proper arrangements.

Before returning to the *Charlotte*, we hire a boat to row us out to the prison barge. The water is rough today, and the little boat can't seem to keep its course, no matter how valiantly the boatman rows. But eventually we reach the sheriff's floating jail. I bang on the hull, just like on my previous visit with Jim, and call out for Hampton.

When his face appears in the porthole, a lump lodges in my throat.

"How are you doing?" I manage to shout.

"If it weren't for the rats and the lousy food, it'd be just like the county fair," he says. The false cheerfulness in his voice doesn't hide the strain. "Come to think of it, the county fair also has rats and lousy food."

"Need anything?" Jefferson calls up, and I give him a sharp look, because that's not like Jefferson at all. It's one of those things that feels good to say, I guess, but I don't know how we'd get Hampton anything he needed.

"I need out! Won't be much longer. Yesterday Jim said they raised enough money to get me free. They just need to take it to the sheriff and sign the papers."

"That's why we came to talk to you," I say. "It's about Jim. I'm afraid we have bad news."

Hampton's face in the porthole is an unreadable mask, like a man so accustomed to bad news it doesn't even land.

"Frank Dilley shot him. It turned out bad."

Anger flashes across his face. Then he pulls away from the porthole. He returns a moment later, wearing the same mask as before. "Shouldn't make a difference. Jim said one of the preachers is handling the money. He has standing in the community, even with the sheriff."

Jefferson and I exchange a look. "That's . . . good news," I say.

"Have you talked to Tom?" Hampton asks.

After too long a pause, Jefferson says, "We haven't seen much of Tom lately."

"He's been working," I add. "We see him at supper and sometimes breakfast."

"You ask him about my Adelaide."

"We'll do that," Jefferson says.

The waves are growing more violent, knocking our boat against the side of the ship. I grip the bench to keep from losing my seat.

"We gotta go," Jefferson says.

Hampton nods once, and his face disappears from the porthole.

We reach shore, pay the oarsman, and trudge home toward the *Charlotte*. The daylight fades early this time of year, especially with the sky so overcast. It's almost dusk by the time we make it home. The wagon is parked outside the ship. Inside the wagon is a huge barrel.

Everyone is gathered in the galley, including Mary. The table is cleared of the Major's and Melancthon's latest project, and fixings for dinner are spread. The Major bounces the baby on his knee, the end of his wooden leg tapping on the floor.

Becky's eyes go straight to the bloodstains on Jefferson's clothes and mine. "How is Mr. Boisclair?"

"He's . . ." I glance at Mary, who nods quietly. Yes, she arranged everything after she left the doctor's office, just as she promised. Even though Helena Russell is nowhere near, I'm afraid to say or even think too much.

"There's going to be a funeral for him tomorrow," Mary says finally. "In the Sailor's Cemetery at the corner of Sansome and Vallejo."

"Oh, Lee, I'm so sorry," Becky says. "I know he was a long-time family friend."

I just nod, unable to form words.

"The view from that spot is positively poetic," Henry says. "I think your friend Jim will approve."

"But . . . Sailor's Cemetery?" Becky says. "He was never a sailor, was he? I thought he was from Dahlonega, like Jefferson and Lee."

"A lot of folks buried there," Mary says. "Indians and Negroes. Chinese. The funeral is going to be a small affair. Henry and I made all the arrangements today."

"Mary is a marvel," Henry says. "Did you know she speaks English, Chinese, *and* Spanish?"

Mary glares at Henry, as if complimenting her is the worst thing ever.

But Becky says, "Of course." As if it's nothing. "She interprets for me all the time at the tavern."

"In any case," I say, "I'd sure appreciate it if everyone could be there tomorrow. Jim is . . . *was* one of my oldest friends."

"Which reminds me," Jefferson adds, looking to the Major. "We'll need to take that barrel off the wagon to make room for a casket. I told Jasper we'd come pick it up tonight. He promised to have it ready."

The Major and Melancthon exchange a glance and a nod. "We can do that right after supper."

"I'd be grateful," I say.

Jefferson and I grab plates. I serve myself a helping of everything on the table—smashed potatoes, green beans with bits of bacon, and a slice of salted ham—but I don't have much of an appetite. I sit beside Mary. She puts her arm around me and gives me a quick squeeze—a rare gesture from her.

"How'd the auction go?" Jefferson asks around a mouthful of food. Nothing affects his appetite.

"Nothing we said, in shouts or whispers, did anything to slow it down," Henry says.

"The starting prices were too good to pass up," Becky

explains. "I think even people who thought Hardwick had robbed them in the past wanted to get a piece of things."

"But did you get your house?" I ask.

Becky brightens. "I think so! I have to pick it up in the next few days. We'll see if the auction . . . holds."

"I'm so relieved to hear it," I say. We needed something to go right for us. "I can't wait to set it up in Glory."

"So Dilley collected all the money and took the strongbox to the bank?" Jefferson asks.

"They were done before noon," Becky says.

"Sold off everything and closed up shop," Henry adds. "I was able to spend the whole afternoon helping Mary arrange things."

I stop playing with my food and put down my knife and fork. "Which means that tonight, a huge portion of his fortune is going to be at Owen and Son, Bankers, right on Portsmouth Square."

"We may have some news about that," Mary says, with a nod toward Henry. "When we were out making funeral arrangements, we had a little trouble finding the help we needed."

Henry adds, "The first two people we asked had already been hired out by Hardwick. To fetch all his safes from various banks around the city."

"Whoa," says Jefferson.

"When?" the Major asks. Melanchthon is looking back and forth between us all, obviously curious about why these details are important, but not butting in. He knows we're up to something, but he hasn't once pestered us with questions. I hope he's trustworthy. The Major assures me that he is.

"Tomorrow," says Mary. "They'll start first thing in the morning, and deliver all of them to Hardwick's house before a big party tomorrow night."

"A party, huh?" I say, and Jefferson draws in a small breath. A party would be perfect. Exactly what we need for the last part of our plan. We'll have to work fast, though, to put everything into place.

Maybe all those safes will . . . I shut my thoughts down as quick as I can. I need to practice *not* thinking about the plan. Then again, it's not like Helena is standing outside the door, hoping to eavesdrop on our thoughts.

"Can you do me a favor?" I ask Mary.

"Of course."

"Any chance you can find the folks Hardwick hired and give them a message?"

"Probably."

"They'll be watched by Hardwick's men every step of the way. They should be warned that the safe at Owen and Son will be the heaviest safe and the hardest to move."

Mary tugs her earlobe. "That is a very good thing for them to know. Thank you."

Jefferson eyes me, but he doesn't say a word. Melanchthon looks at Mary, then me, then back again.

Mary rises. "I need to go. I got myself a job serving drinks in a gambling den tonight."

"Serving drinks?" Becky asks with a raised brow.

Mary has the grace to smile. "Just serving drinks."

"I suppose it's good not to be idle while you're here," Becky says, which I think is a callous and uppity thing to say, as Mary has never been idle a day in her life. But my thoughts toward Becky soften when she adds, "Will you be coming back with me to Glory? After we've finished here? I . . . I've gotten used to having you around the tavern."

Mary looks at her a long moment. "Maybe. I'm not sure."

Becky opens her mouth, but nothing comes out.

To me, Mary says, "Be careful."

"You too. Mary . . . I know you volunteered for these assignments, but I'm not sure it's safe."

Mary shrugs. "I'm the only one who speaks Chinese and Spanish. It has to be me."

Melancthon stands. "I'd be happy to accompany you, ma'am, and see to your safety."

Mary's smile lights up the galley. "I'd like that, sir."

After they leave, the Major hands the baby to Becky, along with her fistful of smashed potatoes. "I should hitch up the wagon and get over to Jasper's before it's too late."

Olive and Andy clear their plates and run off to play hide-and-seek. The sounds of counting and running echo hollowly through the ship. Henry, Becky, Jefferson, and I all linger at the table, unwilling to let the day go.

"What exactly do we know about this party tomorrow night?" I ask.

"Not much," Henry says. "Hardwick has been sending out invitations to all the local politicians and bigwigs, but they take turns hosting parties for each other all the time.

It didn't sound like anything special."

"We'll make it special," Jefferson murmurs.

I think about the city and get the map of it clear in my head. "Hardwick's house is in Pleasant Valley, right? Melancthon says the *Argos* is sailing for New York. It's currently anchored in Mission Bay, which is right next to Pleasant Valley. If all of Hardwick's safes are being delivered to his house, that's the first step to loading them onto the ship."

"If we hadn't hired Melancthon ourselves," Jefferson says, "he'd be on the *Argos* already, overseeing the hold retrofit. The carpenters will be finished soon, and Hardwick could be gone with the tide on Thursday."

"So this is our only chance."

Henry nods.

Becky tries to spoon some green beans into the baby's mouth, but the tiny thing can't be fooled. She tightens up her lips and shakes her head. Becky widens her eyes and grins hugely and says to the baby, "Say 'Hardwick is a baaaaad man!'"

"Bah!" says the baby, and Becky slips a spoonful into her mouth.

Jefferson folds his arms. "It's comeuppance time," he says.

"It is," I agree. "Then home to Glory." With its sunrise hills and golden grass and wide-open space. So different from this busy, rickety city.

"Which reminds me." Becky hands the baby to Henry, who uses his table napkin to wipe at the smeared potatoes on her round cheeks. "You two wait right here. I had time to go shopping after the auction today, and I found something for you."

She disappears and returns with several bundles wrapped in brown paper. She puts the first in front of me and unfolds it to reveal a gold-and-yellow damask linen.

"What's this?" I ask.

"Material for your wedding dress! I realized I was never going to coax you into a dress shop. And then I thought about it—why must you have a boughten dress, anyway? We could get one tailored just for you."

It looks like a tub of butter exploded in a vat of cream. "It's . . . nice."

Becky beams and starts tearing open another package. "And I found the perfect lace to go with it!"

I admire the lace and try not to think about how, when I get married, I'm going to look like a giant pastry covered in spun sugar. "You're so thoughtful, Becky."

"This one is for you," she says to Jefferson, opening the final package to reveal wool and satin in varying shades of plum—unripe plum and juicy plum and nearly prune. I'm going to look like butter and sugar, but Jefferson is going to look like a giant walking bruise. I glance over at Henry, but he's no help at all, because he stares at the nearly prune satin like it's manna from heaven.

"You shouldn't have," Jefferson tells Becky flatly, and I have to stifle a giggle.

"Don't be ridiculous. Glory's first wedding is going to be a special event. Historic. It's the least I could do for the two of you."

"I . . . thank you," Jefferson says, looking at me with panic in his eyes.

"The tailor will be here Friday to take your measurements," Becky says. "I would have scheduled it sooner, but they're very busy right now, finishing up new clothes for Mr. Hardwick's party. I declare, any person with an aptitude in San Francisco right now is bound to make a fortune."

Movement catches my eye, and I look up and see Olive and Andy peering around the corner. I beckon to them, and Olive runs over and climbs onto my lap.

"Do you love it?" Olive asks.

"I love it," I say. "Your ma is a very good friend."

"This is the color I would have picked," Andy announces, grabbing at the fabric for Jefferson's suit. Becky slaps his hands away.

"No touching. You haven't washed your hands," she says.

Andy sticks his fingers in his mouth and licks them vigorously, then wipes his hand on his trousers. "Now can I?" he asks.

I am eager to see the result of this inquiry, but we're interrupted by banging at the door.

"I'll see who it is," Jefferson says, and he heads down the hallway to the entrance.

Before he gets halfway, he starts backing up. Following him is Frank Dilley, his hand on one of his guns.

I slide Olive from my lap and push her behind me.

My Hawken rifle is in my room, beneath my cot. I'll have to get past Dilley.

"I let myself in," he says. "Well, ain't this a proper reunion with you wagon-train bootlickers, the Johnny-come-latelies. I don't suppose Wally Craven is around here somewhere?"

"Your former wagon master and *superior* is momentarily engaged," Becky says. "If you have a message for him, you may leave it and go."

"No, I have a message for you," he replies. "Well, you, specifically," he adds, indicating me. "But I'll extend it to all of you, even the brats."

He reaches into his left vest pocket; Jefferson starts forward.

"Slow down, tiger," Dilley says, and draws his gun just far enough to make Jefferson freeze.

He removes a gilt-edged envelope, which he tosses onto the galley table.

"Mr. Hardwick requests the pleasure of your company, and that of your guests, at a little soirec he is hosting at his home tomorrow night. It's a farewell party for all his business associates before he leaves for New York. He's done business with you, as a representative of the town of Glory, and would like to show his appreciation. The details are in the invitation. Be sure to bring it with you. I'll tell them at the gate to expect you—the children too." He glances at Henry. "Your good pal Tom doesn't need an invitation. He'll be there working for Mr. Hardwick. And I understand the doc deserted you, like he should have a long time ago. But he's still invited."

"Why'd Hardwick send *you*?" I ask. Hardwick knows our history with Dilley.

"Oh, I volunteered. A chance to see some old friends one last time."

He tips his hat and backs out the way he came, keeping his hand on his gun the whole time.

The second he's gone, I run to my room and grab my rifle. I have my powder horn out and I'm shoving a wad of shot and cotton down the muzzle when Jefferson stops me. "You can't shoot him," he says.

"I'm not an idiot. But he was here. In our home. He just walked right in. So I'm keeping this gun loaded."

"Lee, you know better. That gunpowder will get wet. Next time you shoot, it will backfire in your face. There's nothing to be done that we aren't already doing."

I glare at him, hating that he's right. It's exactly what my daddy would have said. "We have to do *something*, damn it."

"You're entirely correct," Becky says softly. "He shouldn't get away with just walking into our home. But the children are listening, and I would still ask you to mind your language."

All the fire goes out of me, doused by the ice-cold water of Becky's words. "I'm sorry."

"Damn it!" Andy says, in perfect mimicry of my voice.

Becky spins on him. "Andrew Joyner Junior! If you ever say that word again, even as a grown man, I will scrub your mouth with soap until it's clean enough for serving Sunday dinner, is that clear?"

"Yes, Ma," he says contritely.

"Besides, you don't want to shoot him, you want to thank him," Henry says.

I spin on him. "What . . . ? Oh. You're right."

He holds up the invitation, which he has unsealed and read. "Now we have a way into Hardwick's house. The final part of our plan, the only part we hadn't figured out yet. Delivered to us on a silver platter. My friends, we are going to a party!"

Becky grins ear to ear. "I haven't attended a proper party since Chattanooga. We have to find something appropriate to wear!"

I recap my powder horn and return the rifle to my room, Jefferson trailing behind me. "Helena Russell will be there," he says.

"Yep." I sit on my cot, and Jefferson settles on the one across from me. "But we'll worry about that tomorrow."

He puts his elbows on his knees and rests his chin on his hands. A tiny bit of soft, dark hair is growing along his jawline now, and I resist the urge to trace it with my fingers. I wonder if he'll choose to grow a beard, like his da, or shave it clean, like his mother's people.

"We have a long night ahead," Jefferson says. "Maybe you should get some shut-eye."

I stare at his lips. "Maybe you should get some with me."

He grins. "I like that idea."

My cot is too small for us both, so we shove two cots together and lie down side by side. He cradles me close, twining my fingers with his, and it reminds me a little of being on the trail, sleeping together beneath the wagon. Back then, I thought he was holding my hand in friendship.

I smile to myself. We aren't just friends, and maybe I

can take liberties now. I reach up and touch the hair on his jawline, because I can.

Hours later, Jefferson shakes me awake. I snap to, shivering with cold. This is our last chance. If we can't do what we plan tonight, we'll run out of time.

I don a skirt—the bright yellow calico, given to me by Lucie Robichaud before she took her leave and went to Oregon Territory. I need to be visible. A distraction.

Jefferson wears dark trousers, brown leather gloves, and a miner's hat, all meant to help him blend in with the night. Together, we exit the *Charlotte* and head toward Portsmouth Square. A few blocks short of our destination, we pause. Jefferson plants a quick kiss on my lips. "Good luck," he whispers.

He'll need luck more than I will tonight. "Be careful," I warn. "Take no chances."

He tips his hat to me and dashes away, into the darkness.

I continue on alone. It's the quietest part of the night, when all the gamblers are abed and a body can hear the water of the bay lapping against the docks just a few blocks away. The sooty wet smell of the city has faded with recent rains, only to be replaced by the more pungent smell of an overflowing outhouse. Everyone has been doing their business wherever they please, and when they're drunk, wherever they please turns out to be wherever they are.

The gallows still stand in the corner of the square, like a tall, angular scarecrow. The body has been removed, but a single crow remains, perched atop the crossbeam, its head tucked under a wing for the night. Near the gallows, a lantern hangs in front of the bank, illuminating not one, but two guards.

Apparently Hardwick learns from his mistakes. With two guards, there's one to spell the other, and no reason to leave the door unguarded even for a second. It reminds me not to underestimate him.

The guards sit quietly in their chairs, positioned on either side of the door. I recognize them instantly: my old friends Large and Larger.

Chimes echo from the harbor. The ships, ringing five bells.

I walk boldly across the square toward the veranda. No short cuts, no misdirection, straight and brisk. "Hello, gentlemen."

They straighten in their chairs, faces brightening. They're likely bored out of their minds, and I provide a welcome diversion. Still, I have to be careful what I say. The moment I cause any trouble, they'll chase me off.

I stop at the edge of the veranda and lean against the post.

"Nice night for a stroll?" Large asks.

"I can't sleep," I admit.

"It's hard to sleep when you're walking around," Larger points out.

"It's usually easier to sleep when you have a bed," Large agrees.

"Why aren't you home in bed?" Larger asks.

Tiles rattle on the rooftop.

"Quite a breeze tonight," I say, which is true, but not the reason for the rattling roof tiles. I jerk a thumb toward the gallows. "I didn't see the hanging. Were either of you here for it?"

"See, that's interesting to me," says Large.

"Me too," says Larger. "The way I heard it, someone fitting your description was loitering the night of the attempted robbery."

"Two people," says Large. "Someone about your height, and a taller, skinny boy. The guard who caught the robber thought they might have been lookouts."

My heart races. Right now I'm giving away more information than I'm getting. "You don't say?"

"I just said," says Larger.

"Yeah, I'm pretty sure he did," adds Large.

"So what are you doing here tonight?" asks Larger.

I'm here to distract them from what Jefferson is doing right this very second, but I think hardest about my second reason for being here, which is knowledge.

And maybe that's not such a bad thing to admit. So I take a chance and try honesty on for size. It's the opposite of what Hardwick would do. "I need information about James Henry Hardwick. He took a bunch of money from me, promised to give my town a charter. Only he never delivered. Now he says there are going to be additional expenses."

Large looks at Larger. Shrugs.

"Sounds like Hardwick," Large says.

"There are always additional expenses with him," Larger agrees.

"And now he's invited me to this big soiree at his house

tomorrow night. I'm wondering what I'm in for if I go, and whether I have any chance at all of getting what he promised me, or if I'm just walking into some sort of awful trap."

The roof tiles rattle again, and I press on, thinking about what Becky would say. "You may have noticed there aren't a lot of woman out here in the territories. It's enough to make a girl downright lonesome. I'd dearly love to make some connections, and this party seems like the place to do it." I do my best to look forlorn and frightened. "But attending might be *dangerous*. Anyway, it was keeping me awake, and so I started walking and ended up here."

The two men look me over, like they're sizing up a stray dog to see if it's going to bite. The night is cold and sharp. The salt-laden wind cuts through everything now, even the latrine scent. Which is the bigger threat, me or boredom? They glance at each other and reach an unspoken consensus. Boredom wins out. Large stands up, fishing a key from his pocket. He turns to open the bank door.

"Mr. Owen lets you go inside his bank?" I practically yell it out, loud enough to wake everyone in the hotel across the square.

"He lets Mr. Hardwick have keys to his bank," says Larger.

"Sort of an apology for what happened the other night," says Large. "Hardwick would never let us have access to the safe, though."

"Never that," Larger agrees.

My heart is in my throat as the door creaks open and Large disappears inside. I shuffle my feet, clear my throat, make any natural noise I can think of. When he reemerges a moment later with a chair, I barely keep from gasping with relief. He drops it on the boardwalk and slides it over toward me. Then he relocks the door.

Larger holds out a hand the size of a paddle. "Have a seat."

I've never been so glad to comply with an order. The roof creaks, so I loudly scrape the chair a little closer to the guards.

Large hikes up his trousers as he sits down again. "What do you want to talk about?"

I cross my arms. "I have a list. . . ."

Two hours later, when I'm yawning too much to keep talking, I thank them for their time and wander home again. The wagon with the casket is parked outside the *Charlotte*. Jefferson sits in the wagon, legs dangling over the side, and I'm so relieved I can hardly breathe. I run forward and throw my arms around his waist.

"Glad you're back safe," he says into my hair.

"It worked!" I say. "I can't believe it actually worked."

"It did." I hear the smile in his voice. "You were out there long enough."

"I wasn't sure how much time it would take. I kept them talking as long as I could think up questions."

He pulls away and holds my shoulders at arm's length. "Well, that's the end of that. No more going anywhere alone in this city. For either of us."

He's probably right. "How are the horses?" I ask.

"I think they were happy to stretch their legs. Did you learn anything interesting from the guards?"

"No. I just pretended to. And then I was suitably grateful afterward." I yawn hugely. "The rest can keep until after I get some shut-eye."

"Did you at least learn their names?" he asks.

"Never thought to ask." And I head inside to bed.

# Chapter Nineteen

I sleep for just a few hours before morning sunlight pours through the new window in my room and wakes me. The rest of the crew is eating a solemn breakfast in the galley, but I don't have any appetite. I pour myself a cup of coffee, then head down to the stables to fetch the team of horses.

Peony and Sorry immediately start to complain. I feed them first and muck out their stalls, but it's not enough to placate them. They're even more restless than usual, as if watching the team head out on an adventure just made them hanker for more. During the long walk from Georgia to California, they got used to being out in the open, under big skies with lots of fresh air.

"Sorry, girl," I tell Peony while I brush her. "But we need the carthorses again today. A couple more days and you'll be on the road again."

The brush does some kind of magic, because she seems more cheerful after, but no amount of grooming or coaxing cheers Sorry. The sorrel just stands there dejected, mane and tail hanging limp, which is more or less the creature's usual state.

I'm probably imagining the way Peony and Sorry glare knives into my back as I fetch their neighbors and lead them up the ramp to the wagon and fresh air. They've made this trip a few times now, and they're all business. Makes me miss the pair Daddy and I trained up back in Dahlonega.

The pair I sold to Jim Bosclair, who knew I had no right to sell them, but bought them anyway to help me out.

The rest of our group gathers outside—everyone but Mary, who insists that she shouldn't be seen with us in the light of day in order for our plan to work. She's right, of course, but I find myself wishing she was here anyway.

Jefferson wears his usual shirt and trousers, but everything is clean and pressed. Henry has donned yet another new suit—I think he must have traded the last one for it—this time in melancholy colors. The Major struggles with his tie, but Henry's deft fingers soon fix it for him. Andy and Olive wear somber wool, their collars freshly pressed. Andy's hair is combed, although nothing can keep a big cowlick from sticking up. Becky wears a deep blue that's almost black, and has the baby wrapped in a navy blanket.

I've donned an ordinary gray dress and a warm sweater that's a little too big. But I decide not to change them. This is how Jim always knew me.

Melancthon emerges from the ship with a wooden cross, which he holds up for us to examine. JAMES BOISCLAIR is carved into the crossbeam, along with yesterday's date.

"It's not much of an offering," he says. "But he's not being buried at sea, so the least he deserves is a decent grave marker."

"Thank you," I tell him. "It's perfect."

We form a sad procession through the streets. The residents of San Francisco are used to death and dying, so folks hardly glance at us twice. It saddens me, that a man's life means so little to them, especially a man like Jim, someone given to helping out strangers.

A small group of four has already gathered in the cemetery. I recognize Jim's friend Isaac, who I met the day Jim took me on his tour of the city. Beside him is the minister who has been raising money to help get Hampton out of jail. The cemetery caretakers, also Negros, stand by with shovels. They've dug a hole for us, and I pay them the amount we agreed on. It's not six feet deep, but I reckon it's deep enough for what we need.

"Is this everyone?" the minister asks.

"I guess so," I say. "Jim didn't have any family when he came west. . . ."

My words die away as several people crest the hill and approach—mostly Negroes, a couple Chinese, one white man with an eye patch.

Isaac moves to greet them all and exchange handshakes. It warms my heart to see folks turning out to pay their respects. Jim was only here a few months, but already he was putting down roots, acting as a leader in his community. Just like back home.

"Isaac tells me you knew Boisclair from Georgia," the minister says to me.

"We both did," I say, indicating Jefferson and myself. "He was good friends with my daddy, and always kind to me. Helped me out of trouble when I needed it most."

"Amen," Isaac says. "That's the kind of man he was."

"Amen," the minister says. "Well, let's get started. Who's going to help lower the coffin?"

Jefferson and I both step forward. With help from Henry and Isaac and the two caretakers, we do a creditable job of lifting it off the wagon and lowering it with ropes into the hole.

"Whew!" says one of the attendants. "He was a heavy fellow."

"He was solid gold," I say, wiping sweat from my forehead. "The stone on which you set your foundation. Worked hard every day of his life."

"Amen," Isaac says.

"Amen," echo the others.

The minister lifts a well-worn pocket Bible, its leather cover flaking at the edges, licks his finger, and opens to the right page without any help from a bookmark.

"Today's word is from Matthew, chapter six, verses nineteen to twenty-one. 'Lay not up for yourselves treasures upon earth, where moth and rust doth corrupt, and where thieves break through and steal.' "

I suffer a brief pang of conscience, and I share a glance with Jefferson, who also lowers his face in what I assume is a fleeting twinge of shame.

"'But lay up for yourselves treasures in heaven, where neither moth nor rust doth corrupt, and where thieves do not break through nor steal. For where your treasure is, there will your heart be also.'"

He delivers a short sermon about people coming to California in search of gold, when what they really need to find is a congregation of souls, a community of like-minded spirits. He says that when the gold fails and the money runs out, as it surely will, God will still be there to help us, and the way he helps us is by surrounding us with the right people.

Brother Jim, he points out, was one of the right people. Even though he'd only been in San Francisco a few months, he'd made it his business to look out for others, like Isaac here, who needed a hand finding a home, or Brother Hampton, who needed the community to lead him out of Babylon and rescue him from unjust imprisonment.

*For where your treasure is, there will your heart be also.*

I glance around at my own small community—Becky and the children, Henry, the Major, and most of all Jefferson. I have treasure richer than gold, if I have friends like these. And it's true; they have my heart.

The minister would say I'm laying up treasure in heaven, where thieves do not break through nor steal, but he'd be wrong. My treasure is still worldly, still vulnerable, and I've already lost too much of it. Theresa and Martin, my parents, and now Jim—all stolen from me.

Maybe I'm just as greedy as any ne'er-do-well taken by gold fever. It's just that I'm greedy for friends. Greedy for a home.

The minister ends by leading us all in a hymn. It's not one that I've ever heard, but I appreciate the sentiment.

"Steer well! The harbor just ahead
Aglow with glory's ray,
Will on thee golden luster shed,
From out the gates of day,
And waiting there are longing hands
That thrill to clasp thine own,
And lead thee through the heav'nly land
Into the bright unknown."

It's fitting we sing this song as we view California's Golden Gate to the bay, still strewn with morning fog, lit on fire by the sunrise. Jim would have loved it.

The minister bows his head and prays. Then we take turns tossing handfuls of dirt onto the casket. Andy enthusiastically throws fistful after fistful, until Becky guides him clear. The two cemetery attendants finish the job with their shovels; I imagine filling a grave goes a lot faster than digging one. When they're done packing down dirt, a little mound remains. I lift Melancthon's cross from the wagon and jab the long, pointed end into the ground, leaning hard until it's firmly set.

I reach into my pocket for gold coins to hand out, two to the minister, and one each to the attendants and to Isaac.

"You don't need to do this," the minister says, but it seems like more of a formal protest than a genuine one. The other coins disappear quickly into their owners' pockets.

"I do, for Jim's sake," I say. "Thank you for coming out today."

"Thank you, and God bless all of you," the minister says.

"When will you know about the fate of Hampton?"

"As soon as the sheriff has time to see me and sign the papers. Seems he's busy at the moment, with the auction just yesterday."

"And evicting people from their houses all week long," Isaac adds.

"We mean to see Hampton free," I say.

"We're handling it," the minister assures us firmly.

"We look out for our own," Isaac adds.

There's a lot of hand-shaking and farewelling, and after all of Jim's friends have trickled away, our group finds itself standing in the cemetery at the foot of Jim's grave. Jefferson just stares at it, shaking his head, as if he can't believe what's just happened.

"So what's next?" Becky asks me.

"We go into the lion's den," I say.

"Might be tricky," Mary says. "The hardest part yet."

Jefferson kicks a clod of dirt at the foot of the grave. "Let's ruin him."

The Major clasps Jefferson on the shoulder. "Even *I'm* willing to put on some frippery and attend a party, so long as there's a chance to set Frank Dilley to rights. That son of a—"

Becky clears her throat abruptly, and the Major jumps.

"Beeswax. That son of a beeswax."

"Ma, what do bees whack?" Andy whispers.

"Hush, darling," Becky says.

Henry is the only one who seems delighted at the prospect. "This is going to be the biggest, most exclusive party in the history of San Francisco. Maybe in the history of California. You couldn't drag me away with horses. And that's before we get to any of the other business."

I can't help grinning at his enthusiasm. "And you, Becky? This all depends on you. I would never do anything to put your children in harm's way, on purpose or by accident. If you have any doubts or reservations, just say the word and we're done."

Becky bites her lower lip, which is never a good sign. She pulls Olive close and gives her a tight hug, puzzling the girl. Then she reaches out for Andy, to tousle his imperfectly combed hair, but he dodges her and starts darting around everyone's legs.

"Bees whack this," he sings. "Bees whack that, bees whack the bear with the bowler hat!"

Becky gazes at her unruly son, her face full of warmth. Full of love. My mama used to look at me like that.

"Oh, of course I'm in," she says at last. "That man's so low he has to reach up to rub the belly of a snake. He should be stepped on like the vermin he is."

"That's what I hoped you'd say." I grab Andy as he runs by and make as if to toss him into the back of the wagon. He squeals in delight. "Let's get ready."

# Chapter Twenty

Henry offered to hire a coach for the evening, something to convey us to Hardwick's soiree in style and comfort—at my expense, of course. But it turns out there are a limited number of carriages to be hired in San Francisco, and we were too late to schedule the lowliest driver with a dung cart.

"I could take all of you in the wagon," Melancthon offers when Henry breaks the news to us.

"I would rather walk a hundred miles," Becky says, "than be bumped around in a wagon like some poor country girl on a hay ride."

She had enough wagon riding to last a lifetime.

I add, "Plus, it's better if you aren't seen with us."

Melancthon presses his lips tight, making me wonder how much he has guessed. But then he nods, and that's that.

So we're going to walk.

As the night falls, we gather in the galley of the *Charlotte*, dressed in our best finery. For Becky and the Major, that means the same clothes they wore to Jim's funeral, but brightened with a few decorative flourishes. Becky paces nervously, irritating Baby Girl Joyner. I don't pretend to know much about babies, but from what I've seen, they must be like cats, sensitive to every fleeting emotion of the person who holds them. Before the tiny girl can get too upset, the Major offers to hold her, and both she and Becky calm right down.

Jefferson sidles up to me. "We might have one of those one day," he whispers in my ear.

"We might have a whole mess of them," I say. "I just hope we can bring them into a world a little safer than this one."

"Becky seems to be doing all right with hers," he points out. "And so will we."

And that's a good thing, because the only thing about children I know for certain is that they tend to follow a wedding the way light follows the sun. I reach out and squeeze Jefferson's hand.

Mary rolls her eyes at us from her seat at the table. She is taking Jasper's place tonight, since the invitation doesn't specify names except to say "Leah Westfall and seven companions." She wears a nondescript dress of brown muslin, and a heavy cloak with a cowl that will hide her face from Frank Dilley.

"You ready for this?" I ask.

She grins. "You know I am."

Henry wears a suit of deep navy blue, with a bright yellow double-breasted waistcoat. He struts around, waiting for someone to notice. Mary has no patience for frippery, and Becky and the Major are too preoccupied—with the children and possibly each other—so I take pity.

"No peacock ever looked finer," I tell him.

He straightens, head held high. "I look dashing, don't I?"

"San Francisco agrees with you."

"I just wish it would agree with me in a more financial capacity." He sighs.

Jefferson is trying to fix the narrow tie that he's added to his shirt.

"It looks like you're tying a halter hitch," I tell him. "You aren't pulling a cow out of a ditch. Here, my daddy taught me. Just"—I slap his hands out of the way—"let me take care of that for you."

He waits patiently while I undo the horrible knot. He says, "If my da owned a tie, I never saw him wear it."

"Your da didn't do a lot of things he ought to have done."

He flinches.

"I mean, you're twice the man he ever was."

"Didn't take it as a criticism. Sometimes it just feels like I'll spend my whole life trying to catch up with all the things he didn't do."

"You've already caught up and run past him," I say, earning a smile. "Here's how my daddy taught me: the long end is a rabbit being chased by a fox, and the short end is a log. The rabbit goes over the log . . . under the log . . . around the log . . . and through the rabbit hole." I make the motions as I talk, tying the knot for him. "Then you slide it up tight, and you're done.

Don't pull on the rabbit; that'll make it too tight. Just slide the knot up like this."

"So the rabbit gets away?"

"Daddy was the type to always pity the frightened rabbit over the hungry fox."

"Tonight we need to be a rabbit who thinks like a fox."

"Or a fox who looks like a rabbit," I say, standing back. "That looks . . ." Sudden shyness hitches my words. "You . . . Jefferson McCauley Kingfisher, I don't mind saying you're the finest-looking young man west of the Mississippi."

He blinks, a little stunned. "And you're beautiful."

I shrug. "The best thing about this dress is it's freshly washed." It's an unremarkable calico, blue to match Becky and Henry, the fabric a little faded. "But I don't mind being a bit ordinary tonight."

"Lee, there's nothing *ordinary* about you," Jefferson says.

Before I can reply, we're interrupted by an overly dramatic sigh. Everyone is staring at us. Mary mimes a huge yawn.

"I offer my enthusiastic support for young love," Becky says. "But can I beg you to hold off on your explorations until tomorrow?"

The Major sits on one of the benches, adjusting the straps that hold his wooden leg—a newer, bulkier design he just finished making. "I think the job that never gets started never gets finished. So let's get started."

Becky says, "Exactly my point. Do you have the invitation?"

I grab it from the table and hold in the air. My hand trembles. "Right here."

The Major hefts Baby Girl Joyner. "Then off we go."

We are solemn and silent as we exit the *Charlotte* and close the door behind us—as if we're still at Jim's funeral. So much hinges on tonight. There are so many things that must go exactly right.

My hand goes to the locket at my throat, but of course it's gone. If all goes according to plan, I'll never see it again, which puts a little ache in my chest. The locket will be nearby for a short while longer, and I reach out with my gold sense toward the Major and discover where he's hidden it. The steady step-*thump* of the Major's gait feels like it could be my own heartbeat.

"I can carry the baby for a spell," Mary says.

The Major gives her up gratefully. He puts on a brave face, but I reckon walking long distances is hard on him, especially with a new leg he's not quite used to yet. I take the lead, with Jefferson walking beside me and everyone else at my back. At the very end of the line, I'm aware of Olive and Andy quietly tagging behind.

Even if I hadn't been to Hardwick's house once already, I'd know which direction to go. Hardwick must have the contents of nearly a dozen gold-filled safes at his house, because it's like a toothache throbbing in my jaw. Blindfold me and bind my hands, and I could still find my way.

But even without my powers, there's no mistaking our path.

First we follow carriages as they rattle past. Then the carriages stop, jamming together at an intersection, waiting in what is only the slightest semblance of a line. We maneuver through the traffic to the place where impatient guests disembark from their assorted rides and join small throngs flowing along the margins of the street. Lanterns light the street and the gardens beyond the wall. Music swells, a Mexican band playing waltzes in the son jalisciense style, with violins, harps, and guitars. Laughter and shouts of delight rise above the music and float toward us.

A line of people awaits entry at the garden gate. Becky takes the baby from Mary.

"I don't mind holding her," Mary says, maybe a little bit wistfully.

"I need something to do right now," Becky replies, clutching the nameless girl to her chest like a shield.

Ahead of us, several people are turned away—first a group of drunken miners, and soon after, a white man and his Indian wife.

"What if they don't let us in?" Becky whispers.

"Then we give up this life of crime and get a good night's sleep?" the Major says.

I glare at him before realizing he's joking.

"They'll let us in," Jefferson says confidently.

"I know the fellows at the gate," I assure them, indicating Large and Larger. But the baby, sensing Becky's anxiety, fusses in her arms, so the Major leans over and sings softly to her.

"There was an old woman tossed up in a basket
Seventeen times as high as the moon
Where she was going, I could not but ask it,
For in her hand she carried a broom

'Old woman, old woman, old woman,' quoth I,
'Oh wither, oh wither, oh wither so high?'
'To sweep the cobwebs from the sky,
But I'll be with you by and by.'"

The baby giggles and grabs at the Major's beard; he leans down farther to let her take hold of it. "That's a silly song," Becky says, and though her words are judgmental, her tone is soft and her gaze fast on his face.

"My father sang it to me," the Major says.

He smiles and Becky smiles back, and I don't say a word, because they are the unlikeliest pair ever, but it seems that slowly and surely they have turned into a pair.

"Hello again," says Large, as we reach the wide iron gate that provides the only entrance into the estate.

"Did you know you would be working here when I inquired about the party last night?" I ask.

They ignore my question. "Do you have your invitation?" asks Larger.

I hand it over.

"We were told to expect eight," Large says, checking a list of names.

Larger looks over our heads. "Counting the young ones and the infant, I see eight."

"I thought the young ones were much younger," Large says as he considers Olive and Andy.

"Children have to grow up fast in California," Becky says smoothly.

"That's the truth," Larger says, waving us in.

We hurry inside before they can change their minds or get a closer look, and then we all stop short, a little overwhelmed. To our left is a lush garden with creeping vines and spired yucca flowers and a single sprawling oak. Beside the oak, the band plays gaily from a temporary stage as couples waltz nearby. Fires glow inside clay ovens, radiating warmth and inviting guests to gather. Lanterns hang from branches and posts, illuminating gaming tables where people are playing Spanish monte and rolling dice. To the right, the doors are thrown open to the rambling wings of the house. Violin music and laughter flow from the windows.

It's a wonderland. A place where magic might happen.

And the thing I notice most, that thing that lights me up from all sides, is my sense of gold. I feel like a fly caught in a spider web of golden strands. The center of the web is inside the house, where the safes must be stored. But strands shoot out in all directions: at the gambling tables, in every purse and pocket, even near the stage, where the band keeps a collection bag.

A young man in a white shirt and a thin black tie approaches with a tray of drinks. Henry snatches up a glass.

"Dancing and games are to your left," the young man says, which we can see very well for ourselves. Then he gestures toward the right. "Food and drink are inside the house."

I follow the direction of his hand. The open double doors frame a familiar profile. The face turns toward us, and the man strides in our direction.

"Frank Dilley," I whisper in warning.

"That's my cue to disappear," Mary says, and she steps away, blending into the swirl of partygoers.

"Olive, Andy," Becky says quickly, "it's time to run and play."

The two of them peel off, their faces hidden by their hats, and disappear into the crowd.

"If you don't mind, I'll follow them," Henry adds, downing his drink in a single gulp and putting the empty glass back on the server's tray.

I glance around for Helena Russell. She is surely in attendance. We all have a job to do here tonight, and right now, my job is to make sure Hardwick and his crew are looking at me. It's the only thing I should be thinking about.

My hand goes to clutch Mama's locket, but of course it's gone. I stride toward Frank as if my knees aren't suddenly wobbling and my heart suddenly pounding. "Thank you for the invitation," I say brightly. "Lovely party."

Frank pretends I don't exist and approaches the Major, glaring down his nose at him. Like he regrets not killing him after the buffalo stampede. Like he might go ahead and correct that mistake right now.

"You showed up," Frank says glumly.

"I thought you'd be glad to see me," the Major replies. "After all, the invitation was delivered by your own hand."

"I can't figure out what drives you, Wally. I guess an old cripple like you is only good for doing women's work and watching children. I'd kill myself before I'd ever do a skirt's job."

The Major smiles at Frank, but the corners of his eyes are as serious as a gunshot. "Dilley, you're neither strong enough nor smart enough to do a skirt's job."

"The Major is the cleverest carpenter in all of California," Becky says. "And he does the work of ten men. We couldn't get by without him."

Frank ignores her too. "We never would have made it across the desert if you were in charge of the wagon train," he says.

The Major's smile disappears. "If I'd stayed in charge, we *all* would have made it across."

Becky opens her mouth but changes her mind about whatever she was going to say. Frank is one of those men who can't feel big unless he's making somebody else smaller. And suddenly, it's like a click in my mind, the way everything settles into place. Frank is lonely. He wanted us here. He needed familiar faces, people he could put down so he could feel better about himself.

"I'm sorry for you, Frank." The words rush out of my mouth before I can stop them, but I decide I don't want to stop them. "You were in charge of the wagon train, and you couldn't keep it together. You worked for my uncle Hiram's mine, and we know how that went. Now you're working for Hardwick, and he's going to leave you behind when he goes to New York. You aren't good enough for anything or anybody."

He puts his hand on his gun. "I was good enough to put your friend Jim in the ground."

And just like that, my pity turns to anger. In fact, I'm so angry now that tears start leaking from my eyes, but a show of tears is probably a good thing.

Jefferson steps forward before I can reply. "You're a murderer, Frank Dilley. Plain and simple."

Frank opens his mouth, taking a menacing step toward us, but he's interrupted by a cheerful greeting.

Hardwick approaches, arm in arm with Helena, who is resplendent in a blue velvet gown. With her auburn hair and pale white skin, she's the colors of the American flag. I focus hard on my anger at Frank, then the scents of beeswax candles and spiced cider, the flickering lanterns and the swirling people.

"Miss Westfall. I was hoping I would get the chance to see you toni—" Hardwick notices Frank's fuming gaze and the hand on his gun. "Go on, Dilley, get out of here."

Frank practically snarls, but he shoots one more angry glance at our group, then strides casually away toward the house, as if that was his plan all along.

"Some dogs you have to keep on a leash," Hardwick says.

"And when the dog bites people anyway?" I ask.

He shrugs. "In one more day, that dog won't be my problem." Hardwick indicates his companion. "You remember my associate, Miss Helena Russell."

We exchange wary nods. Her eyes glitter in the lantern light—merely blue right now. "Pleased to see you again," I lie. "May I introduce my friends . . ." I look around, but Jefferson and the Major have wisely made themselves scarce. "My friend, Mrs. Rebecca Joyner."

Becky curtsies. "We've had the pleasure of meeting once before, Mr. Hardwick, Miss Russell. In the law offices on Portsmouth Square. I was trying to recover possession of my house."

"And did it all work out?" Hardwick asks.

"That remains to be seen," she says.

Hardwick reaches into his pocket and pulls out a pair of solid gold dice. He rolls them in the palm of his hand. I can sense their weight and balance. They are perfect. Beautiful.

"I had them made especially for this evening's festivities," Hardwick says. "Can I persuade you to try your hand at hazard?"

I eye the golden dice. It would be an interesting test of my skills. But I tamp that thought down as soon as it occurs to me. "Hazard? No, thank you, I've faced enough hazards on the road from Georgia to California, and a few more since I arrived."

He has such a patronizing smile. Very like my uncle's when he was eager to explain the world to me. "Hazard is the name of a dice game. I think the origin of our common use of the word comes from the game, and not the other way around."

It's a trap. I'm sure of it. The trap is even called "hazard," which ought to be a warning sign, like the church bells ringing when there's a big fire. But my job tonight is to keep as much attention on me as possible, especially from Hardwick and Helena.

I glance around. Jefferson, the Major, Olive, and Andy are nowhere to be seen. Henry sits at a monte table with the governor and other high rollers. Becky and I are alone. "What do you think, Becky?"

"I think Mr. Joyner loved gambling even though he was never any good at it, and lost far more often than he won."

"But he did love it, right?" I turn back to Hardwick. "I'll give it a try. But you'll have to teach me how."

Something about Hardwick's triumphant smile sets my belly to squirming. He tosses the golden dice in his hand. Helena's eyes gleam; does she already know how this will end?

## Chapter Twenty-One

Hardwick leads us over to a table shaped like a tub, long and narrow with high sides and lined with green felt. We watch players tossing dice into the tub, and he explains the rules to me—something about a main, a chance, a nick, and so on—but I'm not paying close attention because a tapestry hanging on the wall behind the table catches my eye.

It's the new seal of California that's been proposed, hastily embroidered but clear enough to parse. In the background is the sprawling San Francisco Bay. Miners work in the hills around it, hefting their pickaxes. But what really catches my attention is the woman in the foreground. She wears flowing robes and a helmet, and holds a spear in one hand. Like she's ready for war.

"That's Minerva," Becky whispers in my ear. "The Roman goddess of wisdom." I hear the grin in her voice when she adds, "It's appropriate they'd choose a woman for the seal, don't you think? I hope it gets approved."

I sense Hardwick hovering at my back. The gentlemen around the table shift to make room for us. He greets everyone, waving his golden dice, as more gather around. It's a split second before I realize he's started talking about me.

"A young woman lost all her family back home in Georgia and decided to pack up with some of her friends and come west to California to find gold. And she found it! She and all of her friends found gold and established the prosperous town of Glory, one of the jewels of our new state. And this town, with all of its miners and prominent new residents, chose her as its representative. This young lady right here."

The room grows quiet. Everyone is listening to Hardwick.

"Last Christmas," he continues, "she came to me in Sacramento and asked for my help establishing a charter for their town, to protect their claims and their community."

Every eye is on me. I sense disbelief in several, so I lock gazes with them and try to stare them down, each and every one individually. *That's right, folks, eyes right here.*

"Now, what can *I* do to help with a town charter?" Hardwick asks disingenuously. "Yes, I know many of our politicians, but I'm not one myself. But it made me think, maybe I *should* be. If I really want to help people like this little lady right here, I ought to consider politics. I don't mean to cast any aspersions on our local leaders. I think they're the best in the whole United States."

This brings forth murmurs of "Hear, hear!" and "Right you are!"

"But what America needs right now is not another general,

not another tired old politician from the cities back east. What America needs is a true pioneer to lead them. Someone who's been in the wilderness and knows how things work out here in the West, for a change. So I'm not making any promises, gentlemen—leave that to the professional politicians!"

This earns some laughter.

"But I'm going to head east, and if you see my name on a ballot come the next election, I hope you will give your fellow Californian due consideration."

Men cheer and clap. Several promise to support Hardwick on the spot, while a few others hint at all the help his new administration will need. If they're all cut from the same cloth as Hardwick, it promises to be a government of thieves, by thieves, and for thieves.

"That brings me back to our guest here," he says. "The Golden Goddess. That's what the miners called her."

My cheeks flush. Why bring that up? What's he trying to do? Maybe it's a warning. *He knows what I . . .* I shove the thought away as soon as it pops up, concentrating instead on the generously oiled mustache of the gentleman closest to me.

"She represents the opportunity that California provides for all of us—to take our chance, to strike it rich, to make something different of ourselves. I had these golden dice made in her honor." He rattles them in his hand and tosses them on the table so everyone can see them, then snatches them up again. "And now we're all going to teach her to play the game of hazard."

He's using me as a symbol, a way to further his own ends.

It's disgusting. The worst violation. And yet, every single eye is on me, exactly as I need. "I've never played before," I say sweetly. "So I'll need everyone's help."

Various middle-aged men shout advice, telling me exactly what to do. One fellow with long sideburns and a garish red cravat slides in and slips an arm around me, but I wriggle away like a snake, and Becky steps in before he can try again. I give her a glance of gratitude.

Hardwick pulls out a stack of gold coins and places it between himself and the gentleman acting as the bank. He declares lucky number seven as his main and rolls the dice. The golden cubes bounce off the back wall of the tub—almost too fast to track with my gold sense—and land upright, with three pips and four. A seven. The dealer doubles Hardwick's money, and there's a flurry of bets as the viewers wager on his next roll.

This time the dice roll up two single pips.

"Snake eyes," says the dealer, and Hardwick loses.

The banker collects money and pays out a variety of bets while Hardwick gathers up the dice and rattles them in the cup of his hand.

Manipulating the dice will take a lot of concentration. And maybe I shouldn't do it with Helena Russell so nearby. But the dice sing to me, so perfect and clear, that I can't resist. Hardwick rolls them again. I pinch my tongue between my teeth to help myself focus. The dice bounce off the far wall of the table and roll across the velvet. They're going to stop . . . *now!* One lands on five, and I take the tiniest split second to continue the roll, pushing it toward the six.

It plops over to a four. I need to be more delicate.

Everyone cheers Hardwick's success. I force myself to smile.

When my turn comes, I reach into my pocket for my last gold coins. I hesitate before putting them on the table. To keep Hardwick occupied as long as possible, I have to win. I pick a number and rattle the dice in my hand. I'm concentrating so hard on the dice themselves, readying myself to flip them over, that I don't throw them hard enough, and they never reach the wall of the table to bounce back.

"Can I try again?" I beg, and most folks are for giving the little lady a second chance, so the dealer gathers the dice and hands them back to me for another throw. I hold them up to the baby in Becky's arms and make a kissing noise. "For newborn luck," I say.

The baby opens her mouth and tries to eat them, which I take for a good sign.

This time my throw goes better. After the dice bounce, I beckon with my fingers, one on each hand, tugging the dice toward me until I get the nick and double my money.

Feeling nervous, I grab my original coins and pull them back to me, leaving only my winnings. A future stake. If I'm going to bet, from now on it will only be with Hardwick's money.

As Hardwick and I go back and forth, my world shrinks to the volume of two golden dice. At first I make a lot of mistakes, lucky to move the dice at all and make it look natural. But as we take turns, my skills improve, and not coincidentally with it, my luck. Hardwick loses more money than he wins, and I win more than I lose. My focus is razor sharp. Maybe too sharp. Surely Helena can sense what I'm doing.

Becky becomes very tense every time I throw the dice. "I start to see why Mr. Joyner enjoyed the thrill of gambling," she confides to me in a whisper.

"Henry, too," I say. "Sometimes it feels good to take a chance on something."

Though I'm doing my best to make sure no chance is involved. Hardwick has been betting on my throws, and I start betting on his. Even when he wins, I win more. Which deflects attention away from my control of the dice.

After a long winning streak, when I've amassed a large stack of coins, Helena Russell says, "I marvel at how lucky the young lady has been. I don't know that I've ever seen someone so lucky."

Her blue eyes are flecked with violet. Just flecks. What does that mean?

Maybe it means I've pushed it too far. Or lost control of my thoughts. I should lose the next round on purpose.

Hardwick pauses before throwing the dice. "Come on, Miss Westfall," he cajoles. "Bet big. Bet like a grown woman and a true Californian. Give me a chance to win back some portion of the money I've lost tonight."

The crowd is all for this. The bigger the stakes, the more they cheer.

I'm in control of this game now. I push all the coins that I've won toward the banker. "Will that do?" I ask.

"Surely the Golden Goddess has something else to add to the pot?" Hardwick says.

I hold up my empty hands. "That's everything." Except for my original stake, which I'll need for the journey back to Glory.

"You must have something more."

"I'm sorry, but I don't—"

"What about the deed to the *Charlotte*?"

My heart stops. "I couldn't."

"Surely you don't plan to stay in San Francisco anyway. You're going back to Glory soon, right? That's why you wanted the town charter. You'll have no need for the *Charlotte* if you're not here."

"Don't do it," whispers Becky. "I don't trust him."

She's right. This was his endgame all along.

"But the *Charlotte* is my home here in San Francisco," I say, loudly so everyone can hear. "I'll stay there every time I'm in town. I've grown fond of it."

"Yes," Becky says. "It's not Glory, but it's a home of sorts."

If I knew, for sure and certain, that I had provided enough of a distraction already, I would walk away right now. But I don't know, and we won't get another chance. I have to keep playing.

Besides, my head buzzes with the power I've used. The dice are my servants, doing whatever I ask. The crowd is cheering for me to take the risk. "You're on a winning streak!" someone says. "You can't lose!" says another. He's right. With my power, I can't lose.

"I've got this," I whisper to Becky. And louder, for everyone's benefit: "I put my whole stake into the *Charlotte*! What would the good Lord say if I gambled it away?" If I'm going to do this, I have to make a spectacle of it.

"Lee!" Becky pleads.

The governor himself saunters over. "I confess, I'm curious to see the Golden Goddess in action," he says. *In action?* My heart takes a tumble.

I glance over at Helena Russell, whose eyes are suddenly the bright, rich purple of royalty. Something is very not right here.

"Dear governor, don't tell me you believe miners' tall tales!" Becky says with a laugh, and suddenly all eyes are on her. She spreads her smile around, bestowing it graciously on each besotted businessman. More than me, maybe even more than Hardwick, Becky is suited to this atmosphere, this world. She's the one who practically glows in the golden lantern light, and I'm grateful for it. It gives me a chance to catch my breath, to calm my nerves.

Which is a good thing, because the governor's sudden interest, along with Becky's charm, has magnified everyone's enthusiasm, and I hear cries of "Golden Goddess!" and "Minerva!" and "It's your lucky night!"

"But what are *you* wagering?" I ask Hardwick. "What are you putting at risk?"

"Besides my reputation?" he asks, drawing a laugh from the crowd. "I mean, I'm taking a big risk being seen losing to a little lady, even one as charming as yourself."

I grit my teeth. "Toughen up, Hardwick. Put something on the table, or I'll take my winnings and walk."

This electrifies the crowd. Cheers of "No!" and "Do it!" and "Place a wager!" sound all around us. The crowd presses in tight, waiting to see what happens.

I start to gather my coins.

"Hold on," he says. He waves over the crowd to one of his servants, who runs off and returns almost immediately with a rosewood cigar box full of gold coins—I don't need to count it to know it's twice what I have on the table, worth more than I paid for the *Charlotte*. Hardwick starts to unload the coins.

He had this box prepared ahead of time, for it to turn up so fast.

"Throw in the box too," I tell him, my voice shaking a little. "I like that silver inlay."

"Very well." He smiles, puts the coins back inside, closes the lid, and sets it on the table. The same servant returns with a piece of paper, and pen and ink. I scrawl out "Deed for the *Charlotte*," and sign my name, and now everyone knows what a disgrace my penmanship is. I toss the paper onto the table.

"Will that do?" I ask.

"Not usually," Hardwick says. With a sweep of his hand, he adds, "But with all these fine Californians to witness, it'll do just fine."

Echoes of "Hear, hear!" rise around us.

"This is a mistake," Becky whispers anxiously. The baby fusses in her arms.

"Maybe," I whisper back. I'm flexing my fingers under the

table, and focusing my thoughts on the gold dice in Hardwick's hand. "But I'm feeling lucky."

Hardwick rattles the dice in his hand and then pauses. He glances over his shoulder, beckoning for someone. Helena.

Who is there, as always, watching. She squeezes through the crowd to reach him, and he holds out his fist with the dice. "For luck," he says.

She leans in, smiles, and—keeping those shining violet eyes on me—blows on the dice.

Ice cracks down my spine.

Everyone is cheering. Hardwick draws back his arm, and I concentrate, waiting for the moment the dice bounce off the back wall of the table. He flings them hard, and—

One die goes flying over the edge of the table, bounces off the banker, and falls on the ground. The banker ducks down quickly and comes up with it. He starts to hand it back, and then pauses.

"One of the corners is smashed," he says, almost apologetically. "It won't roll evenly."

He switched it. I can sense a third die still near the floor, maybe stuffed into his shoe. Or maybe I'm imagining it. There's so much gold in this room, and none of it as familiar as my locket. I could accuse him of cheating, but if I'm wrong, or if I can't prove it, I'll be in even worse trouble. The banker hands the die around the table, so everyone can see that it's ruined.

"Alas, gold is so much softer than bone," Hardwick says. "I guess we'll have to retire these dice and replace them with an ordinary pair."

My pulse jumps in my throat. "Sure."

Becky grabs my hand and gives it a squeeze.

Hardwick pockets the damaged die, and the banker retrieves a conventional pair. They're passed around for inspection, but I can't focus enough to look at them. My stomach is churning, enough that I might throw up. I've played right into Hardwick's hands again. Hardwick's and Russell's. They've been steps ahead of me the whole time. Hardwick knows what I can do after all, and he knew I'd use my power to cheat.

He makes a show of shaking the dice again, and pauses to hold out his fist for Helena. When she leans in to blow on the dice, he snatches his fist away, making everybody in the crowd laugh.

He pauses to look at me. "I'll make my own luck this time."

I smile, but I'm sure it looks sickly. The dice are undoubtedly weighted to favor his call. There's not a man in the crowd that would admit to it, though.

Hardwick tosses the dice. Perfectly this time.

I close my eyes as they bounce off the back of the table.

They thump along the felt, rumbling to a stop.

Half the crowd cheers. Half the crowd groans in disappointment.

When I open my eyes again, the banker is pushing the stack of coins towards Hardwick. He picks up the deed for the *Charlotte*, snapping the corners.

"Oh," Becky breathes. "This is not good at all."

"You win some, you lose some," Hardwick says, waving the

makeshift deed, taunting me with my own signature. "Let me give this to the source of all my good fortune this year, the woman who deserves it most."

With a flourish, he hands it to Helena. She smiles with gratitude, but there's a tremor at the corner of her mouth, and after she folds the sheet of paper and tucks it into her bodice, she lets her hand linger over her heart for a moment, as if assuring herself the deed is actually there.

"That's all for me here," Hardwick says, with a wave of his hand. "If you gentlemen will excuse me, I need to be a good host and visit with the other guests at my party. I return you all to your previous amusements."

As he turns to go, the governor at his heels, I push through the crowd to follow them. Becky grabs my arm and pulls me back. "Let him go," she says.

"He played me. He played me perfectly."

"He knew exactly what you were going to do," she says.

"Because of his Irish woman," I growl.

"No," Becky says, circling around to stand in front of me and block my view. "No, he knew because the two of you were dancing, and you followed his every lead. You let him dictate the tempo and the steps, every step of the way, right up to the end when . . . why are you grinning like a cat that caught the cream?"

"I . . . I can't say. Or even think it. Not yet."

Becky's eyes narrow. "I see."

Quickly she guides me away from the crowds at the gaming tables to a quieter spot beneath a tree hung with lanterns. From here we have a perfect view through the double door of the proposed seal of California, and Becky stares at it, rocking the baby back and forth.

She says, "In that case, you have to calm down, control your thoughts, keep your eye on the horizon." The baby yawns, which is the most adorable thing I've ever seen. "We still have a ways to go."

"I know." I glance around the garden, trying to reorient myself. Hardwick is giving another speech to a different crowd. Henry is still seated at one of the card tables, laughing like he's winning, or at least having a good time. I see glimpses of Olive and Andy—or rather their hats—in the crowd around the band and dance floor. Maybe Becky should pretend to be more concerned about them.

But Jefferson and the Major are nowhere to be seen. When I turn toward the house looking for them, Helena is walking toward us.

Becky sees her at the same time. Taking hold of my arm, she steers me the other direction. "Let's go. I prefer to be in polite company."

"Wait," Helena says. "I just want a quick word."

I hesitate. Becky gives me a stern look, then hugs the baby closer as the other woman approaches. "Be careful," forms on Becky's lips as she hurries away. "Mind your mind."

I think hard about grief. Over losing the *Charlotte*, Jim getting shot, the loss of my parents, now a year gone. Even the empty space at my chest where my locket used to be. Grief is an easy thing to think about. It fills me up, leaving room for nothing else.

Helena stops a few feet away, near yet wary. An infuriating half smile plays about her lips, as if she's pondering hidden knowledge. Her gown and jewelry sparkle, her red hair stuns. You almost can't tell she's a hardworking mountain girl, just like me.

That's what centers me.

I don't want to be anything like her. I don't want to be the special *associate* of some man. A trophy to be shown off at all the balls and parties. I just want Jefferson, a few friends, and work that makes me happy.

That's the difference between me and Hardwick, I suppose, and people like him, too. No matter how much they have, it'll never be enough. They'll never be satisfied. I don't want to always want.

"Thank you for the ship," she says for an opening sally.

I open my mouth to say something possibly rude and insulting, but Mary catches my eye from across the courtyard. She holds up two fingers. The signal that all is ready.

I laugh.

Helena's eyes—mere blue—flare slightly, the only indication of her shaken confidence. I nod toward her bosom, where she slipped the hastily scrawled deed. "Enjoy your slip of paper."

Her next words are cold as ice. "What are you talking about?"

I can't stop my grin, and I don't want to. "I don't legally own that ship. I never did. It's in a man's name. Even if I did own the ship, I couldn't sign away the deed." I bat my eyelashes. "I'm just a little lady. You see, it's a matter of coverture—"

"Hardwick will testify," she snaps.

"No, he's leaving for New York tomorrow. Going to take his millions and buy his way into a political career. The businessman-become-president. He doesn't care about the *Charlotte*. Or you. Unless he's taking you with him?"

For the first time since I've met her, I see panic in her eyes. "I . . . turned down his offer to accompany him to New York."

"And I don't own the ship."

She pauses, sizing me up. "You're too honorable. You wouldn't use the same laws that are unfair to you to treat another woman unfairly."

"Not usually. But I don't care if you were a poor girl down on her luck who found a way to escape some nasty problems. You allied yourself with a monster, so you don't get concessions."

It could be a trick of the flickering lantern light, but I might see tears shining in her eyes. "Seems I backed the wrong horse," she says.

"Do you see that with your power, or are you just guessing?"

"Neither. I knew justice mattered to you, even before I saw into your mind."

And there it is at last. All our cards on the table, with not a bluff left between us. She does see our thoughts. I suspected it, acted on that suspicion as if it was fact, and yet her admission still chills me. "You can't own the *Charlotte* either, as a woman," I point out. "You'd have to find a man to hold the deed for you. Someone you trust as much as you trusted Hardwick."

She shakes her head. "Oh, I don't trust him at all. I'd never go to New York with him. But you're right. To do business here, I'll have to find someone I trust." She taps a lip thoughtfully.

I admit, it warms my heart a little to know Helena doesn't trust Hardwick either. Maybe we have more in common than I thought. "I had several people to choose from," I say. "It was no problem at all, finding someone to hold the deed for me. Trust is a great benefit of having real friends. I highly recommend trying it."

She glares. "Don't act so holier-than-thou with me. People like us don't have real friends."

*This poor woman.* "They've proven themselves over and over. Whenever I've had trouble that my own abilities couldn't solve, my friends have been there to help me."

"Your abilities." She raises an eyebrow. "Power is more like it. Your *power* is amazing. Like no gift I've ever seen."

I glance around, making sure no one is near enough to hear our conversation. The music of the band provides perfect cover. "And . . . you've seen a lot of gifts?" My question is tentative, even though I want with all my heart to know the answer.

"Not a lot. People like us are very rare. Always women, though. I knew a water dowser who could call water. And I've heard tell of others. Menders, who could fix things with the touch of their hand. Storytellers who could make you believe any lie was true. Weather witches, who knew a storm was coming even with a clear horizon, or pull a few drops of water from a cloudless sky. I once heard about a healer who could call on her powers to save a mother and baby in a childbirth gone bad. But I've never known of any power in the world like yours."

My breath stumbles. Other women with amazing gifts, people who can change the world around them for the better. "But you can see the future! Read thoughts!"

She shakes her head. "I glimpse them, at best. My mother called them the second sight. Claimed they came from the old country, way back. Mother to daughter. That's why she packed up the family and came to the States before the potato famine. She saw nothing but death if she stayed."

"You must have been young." I need to know more.

"Born on the boat over. Mother said being born on water gave my powers extra strength. Said I drew on a deep well."

"She's gone?"

"I saw her death coming, and so did she. We couldn't stop it."

My own mama passed before my very eyes. She always hinted about a childhood gone wrong, got angry whenever I used the word "witch." Now I know she was hiding powers of her own, and something awful must have happened to her in Boston, something I'll probably never know.

Helena's eyes darken with memory—whether hers or mine, I can't know. She turns as if to leave, but I grab her sleeve. "Wait! I have to know . . . how do your powers work?"

She stares down at my hand on her sleeve, and I let go, my face reddening.

"Why should I tell you anything more? We've played nice long enough."

"I'm sorry. It's just . . . I've never met anyone else who . . ."

She turns to go.

"Helena, I will give you the *Charlotte*."

She whirls back around.

"Well, I'll give *half* of it to you," I quickly amend. "If you tell me everything you know, and if you stop helping Hardwick right this instant."

"I thought it wasn't yours to give," she snaps. But she can't hide the sudden hope in her eyes.

"The gentleman who holds it in trust for me would give it away on my word, no questions asked. Look into my mind and know it to be true."

She is silent a long moment, studying me, considering. Her eyes glow violet, and I wish I could see what she was seeing.

"I even know someone who could hold it in trust for you," I coax. "Someone who would never go behind your back."

At last she says, "I believe you."

"Do we have a deal?"

She glances over her shoulder, as if Hardwick might suddenly appear in the gardens. Then she says, "We have a deal."

All the air leaves my body in a rush. "So," I say, grinning. "Tell me how your power works!"

She shrugs, seeming more resigned than happy with our new arrangement. "Let's say a fellow, like your friend Henry, comes into Hardwick's gambling den to win some money. I get glimpses of him—his intent, his need, a direct thought if it's strong enough, sometimes a peek of him at the end of the night. Maybe he's got all the chips, maybe he's about even, or maybe he's flat broke and crying into his mead."

"How does that help Hardwick?"

"I steer him toward the tables with the losers and away from the winners."

I think back to the first time I met her, with Becky in the law offices. "You saw Mrs. Joyner coming with Henry in disguise to claim her house? That's why Frank Dilley was waiting for us."

She smiles. "Yes. One of my clearer visions."

"But you can't change the future, even when you see it?"

"I tried. My mother and I both tried." Bitterness tinges her voice. "I've learned to accept what I see, work *with* it instead of against it. Good men or bad, it doesn't matter—luck flows downhill. There's no point in fighting upstream against it."

The *Charlotte* notwithstanding, she's giving everything away more freely than I expected. Maybe she's lonely. Maybe she's as eager as I am to talk to someone else with witchy gifts. I nod toward the gambling tables. "So what do you see for my friend Henry tonight?"

"Oh, Henry's going away broke, but you don't need to buy him a drink. He'll be perfectly happy." She pauses. "And I'm not sure why."

"Because he's always happy. It's his nature." I glance over my shoulder to look at Henry and smile.

And freeze instead.

Tom is strolling through the tables with an arm around Mr. Keys, who staggers drunkenly. Together, they are singing loud enough to drown out the band.

Henry laughs out loud, delighted to see Tom in his cups. He stands to say hello.

But this is *my* cue. Henry doesn't know this part of the plan. He could ruin everything. I need to reach Tom before Henry does.

I pick up my skirts and run. "Tom! Thomas Bigler!" Becky once used some choice words, and I mine my memory for them. "Thomas Bigler, you no-good, rotten, pusillanimous snake!"

The shocked crowd parts to make way for me. Henry sinks back down to his seat. I reach Tom and shove him in the chest.

"Hello, Lee," Tom says. Mr. Keys shrinks away from us both, eyes wide.

"Don't 'Hello, Lee' to me," I shout. "I can't believe you work for that scoundrel Hardwick. Not after everything he did to us. He just took the roof right from over our heads. Becky lost her house because of *you*! Jim got shot because of *you*!"

I keep advancing on him as I talk, grabbing and pushing, grabbing and pushing, until he has to grab me in return just to keep his balance.

I can't stop now. "You sold us out. You told Hardwick that Becky and Henry were going to pick up her house from the customs officer!"

"Don't blame any of those things on me," he says. "A man has to earn a living."

Party guests gather to watch the show, and a few good Samaritans try to intervene, gently coaxing us apart. Tom and I elbow them back.

"You don't have to work for *him*," I snap.

We're all tangled up, and I'm right in his face, close enough to feel his breath on me. But it's the last thing I get to say. Hands pry us apart, and rough knuckles on my collar drag me back and fling me to the ground.

Frank Dilley looms over me, Mr. Keys at his side. Tom stands beside them like a brother-in-arms, yanking down his vest and checking his pockets.

"You can't talk to Mr. Hardwick's employees that way," Dilley says. "Now get to your feet, so I can throw you out on the street where you belong."

First I smooth my dress and pat my pocket, noticing that all my coins are gone—even the original stake I painstakingly preserved. I take my time rising as the crowd presses in, every eye on us.

A baby's cry penetrates the din. Becky appears, angry infant in her arms, and stands over me like a shelter in a storm. "You can't treat a young lady that way," she says.

"Lee Westfall ain't no lady," Dilley says. "Way I remember it, she prefers to wear pants."

"You're just steamed because I wear them better than you." Dilley raises his hand as if to strike me, but Hardwick arrives, giving Dilley pause. Becky helps me to my feet.

"There's no need for trouble here," Hardwick says.

I back into the crowd, until there's no room to back away farther. Several hands reach out to steady me, and I'm not sure if they're trying to be helpful or just looking for an excuse to lay hands on a young woman. I glare at Hardwick. "You're not content to rob me, you have to threaten me, too! You're a lowdown thief."

"Miss Westfall, you can't be a guest in my home and impugn me with that kind of language," Hardwick says very reasonably.

"It's not impugning if it's the truth," I shout. "You're a thief! You sell land that isn't yours. You kick people out of houses they paid for. You steal people's most treasured possessions, the things they shipped to San Francisco, and then sell them at auction."

"Miss Westfall," Hardwick says. "I've done nothing illegal."

And that's the crux of it, isn't it? The law is always on Hardwick's side.

I glance at Tom, who gives a barely discernable nod. He has dealt with my stash of coins, and it's finally time to play my final card. I say, "You're a thief just the same. And you invited all these people here tonight"—I swing my arm around to indicate every judge, businessman, and politician in the crowd—"to rob them one last time before you leave town. Did you think no one would notice?" There. I've planted the seed. It will be up to Henry to water it and make it grow.

"Friends, friends, I apologize," Hardwick says, addressing the crowd. "Clearly she has had too much to drink. A little beer and little gambling are too much for any lady to handle."

People laugh politely, even though anyone nearby can tell I'm sober as a funeral. "I haven't touched a drop of your cheap watered-down booze."

"Clearly you brought your own," Hardwick says, getting a

few more laughs. He's so slick, nothing sticks to him. It's like watching water slide off a duck. "One of the great things I love about California is its egalitarian promise. Everyone who wants to work hard and earn their way can rise to the top. It will make this the greatest state in the Union. Unfortunately," he pauses to give me a pitying look, "some people try to gamble their way to riches instead, and end up losing everything." He beckons Frank with a wave of his hand. "Please escort the two ladies to the gate. Round up their other friends as you find them, and see them out as well."

Frank grins, reaching out like he means to take us by the collar, but I slap his hand away. "We'll go quietly. Don't you dare touch us."

"I was growing tired of this party anyway," Becky says, rocking the baby against her shoulder. "It's hard to find common interests with such low company as yourself."

"If you want low company, I can put you both in the ground," Dilley says, resting a hand on his gun.

"You might get away with shooting a man at an auction," I say. "But not even Mr. Hardwick will protect you if you shoot a woman in his garden." Henry sure is taking his time. I trust him to know the exact perfect moment, but waiting is nerve-wracking, nonetheless.

"Don't try me," Dilley says. The music and chatter have stopped. Everyone watches as he escorts us to the gates at gunpoint. Large and Larger guard the entrance, and as usual, they appear to be suffering from an excess of boredom, at least until they see us coming. Not that they move, or rise from their chairs, but I think, in the light of the lantern, that I see their eyebrows go up.

"Where are your brats?" Frank asks Becky.

"I'm sure I don't know what you're talking about," she says.

"Your children. The guest log says they came with you."

"Well, they're not here," she says.

"They're very curious children," I say, just to stall. "They could have wandered anywhere. You should probably go look for them."

Finally, a high, operatic tenor rises loud and clear over the garden, from the direction of the gaming tables. "I've been robbed! Help!" the voice sings. "My gold is gone, stolen right out of my pockets! Check your pockets, everyone."

Henry is overdoing it somewhat, but before I can worry, his cry is followed by a second, unfamiliar voice. "My watch is gone!"

There's a sudden babble. Frank Dilley turns to Large and Larger. "Lock the gates. No one leaves until we've got this solved. Especially not these two troublemakers."

Frank takes off to investigate.

"So, are you enjoying the party?" I ask Large and Larger as the commotion in the garden grows louder.

"It's starting to get interesting," says Large.

"But I don't expect it to last," says Larger.

"Somebody would have to be really stupid to steal anything at one of Mr. Hardwick's parties," Large says.

"They'd be sure to get caught," Larger agrees.

I lock eyes with Becky, but I decide not to say a thing. I try to clutch my locket for comfort, but of course it's not there anymore.

One of the waiters runs up to the gate, a young man with his collar undone and his tie loose. "Are you all right, young man?" Becky asks.

"One of those nights," he answers. To the two guards, he says, "Mr. Hardwick says you must run and fetch the sheriff. There's been a theft, and he wants it solved and the thief punished."

Large looks at Larger.

"Do you feel like running?"

"I don't get paid enough to run."

"Me neither."

Larger stands and opens the gate. "You better go and fetch the sheriff," he tells the waiter. "You know all the details anyway."

The young man starts to protest, but Larger put his hand on his Colt revolver. "Sure," the waiter says quickly. "I can do that."

After he dashes through the gate, they drag it closed and lock it again. I ask, "Do you mind if we go see what's happening?"

"Just don't try to leave through this gate," Larger says.

"Because then we'd have to stop you," Large says.

"And it feels like that could take some effort," Larger adds.

Becky and I stroll back toward the crowd, which has gathered around Hardwick's porch. The general sentiment seems to be anger and suspicion, with everyone giving the side-eye to everyone else. Hardwick himself stands in the doorway, backlit by a fire in the hearth of the room behind him, while various prominent men deliver complaints. The governor points to the missing pocket watch at the end of his gold chain. The wife of a senator complains about her absent necklace and bracelets. A judge wants Hardwick to know that his pocket has been picked clean of golden eagles.

Hardwick is doing his best to calm everyone down when Mr. Keys appears at his shoulder to whisper something in his ear.

"I can't hear you," Hardwick says.

The whole crowd falls silent just as Mr. Keys, still clearly tipsy, shouts, "We have a problem inside—someone broke into one of our safes!"

The timing could not be better, and it's hard to resist clapping. For once, luck is with us.

Hardwick follows Mr. Keys into the house, and the crowd surges forward. I make sure I'm near the front as we push in and chase him through the house to a large storeroom behind the kitchen. Eleven safes stand neatly in two rows against the wall. Being this close to that much gold is nearly enough to make my knees buckle.

The largest safe, from Owen and Son, Bankers, stands with its door wide open and its shelves completely empty. Almost two hundred thousand dollars in gold was held in that safe. An unimaginable amount. And now it's all gone.

I grin in spite of myself.

"Is there something amusing about this?" Hardwick asks me. His voice cracks, which widens my grin. He's finally losing his composure.

"I told you to stay by the gate," Frank yells when he spots me.

"You didn't, actually. You just said we couldn't leave—"

An unfamiliar voice hollers, "Look at all those safes! If Hardwick has so much money, why'd he steal from us?"

"Thief!" someone else shouts.

"Yeah, thief!" I chime in.

Hardwick raises his hands. "Hold on, friends. The sheriff will be here any moment, and we'll sort this out. Now, please, please, all of you go back to the parlor. We have wine, whiskey, hors d'oeuvres . . ."

California is still too new and wild for people to ignore free food. A bit mollified, we all wait, crowded inside and around the front of his mansion, until Sheriff Purcell storms in, accompanied by several deputies.

Somehow, I thought he'd be larger. Imposing. Instead, the sheriff is of medium height and weight, with curly light brown hair turning to gray. He has a hornet's-nest-poked-with-a-stick kind of look about him, thanks to his unkempt hair and beard, which bodes either very well or very ill.

"You have some nerve, hauling me down here," Purcell says to Hardwick.

A puzzled look flits across Hardwick's face. "Perhaps we should discuss the situation in private."

Purcell glances around, noting all the familiar faces in the crowd. "No, I think I'm fine discussing it in front of witnesses."

"Something has upset you," Hardwick observes.

"You left me with a colossal mess after the auction yesterday. I'm still sorting out all the complaints!"

"What complaints?" Hardwick seems truly baffled, and I'm not ashamed to say I don't feel sorry for him in the least.

"Theirs and mine," Purcell says. "Their complaints are that you sold a bunch of property that was already owned by other people. I've got two sets of owners for all these different plots of land lined up in my office, wanting a resolution."

"Thief!" someone shouts behind me. Jefferson's voice, unless I miss my guess. Whispered echoes of "thief" ripple through the crowd.

"That's not what I . . . that's not right," Hardwick says.

"No, James, it's not right at all. *My* complaint is that you set the prices for the last auction so low that my office's cut of the proceeds is just a fraction of what we need this month. I'm going to have to let deputies go, because I can't afford to pay them, and that's on you." Purcell sticks a finger in Hardwick's chest.

"That's a lie," Hardwick says furiously. "I chose those prices myself."

"So you admit it's your fault," Purcell says.

"I admit nothing," Hardwick says. "But if you help me figure out who the thief is tonight, I promise I'll make it right with you."

"Your promises are worth squat," the sheriff says.

This is working out far better than I had hoped or dreamed.

The governor steps forward and rests a hand on Purcell's shoulder. "What about *my* promises? Help us find the culprit tonight, resolve this situation, and *I* will make it right with you."

The sheriff's outrage melts away like a spring snowfall. "Yes, sir," Purcell says. He waves over some deputies. "Make a list of everything that's been stolen, and then start searching everyone."

This process moves quickly, more quickly than I expected, because the party is no longer any fun, the whiskey is no longer flowing, and people are eager to wrap up this problem and leave. When my turn comes, I report that I've lost a few five-dollar pieces, and a quick search of my pockets and purse turn up empty. I'm herded toward a group of folks who have already been searched.

"Miss Westfall?" asks a voice.

I look up to see the governor again. "Hello, sir," I say, wondering if the sheriff really had the gumption to search the governor, or if it was all a pretense. "This is a terrible situation." I hope my face matches the solemnity of my voice.

"I'm sure you remember when we first met," he says.

"In Sacramento, at the Christmas ball," I offer.

"You were already the Golden Goddess, but a goddess without a realm. Did you receive a happy resolution to your problem that day?"

"No, sir, I did not," I answer. "Me and the miners of Glory, we raised all the gold we had, and gave it to Mr. Hardwick, who promised to make sure we had a town charter. Something that would protect our claims, and protect our right to govern ourselves. Only it turned out he made a promise he couldn't deliver."

"I'm getting the impression that he has made many promises he's incapable of delivering," the governor says, his face grave.

Everyone is jumping ship now, even Hardwick's closest associates.

The governor's scrutiny becomes intense, making me fidget. "You're still interested in that town charter, I presume?" he says.

My breath catches. "Yes, sir. Naturally, sir."

"Good to know," he says noncommittally.

Frank Dilley drags two small forms by the scruffs of their necks, and throws them to the ground at the sheriff's feet. It's Sonia, the pickpocket, and her little towheaded companion, Billy. Naturally, I'm shocked to see them.

"I caught these two lingering near the gate," Frank says. "I recognized them for cutpurses who hang around the docks. If anyone is guilty of theft, it's them."

People in the crowd draw back from the two as if they're infected with measles. Sonia looks up at thc sheriff, eyes wide with innocence. "That's not true, sir. We just came for the music and the food."

"I was hungry," Billy adds, with his sad puppy-dog eyes.

"Search us, sir," Sonia says, holding up her arms. "You won't find anything."

"Well," Billy says. "I've got a couple sausages in my pocket. But they're small sausages. And some cheese."

"Billy!"

"Search them," the sheriff tells his deputies, but their careful patting down, including a search for any hidden pockets, turns up only lint-covered sausages, smooshed cheese, and a slice of dried apple.

"They're clean," the deputy reports. He wrinkles his nose. "Well, not clean, but they don't have any valuables on them."

"How'd you get into the party?" the sheriff asks. "Climb over a wall? Sneak in?"

"We came right in through the front gate," Billy says earnestly, as he sticks the cheese and sausages back in his pockets, and shoves the browned apple slice into his mouth.

"That's the honest truth, sir," Sonia says. "We came with an invitation from Mr. Dilley, here."

"Frank?" Hardwick says, his voice hard.

"That's a damn lie!" Frank answers.

"We've searched all the guests and the grounds," one of the deputies reports to the sheriff. "The stolen items are nowhere to be found."

"Then maybe we should search inside the house," the sheriff says.

Helena sidles up to him. "You won't find anything in there," she says to him. "Nobody's been in the private quarters, except Hardwick and his staff."

She must have sussed out part of our plan. I give Helena a grateful look. All I demanded was that she stop helping Hardwick, not that she help us instead. But I'll take it.

"It's true," Hardwick says. "No one has been inside the private wing."

"You'd swear to that?" the sheriff answers.

Hardwick opens his mouth. Closes it. The trap has been set, and he has no answer.

The sheriff and deputies go from room to room. After only a few minutes, a cry reaches us from one of the bedrooms. Footsteps hurry to investigate. The sheriff and his men return carrying the governor's gold watch, the senator's wife's ruby bracelet, and a handful of other items.

"We found the jewelry under the mattress," he says. "It's all there."

They lay out everything on a long serving table. The last two items are an iron key, which I would bet money fits the open safe in the storeroom, and the burned fragment of a safe ledger, still smoking, as though just rescued from the cinders.

"Whose room is along the west wall?" the sheriff asks. "The one with red velvet curtains and the beehive fireplace?"

Hardwick stares at Frank. "Where's the gold, Dilley? Where's the gold from the safe?"

"I don't know what you're talking about," Frank says.

"That was Frank Dilley's room," Hardwick says. "And the key and ledger match a very specific safe. I want to know where he put my two hundred thousand dollars."

"I never stole anything you didn't tell me to steal," Frank sneers as the deputies close around him.

"So you're saying it wasn't your fault?" the sheriff prompts. "Hardwick ordered you to steal the jewelry?"

Silence. Frank looks back and forth between Hardwick and the sheriff.

"Don't take the fall for Hardwick," I tell him.

Everyone in the room is listening closely. It's so quiet you could hear a flea sneeze.

I see the exact moment Frank makes his decision. "Yes. Hardwick made me do it."

"That's a lie!" Hardwick yells.

Quicker than a blink, Frank draws his gun and aims it at Hardwick. Someone shouts a warning. The deputies tackle Frank, and the gun fires into the ceiling, raining plaster onto Hardwick's head.

Hardwick's face goes from terrified to controlled in the space of a breath. He has the poise and presence of a leader. A president. "Please claim your items, people," Hardwick says, his face white from plaster dust, but just as composed as you please. "I'm very sorry for the problem here tonight."

"You're only sorry you got caught," I say. There's no proof Hardwick did it, just the confession of a desperate man. But my words are bound to be repeated.

We gather at the gate. Becky is there waiting, along with a couple of droopy heads hiding under Olive's and Andy's hats. The Major stands beside them, rocking the baby in his arms. She's sleeping hard, with one hand tangled in his beard, and a thumb jammed firmly into her mouth. Jefferson and Henry show up just as I do. I scan the crowd for Mary and spot her clearing empty platters from a refreshment table, making herself useful as always.

Guests stream past us, muttering that the only thing Hardwick is sorry for is finally getting caught.

"It's just as well Hardwick is leaving," the governor tells

someone. "He won't be our problem anymore."

Jefferson and I exchange a grin.

"Well, for once, we had a spot of luck," Jefferson says.

"Yep," I agree. "Thanks to Helena and Frank."

"Could it have gone any better?" Becky adds, and she can't keep the glee from her voice.

The sheriff and his deputies come by, dragging a kicking and protesting Frank Dilley by his elbows.

"So it was him?" asks Larger.

"What's going to happen to Dilley?" asks Large.

"He'll be treated the way we treat any other thief," the sheriff says. "After he tells us where he hid all the gold coins from Mr. Hardwick's safe."

I can't help thinking about the gallows standing in Portsmouth Square. Or the way they cast a shadow over the spot where Jim was shot, where he lay bleeding in the mud. "He has legitimately earned anything this city can dish out," I say. "Right?"

The Major says, "If Frank swings, I won't be shedding any tears."

"If he had swung earlier, a whole lot of good folks would still be alive," Jefferson says.

"This is a good night," Henry assures me. "We did a good thing."

But there are ten full safes sitting in Hardwick's storeroom, holding close to two million dollars' worth of gold. And he has a ship chartered to take him to New York, along with his fortune. "We aren't done," I say. "Not quite yet."

## Chapter Twenty-Two

We return to the *Charlotte*, but I hardly sleep at all, and I wake too early. The *Argos* won't leave until the evening tide, so I have plenty of time. I force myself to enjoy a leisurely breakfast, but I don't taste a single bite. Finally I can't take it anymore, and I pop up from the table, don a wool coat, and climb down to the stable to saddle Peony.

She's so excited to see me grab her bridle that she tosses her head, whinnying and stomping her hooves. I can hardly hold her still enough to cinch the saddle. I lead her from the hold, up the ramp, and into the street, and by the time I mount her she's almost shaking with anticipation.

The tiniest nudge with my heels sends her into a fast trot, and together we head uphill. People gape as we pass, and I soak up their attention. Peony is the most beautiful horse I ever knew, with her caramel-sugar coat and her mane and tail blond like spun sunshine. I'm proud to ride her, and after everything we've done here in San Francisco, it's finally okay to draw a little attention.

Together we crest a green hill near the Soldier's Cemetery and Jim's grave, where I'm certain to have the very best view. I dismount and turn her loose to graze on fresh grass for a change.

The bay is a wonder—fog sends opaque fingers through the Golden Gate into the bay, and the eastern sunrise sets it all on fire. The fog makes my view of the *Argos* blurry, but I can see enough. Crews are already loading Hardwick's fortune on board. A safe dangles from a boom, wrapped in ropes. The boom lifts it away from the dock and swings it over the deck toward the open hold. It's a slow, careful, dangerous process.

I stretch out my hand. It would be so easy to call that gold to me, to make it snap the ropes and drop through the dock or even the deck of the ship. But what good would that do? Not enough, that's for sure.

If a single safe broke open, Hardwick's men would just gather the coins and start over. He could hire another ship. Repair the damage. It would slow him down, but not stop him.

I sit for hours, watching. As they raise and swivel each safe into place, I wrap my head around the shape and weight of its contents. When they lower it belowdecks, out of my sight, I can still sense it down in the hold. I can tell where they place the first one, right along the keel line. The second one is lashed against it so tight that the two volumes become one. A voice, a voice, and then a harmony.

By the time they're lowering the third safe, Jefferson appears, riding Sorry. He dismounts and retrieves a canteen and a bit of hardtack from his saddlebag. The water feels good sliding down my throat. "Thanks."

"I figured I'd find you here."

"One thing left to do," I say.

"You should have told me you were going."

"I didn't want to wake you."

"Which would have been no big deal at all. Lee. We're going to be *married*. You're not alone anymore. You have to stop thinking like an alone person."

"I . . . you're right. I'm sorry."

"You've been through a lot. I understand."

And I believe he really does. "Keep reminding me," I say. "Keep lecturing. I agree with you. It's just that, like with the gold, I need practice."

He wraps an arm around my shoulders and plants a kiss on the top of my head.

I watch every safe swing into the ship. I stretch out my hand, close my eyes, and get the shape and feel of it all. So much gold. All in one place. My practice must be paying off, because a year ago, maybe even a month ago, so much gold nearby would have rendered me senseless.

The fog is burning away, and the breeze is picking up when one of the safes clangs like a cymbal in my head. I gasp.

"Lee? What's wrong?"

"I . . . nothing." My breath comes in pants. "It's *the* safe. The one I was waiting for."

His face breaks into a grin. "So it worked! You can sense that one just fine, then?"

"Oh, yes. Oh, my. It's . . . intense." I close my eyes and follow the safe and its contents as it's lowered into place. It's near the keel line now, lashed to the other safes. Perfect.

"Are you going to be okay?"

"Yes."

"You've given up so much already, Lee. I hate to see you lose this, too."

I yawn and rub my eyes. Those golden dice were small, but it took so much effort and concentration to control them last night that I'm exhausted. Like I climbed the Rockies again instead of just playing a few hands of cards. "It will be worth it," I tell him. "I started my journey with that locket. It's only fitting I end with it." *It will be worth it,* I repeat silently to myself.

Jefferson collects Sorry, and they leave to refill his canteen and fetch more food.

I'm glad, because I need this moment alone to say good-bye. After today, the very last tangible memory of my mother will be gone. *Thank you, Mama,* I say, hoping she can hear me from wherever she is.

The ship is almost fully loaded by the time Jefferson and Sorry return. He carries a basket of still-warm biscuits, but I only take a few bites. I don't want nature calling me away. I don't want to miss a thing.

As gold fills the hold of the ship, the temptation to do something grows stronger, but I have to wait a little longer.

Hardwick arrives with a wagon carrying the last pair of safes. Mr. Keys is with him, slumped over as though half drunk and twice as miserable as the night before. As the penultimate safe swings into the air, I stretch out my hand and think about how easy it would be. Just push and pull, get the rope swinging back and forth in the right direction, then yank it off so it lands right on Hardwick's head.

But I'm not a murderer. I'm not that coldhearted. Am I?

Plenty of folks have gotten hurt around me. Daddy and Mama, gunned down like animals in their own home. Poor Mr. Joyner, crushed when the wagon rolled down the mountainside. Therese, dying in the desert, giving up her life to save her family. Her brother Martin, killed by my uncle's men. All of Muskrat's people, dying in the mining camp—maybe even Muskrat himself, since no one has seen him since that terrible night. Jim, shot before my very eyes, bleeding in the mud at my feet. And Frank Dilley, who even now might be hanging at Portsmouth Square.

The last safe swings over the ship and gradually lowers into the hold, and I let it. I don't do a thing about it.

Beside me, Jefferson uses his pocketknife to slide a bit of cheese from a wedge. "Want some?" he asks.

"Not just yet."

This is my last chance to fix that final safe full of gold in my mind, to feel where it fits with the others in the hold of the ship. The ship rocks on the waves, but the safes are tied down tightly. I sense them moving with the flow of water, but their weights don't shift one bit relative to one another. In the center of it all is the familiar chest, containing a stack of gold bars, all wrapped tight with rope around the centerpiece of my mama's locket.

I know from Melancthon that the captain wants to take the ship out with the ebb tide, as the moon rises late this afternoon. I feel hollow inside, from all the gold I moved yesterday, from the lack of sleep and food, from the final choice I know I'm about to make.

Hardwick stands on the deck, with only Mr. Keys at his side. Hardwick is smaller than a toy soldier, but I still recognize him. Two days ago, he was arguably the most powerful man in California. Today, no one shows up to wish him farewell.

But it's not enough to sully his reputation and cast suspicion. The people of New York don't know him like we do. When he shows up with all the gold he's collected in California, they'll fall all over themselves to make him feel at home.

A few loyal underlings wander the deck. I recognize the fellow who was guarding the bank the night they caught the robber. But I'm glad Large and Larger are not among them. I never saw them do anything cruel.

The captain calls out to the crew, and they cast off from the dock. A boat with long oars tugs them out of the harbor and into the bay.

I stand as the ship goes by. "I need to keep my eyes on it," I tell Jefferson. "Time to mount up."

Jefferson shoves leftovers back into his saddlebag, and we both return to our saddles. I direct Peony so I can follow the ship around the bay line, always keeping it in sight, never releasing my mental grip on all that gold. As the ship rounds the mouth of the bay, I coax Peony into a trot. Sorry's hooves clatter behind me.

The air turns cold with the evening, and the bellies of the clouds are burnished red gold with the setting sun. The lighthouse at Alcatraz Island winks on, and behind it stretch the green hills of Rancho Saucelito. The sea is choppy. The waves rock the ship back and forth as it sails toward the Golden Gate and the Pacific Ocean.

I pull Peony up, to give her a quick rest and to reach out with my gold sense. The ship is moving faster than we are, stretching the distance between us, but I can still feel its golden cargo, especially Mama's precious locket. It's like a song wafting toward me from a great distance, through a valley in the mountains.

"It's not far enough," I whisper to myself.

"What's not far enough?" Jefferson asks.

"The ship. There are islands. Like Alcatraz. Places it can put into shore."

"That's a good thing, right? We don't want anyone to die."

"Melancthon took care of that," I assure him. "The *Argos* needs to be close enough to shore that lifeboats can reach safety, but far enough away that the ship itself can't."

"I suppose you're right."

"I—we—have to get to the fort at the Presidio," I tell him. "We have to see her through the Golden Gate."

"Then we'd better move. Fast."

But I'm already urging Peony forward, and Jefferson quickly falls in behind. It's almost a mile from here to the army fort at the Presidio, but we're on land and the ship is going with the tide. Thank goodness it's sailing directly into a west wind.

I give Peony a light kick with my heels, and she eagerly stretches into a full gallop. She is a wonder, game to run and giving it her all in spite of being cooped up for so long. I lean forward onto her withers, where my weight will be easiest to bear. She recognizes the weight shift and what it means. Without any further coaxing, she lowers her head like a thoroughbred and runs even faster.

Still, it's going to be a close thing.

Wind chaps my face, and my hair loosens from its braid. People stare as we fly by, and we must be a sight—two people breezing their horses through the San Francisco streets, dodging carts and amblers and puddles. Sorry begins to fall a little behind, but I don't dare slow down so she and Jeff can catch up.

If we do get there in time, what if my gold sense isn't up to the task? I've done some amazing things with it, for sure and certain. I found a lost boy in the middle of the night on the wide-open prairie. I collapsed my uncle's mine. Of course, that mine was only a stone's throw away, and my gold sense was aided by a liberal application of gunpowder. By the time I reach the fort, the *Argos* will be halfway to the setting sun.

I just don't know if my second sight, or whatever it is, will be enough.

The white walls of the Presidio rise before us. The flagpoles fly the banners of California and the United States.

"Whoa," I say, pulling back on the reins. Peony slows, and I dismount. Her coat is damp now. She'll need a good rubdown as soon as I get a chance.

The flags snap in the wind, which is changing direction to favor the *Argos*.

But I can still see her. She's in the middle of the Golden Gate now, pinched between two peninsulas, a quarter mile away. From here, at last, I can see the Pacific, and the sight catches my breath, makes me feel like we've run a hundred miles instead of one.

"Have you ever seen its like?" Jefferson says breathlessly, riding up on Sorry. The sun is setting over the ocean, skipping coins of gleaming light across the waves. The watery horizon stretches forever, slightly curved, and finally I understand how big the world is.

The ebb tide runs rough, and the waves are high, tossing the ship back and forth as it doggedly pushes for the open sea. Seabirds circle and dart. A few have landed on the mast, but they are barely more than black dots at this distance.

I close my eyes and stretch out my right hand, find the shape of the gold. It's easy. Mama's locket jumps out at me in particular. Even through the haze of gold surrounding it, I feel its gentle curve, its tiny latch, its flower etching.

I squeeze my fist around the heart shape, and I pull it toward me.

Nothing happens.

I concentrate again, and push it away with all my power.

Still nothing.

I've waited too long. My plan was never going to work.

"Don't give up, Lee," Jefferson says. He has dismounted and now stands at my side.

I grab the gold and pull it toward me with all my strength. I hold my fist up tight against my chest, then I fling it away, as hard as I can.

The ship slips past us, toward open water.

There's nothing complex about this part of my plan. It should be as simple as sensing a broken coin in someone's pocket, and pulling and pushing it, back and forth, until the coin rips the seam. As easy as pushing a saddlebag full of gold back and forth across a bedroom floor. As easy as flipping over a pair of golden dice.

I reach out with both hands, close my eyes. Ten safes. Almost two million dollars in gold coins. More money than I ever imagined. All tied down around the heart of my mama's final gift to me. And using that final gift as a focus, I pull my hands against my chest and squeeze, like I'm giving all that gold the fiercest bear hug of my life.

To anyone watching, I must appear to have taken leave of my sense, but I don't care. I punch my fists out, like I'm trying to knock an attacker down to save my life.

Something moves.

My eyes shoot open. The ship is farther away, heading toward deep water.

I stretch out my arms again, and pull the gold toward me. I feel it skew, unevenly, as something breaks. I shove it away again, and the mass lurches hard.

The cargo is no longer tied down, and the ship rolls in the waves.

I remember what Melancthon told me about the capsized ship: the waves and the cargo together were what sank it. So I wait—just a moment—until the ship is listing toward my shore, and I pull with all my strength, working with the waves instead of against. I release it, and when the hull begins to tip back in the other direction, I push as hard as I can.

Now the loose cargo is doing half the work, sliding on its own as the ship tosses in the rough tide.

"Lee," Jefferson whispers. "Your nose is bleeding."

"Tell me if my eyes start bleeding," I snap. But I lick my lips and taste raw copper on my tongue, thinking of the story Becky told me, about the man who moved the tree and caused his heart to burst.

But I can't quit now, with the job half done. If I do, the crew will just go down into the hold and secure the cargo.

So I stand here, pushing and pulling, one way and then the other, as the ship rides off into the distance. My legs start to wobble. I'm vaguely aware when Jefferson closes the gap between our bodies, and suddenly I realize I'm no longer standing on my own strength, that his arm is wrapped around my waist.

The *Argos* is rolling so violently now that the masts nearly kiss the waves. Dark specks flee the tossing ship—the crew has managed to launch several of the lifeboats.

The ship is so far away now, I can barely sense the locket at all. It feels like a nugget, lost in a rushing creek, beneath gravel and ice. It's going to get away.

My luck changes. The ship slows. The captain, either in a

panic, or under orders from Hardwick, is trying to turn the ship back. To put to shore before all is lost.

It gives me a chance. A large wave hits it nearly broadside. I grab the gold and pull it as hard as I can. The ship rolls right over. The mast breaks as it hits the water. A split second after I see it, I hear the sharp snap of cracking wood.

I sink to my knees.

"Lee," Jefferson says. "Lee . . . Lee, are you *all right*?"

I reach out one last time with both fists, and yank down as hard as I can, hurling that gold down to the bottom of the ocean. I hope the water is a mile deep. Or at least too deep for any divers to reach it.

"Lee!"

Bloods gushes out of my nose and runs down over my lips and chin.

"I . . ."

I don't remember falling over, but I'm lying sideways, and my head hurts where it hit the ground. Gravel presses tiny dots of pain into my cheek.

*"Lee!"*

Jefferson's hands grasp me, but they feel faraway, almost like they're touching someone else. So tired. Hollowed out. Sun fading away.

"S'okay," I tell him, from a distance. "Trust you . . . help me home?" Arms wrap me tight, bolster me. I'm barely conscious as he helps me into my saddle. Fortunately, riding Peony is something I can almost do in my sleep, and we start a slow, careful trek back toward the *Charlotte*.

## Chapter Twenty-Three

I'm feeling better by the time we return, but I still fall into my cot and sleep like the dead. When I wake, morning shines bright through the window Melancthon made for me. I scratch my itchy upper lip and discover that more blood caked there overnight. The bleeding seems to have stopped for good, though, so I force myself out of bed, wash quickly, and fetch Jefferson, who is hugely relieved to see me awake and hale. Everyone else has left already; Jefferson convinced them to let me sleep.

Dawn chills the air as we return to the cemetery on Peony and Sorry, following the same road we galloped along just hours before. The horses are delighted to be out again so soon. Peony kicks up her heels and tosses her head at every bird and bug. I'm glad one of us has some spunk; I'm so tired I could die.

"I don't think you should be up and about," Jefferson says. "In fact, maybe you should stay in bed for a week. Possibly a month."

"After the meeting," I promise. "I'll sleep then."

To be fair to him and his concerns, my head is throbbing, like there's an arrastra inside my skull, and a mule is dragging a grindstone around and around in a circle. My knees are weak, and my arms feel twisted and limp as a hen's wry neck.

"If I'm this exhausted," Jefferson says, "you must be about to faint."

"I promise I won't try to roll over any ships today," I say.

Jefferson shakes his head. "If I hadn't been there to see it, I wouldn't believe it."

"I hope everyone is all right."

"Saw Melancthon at breakfast," Jefferson says. "He said the crew got safely ashore. The ebb tide carried the smaller boats out to sea, but other ships were there to pick them up. Hardwick's pinnace made it into shore this morning, right before we left."

"But the *Argos* did sink, right?" I'd hate to hear it was all for naught, that the ship somehow survived.

"The officer said they expect some light wreckage to drift ashore, but I don't reckon it will include any gold-filled safes. The water in that part of the bay is more than fifty fathoms deep."

"Is fifty fathoms deep?"

"Deep enough to sink Hardwick's fortune."

Sorry shakes her ruddy head, jangling her bridle, as if putting an end to the matter. As the sun rises across the bay, I feel a little warmer and a lot more whole again.

"We really did it, didn't we?" Jefferson says.

"Yep. Nobody in California will trust Hardwick again. And

he'll find it a lot harder to start rebuilding his fortune from scratch."

"Looks like almost everyone is here already," Jefferson says.

The Sailor's Cemetery stretches before us, green as an emerald with all the recent rain. A small crowd gathers around Jim's grave. A final chance to say good-bye. The wagon is here, and it looks like it's carrying a full load of lumber—Becky's house, if I don't miss my guess. Breath rises like fog from the carthorses' nostrils.

"There you are!" Becky says when she sees us.

"I needed a little extra sleep," I admit.

"See, Wally?" Becky says to the Major. "Just a touch of lethargy. She's always that way after using her gift."

He reaches out and quietly squeezes her hand. She squeezes back like she has no intention of letting go.

Mary steps forward, wearing her traveling dress. I hope that means she's planning to rcturn with us.

I smile at her. "Thank you for coming. And for working so hard."

"Glad to see you didn't kill yourself," she says.

Henry leans against the wagon. He's wearing another new suit, this one a brown tweed, a little plainer and more practical than the one he wore to Hardwick's party. "The news around the city this morning is that the *Argos* capsized on its way out of the bay last night. All of Hardwick's gold sank to the bottom of the ocean."

"We might have heard a thing or two about that," Jefferson said.

Melancthon reaches up to calm one of the carthorses. "A shipwreck is a bad business," he says. "And capsizing is one of the worst."

I nod solemnly. "I was glad to learn the crew survived."

"Still," he says. "Makes a fellow glad he didn't accept that job."

"Other ships will be headed east soon enough," I tell him.

"True enough. But I might find a reason to stay."

Two figures enter the cemetery and walk toward us through the fog. It's Tom, along with Hampton.

Andy runs forward, arms outstretched. "Hampton! You're back!"

Hampton lifts the boy into his arms. "I missed you too, my friend." Hampton is thin and haggard, but he grins like it's Christmas. Everyone rushes forward to clap him on the back or shake his hand.

"It does my heart good to see you safe," Becky says.

"Here come the last of the stragglers," I say.

Jasper approaches, hands in the pockets of his waistcoat, while his companion makes his way with the help of a crutch. I've never been so happy to see anyone in my whole life.

"Jim!" I say, running to greet him. At his warning look, I stop short of wrapping him in a hug.

"I'm still prone to toppling over," Jim cautions.

I settle for grasping his shoulder and grinning like a fool.

"He's lucky to be alive and walking at all," Jasper says. "I'd hate to see him fall down and undo all the amazing surgery

I did to save his life. My recommendation was that he stay in bed today."

"I told *her* the same thing," Jefferson said, jerking his thumb at me.

"Some folks make the worst patients," Jasper says.

"All right, now that everybody's here, let's be quick," I say. Henry is already grabbing shovels from the wagon and handing them out. I take one, eager to get started.

"Wait a second," says Hampton. "Boisclair . . . you're alive?" His eyes are as wide as saucers.

"Alive and kicking," Jim says. "Well, I'll be kicking in a few weeks, I'm sure."

"Not that I'm complaining, but . . . could someone explain this, please?" Hampton says. Relief and anger do battle across his face. I hate that we caused him any more suffering, and I wouldn't blame him one bit if he decided to be mad as a wet cat.

"I'm pretty sure none of us knows the whole story," Jefferson says. He yanks the shovel out of my hand and gives me a stay-put-or-else look.

"Then this is a good time to put it together," I say, and everyone nods agreement.

"First," Becky says, "I want to know how Hardwick was able to set a trap for us that day at the Custom House. How did he know I'd try to reclaim my house? Was it that mind reader of his?"

Henry stops digging long enough to wipe sweat from his forehead. "I've wondered the same thing."

"Wait," Hampton says. "Mind reader?"

I nod. "Miss Helena Russell. When she sees people, she gets glimpses of the future, sometimes the thoughts in their heads. So when she met us in the law offices, she got a picture in her head of Becky returning with Henry in tow. She warned Hardwick, who sent his guards."

"Is that what she told you at the party?" Becky asks.

"I asked her outright, and she admitted it. After our failed attempt to reclaim the house, Hardwick's men kidnapped Hampton." I nod toward my friend.

"That's when we decided to ruin Hardwick," Mary says smugly.

"I knew you were up to something big, something that involved Hardwick," Melancthon says. "But . . . this is a lot for a fellow to swallow. A mind reader?"

I'm so glad we decided to trust the sailor. He ended up playing an important role. I say, "That was the hardest part—deciding how to act when Hardwick had someone who could pluck our thoughts right out of our heads. We had to divide the plan into parts, and give each person a single part to figure out on their own."

Tom says, "I pretended to be at odds with everyone, and I went to work for Hardwick."

"In the meantime," I say, "we spied on the banks where he kept his money."

"I loitered around the docks to spread word about how much money he had," Jefferson says. He's standing knee-deep in a hole, with his jacket off and his shirtsleeves rolled to his elbows.

"I helped with that!" Henry says. "I spread the word at gambling houses throughout the city."

"I even suggested that some people might be planning to steal it," Jefferson adds. "The idea was to have the rumors get back to Hardwick, so we could see what protection measures he'd put in place. But that part backfired a little. When we went to the bank that night to check it out, a couple of ambitious knuckleheads got there first."

"We did find out exactly how his money was guarded," I say. "But I couldn't let the robbers get away with the safe—we needed that safe intact." The shadow of the gallows passes across my thoughts.

"In the meantime," Tom says, "I learned everything I could about the sheriff's auctions. Hardwick managed them, and Sheriff Purcell took a cut of the money. I soon discovered that Purcell felt he wasn't getting his fair share."

"So Jefferson sabotaged the auction," I say. "All the prices were too low, only a fraction of what Hardwick wanted. And every single lot he had sold at the last auction was listed again. But, Jefferson . . ." I turn toward him. Sweat runs down his neck. "How did you do it?"

His self-satisfied grin is the best thing I've seen in days. "I paid a printer to run off phony auction sheets," he says. "Billy, the pickpocket, was already working at the auctions, handing out price sheets every month. So Hardwick's printer handed him the real price sheets, and then we replaced them with fake ones we commissioned, and Billy distributed them, just like always."

"Custom House lot twenty-three!" Becky says.

"Huh?" I say.

"Custom House lot twenty-three, that was the other thing you changed. The original bid sheet said 'one house, from Tennessee, complete with furnishings and ready for assembly.' But the fake one said 'one small load of wood, somewhat water damaged.'"

I grin. "That probably made it easier to buy."

"We were the only bidders," Henry says, looking up from the hole again, which is now almost waist-deep. "Imagine that!"

"My job was to create a distraction," Jim says. "To keep the auctioneer from paying close attention to the false bid sheets, and to put the crowd on edge." He winces. "That proved to be an even better distraction than anticipated."

"You mean *worse*," I say, glaring.

"After Jim was shot," Becky says, "Henry and I stuck around for a while, sowing discord."

"We put on a fine bit of theater, if you ask me," Henry says. "We didn't know what kind of shape Jim was in, but we soldiered on."

"Ideally, the plan should have worked either way," I say. "If they didn't catch the substitution, then the sale proceeded and the sheriff would think Hardwick was trying to cheat him. If the auctioneer did notice something wrong and called off the auction, then both Hardwick and the sheriff would come up empty-handed." I turn to Jim and say, "But neither one was worth your life. If Frank Dilley had killed you, I don't know what I would have done."

"I didn't come all the way out to California just to die," Jim says. He stretches out his crutch and taps the name on the grave marker. "But since everyone thinks I did, I might try being someone else for a while."

"Well, you're welcome in Glory, Mr. Boisclair," says the Major.

"But why?" Hampton says. "Why let people go on thinking Jim was dead? I'm still so confused."

"We're getting to that," Mary assures him.

Hampton's frown deepens. I open my mouth to assure him, to explain, but he jumps into the muddy hole and takes Jefferson's shovel. "I have no idea what's going on here, but let me spell you a bit."

"Thanks, Hampton." Jeff wipes his forehead with his sleeve and climbs out.

Following Hampton's lead, Jasper rolls up his sleeves and jumps in to spell Henry.

"The best thing about the auction," Tom says, "is that it made Sheriff Purcell steaming mad at Hardwick, even before he got called out to the party."

"Party?" says Hampton. He pauses midshovel, and dirt clods topple back into the hole.

"I bet the sheriff expected to confiscate all the money Frank Dilley stole," the Major says.

"Frank Dilley stole a bunch of money?" Jasper asks, exchanging a baffled look with Hampton.

"Don't stop digging!" Mary says. "We have to get this done before anyone comes along."

As they resume their attack on the hole, I say, "*We* stole the money. But we made it look like Frank Dilley did it."

"That's the best news I've heard all month," Hampton says.

"Tell me how you did it," Jasper demands.

"Well, we needed your help for that," Henry says.

"Ah," Jasper says. "That's what all the fuss with Jim was about."

"Yep," I say. "After Jim was shot, Mary had the *best* idea."

Mary grins. "It turned out pretty well, if I do say so myself. Once we had the keys for Hardwick's safes—"

"Hold on, hold on, hold on," Tom interrupts. "How did you get the keys to Hardwick's safes? I've been dying to know how you managed it. They were never out of Ichabod's hands."

"Ichabod?" I ask.

"His accountant."

"Mr. Keys!" Jefferson says. He's leaning against the wagon now, taking a breather. "That was a tough one. He checked those keys every time he sat down and again the second he stood up. So I paid Sonia to help us. One day when Mr. Keys . . . Ichabod . . . stopped for lunch, she lifted his key ring. We had wax trays ready so she could make impressions of all the keys in just a few minutes."

"Like the locksmith who worked on the *Charlotte*," Melancthon says.

Jefferson nods. "By the time his food was served, the ring was back on his belt; he never noticed it was gone."

"Once we had the keys for Hardwick's safes," the Major continues, "we needed a way to get the gold out quickly and efficiently, and then transport it without it being noticed."

"Aha!" Melancthon interjects. "That's what you needed that bilge hose for. They're heavy when full, but easy to move."

"We were going fill the hose with gold coins, and then store them all in the *Charlotte* in a barrel," the Major says. "But it's a good thing we didn't. After he was arrested, Frank Dilley told the sheriff that *we* stole the money, and Purcell came and searched the *Charlotte* from stem to stern yesterday. If we'd had a single coin hidden aboard the ship, he would have found it."

"I still don't understand how you got the money out of the bank," Jasper says.

"That was me, too," Jefferson says. "The bank has a tile roof. I climbed up, removed a few tiles, and slipped directly into the cage. Took me a minute to figure out which key opened the safe. Then I stuffed the gold coins into the bilge hose."

"Which was why Major Craven had me line it with cotton padding," Melancthon says, running a hand through his whisk-broom hair. "To muffle the sound."

"Exactly," the Major says.

"My job was to talk to the guards," I say. "Keep them from walking around the back of the building or paying too much attention to any odd noises." I helped in another way, too, by giving all that gold a little push, making the bilge hose easier to handle. But I'm not sure I should say so aloud. Melancthon doesn't need to know *all* our secrets.

"I thought for sure they were going to catch me when they opened the door," Jefferson says. "There was just enough time to close the safe door and crouch behind it. If it hadn't been cloudy and dark, he might have noticed the hole in the roof." He looks at me. "You did a great job distracting them."

I shrug. "Those fellows weren't too bad."

"Once the safe was empty," Jefferson continues. "I climbed back up to the roof, holding one end of the hose. I pulled it over the edge and loaded it onto the wagon. Then I replaced the roof tiles, and it was like I'd never been there."

Mary is all grins. "The next day, I paid Hardwick's Chinese workers—the ones who moved all his safes—to pretend that one safe was just as heavy as the others, even though it was empty."

"He never suspected a thing," Tom says. "*I* never suspected a thing."

"So, back to Jim," I say. "Once he was shot, Mary recognized an opportunity. A way to hide all the gold we planned to steal."

Jasper says, "So *that's* why she told me to keep Jim hidden."

"She made all the arrangements," Henry adds. "She organized everything."

"I came to San Francisco alone," Mary says. "So I didn't think Hardwick would realize I was part of the group. I had to keep out of sight around the *Charlotte*, though, sneaking in and out through the hold. I was afraid Frank Dilley would recognize me from Hiram's Gulch."

"It worked out," I say. "Mary was able to get things done without Hardwick ever catching wind."

Becky stares at Mary. "I thought . . . I thought you were avoiding me."

Mary stares back, not answering.

"So that's why we're digging," Jasper says, attacking the hole with renewed enthusiasm.

"Because you did bury something here," Hampton agrees. "But it's not Jim."

A sharp crack sounds. Hampton and Jasper use their shovels to scrape dirt away, revealing a muddy wooden casket.

"Go ahead, Hampton," I say. "You do the honors."

He shoves the tip of his shovel beneath the lid and levers it off.

We all crowd around and peer down into the hole. About four thousand coins sit piled inside the casket, all fifty-dollar pieces. There's a moment of silence, as if someone has died and we're all showing respect. It's not inappropriate, I think. People probably did die to collect this gold. The Indians who had their land stolen. The forty-niners who died on the wagon trail west. The miners who worked themselves sick. The people Hardwick kicked out of their homes to live in the cold, wet San Francisco streets.

Jim gives a low, appreciative whistle.

"Hampton, I'm so sorry we lied to you," I say. "It was meant to protect Jim from any further reprisals, and we weren't sure how to get the real information to you."

"I have to admit," Hampton says, "after getting my freedom papers, then having my freedom taken away again . . . more bad news was awful hard to take in." He takes a good long gander at all that gold. "But it also gave you a casket and a reason to bury it," he adds graciously.

Becky says, "It comes to about three hundred and thirty coins per portion. We'd better get them counted out quick."

"Already on it," Jefferson says. He climbs back into the hole with a dozen bags, and he and Hampton start counting out the coins.

"So what happened at the party last night?" Jasper asks. "You know, the one I missed so Mary could go in my place?" He says it with mock effrontery, as if he was the type of fellow to actually care about a party.

"All I know is that I was supposed to debauch Ichabod yesterday," Tom says. "If anyone was going to sense something amiss, it was going to be him. I was successful, and I hesitate to share all the details, although I confess that we opened the first bottle of wine before lunch. He's a decent enough fellow. I was glad to hear he escaped the sinking of the *Argos*."

"At the party, we had to get inside one of the safes *and* frame Frank Dilley," I say. "But I don't know this part. The Major took care of that." I turn to him. "Please tell me how you did it!"

"We needed to use those copied keys again," the Major says. "So many people are abandoning steady employment and running for the golden hills that the caterers were understaffed. They were thrilled when Mary and I volunteered to help out."

"It took a long time for us to figure out which room was Frank's," Mary says.

"Almost too long," the Major says. "By the way, this crutch

is noisy as all get-out. I stepped on rugs whenever possible, but I don't mind saying that getting in and out of Frank's room is one of the most hair-raising things I've ever done."

Becky pats his arm. "You're a brave man."

"So we found the safes first. We opened one and put Lee's little bundle inside, then I marked it with a bit of chalk so the dockhands would know which one to put in the center of the hold."

"Huh?" says Melancthon. "'Little bundle?'"

"Just a keepsake," I hurry to say. "A locket I carried west with me. It belonged to my mother. I wanted to give it a ceremonial burial at sea, in her honor."

Henry gives me an admiring look, and Mary coughs to cover a laugh.

"Then we found Frank's room," the Major continues, "and we left the key there, along with some other incriminating evidence."

"Where did you hide the duplicate key?" Tom asks. "Everyone at the party was searched closely, and staff was searched *twice*."

The Major hands the baby to Becky and sits down on the edge of the wagon. He pops open a small door on his wooden leg to reveal a secret compartment within. "I carried it here, along with everything else. They searched my pockets, and the seams of my clothes, but they didn't even want to touch my wooden leg."

"You're so clever," Becky says.

"I manage."

Jefferson and Hampton finish dividing the last of the coins. They stack the bags beside the grave and climb out of the hole. Jeff offers the first bag to Hampton. "For all your trouble," he says.

"I've had a lot more trouble than this in my life," Hampton says. "But I'll take some of that gold, I'm not ashamed to say."

Jefferson hands the second bag to Tom.

"As an officer of the court, who may have to testify under oath at some point in the future, I cannot in good conscience accept stolen property." Jefferson starts to withdraw the bag, but Tom grabs it. "I can, however, with a clear heart, give it to someone who should never have been treated as property in the first place, as a first step toward making things right. So I shall hold it in trust for Adelaide."

Hampton beams. "Any word of her while I was gone?" he says.

Tom's smile is sympathetic. "You know it's too early, Hampton. It takes months for these things to happen."

"Well, this ought to help me open that general store," Jim says, taking his bag.

Jasper says it'll help him start his own practice and provide services to the people of California who can't afford a doctor. Mary, Melancthon, the Major, and Henry all accept their shares.

When it's Becky's turn, she opens the bag, removes a few coins, and then hands it back. Holding up the coins, she says, "This is reimbursement from Mr. Hardwick, to repay the cost of recovering my house at auction. But otherwise, I don't feel comfortable stealing from anyone, not even a man as terrible as he was. He's been ruined, and that's enough for me."

Jefferson hesitates, glancing at me uncertainly.

The Major reaches out and grabs the bag. "I'll take it and invest it for the children. We'll plant it like a seed and let it grow, so that they have something to inherit when they're older."

"Wally!"

"Don't try to talk me out of it. My old man left me nothing but a bunch of debt and some bad memories. I figure these little ones already have good memories of their father, all except for the babe here. But there's no reason they can't have a little money. It's what your husband would do if he was still here."

"I'm pretty sure he would gamble it all away," Becky says.

I'm pretty sure she's right.

"So, I think I understand the whole story now," Jasper says. "Except for one thing. How did you steal all those jewels? The pocket watches and gold coins?"

"It was us," says a sulky voice.

"Sonia!" She has arrived with Billy, which I expected, and with Helena, who I wasn't sure would show up.

Jefferson, Hampton, and Jasper clamber out of the hole, and they work fast to shovel all the dirt back in. Everyone gives Helena a wide berth, even though she's here at my invitation.

"These are our new friends, Sonia and Billy," I say. "They helped us all along, mostly by working with Jefferson and

Mary. They also joined us at Hardwick's party, disguised as Becky's children."

"That's why the children stayed with me all night on the *Charlotte*," Melancthon says.

"They were supposed to be us?" Olive asks, running up to Sonia. "You're so big!"

"You'll be big soon enough," Sonia says, chucking her under the chin. "Don't rush it."

"Nobody but Frank Dilley knew what Becky's children looked like," I explain. "So we were able to sneak them in."

"Which I might have foreseen," Helena says. "But I don't think you ever really looked at them."

"I tried to think of them as Olive and Andy," I say. "It was hard."

"But it worked."

"So you're the mind reader," Melancthon says to Helena.

Helena just smiles at him.

"You've counted out all the portions," Sonia says, her voice suddenly cracking with anger. "And you weren't going to leave any for us."

"A promise is a promise," I say, bending over to pick up one of the remaining bags. "I trust you'll use it to look after Billy."

The fight melts out of her. "And maybe a few other kids," she says, cradling the gold to her chest, a shy smile forming.

"It'd help if you had a decent roof over your heads and some honest work," I say.

Her smile disappears. "It'd help if someone would give us honest work."

"We'll see," I say, and I glance over at Helena. "I think the *Charlotte* would make a fine hotel. It already has a good carpenter, who is also an excellent cook, but he needs someone who can manage the business side of things. Someone who is good at working with people, and who can see trouble coming before it arrives."

"You gave *him* the deed for the *Charlotte*," Helena says fiercely.

"No. I gave it to my good friend Wally Craven."

The Major steps forward, pulling a bit of paper from his pocket. "And I'd like to give it to our new friends, Helena Russell and Melancthon Jones," he says. "Miss Russell, you need a man to hold the deed in trust for you, and I can't think of a more trustworthy fellow than Mr. Jones."

"Either one of you can buy the other out at any time, of course," Tom adds.

Helena snatches the deed from the Major's hand. Melancthon and Helena regard each other like a pair of alley cats who discover themselves in a corner.

After a moment, Helena says, "I can see myself working with him," and I wonder if she means it literally or figuratively. "Mr. Jones, it looks like we're going into business together."

Melancthon's eyes are wide with amazement. "I can hardly believe it."

"You've been such a help, sir," I tell him. "We couldn't have done this without you. You worked hard getting the *Charlotte* into livable shape. You watched the children during the party.

Most importantly, you convinced the crew of the *Argos* to have plenty of lifeboats ready."

"I . . . yes . . . I mean, sailors are a superstitious lot. All I had to say was I'd heard omens about it being a bad day for sailing and . . . really? You're giving us the ship?"

With a glance at Jefferson, I say, "I can't own property, being a woman. And my future husband can't own property either, being half Cherokee."

"And I have no use for a ship," the Major says, staring at Becky. "My home is in Glory."

I say, "So the *Charlotte* belongs to Melancthon and Helena now. If you rent out rooms, you'll need someone to clean them, run errands, and the like. May I introduce you to my friends Sonia and Billy? They are currently in possession of their own means of support, but could use some stability and a future."

The four of them regard one another uncertainly.

"Lee," Jefferson says, pausing to toss his shovels back on the wagon. "It's time to be on our way."

I turn toward my mare.

"Wait," Melancthon says. "I have one more big question."

All of us wait expectantly.

"How did you sink the *Argos*?"

The air is suddenly taut. Everyone stares at me, wondering what I'll tell him. The wind is picking up, clearing the morning fog. A sea hawk screeches overhead.

I smile. "Melancthon," I say, "I'm afraid that's one secret we're not willing to share."

Before he can press, Jasper says, "I need to get back to work. But I'll be in Glory for the wedding, don't think I won't."

Tom and Henry take their leave, insisting that this is "not a real good-bye," promising to be in touch soon. Jim declares that he's fetching his things and heading for Glory, that staying in this city might be bad for his health, and Hampton offers to help him along.

Becky and the Major are on the wagon bench, the children in the back, all waiting for Jefferson and me to finish up. Mary stands beside the wagon, looking a little lost.

"If the *Charlotte* makes a successful hotel," Melancthon says, "there might be funds waiting for you. I could hold them in escrow—"

I wave my hand at him. "The deed is in your name. The ship is yours."

He gapes at me. "But—"

Helena puts a hand on his arm. "She has resources," she says. "The girl will be just fine."

Jefferson puts our gold into Peony's saddlebags. He hefts the bag, gauging its weight. "This is less than we had when we arrived in San Francisco."

"But still more than we need." I put a foot in the stirrup and swing myself up onto Peony's back. "Mary, are you staying in the city or coming home with us?"

She hesitates.

"Mary?" I say.

Mary and Becky are staring at each other. Becky's jaw twitches.

Finally Becky says, "Mary, don't be daft. You know I can't run that restaurant without you." She lifts her chin. "You're the *third best* employee I've ever had, and I've grown fond of y— your company." After another too-long pause, Becky adds, "And fine. I'll raise your wages."

Mary's smile could light up the bay. "Glory is my home."

"Oh, Mary, I'm so glad," I tell her, nudging Peony forward. "Jefferson, are you ready to go home?"

Jefferson climbs onto Sorry's back, and I swear the horse sighs. "More than ready."

# April 1850

## Chapter Twenty-Four

Our first spring in California is glorious. It's like the sun dropped dollops of its very own self all over our claims, because the land bursts with yellow mustard and bright orange poppies. The oaks grow heavy with soft gray-green leaves, and everywhere the air is filled with the sounds of birdsong and trickling water. Truly, we have come to the promised land.

The morning before our wedding, a small letter-shaped parcel reaches me from San Francisco. It's made of beautiful, thick parchment, sealed with a splotch of red wax, stamped with the words OFFICE OF THE GOVERNOR OF CALIFORNIA.

I'm serving coffee in the Worst Tavern. It's another busy day, because a group of Chinese miners are traveling through again, and the whole lot of them decided to stop for biscuits and gravy. Letters aren't too uncommon since the weather turned; it seems the peddler or some other traveler stops by with a bundle at least twice a week now. So Mary is the only one paying attention as I break the seal with my fingernail and open it.

I gasp.

"What?" Mary says. "What is it?"

"It's . . ." Two pieces of paper. One is a letter from the governor himself, which I quickly skim. The other . . . "Mary, I think this is a town charter."

"What? Let me see." She snatches the charter from my hand.

Becky sidles over to find out why we've stopped working.

"That sure is a fancy seal," Mary says, gazing down at the charter. "And look at all those signatures!"

Becky snatches the letter from my other hand, so I'm holding nothing.

"The governor thanks you for ridding California of the problem of James Henry Hardwick," she says, reading quickly. "He doesn't know what you did exactly, but he knows where credit is due. It's his pleasure to do you this favor, blah, blah, flattery and more flattery, and he hopes you will remember him in the first election after California attains statehood. . . ." She looks up at me, grinning ear to ear. "He did this to cultivate you as an ally," she says. "He thinks you're *important*."

"I'm happy to not dissuade him," I say, and I'm grinning ear to ear, too. A town charter. Signed by the governor himself and several others, probably delegates from California's constitutional convention, which is what passes for a government in these lawless lands.

Becky takes it from Mary's hand. "After the breakfast rush, I'll frame it and post it in the tavern so everyone can see it," she says brightly. She tucks the charter and letter into her apron pocket. "Now, get back to work, both of you. These miners won't feed themselves."

We've barely served a handful of people before Jefferson arrives, looking more proper and well-groomed than he usually does before a hard day of prospecting. I'm about to tell him about our shiny new charter, but he preempts me in an overly loud voice. "Leah Elizabeth Westfall!"

I'm so startled that I almost drop the coffeepot.

He grins. "Maybe you should set that down."

I do, slowly, as the sound of scraping forks ceases and everyone—Becky, the Buckeyes, the Chinese, and Mary—all turn to stare.

"Um. Good morning, Jeff?"

Still grinning, he reaches into his pocket while dropping to one knee. "I know you already proposed to me, and I know we're getting hitched tomorrow, one way or the other. But I still reckon it's right and proper to give you this." He reaches up, and my gold sense knows what he holds in his hand even before my eyes take it in. A gold band, shiny and new.

I pinch it between thumb and forefinger, holding it up to the light. "Jeff," I say. "You know I don't need fancies. Or any more gold."

"I know. But that ring is special, see. Remember that nugget you gave me? Seems like a long time ago now. You tracked a wounded deer onto our homestead and chanced upon that nugget in a stream. And you gave it to me the day your mama and daddy died, said it wasn't yours by right."

"I remember."

"Well, this is me, giving it back to you."

I blink at him, my knees suddenly quivery. I knew he had kept it. I found it in a box of his things the night Frank Dilley set our camp on fire, but I'd had no idea *why* he kept it. Tears prick at my eyes. "Jefferson, this is the nicest thing. Making that nugget into a ring . . ."

"Put it on."

I do, and it slips onto my finger and sends tingling warmth through my whole hand, like it was meant to be there all along. I hold it up, admiring the way it shines in the light. A little piece of home, a bit of shared history, tying us together as powerfully as any wedding vow.

"Thank you."

"So does this mean you'll marry me after all?"

As if there was any question. I lean down and throw my arms around him, almost knocking him back. Everyone around us cheers like it was a proper proposal, even the Chinese miners.

Jefferson gets to his feet and hugs me back, his face nuzzling my hair. Reluctantly, I disentangle myself. There's a lot to do before our wedding tomorrow, and I need to get back to work.

Someone clears his throat. It's Old Tug, standing from the table, hat crumpled tight in his hand. His friends give him nods of encouragement. "You can do it, Tug," says one, as another slaps him on the back.

"I guess this is as fine a moment as any," he says. For once, he wears a clean shirt and pressed trousers, and he's obviously made an attempt at combing his thistly hair. He takes a deep breath.

Jefferson and I exchange a puzzled glance and sit on the nearest bench, glad to cede the stage to someone else.

"Miss Mary," Tug begins, and he starts twisting that hat in his hand.

Mary freezes, like a rabbit who's sighted a fox. Slowly, carefully, she sets her basket of biscuits on the table and folds her hands together over her apron.

*Twist, twist, twist,* goes Tug's hat. "I know I'm not a fancy man. And even though I'm mighty fine looking, I concede that I am but the fourth best-looking fellow in this town."

Fourth? At least he doesn't lack optimism.

"But I work hard, and I'm healthy and strong," Tug continues. "A catch for any woman. But, see, I don't want any woman. I want you, Miss Mary. To be my wife. You're the nicest, handsomest, uppittiest woman I ever knew, and it'd make me the happiest man in the world if you said yes."

And then, Tug shocks us all by clearing his throat again and letting loose a long string of Chinese. No one gapes more than Mary.

Tug grins. "Been practicing that for months, with the help of some of my friends here. You'll always be smarter than me, and I'm sure I bungled that a fair piece, but . . . maybe you can teach me true?"

Silence reigns in the tavern.

I lean toward Jefferson and whisper, "He's never proposed like that before. He must really love her."

Jefferson whispers back, "Mary is the only thing he's been talking about for the last two months."

Finally Mary unclenches her hands, lifts her chin, and says, "Mr. Tuggle, I would be honored to become your wife."

Tears brim over in Tug's eyes, and suddenly all the Buckeyes are whooping and hollering like it's the Fourth of July.

"Two weddings in Glory this year!" I say, delighted.

"Three," says a voice at my ear. It's the Major, slipping onto the bench beside Jeff and me. "Becky said yes," he explains. "But we prefer to keep things quiet for now. We'll wait until her husband has been gone from us a whole year, God rest his soul."

Jefferson claps him on the back, as I reach out to take his hand. "That's wonderful news, Major," I tell him.

From her place at the stove, Becky bangs a pair of tongs against a kettle, creating enough racket that everyone falls silent again.

She announces, "In honor of the upcoming nuptials of my dearest friends, everyone gets free seconds today!"

And once again, the miners cheer wildly. I get to my feet. "Becky is going to need my help," I say to Jefferson.

"And mine," Jefferson says. "Just put me to work."

The next afternoon, Becky helps me don my ridiculous spun-sugar wedding gown. We're getting ready inside her brand-new house—well, old house, I suppose—which has a porch, two rooms, a loft, and three windows. Her honeymoon cottage, shipped all the way from Tennessee.

We stand before a long floor mirror in a silver frame, and I can hardly believe such a fragile, frivolous thing made it to California unscathed.

"You sure you don't mind?" I ask Becky as she cinches my waist so tight I can hardly breathe.

"Of course not. This is the nicest house in all of Glory. You and Jefferson should enjoy it as newlyweds for at least a week." She works the ribbons in back, forming a perfect bow. "I'll take the house back soon enough, don't you worry. But Wally and Wilhelm and the Buckeyes worked so hard putting this place together; I reckon the whole town will want to see it put to good use right away."

I stare at my reflection in the mirror. It seems as though Mama is looking back at me—those same golden-brown eyes, the same golden-brown hair, that strong, stubborn chin. My hand goes toward my throat, reaching for a locket that's no longer there. I don't imagine that I'll ever get used to its absence.

Olive steps forward with a bouquet of wildflowers—mustard, poppies, blue lupine, and purple paintbrush. "I made this for you," she says shyly.

"Olive, this is beautiful. The best wedding bouquet I've ever seen."

The girl's cheeks blush rosy. "I made a littler one for Minnie, too," she says.

"Minnie?" I give Becky a questioning look.

Becky frowns at her oldest, but it's empty of true vexation. "I was going to wait until after the wedding to tell you," she says. "I've named my daughter."

I can hardly believe it. After all this time. "Becky, that's wonderful. Minnie, is it?"

"Minerva."

"From the California seal."

"Exactly. I wanted a strong name for her."

"Minerva is the Roman goddess of wisdom," Olive informs me solemnly. "I'm the big sister, so I have to teach her to be wise."

"I can't think of a better teacher."

The dinner bell rings, even though no meal is being served right now.

"It's time!" Becky says. "You look lovely. Ready to go?"

"I've kept that boy waiting long enough." I just hope I don't drown in lace before I can get myself properly hitched.

Becky leads me from the house, Olive following behind. Mary meets me at the door, dressed in a pretty gown of soft yellow. We are the four women of Glory, and we make a brightly colored but careful procession toward the Worst Tavern.

All the people I love in the world are already seated—Jim Boisclair, who has opened up a new general store right here in Glory, the Major with his future stepdaughter in his arms, Hampton, even Wilhelm and the Buckeyes. The college men have returned: Henry and Tom for a visit, but Jasper is here to stay. Tom waits at the front beneath the awning. He is licensed to perform wedding ceremonies now, and I'll have no one else. Henry gazes up at him adoringly from the first row.

Beside Tom stands Jefferson, and my heart tumbles a little. His straight black hair is fresh from a wash, his skin bronzed from working outside so much, his eyes bright with anticipation. I hate to admit it, but Becky and Henry were right. Plum is the perfect color for him, and I etch this moment in my mind, so that later I'll be able to pull it from my memory and treasure it.

Nailed to the wall behind Tom is our town charter, neatly framed. At Jeff's feet sit Nugget and Coney. I can safely say I've never attended a wedding with dogs before, but everything is different in California.

As I reach the front, Jefferson whispers, "You're right. You look like a pastry."

I grin up at him, wondering if any moment could be more golden than this one.

"I mean, you look really pretty, Lee. The prettiest girl in the land." He would know. He's seen a whole continent.

Tom begins. "Dearly beloved . . ."

It's going to be a quick ceremony, because Jefferson and I aren't fancy people. It's not the wedding that's important to us, it's the marriage. It's working together for the rest of our lives. It's knowing someone so deeply that facing the unknown together isn't dark and dangerous, but instead beautiful and bright.

I place my hand in Jefferson's, mouthing the words I hardly ever say, even though I feel them with my whole heart, for him, for my friends, for my home.

# *Author's Note*

The descriptions of San Francisco owe much to the careful attention of journalist Bayard Taylor and his book *Eldorado*, originally published in 1850. Taylor traveled from New York to California in 1849 to report for the *New York Tribune*. I relied on the annotated edition, *Eldorado: Adventures in the Path of Empire*, published in 2000 by Santa Clara University and Heydey Books.

Coverture, the legal doctrine whereby a married woman's legal rights were entirely subsumed by her husband, was a real part of American history, though the specific laws varied by state and over time, in more complicated ways than I can cover here. One of the first goals of early feminists was to eliminate the doctrine of coverture. The Supreme Court finally struck down the last state law based on coverture in 1981, when I was eight years old.

Hampton's kidnapping was inspired by several historical instances, in particular, the account of Stephen Hill, a free black man kidnapped by slave catchers, whose freedom papers were destroyed. Delilah Beasley's *The Negro Trail Blazers of California,* originally published in 1919, is one of the earliest books to describe the many instances of free blacks who were held by slave catchers, as well as the black community's efforts to free them. She also described former slaves, like Hampton, who mined gold to buy family members out of slavery.

The *Charlotte*, run aground and converted into a residence, is loosely based on accounts of the whaling ship *Niantic*, one of the finest hotels in the early days of San Francisco. The Apollo saloon was a real saloon in San Francisco that also started out as a grounded ship.

The land-fraud schemes attributed to Hardwick all took place in San Francisco during the Gold Rush. In particular, several fortunes were built by selling titles to "water lots" in the bay. The practice of sinking ships to claim lots and begin the landfill process was very common, especially during 1851 and 1852, and was more mechanized than I've described in this book.

Sheriff Purcell was inspired by two early sheriffs in San Francisco, William Landers and John C. Pulis, both of who came west during the Mexican War as part of the New York Volunteers military unit.

The attempted bank robbery and the hanging that followed was inspired by a contemporary account of John Jenkins, an Australian who stole an entire safe from a bank and was captured during his escape and executed by a vigilance committee without a trial.

I hope the reader can forgive me, because the hymn "O Sleepless Nights, O Cheerless Days," from which the book's title is taken, was not published until well after the Gold Rush. It was written by Helen Smith Arnold, who was born in 1849. Arnold wrote two other hymns, and died in 1873 at the age of twenty-three.

James Boisclair is one of the few historical figures to appear in these novels. After buying his freedom and opening a successful general store in Dahlonega, Georgia, Boisclair packed up and joined the Gold Rush to California. Very little is known about what happened after he arrived, only that he was shot and killed. One of the best historical accounts of Boisclair is found in "Georgia's Forgotten Miners: African Americans and the Georgia Gold Rush of 1829," by David Williams, published in *Appalachians and Race: The Mountain South from Slavery to Segregation*, edited by John C. Inscoe (University Press of Kentucky, 2001).

A special thank-you goes to Dr. Shirley Ann Wilson Moore, Professor Emerita of History at California State University, Sacramento, who reviewed this manuscript and applied her vast knowledge to the text. For further reading on this time period, I recommend her outstanding book, *Sweet Freedom's Plains: African Americans on the Overland Trails 1841–1869* (University of Oklahoma Press, 2016).

In telling Mary's story, I was influenced by the historical accounts of Polly Bemis, a Chinese immigrant who came to San Francisco as a concubine, lived in the gold-mining camps of Idaho, and wedded Charlie Bemis, a white saloonkeeper, in a marriage of convenience. Her story can be found in *The Poker Bride: The First Chinese in the Wild West,* by Christopher Corbett (Atlantic Monthly Press, 2010). Mrs. Bemis remained independent throughout her life, controlling her own destiny. Though I didn't use specific details about Mrs. Bemis's life, I wanted Mary's story to illustrate both the opportunities briefly available to nonwhite women during the early Gold Rush period, as well as the challenges they encountered that forced them to make hard choices.

Books are hard to write. Trilogies are harder. I couldn't have written this one without my team, which includes my husband and researcher, C. C. Finlay; my indefatigable editor, Martha Mihalick; and my agent-cheerleader, Holly Root. I also owe a huge debt to my readers. Thank you for your tweets, your emails, your Facebook messages, and most of all for hanging out with me at events all over the country. You make this job the best in the world.

# DON'T MISS A SECOND OF THE ROMANCE AND POWER!

"Carson joins the ranks of writers like Kristin Cashore, Megan Whalen Turner, and Tamora Pierce as one of YA's best writers of high fantasy."
—*Locus Magazine*

www.epicreads.com

special blend of papaya, lime, lemon, and rum. As if to destroy evidence, he drank it down quickly.

I walked over to three doors in a wall and touched one.

"That's a closet, dear boy." I put my hand on the second door.

"Don't go in. You'll be sorry what you see." I didn't go in.

I put my hand on the third door. "Oh, dear, well, go ahead," said Shelley petulantly. I opened the door.

Beyond it was a small anteroom with a mere cot and a table near the window.

On the table sat a bird cage with a shawl over it. Under the shawl I could hear the rustle of feathers and the scrape of a beak on the wires.

Shelley Capon came to stand small beside me, looking in at the cage, a fresh drink in his little fingers.

"What a shame you didn't arrive at seven tonight," he said.

"Why seven?"

"Why, then, Raimundo, we would have just finished our curried fowl stuffed with wild rice. I wonder, is there much white meat, or any at all, under a parrot's feathers?"

"You wouldn't!?" I cried.

I stared at him.

"You would," I answered myself.

I stood for a moment longer at the door. Then, slowly, I walked across the small room and stopped by the cage with the shawl over it. I saw a single word embroidered across the top of the shawl: MOTHER.

I glanced at Shelley. He shrugged and looked shyly at his boot tips. I took hold of the shawl. Shelley said, "No. Before you lift it . . . ask something."

"Like what?"

"DiMaggio. Ask DiMaggio."

A small ten-watt bulb clicked on in my head. I nodded. I leaned near the hidden cage and whispered: "DiMaggio. 1939."

There was a sort of animal-computer pause. Beneath the word MOTHER some feathers stirred, a beak tapped the cage bars. Then a tiny voice said:

"Home runs, thirty. Batting average, .381."

I was stunned. But then I whispered: "Babe Ruth. 1927."

Again the pause, the feathers, the beak, and: "Home runs, sixty. Batting average, .356. Awk."

"My God," I said.

"My God," echoed Shelley Capon.

"That's the parrot who met Papa, all right."

"That's who it is."

And I lifted the shawl.

I don't know what I expected to find underneath the embroidery. Perhaps a miniature hunter in boots, bush jacket, and wide-brimmed hat. Perhaps a small, trim fisherman with a beard and turtleneck sweater perched there on a wooden slat. Something tiny, something literary, something human, something fantastic, but not really a parrot.

But that's all there was.

And not a very handsome parrot, either. It looked as if it had been up all night for years; one of those disreputable birds that never preens its feathers or shines its beak. It was a kind of rusty green and black with a dull-amber snout and rings under its eyes as if it were a secret drinker. You might see it half flying, half hopping out of café-bars at three in the morning. It was the bum of the parrot world.

Shelley Capon read my mind. "The effect is better," he said, "with the shawl over the cage."

I put the shawl back over the bars.

I was thinking very fast. Then I thought very slowly. I bent and whispered by the cage:

"Norman Mailer."

"Couldn't remember the alphabet," said the voice beneath the shawl.

"Gertrude Stein," I said.

"Suffered from undescended testicles," said the voice.

"My God," I gasped.

I stepped back. I stared at the covered cage. I blinked at Shelley Capon.

"Do you really *know* what you have here, Capon?"

"A *gold* mine, dear Raimundo!" he crowed.

"A *mint!*" I corrected.

"Endless opportunities for blackmail!"

"Causes for murder!" I added.

"Think!" Shelley snorted into his drink. "Think what Mailer's publishers *alone* would pay to shut this bird up!"

I spoke to the cage:

"F. Scott Fitzgerald."

Silence.

"Try 'Scottie,' " said Shelley.

"Ah," said the voice inside the cage. "Good left jab but couldn't follow through. Nice contender, but—"

"Faulkner," I said.

"Batting average fair, strictly a singles hitter."

"Steinbeck!"

"Finished last at end of season."

"Ezra Pound!"

"Traded off to the minor leagues in 1932."

"I think . . . I need . . . one of those drinks." Someone put a drink in my hand. I gulped it and nodded. I shut my eyes and felt the world give one turn, then opened my eyes to look at Shelley Capon, the classic son of a bitch of all time.

"There is something even more fantastic," he said. "You've heard only the first half."

"You're lying," I said. "What could there be?"

He dimpled at me—in all the world, only Shelley Capon can dimple at you in a completely evil way. "It was like this," he said. "You remember that Papa had trouble actually getting his stuff down on paper in those last years while he lived here? Well, he'd planned another novel after *Islands in the Stream*, but somehow it just never seemed to get written.

"Oh, he had it in his mind, al right—the story was

there and lots of people heard him mention it—but he just couldn't seem to write it. So he would go to the Cuba Libre and drink many drinks and have long conversations with the parrot. Raimundo, what Papa was telling El Córdoba all through those long drinking nights was the story of his last book. And, in the course of time, the bird has memorized it."

"*His very last book!*" I said. "The final Hemingway novel of all time! Never written but recorded in the brain of a parrot! Holy Jesus!"

Shelley was nodding at me with the smile of a depraved cherub.

"How much you want for this bird?"

"Dear, dear Raimundo." Shelley Capon stirred his drink with his pinkie. "What makes you think the creature is for sale?"

"You sold your mother once, then stole her back and sold her again under another name. Come off it, Shelley. You're onto something big." I brooded over the shawled cage. "How many telegrams have you sent out in the last four or five hours?"

"Really! You horrify me!"

"How many long-distance phone calls, reverse charges, have you made since breakfast?"

Shelley Capon mourned a great sigh and pulled a crumpled telegram duplicate from his velveteen pocket. I took it and read:

FRIENDS OF PAPA MEETING HAVANA TO REMINISCE OVER BIRD AND BOTTLE. WIRE BID OR BRING CHECKBOOKS AND OPEN MINDS. FIRST COME FIRST SERVED. ALL WHITE MEAT BUT CAVIAR PRICES. INTERNATIONAL PUBLICATION, BOOK, MAGAZINE, TV, FILM RIGHTS AVAILABLE. LOVE. SHELLEY YOU-KNOW-WHO.

My God again, I thought, and let the telegram fall to the floor as Shelley handed me a list of names the telegram had been sent to:

*Time. Life. Newsweek.* Scribner's. Simon & Schuster. *The New York Times. The Christian Science Monitor. The Times of London. Le Monde. Paris-Match.* One of the Rockefellers. Some of the Kennedys. CBS. NBC. MGM. Warner Bros. 20th Century-Fox. And on and on and on. The list was as long as my deepening melancholy.

Shelley Capon tossed an armful of answering telegrams onto the table near the cage. I leafed through them quickly.

Everyone, but everyone, was in the air, right now. Jets were streaming in from all over the world. In another two hours, four, six at the most, Cuba would be swarming with agents, publishers, fools, and plain damn fools, plus counterespionage kidnapers and blonde starlets who hoped to be in front-page photographs with the bird on their shoulders.

I figured I had maybe a good half-hour left in which to do something, I didn't know what.

Shelley nudged my arm. "Who sent you, dear boy? You *are* the very first, you know. Make a fine bid and you're in free, maybe. I must consider other offers, of course. But it might get thick and nasty here. I begin to panic at what I've done. I may wish to sell cheap and flee. Because, well, think, there's the problem of getting this bird out of the country, yes? And, simultaneously, Castro might declare the parrot a national monument or work of art, or, oh, hell, Raimundo, who *did* send you?"

"Someone, but now no one," I said, brooding. "I came on behalf of someone else. I'll go away on my own. From now on, anyway, it's just me and the bird. I've read Papa all my life. Now I know I came just because I had to."

"My God, an altruist!"

"Sorry to offend you, Shelley."

The phone rang. Shelley got it. He chatted happily for a moment, told someone to wait downstairs, hung up, and cocked an eyebrow at me: "NBC is in the lobby. They want an hour's taped interview with El Córdoba there. They're talking six figures."

My shoulders slumped. The phone rang. This time I picked it up, to my own surprise. Shelley cried out. But I said, "Hello. Yes?"

"*Señor*," said a man's voice. "There is a *Señor* Hobwell here from *Time*, he says, magazine." I could see the parrot's face on next week's cover, with six follow-up pages of text.

"Tell him to wait." I hung up.

"*Newsweek?*" guessed Shelley.

"The other one," I said.

"The snow was fine up in the shadow of the hills," said the voice inside the cage under the shawl.

"Shut up," I said quietly, wearily. "Oh, shut up, damn you."

Shadows appeared in the doorway behind us. Shelley Capon's friends were beginning to assemble and wander into the room. They gathered and I began to tremble and sweat.

For some reason, I began to rise to my feet. My body was going to do something, I didn't know what. I watched my hands. Suddenly, the right hand reached out. It knocked the cage over, snapped the wire-frame door wide, and darted in to seize the parrot.

"No!"

There was a great gasping roar, as if a single thunderous wave had come in on a shore. Everyone in the room seemed knocked in the stomach by my action. Everyone exhaled, took a step, began to yell, but by then I had the parrot out. I had it by the throat.

"No! No!" Shelley jumped at me. I kicked him in the shins. He sat down, screaming.

"Don't anyone move!" I said and almost laughed, hearing myself use the old cliché. "You ever see a chicken killed? This parrot has a thin neck. One twist, the head comes off. Nobody move a hair." Nobody moved.

"You son of a bitch," said Shelley Capon, on the floor.

For a moment, I thought they were all going to rush me. I saw myself beaten and chased along the beach, yelling, the cannibals ringing me in and eating me, Tennessee Williams style, shoes and all. I felt sorry for my skeleton, which would be found in the main Havana plaza at dawn tomorrow.

But they did not hit, pummel, or kill. As long as I had my fingers around the neck of the parrot who met Papa, I knew I could stand there forever.

I wanted with all my heart, soul, and guts to wring the bird's neck and throw its disconnected carcass into those pale and gritty faces. I wanted to stop up the past and destroy Papa's preserved memory forever, if it was going to be played with by feeble-minded children like these.

But I could not, for two reasons. One dead parrot would mean one dead duck: me. And I was weeping inside for Papa. I simply could not shut off his voice transcribed here, held in my hands, still alive, like an old Edison record. I could not kill.

If these ancient children had known that, they would have swarmed over me like locusts. But they didn't know. And, I guess, it didn't show in my face.

"Stand back!" I cried.

It was that beautiful last scene from *The Phantom of the Opera* where Lon Chaney, pursued through midnight Paris, turns upon the mob, lifts his clenched fist as if it contained an explosive, and holds the mob at bay for one terrific instant. He laughs, opens his hand to show it empty, and then is driven to his death in the river. . . . Only I had no intention of letting them see an empty hand. I kept it close around El Córdoba's scrawny neck.

"Clear a path to the door!" They cleared a path.

"Not a move, not a breath. If anyone so much as swoons, this bird is dead forever and no rights, no movies, no photos. Shelley, bring me the cage and the shawl."

Shelley Capon edged over and brought me the cage and its cover. "Stand off!" I yelled.

Everyone jumped back another foot.

"Now, hear this," I said. "After I've got away and have hidden out, one by one each of you will be called to have his chance to meet Papa's friend here again and cash in on the headlines."

I was lying. I could hear the lie. I hoped they couldn't. I spoke more quickly now, to cover the lie: "I'm going to start walking now. Look. See? I have the parrot by the neck. He'll stay alive as long as you play 'Simon says' my way. Here we go, now. One, two. Halfway to the door." I walked among them and they did not breathe. "One, two," I said, my heart beating in my mouth. "At the door. Steady. No sudden moves. Cage in one hand. Bird in the other—"

"The lions ran along the beach on the yellow sand," said the parrot, his throat moving under my fingers.

"Oh, my God," said Shelley, crouched there by the table. Tears began to pour down his face. Maybe it wasn't all money. Maybe some of it was Papa for him, too. He put his hands out in a beckoning, come-back gesture to me, the parrot, the cage. "Oh, God, oh, God." He wept.

"There was only the carcass of the great fish lying by the pier, its bones picked clean in the morning light," said the parrot.

"Oh," said everyone softly.

I didn't wait to see if any more of them were weeping. I stepped out. I shut the door. I ran for the elevator. By a miracle, it was there, the operator half-asleep inside. No one tried to follow. I guess they knew it was no use.

On the way down, I put the parrot inside the cage and put the shawl marked MOTHER over the cage. And the elevator moved slowly down through the years. I thought of those years ahead and where I might hide the parrot and keep him warm against any weather and feed him properly and once a day go in and talk through the shawl, and nobody ever to see him, no papers, no magazines, no cameramen, no Shelley Capon, not even Antonio from the Cuba Libre. Days might go by or weeks and sudden fears might come over me that the parrot had gone dumb. Then, in the middle of the night, I might wake and shuffle in and stand by his cage and say:

"Italy, 1918 . . . ?"

And beneath the word MOTHER, an old voice would say: "The snow drifted off the edges of the mountain in a fine white dust that winter. . . ."

"Africa, 1932."

"We got the rifles out and oiled the rifles and they were blue and fine and lay in our hands and we waited in the tall grass and smiled—"

"Cuba. The Gulf Stream."

"That fish came out of the water and jumped as high as the sun. Everything I had ever thought about a fish was in that fish. Everything I had ever thought about a single leap was in that leap. All of my life was there. It was a day of sun and water and being alive. I wanted to hold it all still in my hands. I didn't want it to go away, ever. Yet there, as the fish fell and the waters moved over it white and then green, there it went. . . ."

By that time, we were at the lobby level and the elevator doors opened and I stepped out with the cage labeled MOTHER and walked quickly across the lobby and out to a taxicab.

The trickiest business—and my greatest danger—remained. I knew that by the time I got to the airport, the guards and the Castro militia would have been alerted. I wouldn't put it past Shelley Capon to tell them that a national treasure was getting away. He might even cut Castro in on some of the Book-of-the-Month Club revenue and the movie rights. I had to improvise a plan to get through customs.

I am a literary man, however, and the answer came

to me quickly. I had the taxi stop long enough for me to buy some shoe polish. I began to apply the disguise to El Córdoba. I painted him black all over.

"Listen," I said, bending down to whisper into the cage as we drove across Havana. "*Nevermore.*"

I repeated it several times to give him the idea. The sound would be new to him, because, I guessed, Papa would never have quoted a middleweight contender he had knocked out years ago. There was silence under the shawl while the word was recorded.

Then, at last, it came back to me. "Nevermore," in Papa's old, familiar, tenor voice, "nevermore," it said.

# The Burning Man

The rickety Ford came along a road that plowed up dust in yellow plumes which took an hour to lie back down and move no more in that special slumber that stuns the world in mid-July. Far away, the lake waited, a cool-blue gem in a hot-green lake of grass, but it was indeed still far away, and Neva and Doug were bucketing along in their barrelful of red-hot bolts with lemonade slopping around in a thermos on the back seat and deviled-ham sandwiches fermenting on Doug's lap. Both boy and aunt sucked in hot air and talked out even hotter.

"Fire-eater," said Douglas. "I'm eating fire. Heck, I can hardly *wait* for that lake!"

Suddenly, up ahead, there was a man by the side of the road.

Shirt open to reveal his bronzed body to the waist, his hair ripened to wheat color by July, the man's eyes burned fiery blue in a nest of sun wrinkles. He waved, dying in the heat.

Neva tromped on the brake. Fierce dust clouds rose to make the man vanish. When the golden dust sifted away his hot yellow eyes glared balefully, like a cat's, defying the weather and the burning wind.

He stared at Douglas.

Douglas glanced away, nervously.

For you could see where the man had come across a field high with yellow grass baked and burnt by eight weeks of no rain. There was a path where the man had broken the grass and cleaved a passage to the road. The path went as far as one could see down to a dry swamp and an empty creek bed with nothing but baked hot stones in it and fried rock and melting sand.

"I'll be damned, you stopped!" cried the man, angrily.

"I'll be damned, I did," Neva yelled back. "Where you going?"

"I'll think of someplace." The man hopped up like a cat and swung into the rumble seat. "Get going. It's *after* us! The sun, I mean, of course!" He pointed straight up. "Git! Or we'll *all* go mad!"

Neva stomped on the gas. The car left gravel and glided on pure white-hot dust, coming down only now and then to careen off a boulder or kiss a stone. They cut the land in half with racket. Above it, the man shouted:

"Put 'er up to seventy, eighty, hell, why not ninety!"

Neva gave a quick, critical look at the lion, the intruder in the back seat, to see if she could shut his jaws with a glance. They shut.

And that, of course, is how Doug felt about the beast. Not a stranger, no, not hitchhiker, but intruder. In just two minutes of leaping into the red-hot car, with his jungle hair and jungle smell, he had managed to disingratiate himself with the climate, the automobile, Doug, and the honorable and perspiring aunt. Now she hunched over the wheel and nursed the car through further storms of heat and backlashes of gravel.

Meanwhile, the creature in the back, with his great

lion ruff of hair and mint-fresh yellow eyes, licked his lips and looked straight on at Doug in the rearview mirror. He gave a wink. Douglas tried to wink back, but somehow the lid never came down.

"You ever try to figure—" yelled the man.

"What?" cried Neva.

"You ever try to figure," shouted the man, leaning forward between them "—whether or not the weather is driving you crazy, or you're crazy *already?*"

It was a surprise of a question, which suddenly cooled them on this blast-furnace day.

"I don't quite understand—" said Neva.

"Nor does anyone!" The man smelled like a lion house. His thin arms hung over and down between them, nervously tying and untying an invisible string. He moved as if there were nests of burning hair under each armpit. "Day like today, all hell breaks loose inside your head. Lucifer was born on a day like this, in a wilderness like this," said the man. "With just fire and flame and smoke everywhere," said the man. "And everything so hot you can't touch it, and people not wanting to be touched," said the man.

He gave a nudge to her elbow, a nudge to the boy.

They jumped a mile.

"You see?" The man smiled. "Day like today, you get to thinking lots of things." He smiled. "Ain't this the summer when the seventeen-year locusts are supposed to come back like pure holocaust? Simple but multitudinous plagues?"

"Don't know!" Neva drove fast, staring ahead.

"This *is* the summer. Holocaust just around the bend. I'm thinking so swift it hurts my eyeballs, cracks my head. I'm liable to explode in a fireball with just plain disconnected thought. Why—why—why—"

Neva swallowed hard. Doug held his breath.

Quite suddenly they were terrified. For the man simply idled on with his talk, looking at the shimmering green fire trees that burned by on both sides, sniffing the rich hot dust that flailed up around the tin car, his voice neither high nor low, but steady and calm now in describing his life:

"Yes, sir, there's more to the world than people appreciate. If there can be seventeen-year locusts, why not seventeen-year people? Ever *thought* of that?"

"Never did," said someone.

Probably me, thought Doug, for his mouth had moved like a mouse.

"Or how about twenty-four-year people, or fifty-seven-year people? I mean, we're all so used to people growing up, marrying, having kids, we never stop to think maybe there's other ways for people coming into the world, maybe like locusts, once in a while, who can tell, one hot day, middle of summer!"

"Who can tell?" There was the mouse again. Doug's lips trembled.

"And who's to say there ain't genetic evil in the world?" asked the man of the sun, glaring right up at it without blinking.

"*What* kind of evil?" asked Neva.

"Genetic, ma'am. In the blood, that is to say. People born evil, growed evil, evil, no changes all the way down the line."

"Whew!" said Douglas. "You mean people who start out mean and stay *at* it?"

"You got the sum, boy. Why not? If there are people everyone thinks are angel-fine from their first sweet breath to their last pure declaration, why not sheer orneriness from January first to December, three hundred sixty-five days later?"

"I never thought of that," said the mouse.

"Think," said the man. "*Think.*"

They thought for above five seconds.

"Now," said the man, squinting one eye at the cool lake five miles ahead, his other eye shut into darkness and ruminating on coal-bins of fact there, "listen. What if the intense heat, I mean the really hot hot heat of a month like this, week like this, day like today, just baked the Ornery Man right out of the river mud. Been there buried in the mud for forty-seven years, like a damn larva, waiting to be born. And he shook himself awake and looked around, full grown, and climbed out of the hot mud into the world and said, 'I think I'll eat me some summer.' "

"How's that again?"

"Eat me some summer, boy, summer, ma'am. Just devour it whole. Look at them trees, ain't they a whole dinner? Look at that field of wheat, ain't that a feast? Them sunflowers by the road, by golly, there's breakfast. Tarpaper on top that house, there's lunch. And the lake, way up ahead, Jehoshaphat, that's dinner wine, drink it all!"

"I'm thirsty, all right," said Doug.

"Thirsty, hell, boy, thirst don't begin to describe the state of a man, come to think about him, come to talk, who's been waiting in the hot mud thirty years and is born but to die in one day! Thirst! Ye Gods! Your ignorance is complete."

"Well," said Doug.

"Well," said the man. "Not only thirst but hunger. Hunger. Look around. Not only eat the trees and then the flowers blazing by the roads but then the white-hot panting dogs. There's one. There's another! And all the cats in the country. There's two, just passed three! And then just glutton-happy begin to why, why not, begin to get around to, let me tell you, how's this strike you, eat people? I mean—people! Fried, cooked, boiled, and parboiled people. Sunburnt beauties of people. Old men, young. Old ladies' hats and then old ladies under their hats and then young ladies' scarves and young ladies, and then young boys' swim-trunks, by God, and young boys, elbows, ankles, ears, toes, and eyebrows! Eyebrows, by God, men, women, boys, ladies, dogs, fill up the menu, sharpen your teeth, lick your lips, dinner's *on!*"

"Wait!" someone cried.

Not me, thought Doug. I said nothing.

"Hold on!" someone yelled.

It was Neva.

He saw her knee fly up as if by intuition and down as if by finalized gumption.

Stomp! went her heel on the floor.

The car braked. Neva had the door open, pointing, shouting, pointing, shouting, her mouth flapping, one hand seized out to grab the man's shirt and rip it.

"Out! Get out!"

"*Here*, ma'am?" The man was astonished.

"Here, here, here, out, out, out!"

"But, ma'am . . . !"

"Out, or you're finished, through!" cried Neva, wildly. "I got a load of Bibles in the back trunk, a pistol with a silver bullet here under the steering wheel. A box of crucifixes under the seat! A wooden stake taped to the axle, with a hammer. I got holy water in the carburetor, blessed before it boiled early this morning at three churches on the way: St. Matthew's Catholic, the Green Town Baptist, and the Zion City High Episcopal. The steam from that will get you alone. Following us, one mile behind, and due to arrive in one minute, is the Revered Bishop Kelly from Chicago. Up at the lake is Father Rooney from Milwaukee, and Doug, why, Doug here has in his back pocket at this minute one sprig of wolfbane and two chunks of mandrake root. Out! out! out!"

"Why, ma'am," cried the man. "I *am!*"

And he was.

He landed and fell rolling in the road.

Neva banged the car into full flight.

Behind, the man picked himself up and yelled, "You must be nuts. You must be crazy. Nuts. Crazy."

"*I'm* nuts? *I'm* crazy?" said Neva, and hooted. "Boy!"

". . . nuts . . . crazy . . ." The voice faded.

Douglas looked back and saw the man shaking his fist, then ripping off his shirt and hurling it to the gravel and jumping big puffs of white-hot dust out of it with his bare feet.

The car exploded, rushed, raced, banged pell-mell ahead, his aunt ferociously glued to the hot wheel, until the little sweating figure of the talking man was lost in sun-drenched marshland and burning air. At last Doug exhaled:

"Neva, I never heard you talk like that before."

"And never will again, Doug."

"Was what you said *true?*"

"Not a word."

"You lied, I mean, you *lied?*"

"I lied." Neva blinked. "Do you think *he* was lying, too?"

"I don't know."

"All I know is sometimes it takes a lie to kill a lie, Doug. This time, anyway. Don't let it become customary."

"No, ma'am." He began to laugh. "Say the thing about mandrake root again. Say the thing about wolfbane in my pocket. Say it about a pistol with a silver bullet, say it."

She said it. They both began to laugh.

Whooping and shouting, they went away in their tin-bucket-junking car over the gravel ruts and humps, her saying, him listening, eyes squeezed shut, roaring, snickering, raving.

They didn't stop laughing until they hit the water in their bathing suits and came up all smiles.

The sun stood hot in the middle of the sky and they dog-paddled happily for five minutes before they began to really swim in the menthol-cool waves.

Only at dusk when the sun was suddenly gone and the shadows moved out from the trees did they remember that now they had to go *back* down that lonely road through all the dark places and past that empty swamp to get to town.

They stood by the car and looked down that long road. Doug swallowed hard.

"*Nothing* can happen to us going home."

"Nothing."

"Jump!"

They hit the seats and Neva kicked the starter like it was a dead dog and they were off.

They drove along under plum-colored trees and among velvet purple hills.

And nothing happened.

They drove along a wide raw gravel road that was turning the color of plums and smelled the warm-cool air that was like lilacs and looked at each other, waiting.

And nothing happened.

Neva began at last to hum under her breath.

The road was empty.

And then it was not empty.

Neva laughed. Douglas squinted and laughed with her.

For there was a small boy, nine years old maybe, dressed in a vanilla-white summer suit, with white shoes and a white tie and his face pink and scrubbed, waiting by the side of the road. He waved.

Neva braked the car.

"Going in to town?" called the boy, cheerily. "Got lost. Folks at a picnic, left without me. Sure glad you came along. It's *spooky* out here."

"Climb in!"

The boy climbed and they were off, the boy in the back seat, and Doug and Neva up front glancing at him, laughing, and then getting quiet.

The small boy kept silent for a long while behind them, sitting straight upright and clean and bright and fresh and new in his white suit.

And they drove along the empty road under a sky that was dark now with a few stars and the wind getting cool.

And at last the boy spoke and said something that Doug didn't hear but he saw Neva stiffen and her face grow as pale as the ice cream from which the small boy's suit was cut.

"What?" asked Doug, glancing back.

The small boy stared directly at him, not blinking,

and his mouth moved all to itself as if it were separate from his face.

The car's engine missed fire and died.

They were slowing to a dead stop.

Doug saw Neva kicking and fiddling at the gas and the starter. But most of all he heard the small boy say, in the new and permanent silence:

"Have either of you ever wondered—"

The boy took a breath and finished:

"—if there is such a thing as genetic evil in the world?"

# A Piece of Wood

"Sit down, young man," said the Official.

"Thanks." The young man sat.

"I've been hearing rumors about you," the Official said pleasantly. "Oh, nothing much. Your nervousness. Your not getting on so well. Several months now I've heard about you, and I thought I'd call you in. Thought maybe you'd like your job changed. Like to go overseas, work in some other War Area? Desk job killing you off, like to get right in on the old fight?"

"I don't think so," said the young sergeant.

"What *do* you want?"

The sergeant shrugged and looked at his hands. "To live in peace. To learn that during the night, somehow, the guns of the world had rusted, the bacteria had turned sterile in their bomb casings, the tanks had sunk like prehistoric monsters into roads suddenly made tar pits. That's what I'd like."

"That's what we'd all like, of course," said the Official. "Now stop all that idealistic chatter and tell me where you'd like to be sent. You have your choice —the Western or the Northern War Zone." The Official tapped a pink map on his desk.

But the sergeant was talking at his hands, turning them over, looking at the fingers: "What would you officers do, what would we men do, what would the *world* do if we all woke tomorrow with the guns in flaking ruin?"

The Official saw that he would have to deal carefully with the sergeant. He smiled quietly. "That's an interesting question. I like to talk about such theories, and my answer is that there'd be mass panic. Each nation would think itself the only unarmed nation in the world, and would blame its enemies for the disaster. There'd be waves of suicide, stocks collapsing, a million tragedies."

"But *after* that," the sergeant said. "After they realized it was true, that every nation was disarmed and there was nothing more to fear, if we were all clean to start over fresh and new, what then?"

"They'd rearm as swiftly as possible."

"What if they could be stopped?"

"Then they'd beat each other with their fists. If it got down to that. Huge armies of men with boxing gloves of steel spikes would gather at the national borders. And if you took the gloves away they'd use their fingernails and feet. And if you cut their legs off they'd *spit* on each other. And if you cut off their tongues and stopped their mouths with corks they'd fill the atmosphere so full of hate that mosquitoes would drop to the ground and birds would fall dead from telephone wires."

"Then you don't think it would do any good?" the sergeant said.

"Certainly not. It'd be like ripping the carapace off a turtle. Civilization would gasp and die from the shock."

The young man shook his head. "Or are you lying to yourself and me because you've a nice comfortable job?"

"Let's call it ninety percent cynicism, ten percent rationalizing the situation. Go put your Rust away and forget about it."

The sergeant jerked his head up. "How'd you know I *had* it?" he said.

"Had what?"

"The Rust, of course."

"What're you talking about?"

"I *can* do it, you know. I could start the Rust tonight if I wanted to."

The Official laughed. "You can't be serious."

"I am. I've been meaning to come talk to you. I'm glad you called me in. I've worked on this invention for a long time. It's been a dream of mine. It has to do with the structure of certain atoms. If you study them you find that the arrangement of atoms in steel armor is such-and-such an arrangement. I was looking for an imbalance factor. I majored in physics and metallurgy, you know. It came to me, there's a Rust factor in the air all the time. Water vapor. I had to find a way to give steel a 'nervous breakdown.' Then the water vapor everywhere in the world would take over. Not on all metal, of course. Our civilization is built on steel, I wouldn't want to destroy most buildings. I'd just eliminate guns and shells, tanks, planes, battleships. I can set the machine to work on copper and brass and aluminum, too, if necessary. I'd just walk by all of those weapons and just being near them I'd make them fall away."

The Official was bending over his desk, staring at the sergeant. "May I ask you a question?"

"Yes."

"Have you ever thought you were Christ?"

"I can't say that I have. But I have considered that God was good to me to let me find what I was looking for, if that's what you mean."

The Official reached into his breast pocket and drew out an expensive ball-point pen capped with a rifle shell. He flourished the pen and started filling in a form. "I want you to take this to Dr. Mathews this afternoon, for a complete checkup. Not that I expect anything really bad, understand. But don't you feel you *should* see a doctor?"

"You think I'm lying about my machine," said the sergeant. "I'm not. It's so small it can be hidden in this cigarette package. The effect of it extends for nine hundred miles. I could tour this country in a few days, with the machine set to a certain type of steel. The other nations couldn't take advantage of us because I'd rust their weapons as they approach us. Then I'd fly to Europe. By this time next month the world would be free of war forever. I don't know how I found this invention. It's impossible. Just as impossible as the atom bomb. I've waited a month now, trying to think it over. I worried about what would happen if I did rip off the carapace, as you say. But now I've just about decided. My talk with you has helped clarify things. Nobody thought an airplane would ever fly, nobody thought an atom would ever explode, and nobody thinks that there can ever be Peace, but there *will* be."

"Take that paper over to Dr. Mathews, will you?" said the Official hastily.

The sergeant got up. "You're not going to assign me to any new Zone then?"

"Not right away, no. I've changed my mind. We'll let Mathews decide."

"I've decided then," said the young man. "I'm leaving the Post within the next few minutes. I've a pass. Thank you very much for giving me your valuable time, sir."

"Now look here, Sergeant, don't take things so seriously. You don't have to leave. Nobody's going to hurt you."

"That's right. Because nobody would believe me. Good-bye, sir." The sergeant opened the office door and stepped out.

The door shut and the Official was alone. He stood for a moment looking at the door. He sighed. He rubbed his hands over his face. The phone rang. He answered it abstractedly.

"Oh, *hello*, Doctor. I was just going to call you." A pause. "Yes, I was going to send him over to you. Look, is it all right for that young man to be wandering about? It *is* all right? If you say so, Doctor. Probably needs a rest, a good long one. Poor boy has a delusion of rather an interesting sort. Yes, yes. It's a shame. But that's what a Sixteen-Year War can do to you, I suppose."

The phone voice buzzed in reply.

The Official listened and nodded. "I'll make a note on that. Just a second." He reached for his ball-point pen. "Hold on a moment. Always mislaying things." He patted his pocket. "Had my pen here a moment ago. Wait." He put down the phone and searched his desk, pulling out drawers. He checked his blouse pocket again. He stopped moving. Then his hands twitched slowly into his pocket and probed down. He poked his thumb and forefinger deep and brought out a pinch of something.

He sprinkled it on his desk blotter: a small filtering powder of yellow-red rust.

He sat staring at it for a moment. Then he picked up the phone. "Mathews," he said, "get off the line, quick." There was a click of someone hanging up and then he dialed another call. "Hello, Guard Station, listen, there's a man coming past you any minute now, you know him, name of Sergeant Hollis, stop him, shoot him down, kill him if necessary, don't ask any questions, kill the son of a bitch, you heard me, this is the Official talking! Yes, kill him, you hear!"

"But, sir," said a bewildered voice on the other end of the line. "I can't, I just *can't*. . . ."

"What do you mean you can't, God damn it!"

"Because . . ." The voice faded away. You could hear the guard breathing into the phone a mile away.

The Official shook the phone. "Listen to me, listen, get your gun ready!"

"I can't shoot anyone," said the guard.

The Official sank back in his chair. He sat blinking for half a minute, gasping.

Out there even now—he didn't have to look, no one had to tell him—the hangars were dusting down in soft red rust, and the airplanes were blowing away on a brown-rust wind into nothingness, and the tanks were sinking, sinking slowly into the hot asphalt roads, like dinosaurs (isn't that what the man had said?) sinking into primordial tar pits. Trucks were blowing away into ocher puffs of smoke, their drivers dumped by the road, with only the tires left running on the highways.

"Sir . . ." said the guard, who was seeing all this, far away. "Oh, God . . ."

"Listen, listen!" screamed the Official. "Go after him, get him, with your hands, choke him, with your fists, beat him, use your feet, kick his ribs in, kick him to death, do anything, but get that man. I'll be right out!" He hung up the phone.

By instinct he jerked open the bottom desk drawer to get his service pistol. A pile of brown rust filled the new leather holster. He swore and leaped up.

On the way out of the office he grabbed a chair. It's wood, he thought. Good old-fashioned wood, good old-fashioned maple. He hurled it against the wall twice, and it broke. Then he seized one of the legs, clenched it hard in his fist, his face bursting red, the breath snorting in his nostrils, his mouth wide. He struck the palm of his hand with the leg of the chair, testing it. "All right, God damn it, come on!" he cried.

He rushed out, yelling, and slammed the door.

# The Messiah

"We all have that special dream when we are young," said Bishop Kelly.

The others at the table murmured, nodded.

"There is no Christian boy," the Bishop continued, "who does not some night wonder: am I Him? Is this the Second Coming at long last, and am I It? What, what, oh, what, dear God, if I *were* Jesus? How grand!"

The Priests, the Ministers, and the one lonely Rabbi laughed gently, remembering things from their own childhoods, their own wild dreams, and being great fools.

"I suppose," said the young Priest, Father Niven, "that Jewish boys imagine themselves Moses?"

"No, no, my dear friend," said Rabbi Nittler. "The Messiah! The *Messiah!*"

More quiet laughter, from all.

"Of course," said Father Niven out of his fresh pink-and-cream face, "how stupid of me. Christ *wasn't* the Messiah, was he? And your people are still waiting for Him to arrive. Strange. Oh, the ambiguities."

"And nothing more ambiguous than this." Bishop Kelly rose to escort them all out onto a terrace which had a view of the Martian hills, the ancient Martian towns, the old highways, the rivers of dust, and Earth, sixty million miles away, shining with a clear light in this alien sky.

"Did we ever in our wildest dreams," said the Reverend Smith, "imagine that one day each of us would have a Baptist Church, a St. Mary's Chapel, a Mount Sinai Synagogue here, here on Mars?"

The answer was no, no, softly, from them all.

Their quiet was interrupted by another voice which moved among them. Father Niven, as they stood at the balustrade, had tuned his transistor radio to check the hour. News was being broadcast from the small new American-Martian wilderness colony below. They listened:

"—rumored near the town. This is the first Martian reported in our community this year. Citizens are urged to respect any such visitor. If—"

Father Niven shut the news off.

"Our elusive congregation," sighed the Reverend Smith. "I must confess, I came to Mars not only to work with Christians, but hoping to invite *one* Martian to Sunday supper, to learn of his theologies, *his* needs."

"We are still too new to them," said Father Lipscomb. "In another year or so I think they will understand we're not buffalo hunters in search of pelts. Still, it *is* hard to keep one's curiosity in hand. After all, our *Mariner* photographs indicated no life whatsoever here. Yet life there is, very mysterious and half-resembling the human."

"Half, Your Eminence?" The Rabbi mused over his coffee. "I feel they are even more human than ourselves. They have *let* us come in. They have hidden in the hills, coming among us only on occasion, we guess, disguised as Earthmen—"

"Do you really believe they have telepathic powers,

then, and hypnotic abilities which allow them to walk in our towns, fooling us with masks and visions, and none of us the wiser?"

"I do so believe."

"Then this," said the Bishop, handing around brandies and crème-de-menthes, "is a true evening of frustrations. Martians who will not reveal themselves so as to be Saved by Us the Enlightened—"

Many smiles at this.

"—and Second Comings of Christ delayed for several thousand years. How long must we wait, O Lord?"

"As for myself," said young Father Niven, "I never wished to *be* Christ, the Second Coming. I just always wanted, with all my heart, to *meet* Him. Ever since I was eight I have thought on that. It might well be the first reason I became a priest."

"To have the inside track just in case He ever *did* arrive again?" suggested the Rabbi, kindly.

The young Priest grinned and nodded. The others felt the urge to reach and touch him, for he had touched some vague small sweet nerve in each. They felt immensely gentle.

"With your permission, Rabbi, gentlemen," said Bishop Kelly, raising his glass. "To the First Coming of the Messiah, or the Second Coming of Christ. May they be more than some ancient, some foolish dreams."

They drank and were quiet.

The Bishop blew his nose and wiped his eyes.

The rest of the evening was like many another for the Priests, the Reverends, and the Rabbi. They fell to playing cards and arguing St. Thomas Aquinas, but failed under the onslaught of Rabbi Nittler's educated logic. They named him Jesuit, drank nightcaps, and listened to the late radio news:

"—it is feared this Martian may feel trapped in our community. Anyone meeting him should turn away, so as to let the Martian pass. Curiosity seems his motive. No cause for alarm. That concludes our—"

While heading for the door, the Priests, Ministers, and Rabbi discussed translations they had made into various tongues from Old and New Testaments. It was then that young Father Niven surprised them:

"Did you know I was once asked to write a screenplay on the Gospels? They needed an *ending* for their film!"

"Surely," protested the Bishop, "there's only *one* ending to Christ's life?"

"But, Your Holiness, the Four Gospels tell it with four variations. I compared. I grew excited. Why? Because I rediscovered something I had almost forgotten. The Last Supper isn't really the Last Supper!"

"Dear me, what is it then?"

"Why, Your Holiness, the first of several, sir. The first of several! After the Crucifixion and Burial of Christ, did not Simon-called-Peter, with the Disciples, fish the Sea of Galilee?"

"They did."

"And their nets were filled with a miracle of fish?"

"They were."

"And seeing on the shore of Galilee a pale light, did they not land and approach what seemed a bed of white-hot coals on which fresh-caught fish were baking?"

"Yes, ah, yes," said the Reverend Smith.

"And there beyond the glow of the soft charcoal fire, did they not sense a Spirit Presence and call out to it?"

"They did."

"Getting no answer, did not Simon-called-Peter whisper again, 'Who is there?' And the unrecognized Ghost upon the shore of Galilee put out its hand into the firelight, and in the palm of that hand, did they not see the mark where the nail had gone in, the stigmata that would never heal?

"They would have fled, but the Ghost spoke and said, 'Take of these fish and feed thy brethren.' And Simon-called-Peter took the fish that baked upon the white-hot coals and fed the Disciples. And Christ's frail Ghost then said, 'Take of my word and tell it among the nations of all the world and preach therein forgiveness of sin.'

"And then Christ left them. And, in my screenplay, I had Him walk along the shore of Galilee toward the horizon. And when anyone walks toward the horizon, he seems to ascend, yes? For all land rises at a distance. And He walked on along the shore until He was just a small mote, far away. And then they could see Him no more.

"And as the sun rose upon the ancient world, all His thousand footprints that lay along the shore blew away in the dawn winds and were as nothing.

"And the Disciples left the ashes of that bed of coals to scatter in sparks, and with the taste of Real and Final and True Last Supper upon their mouths, went away. And in my screenplay, I had my CAMERA drift high above to watch the Disciples move some north, some south, some to the east, to tell the world what Needed to Be Told about One Man. And their footprints, circling in all directions, like the spokes of an immense wheel, blew away out of the sand in the winds of morn. And it was a new day. THE END."

The young Priest stood in the center of his friends, cheeks fired with color, eyes shut. Suddenly he opened his eyes, as if remembering where he was:

"Sorry."

"For what?" cried the Bishop, brushing his eyelids with the back of his hand, blinking rapidly. "For making me weep twice in one night? What, self-conscious in the presence of your own love for Christ? Why, you have given the Word back to me, *me!* who has known the Word for what seems a thousand years! You have freshened my soul, oh good young man with the heart of a boy. The eating of fish on Galilee's shore *is* the True Last Supper. Bravo. You deserve to meet Him. The Second Coming, it's only fair, must be for you!"

"I am unworthy!" said Father Niven.

"So are we all! But if a trade of souls were possible, I'd loan mine out on this instant to borrow yours fresh from the laundry. Another toast, gentlemen? To Father Niven! And then, good night, it's late, good night."

The toast was drunk and all departed; the Rabbi and the Ministers down the hill to their holy places, leaving the Priests to stand a last moment at their door looking out at Mars, this strange world, and a cold wind blowing.

Midnight came and then one and two, and at three in the cold deep morning of Mars, Father Niven stirred. Candles flickered in soft whispers. Leaves fluttered against his window.

Suddenly he sat up in bed, half-startled by a dream of mob-cries and pursuits. He listened.

Far away, below, he heard the shutting of an outside door.

Throwing on a robe, Father Niven went down the dim rectory stairs and through the church where a dozen candles here or there kept their own pools of light.

He made the rounds of all the doors, thinking: Silly, why lock churches? What is there to steal? But still he prowled the sleeping night . . .

. . . and found the front door of the church unlocked, and softly being pushed in by the wind.

Shivering, he shut the door.

Soft running footsteps.

He spun about.

The church lay empty. The candle flames leaned now this way, now that in their shrines. There was only the ancient smell of wax and incense burning, stuffs left over from all the marketplaces of time and history; other suns, and other noons.

In the midst of glancing at the crucifix above the main altar, he froze.

There was a sound of a single drop of water falling in the night.

Slowly he turned to look at the baptistery in the back of the church.

There were no candles there, yet—

A pale light shone from that small recess where stood the baptismal font.

"Bishop Kelly?" he called, softly.

Walking slowly up the aisle, he grew very cold, and stopped because—

Another drop of water had fallen, hit, dissolved away.

It was like a faucet dripping somewhere. But there were no faucets. Only the baptismal font itself, into which, drop by drop, a slow liquid was falling, with three heartbeats between each sound.

At some secret level, Father Niven's heart told itself something and raced, then slowed and almost stopped. He broke into a wild perspiration. He found himself unable to move, but move he must, one foot after the other, until he reached the arched doorway of the baptistery.

There was indeed a pale light within the darkness of the small place.

No, not a light. A shape. A figure.

The figure stood behind and beyond the baptismal font. The sound of falling water had stopped.

His tongue locked in his mouth, his eyes flexed wide in a kind of madness, Father Niven felt himself struck blind. Then vision returned, and he dared cry out:

"Who!"

A single word, which echoed back from all around the church, which made candle flames flutter in reverberation, which stirred the dust of incense, which frightened his own heart with its swift return in saying: Who!

The only light within the baptistery came from the pale garments of the figure that stood there facing him. And this light was enough to show him an incredible thing.

As Father Niven watched, the figure moved. It put a pale hand out upon the baptistery air.

The hand hung there as if not wanting to, a separate thing from the Ghost beyond, as if it were seized and pulled forward, resisting, by Father Niven's dreadful and fascinated stare to reveal what lay in the center of its open white palm.

There was fixed a jagged hole, a cincture from which, slowly, one by one, blood was dripping, falling away down and slowly down, into the baptismal font.

The drops of blood struck the holy water, colored it, and dissolved in slow ripples.

The hand remained for a stunned moment there before the Priest's now-blind, now-seeing eyes.

As if struck a terrible blow, the Priest collapsed to his knees with an outgasped cry, half of despair, half of revelation, one hand over his eyes, the other fending off the vision.

"No, no, no, no, no, no, no, it *can't!*"

It was as if some dreadful physician of dentistry had come upon him without narcotic and with one seizure entire-extracted his soul, bloodied raw, out of his body. He felt himself prized, his life yanked forth, and the roots, O God, were . . . *deep!*

"No, no, no, no!"

But, yes.

Between the lacings of his fingers, he looked again.

And the Man was there.

And the dreadful bleeding palm quivered dripping upon the baptistery air.

"Enough!"

The palm pulled back, vanished. The Ghost stood waiting.

And the face of the Spirit was good and familiar. Those strange beautiful deep and incisive eyes were as he knew they always must be. There was the gentleness of the mouth, and the paleness framed by the flowing locks of hair and beard. The Man was robed in the simplicity of garments worn upon the shores and in the wilderness near Galilee.

The Priest, by a great effort of will, prevented his tears from spilling over, stopped up his agony of surprise, doubt, shock, these clumsy things which rioted within and threatened to break forth. He trembled.

And then saw that the Figure, the Spirit, the Man, the Ghost, Whatever, was trembling, too.

No, thought the Priest, He can't be! Afraid? Afraid of . . . *me?*

And now the Spirit shook itself with an immense agony not unlike his own, like a mirror image of his own concussion, gaped wide its mouth, shut up its own eyes, and mourned:

"Oh, please, let me go."

At this the young Priest opened his eyes wider and gasped. He thought: But you're free. No one keeps you here!

And in that instant: "Yes!" cried the Vision. "*You* keep me! Please! Avert your gaze! The more you look the more I become *this!* I am *not* what I seem!"

But, thought the Priest, I did not speak! My lips did not move! How does this Ghost know my mind?

"I know all you think," said the Vision, trembling, pale, pulling back in baptistery gloom. "Every sentence, every word. I did not mean to come. I ventured into town. Suddenly I was many things to many people. I ran. They followed. I escaped here. The door was open. I entered. And then and then—oh, and then was trapped."

No, thought the Priest.

"Yes," mourned the Ghost. "By you."

Slowly now, groaning under an even more terrible weight of revelation, the Priest grasped the edge of the font and pulled himself, swaying, to his feet. At last he dared force the question out:

"You are not . . . what you seem?"

"I am not," said the other. "Forgive me."

I, thought the Priest, shall go mad.

"Do not," said the Ghost, "or I shall go down to madness with you."

"I can't give you up, oh, dear God, now that you're here, after all these years, all my dreams, don't you see, it's asking too *much*. Two thousand years, a whole race of people have waited for your return! And I, I am the one who meets you, sees you—"

"You meet only your own dream. You see only your own need. Behind all this—" the figure touched its own robes and breast, "I am another thing."

"What must I *do!*" the Priest burst out, looking now at the heavens, now at the Ghost which shuddered at his cry. "*What?*"

"Avert your gaze. In that moment I will be out the door and gone."

"Just—just like that?"

"Please," said the Man.

The Priest drew a series of breaths, shivering.

"Oh, if this moment could last for just an hour."

"Would you kill me?"

"No!"

"If you keep me, force me into this shape some little while longer, my death will be on your hands."

The Priest bit his knuckles, and felt a convulsion of sorrow rack his bones.

"You—you are a Martian, then?"

"No more. No less."

"And I have done this to you with my thoughts?"

"You did not mean. When you came downstairs, your old dream seized and made me over. My palms still bleed from the wounds you gave out of your secret mind."

The Priest shook his head, dazed.

"Just a moment more . . . wait . . ."

He gazed steadily, hungrily, at the darkness where the Ghost stood out of the light. That face was beautiful. And, oh, those hands were loving and beyond all description.

The Priest nodded, a sadness in him now as if he had within the hour come back from the true Calvary. And the hour was gone. And the coals strewn dying on the sand near Galilee.

"If—if I let you go—"

"You must, oh you must!"

"If I let you go, will you promise—"

"What?"

"Will you promise to come back?"

"Come back?" cried the figure in the darkness.

"Once a year, that's all I ask, come back once a year, here to this place, this font, at the same time of night—"

"Come back . . . ?"

"Promise! Oh, I must know this moment again. You don't know how important it is! Promise, or I won't let you go!"

"I"—

"Say it! Swear it!"

"I promise," said the pale Ghost in the dark. "I swear."

"Thank you, oh thanks."

"On what day a year from now must I return?"

The tears had begun to roll down the young Priest's face now. He could hardly remember what he wanted to say and when he said it he could hardly hear:

"Easter, oh, God, yes, Easter, a year from now!"

"Please, don't weep," said the figure. "I will come. Easter, you say? I know your calendar. Yes. Now—" The pale wounded hand moved in the air, softly pleading. "May I go?"

The Priest ground his teeth to keep the cries of woe from exploding forth. "Bless me, and go."

"Like this?" said the voice.

And the hand came out to touch him ever so quietly.

"Quick!" cried the Priest, eyes shut, clenching his fists hard against his ribs to prevent his reaching out to seize. "Go before I keep you forever. Run. Run!"

The pale hand touched him a last time upon his brow. There was a soft run of naked feet.

A door opened upon stars; the door slammed.

There was a long moment when the echo of the slam made its way through the church, to every altar, into every alcove and up like a blind flight of some single bird seeking and finding release in the apse. The church stopped trembling at last, and the Priest laid his hands on himself as if to tell himself how to behave, how to breathe again; be still, be calm, stand tall. . . .

Finally, he stumbled to the door and held to it, wanting to throw it wide, look out at the road which must be empty now, with perhaps a figure in white, far fleeing. He did not open the door.

He went about the church, glad for things to do, finishing out the ritual of locking up. It was a long way around to all the doors. It was a long way to next Easter.

He paused at the font and saw the clear water with no trace of red. He dipped his hand and cooled his brow and temples and cheeks and eyelids.

Then he went slowly up the aisle and laid himself out before the altar and let himself burst forth and really weep. He heard the sound of his sadness go up and come back in agonies from the tower where the bell hung silent.

And he wept for many reasons.

For himself.

For the Man who had been here a moment ago.

For the long time until the rock was rolled back and the tomb found empty again.

Until Simon-Called-Peter once more saw the Ghost upon the Martian shore, and himself Simon-Peter.

And most of all he wept because, oh, because, because . . . never in his life could he speak of this night to anyone. . . .

# G. B. S.—Mark V

"Charlie! Where you going?"

Members of the rocket crew, passing, called.

Charles Willis did not answer.

He took the vacuum tube down through the friendly humming bowels of the spaceship. He fell, thinking: This is thc grand hour.

"Chuck! Where traveling?" someone called.

To meet someone dead but alive, cold but warm, forever untouchable but reaching out somehow to touch.

"Idiot! Fool!"

The voice echoed. He smiled.

Then he saw Clive, his best friend, drifting up in the opposite chute. He averted his gaze, but Clive sang out through his sea shell ear-pack radio:

"I want to see you!"

"Later!" Willis said.

"I *know* where you're going. Stupid!"

And Clive was gone up away while Willis fell softly down, his hands trembling.

His boots touched surface. On the instant he suffered renewed delight.

He walked down through the hidden machineries of the rocket. Lord, he thought, crazy. Here we are one hundred days gone away from the Earth in Space, and, this very hour, most of the crew, in fever, dialing their aphrodisiac animatronic devices that touched and hummed to them in their shut clamshell beds. While, what do *I* do? he thought. *This.*

He moved to peer into a small storage pit.

There, in an eternal dusk, sat the old man.

"Sir," he said, and waited.

"Shaw," he whispered. "Oh, Mr. George Bernard Shaw."

The old man's eyes sprang wide as if he had swallowed an Idea.

He seized his bony knees and gave a sharp cry of laughter.

"By God, I *do* accept it *all!*"

"Accept *what*, Mr. Shaw?"

Mr. Shaw flashed his bright blue gaze upon Charles Willis.

"The Universe! *It* thinks, therefore I *am!* So I had *best* accept, eh? Sit."

Willis sat in the shadowed areaway, clasping his knees and his own warm delight with being here again.

"Shall I read your mind, young Willis, and tell you what you've been up to since last we conversed?"

"*Can* you read minds, Mr. Shaw?"

"No, thank God. Wouldn't it be awful if I were not only the cuneiform-tablet robot of George Bernard Shaw, but could also scan your head-bumps and spell your dreams? Unbearable."

"You already *are*, Mr. Shaw."

"*Touché!* Well, now." The old man raked his reddish beard with his thin fingers, then poked Willis gently in the ribs. "How is it you are the only one aboard this starship who ever visits me?"

"Well, sir, you see—"

The young man's cheeks burnt themselves to full blossom.

"Ah, yes, I do see," said Shaw. "Up through the honeycomb of the ship, all the happy male bees in their hives with their syrupy wind-up soft-singing nimble-nibbling toys, their bright female puppets."

"Mostly *dumb*."

"Ah, well. It was not always thus. On my last trip the Captain wished to play Scrabble using only names of characters, concepts and ideas from my plays. Now, strange boy, why do *you* squat here with this hideous old ego? Have you no need for that soft and gentle company abovestairs?"

"It's a long journey, Mr. Shaw, two years out beyond Pluto and back. Plenty of time for abovestairs company. Never enough for this. I have the dreams of a goat but the genetics of a saint."

"Well said!" The old man sprang lightly to his feet and paced about, pointing his beard now toward Alpha Centauri, now toward the nebula in Orion.

"How runs our menu today, Willis? Shall I preface Saint Joan for you? Or . . . ?"

"Chuck . . . ?"

Willis's head jerked. His seashell radio whispered in his ear. "Willis! Clive calling. You're late for dinner. I know where you are. I'm coming down. Chuck—"

Willis thumped his ear. The voice cut off.

"Quick, Mr. Shaw! Can you—well—*run*?"

"Can Icarus fall from the sun? Jump! I shall pace you with these spindly cricket legs!"

They ran.

Taking the corkscrew staircase instead of the air-tube, they looked back from the top platform in time to see Clive's shadow dart into that tomb where Shaw had died but to wake again.

"Willis!" cried his voice.

"To hell with him," said Willis.

Shaw beamed. "Hell? I know it well. Come. I'll show you around!"

Laughing, they jumped into the feather-tube and fell *up*.

This was the place of stars.

Which is to say the one place in all the ship where, if one wished, one could come and truly look at the Universe and the billion billion stars which poured across it and never stopped pouring, cream from the mad dairies of the gods. Delicious frights or outcrops, on the other hand, if you thought it so, from the sickness of Lord God Jehovah turned in his sleep, upset with Creation, and birthing dinosaur worlds spun about satanic suns.

"It's all in the thinking," observed Mr. Shaw, sidling his eyes at his young consort.

"Mr. Shaw! You *can* read minds?"

"Poppycock. I merely read faces. Yours is clear glass. I glanced just now and saw Job afflicted, Moses and the Burning Bush. Come. Let us look at the Deeps and see what God has been up to in the ten billion years since He collided with Himself and procreated Vastness."

They stood now, surveying the Universe, counting the stars to a billion and beyond.

"Oh," moaned the young man, suddenly, and tears fell from his eyes. "How I wish I had been alive when you were alive, sir. How I wish I had *truly* known you."

"*This* Shaw is best," retorted the old man, "all of the mincemeat and none of the tin. The coattails are better than the man. Hang to them and survive."

Space lay all about, as vast as God's first thought, as deep as His primal breathing.

They stood, one of them tall, one short, by the scanning window, with a fine view of the great Andromeda

Nebula whenever they wished to focus it near with a touch of the button which made the Eye magnify and suck things close.

After a long moment of drinking stars, the young man let out his breath.

"Mr. Shaw . . . ? *Say* it. You know what I like to hear."

"Do I, my boy?" Mr. Shaw's eyes twinkled.

All of Space was around them, all of the Universe, all of the night of the celestial Being, all the stars and all the places between the stars, and the ship moving on its silent course, and the crew of the ship busy at work or games or touching their amorous toys, so these two were alone with their talk, these two stood viewing the Mystery and saying what must be said.

"Say it, Mr. Shaw."

"Well, now . . ."

Mr. Shaw fixed his eyes on a star some twenty light-years away.

"What *are* we?" he asked. "Why, we are the miracle of force and matter making itself over into imagination and will. Incredible. The Life Force experimenting with forms. You for one. Me for another. The Universe has shouted itself alive. We are one of the shouts. Creation turns in its abyss. We have bothered it, dreaming ourselves to shapes. The void is filled with slumbers; ten billion on a billion on a billion bombardments of light and material that know not themselves, that sleep moving and move but finally to make an eye and waken on themselves. Among so much that is flight and ignorance, we are the blind force that gropes like Lazarus from a billion-light-year tomb. We summon ourselves. We say, O Lazarus Life Force, truly come ye forth. So the Universe, a motion of deaths, fumbles to reach across Time to feel its own flesh and know it to be ours. We touch both ways and find each other miraculous because we are One."

Mr. Shaw turned to glance at his young friend.

"There you have it. Satisfied?"

"Oh, yes! I—"

The young man stopped.

Behind them, in the viewing-cabin door, stood Clive. Beyond him, they could hear music pulsing from the far cubicles where crewmen and their huge toys played at amorous games.

"Well," said Clive, "what goes on—?"

"Here?" interjected Shaw, lightly. "Why, only the confounding of two energies making do with puzzlements. This contraption—" he touched his own breast, "speaks from computerized elations. That genetic conglomeration—" he nodded at his young friend, "responds with raw, beloved, and true emotions. The sum of us? Pandemonium spread on biscuits and devoured at high tea."

Clive swiveled his gaze to Willis.

"Damn, you're nuts. At dinner you should have *heard* the laughter! You and this old man, and just talk! they said. Just talk, talk! Look, idiot, it's your stand-watch in ten minutes. Be there! God!"

And the door was empty. Clive was gone.

Silently, Willis and Mr. Shaw floated down the drop-tube to the storage pit beneath the vast machineries.

The old man sat once again on the floor.

"Mr. Shaw." Willis shook his head, snorting softly. "Hell. Why is it you seem more alive to me than anyone I have ever known?"

"Why, my dear young friend," replied the old man, gently, "what you warm your hands at are Ideas, eh? I am a walking monument of concepts, scrimshaws of thought, electric deliriums of philosophy and wonder. You love concepts. I am their receptacle. You love dreams in motion. I move. You love palaver and jabber. I am the consummate palaverer and jabberer. You and I, together, masticate Alpha Centauri and spit forth universal myths. We chew upon the tail of Halley's Comet and worry the Horsehead Nebula until it cries a monstrous Uncle and gives over to our creation. You love libraries. I am a library. Tickle my ribs and I vomit forth Melville's Whale, Spirit Spout and all. Tic my ear and I'll build Plato's *Republic* with my tongue for you to run and live in. You love Toys. I am a Toy, a fabulous plaything, a computerized—"

"—friend," said Willis, quietly.

Mr. Shaw gave him a look less of fire than of hearth. "Friend," he said.

Willis turned to leave, then stopped to gaze back at that strange old figure propped against the dark storage wall.

"I—I'm afraid to go. I have this fear something may *happen* to you."

"I shall survive," replied Shaw tartly, "but if you warn your Captain that a vast meteor shower approaches. He must shift course a few hundred thousand miles. Done?"

"Done." But still Willis did not leave.

"Mr. Shaw," he said, at last. "What . . . what do you *do* while the rest of us sleep?"

"Do? Why, bless you. I listen to my tuning fork. Then, I write symphonies between my ears."

Willis was gone.

In the dark, alone, the old man bent his head. A soft hive of dark bees began to hum under his honey-sweet breath.

Four hours later, Willis, off watch, crept into his sleep-cubicle.

In half-light, the mouth was waiting for him.

Clive's mouth. It licked its lips and whispered:

"Everyone's talking. About you making an ass out of yourself visiting a two-hundred-year-old intellectual relic, you, you, you. Jesus, the psycho-med'll be out tomorrow to X-ray your stupid skull!"

"Better that than what you men do all night every night," said Willis.

"What we do is us."

"Then why not let me be *me?*"

"Because it's unnatural." The tongue licked and darted. "We all *miss* you. Tonight we piled all the grand toys in the midst of the wild room and—"

"I don't want to hear it!"

"Well, then," said the mouth, "I might just trot down and tell all this to your old gentleman friend—"

"Don't go *near* him!"

"I might." The lips moved in the shadows. "You can't stand guard on him forever. Some night soon, when you're asleep, someone might—tamper with him, eh? Scramble his electronic eggs so he'll talk vaudeville instead of *Saint Joan?* Ha, yes. Think. Long journey. Crew's bored. Practical joke like that, worth a million to see you froth. Beware, Charlie. Best come play with us."

Willis, eyes shut, let the blaze out of him.

"Whoever dares to touch Mr. Shaw, so help me God, I'll kill!"

He turned violently on his side, gnawing the back of his fist.

In the half-dark, he could sense Clive's mouth still moving.

"Kill? Well, well. Pity. Sweet dreams."

An hour later, Willis gulped two pills and fell stunned into sleep.

In the middle of the night he dreamed that they were burning good Saint Joan at the stake and, in the midst of burning, the plain-potato maiden turned to an old man stoically wrapped around with ropes and vines. The old man's beard was fiery red even before the flames reached it, and his bright blue eyes were fixed fiercely upon Eternity, ignoring the fire.

"Recant!" cried a voice. "Confess and recant! Recant!"

"There is nothing to confess, therefore no need for recantation," said the old man quietly.

The flames leaped up his body like a mob of insane and burning mice.

"Mr. Shaw!" screamed Willis.

He sprang awake.

*Mr. Shaw.*

The cabin was silent. Clive lay asleep.

On his face was a smile.

The smile made Willis pull back, with a cry. He dressed. He ran.

Like a leaf in autumn he fell down the air-tube, growing older and heavier with each long instant.

The storage pit where the old man "slept" was much more quiet than it had a right to be.

Willis bent. His hand trembled. At last, he touched the old man.

"Sir—?"

There was no motion. The beard did not bristle. Nor the eyes fire themselves to blue flames. Nor the mouth tremble with gentle blasphemies . . .

"Oh, Mr. Shaw," he said. "Are you dead, then, oh God, are you really dead?"

The old man was what they called dead when a machine no longer spoke or tuned an electric thought or moved. His dreams and philosophies were snow in his shut mouth.

Willis turned the body this way and that, looking for some cut, wound, or bruise on the skin.

He thought of the years ahead, the long traveling years and no Mr. Shaw to walk with, gibber with, laugh with. Women in the storage shelves, yes, women in the cots late at night, laughing their strange taped laughters and moving their strange machined motions, and saying the same dumb things that were said on a thousand worlds on a thousand nights.

To be alone. To fall.

"Oh, Mr. Shaw," he murmured at last. "Who *did* this to you?"

Silly boy, whispered Mr. Shaw's memory voice. You *know*.

I know, thought Willis.

He whispered a name and ran away.

"Damn you, you killed him!"

Willis seized Clive's bedclothes, at which instant Clive, like a robot, popped wide his eyes. The smile remained constant.

"You can't kill what was never alive," he said.

"Son of a bitch!"

He struck Clive once in the mouth, after which Clive was on his feet, laughing in some strange wild way, wiping blood from his lips.

"What did you do to him?" cried Willis.

"Not much, just—"

But that was the end of their conversation.

"On posts!" a voice cried. "Collision course!"

Bells rang. Sirens shrieked.

In the midst of their shared rage, Willis and Clive turned cursing to seize emergency spacesuits and helmets off the cabin walls.

"Damn, oh, damn, oh—d—"

Half-through his last damn, Clive gasped. He vanished out a sudden hole in the side of the rocket.

The meteor had come and gone in a billionth of a second. On its way out, it had taken all the air in the ship with it through a hole the size of a small car.

My God, thought Willis, he's gone forever.

What saved Willis was a ladder he stood near, against which the swift river of air crushed him on its way into Space. For a moment he could not move or breathe. Then the suction was finished, all the air in the ship gone. There was only time to adjust the pressure in his suit and helmet, and glance wildly around at the veering ship which was being bombarded now as in a space war. Men ran, or rather floated, shouting wildly, everywhere.

Shaw, thought Willis unreasonably, and had to laugh. Shaw.

A final meteor in a tribe of meteors struck the motor section of the rocket and blew the entire ship apart. Shaw, Shaw, oh, Shaw, thought Willis.

He saw the rocket fly apart like a shredded balloon, all its gases only impelling it to more disintegration. With the bits and pieces went wild crowds of men, dismissed from school, from life, from all and everything, never to meet face to face again, not even to say farewell, the dismissal was so abrupt and their deaths and isolation such a swift surprise.

Good-bye, thought Willis.

But there was no true good-bye. He could hear no weeping and no laments over his radio. Of all the crew, he was the last and final and only one alive, because of his suit, his helmet, his oxygen, miraculously spared. For what? To be alone and fall?

Oh, Mr. Shaw, oh, sir, he thought.

"No sooner called than delivered," whispered a voice.

It was impossible, but . . .

Drifting, spinning, the ancient doll with the wild red beard and blazing blue eyes fell across darkness as if impelled by God's breath, on a whim.

Instinctively, Willis opened his arms.

And the old party landed there, smiling, breathing heavily, or pretending to breathe heavily, as was his bent.

"Well, well, Willis! Quite a treat, eh?"

"Mr. Shaw! You were *dead!*"

"Poppycock! Someone bent some wires in me. The collision knocked things back together. The disconnection is here below my chin. A villain cut me there. So if I fall dead again, jiggle under my jaw and wire me up, eh?"

"Yes, sir!"

"How much food do you carry at this moment, Willis?"

"Enough to last two hundred days in Space."

"Dear me, that's fine, fine! And self-recycling oxygen units, also, for two hundred days?"

"Yes, sir. Now, how long will *your* batteries last, Mr. Shaw?"

"Ten thousand years!" the old man sang out happily. "Yes, I vow, I swear! I am fitted with solar-cells which will collect God's universal light until I wear out my circuits."

"Which means you will outtalk me, Mr. Shaw, long after I have stopped eating and breathing."

"At which point you must dine on conversation, and breathe past participles instead of air. But, we must hold the thought of rescue uppermost. Are not the chances good?"

"Rockets *do* come by. And I am equipped with radio signals—"

"Which even now cry out into the deep night: I'm here with ramshackle Shaw, eh?"

I'm here with ramshackle Shaw, thought Willis, and was suddenly warm in winter.

"Well, then, while we're waiting to be rescued, Charles Willis, what next?"

"Next? Why—"

They fell away down Space alone but not alone, fearful but elated, and now grown suddenly quiet.

"*Say* it, Mr. Shaw."

"Say what?"

"You know. Say it again."

"Well, then." They spun lazily, holding to each other. "Isn't life miraculous? Matter and force, yes, matter and force making itself over into intelligence and will."

"Is *that* what we are, sir?"

"We are, bet ten thousand bright tin-whistles on it, we are. Shall I say *more*, young Willis?"

"Please, sir," laughed Willis. "I want some more!"

And the old man spoke and the young man listened and the young man spoke and the old man hooted and they fell around a corner of Universe away out of sight, eating and talking, talking and eating, the young man biting gumball foods, the old man devouring sunlight with his solar-cell eyes, and the last that was seen of them they were gesticulating and babbling and conversing and waving their hands until their voices faded into Time and the solar system turned over in its sleep and covered them with a blanket of dark and light, and whether or not a rescue ship named Rachel, seeking her lost children, ever came by and found them, who can tell, who would truly ever want to know?

# The Utterly Perfect Murder

It was such an utterly perfect, such an incredibly delightful idea for murder, that I was half out of mind all across America.

The idea had come to me for some reason on my forty-eighth birthday. Why it hadn't come to me when I was thirty or forty, I cannot say. Perhaps those were good years and I sailed through them unaware of time and clocks and the gathering of frost at my temples or the look of the lion about my eyes. . . .

Anyway, on my forty-eighth birthday, lying in bed that night beside my wife, with my children sleeping through all the other quiet moonlit rooms of my house, I thought:

I will arise and go now and kill Ralph Underhill.

Ralph Underhill! I cried, who in God's name is *he?*

Thirty-six years later, kill him? For *what?*

Why, I thought, for what he did to me when I was twelve.

My wife woke, an hour later, hearing a noise.

"Doug?" she called. "What are you doing?"

"Packing," I said. "For a journey."

"Oh," she murmured, and rolled over and went to sleep.

"Board! All aboard!" the porter's cries went down the train platform.

The train shuddered and banged.

"See you!" I cried, leaping up the steps.

"Someday," called my wife, "I wish you'd *fly!*"

Fly? I thought, and spoil thinking about murder all across the plains? Spoil oiling the pistol and loading it and thinking of Ralph Underhill's face when I show up thirty-six years late to settle old scores? Fly? Why, I would rather pack cross-country on foot, pausing by night to build fires and fry my bile and sour spit and eat again my old, mummified but still-living antagonisms and touch those bruises which have never healed. Fly? !

The train moved. My wife was gone.

I rode off into the Past.

Crossing Kansas the second night, we hit a beaut of a thunderstorm. I stayed up until four in the morning, listening to the rave of winds and thunders. At the height of the storm, I saw my face, a darkroom negative-print on the cold window glass, and thought:

Where is that fool going?

To kill Ralph Underhill!

Why? Because!

Remember how he hit my arm? Bruises. I was covered with bruises, both arms; dark blue, mottled black, strange yellow bruises. Hit and run, that was Ralph, hit and run—

And yet . . . you loved him?

Yes, as boys love boys when boys are eight, ten, twelve, and the world is innocent and boys are evil beyond evil because they know not what they do, but do it anyway. So, on some secret level, I *had* to be hurt.

We dear fine friends needed each other. I to be hit. He to strike. My scars were the emblem and symbol of our love.

What else makes you want to murder Ralph so late in time?

The train whistle shrieked. Night country rolled by.

And I recalled one spring when I came to school in a new tweed knicker suit and Ralph knocking me down, rolling me in snow and fresh brown mud. And Ralph laughing and me going home, shame-faced, covered with slime, afraid of a beating, to put on fresh dry clothes.

Yes! And what *else?*

Remember those toy clay statues you longed to collect from the Tarzan radio show? Statues of Tarzan and Kala the Ape and Numa the Lion, for just twenty-five cents?! Yes, yes! Beautiful! Even now, in memory, O the sound of the Ape man swinging through green jungles far away, ululating! But who had twenty-five cents in the middle of the Great Depression? No one.

Except Ralph Underhill.

And one day Ralph asked you if you wanted one of the statues.

Wanted! you cried. Yes! Yes!

That was the same week your brother in a strange seizure of love mixed with contempt gave you his old, but expensive, baseball-catcher's mitt.

"Well," said Ralph, "I'll give you my extra Tarzan statue if you'll give me that catcher's mitt."

Fool! I thought. The statue's worth twenty-five cents. The glove cost two dollars! No fair! Don't!

But I raced back to Ralph's house with the glove and gave it to him and he, smiling a worse contempt than my brother's, handed me the Tarzan statue and, bursting with joy, I ran home.

My brother didn't find out about his catcher's mitt and the statue for two weeks, and when he did he ditched me when we hiked out in farm country and left me lost because I was such a sap. "Tarzan statues! Baseball mitts!" he cried. "That's the last thing I *ever* give you!"

And somewhere on a country road I just lay down and wept and wanted to die but didn't know how to give up the final vomit that was my miserable ghost.

The thunder murmured.

The rain fell on the cold Pullman-car windows.

What *else?* Is that the list?

No. One final thing, more terrible than all the rest.

In all the years you went to Ralph's house to toss up small bits of gravel on his Fourth of July six-in-the-morning fresh dewy window or to call him forth for the arrival of dawn circuses in the cold fresh blue railroad stations in late June or late August, in all those years, never once did Ralph run to your house.

Never once in all the years did he, or anyone else, prove their friendship by coming by. The door never knocked. The window of your bedroom never faintly clattered and belled with a high-tossed confetti of small dusts and rocks.

And you always knew that the day you stopped going to Ralph's house, calling up in the morn, that would be the day your friendship ended.

You tested it once. You stayed away for a whole week. Ralph never called. It was as if you had died, and no one came to your funeral.

When you saw Ralph at school, there was no surprise, no query, not even the faintest lint of curiosity to be picked off your coat. Where *were* you, Doug? I need someone to beat. Where you *been*, Doug, I got no one to *pinch!*

Add all the sins up. But especially think on the last:

He never came to my house. He never sang up to my early-morning bed or tossed a wedding rice of gravel on the clear panes to call me down to joy and summer days.

And for this last thing, Ralph Underhill, I thought, sitting in the train at four in the morning, as the storm faded, and I found tears in my eyes, for this last and final thing, for that I shall kill you tomorrow night.

Murder, I thought, after thirty-six years. Why, God, you're madder than Ahab.

The train wailed. We ran cross-country like a mechanical Greek Fate carried by a black metal Roman Fury.

They say you can't go home again.

That is a lie.

If you are lucky and time it right, you arrive at sunset when the old town is filled with yellow light.

I got off the train and walked up through Green Town and looked at the courthouse, burning with sunset light. Every tree was hung with gold doubloons of color. Every roof and coping and bit of gingerbread was purest brass and ancient gold.

I sat in the courthouse square with dogs and old men until the sun had set and Green Town was dark. I wanted to savor Ralph Underhill's death.

No one in history had ever done a crime like this.

I would stay, kill, depart, a stranger among strangers.

How would anyone dare to say, finding Ralph Underhill's body on his doorstep, that a boy aged twelve, arriving on a kind of Time Machine train, traveled out of hideous self-contempt, had gunned down the Past? It was beyond all reason. I was safe in my pure insanity.

Finally, at eight-thirty on this cool October night, I walked across town, past the ravine.

I never doubted Ralph would still be there.

People do, after all, move away. . . .

I turned down Park Street and walked two hundred yards to a single streetlamp and looked across. Ralph Underhill's white two-story Victorian house waited for me.

And I could feel him *in* it.

He was there, forty-eight years old, even as I felt myself here, forty-eight, and full of an old and tired and self-devouring spirit.

I stepped out of the light, opened my suitcase, put

the pistol in my right-hand coat pocket, shut the case, and hid it in the bushes where, later, I would grab it and walk down into the ravine and across town to the train.

I walked across the street and stood before his house and it was the same house I had stood before thirty-six years ago. There were the windows upon which I had hurled those spring bouquets of rock in love and total giving. There were the sidewalks, spotted with firecracker burn marks from ancient July Fourths when Ralph and I had just blown up the whole damned world, shrieking celebrations.

I walked up on the porch and saw on the mailbox in small letters: UNDERHILL.

What if his wife answers?

No, I thought, he himself, with absolute Greek-tragic perfection, will open the door and take the wound and almost gladly die for old crimes and minor sins somehow grown to crimes.

I rang the bell.

Will he know me, I wondered, after all this time? In the instant before the first shot, *tell* him your name. He must know who it is.

Silence.

I rang the bell again.

The doorknob rattled.

I touched the pistol in my pocket, my heart hammering, but did not take it out.

The door opened.

Ralph Underhill stood there.

He blinked, gazing out at me.

"Ralph?" I said.

"Yes—?" he said.

We stood there, riven, for what could not have been more than five seconds. But, O Christ, many things happened in those five swift seconds.

I saw Ralph Underhill.

I saw him clearly.

And I had not seen him since I was twelve.

Then, he had towered over me to pummel and beat and scream.

Now he was a little old man.

I am five foot eleven.

But Ralph Underhill had not grown much from his twelfth year on.

The man who stood before me was no more than five feet two inches tall.

I *towered* over him.

I gasped. I stared. I saw more.

I was forty-eight years old.

But Ralph Underhill, forty-eight, had lost most of his hair, and what remained was threadbare gray, black and white. He looked sixty or sixty-five.

I was in good health.

Ralph Underhill was waxen pale. There was a knowledge of sickness in his face. He had traveled in some sunless land. He had a ravaged and sunken look. His breath smelled of funeral flowers.

All this, perceived, was like the storm of the night before, gathering all its lightnings and thunders into one bright concussion. We stood in the explosion.

So this is what I came for? I thought. This, then, is the truth. This dreadful instant in time. Not to pull out the weapon. *Not* to kill. No, no. But simply—

To see Ralph Underhill as he *is* in this hour.

That's all.

Just to be here, stand here, and look at him as he has become.

Ralph Underhill lifted one hand in a kind of gesturing wonder. His lips trembled. His eyes flew up and down my body, his mind measured this giant who shadowed his door. At last his voice, so small, so frail, blurted out:

"Doug—?"

I recoiled.

"Doug?" he gasped, "is that *you?*"

I hadn't expected that. People don't remember! They can't! Across the years? Why would he know, bother, summon up, recognize, call?

I had a wild thought that what had happened to Ralph Underhill was that after I left town, half of his life had collapsed. I had been the center of his world, someone to attack, beat, pummel, bruise. His whole life had cracked by my simple act of walking away thirty-six years ago.

Nonsense! Yet, some small crazed mouse of wisdom scuttered about my brain and screeched what it knew: You needed Ralph, but, *more!* he needed *you!* And you did the only unforgivable, the wounding, thing! You vanished.

"Doug?" he said again, for I was silent there on the porch with my hands at my sides. "Is that you?"

This was the moment I had come for.

At some secret blood level, I had always known I would not use the weapon. I had brought it with me, yes, but Time had gotten here before me, and age, and smaller, more terrible deaths. . . .

Bang.

Six shots through the heart.

But I didn't use the pistol. I only whispered the sound of the shots with my mouth. With each whisper, Ralph Underhill's face aged another ten years. By the time I reached the last shot he was one hundred and ten years old.

"Bang," I whispered. "Bang. Bang. Bang. Bang. Bang."

His body shook with the impact.

"You're dead. Oh, God, Ralph, you're dead."

I turned and walked down the steps and reached the street before he called:

"Doug, is that *you?*"

I did not answer, walking.

"Answer me?" he cried, weakly. "Doug! Doug Spaulding, is that you? Who is that? Who are you?"

I got my suitcase and walked down into the cricket night and darkness of the ravine and across the bridge and up the stairs, going away.

"Who is that?" I heard his voice wail a last time.

A long way off, I looked back.

All the lights were on all over Ralph Underhill's house. It was as if he had gone around and put them all on after I left.

On the other side of the ravine I stopped on the lawn in front of the house where I had been born.

Then I picked up a few bits of gravel and did the thing that had never been done, ever in my life.

I tossed the few bits of gravel up to tap that window where I had lain every morning of my first twelve years. I called my own name. I called me down in friendship to play in some long summer that no longer was.

I stood waiting just long enough for my other young self to come down to join me.

Then swiftly, fleeing ahead of the dawn, we ran out of Green Town and back, thank you, dear Christ, back toward Now and Today for the rest of my life.

# Punishment Without Crime

"You wish to kill your wife?" said the dark man at the desk.

"Yes. No . . . not exactly. I mean . . ."

"Name?"

"Hers or mine?"

"Yours."

"George Hill."

"Address?"

"Eleven South St. James, Glenview."

The man wrote this down, emotionlessly. "Your wife's name?"

"Katherine."

"Age?"

"Thirty-one."

Then came a swift series of questions. Color of hair, eyes, skin, favorite perfume, texture and size index. "Have you a dimensional photo of her? A tape recording of her voice? Ah, I see you do. Good. Now—"

An hour later, George Hill was perspiring.

"That's all." The dark man arose and scowled. "You still want to go through with it."

"Yes."

"Sign here."

He signed.

"You know this is illegal?"

"Yes."

"And that we're in no way responsible for what happens to you as a result of your request?"

"For God's sake!" cried George. "You've kept me long enough. Let's get on!"

The man smiled faintly. "It'll take nine hours to prepare the marionette of your wife. Sleep awhile, it'll help your nerves. The third mirror room on your left is unoccupied."

George moved in a slow numbness to the mirror room. He lay on the blue velvet cot, his body pressure causing the mirrors in the ceiling to whirl. A soft voice sang, "Sleep . . . sleep . . . sleep . . ."

George murmured, "Katherine, I didn't want to come here. You forced me into it. You made me do it. God, I wish I weren't here. I wish I could go back. I don't want to kill you."

The mirrors glittered as they rotated softly.

He slept.

He dreamed he was forty-one again, he and Katie running on a green hill somewhere with a picnic lunch, their helicopter beside them. The wind blew Katie's hair in golden strands and she was laughing. They kissed and held hands, not eating. They read poems; it seemed they were always reading poems.

Other scenes. Quick changes of color, in flight. He and Katie flying over Greece and Italy and Switzerland, in that clear, long autumn of 1997! Flying and never stopping!

And then—nightmare. Katie and Leonard Phelps. George cried out in his sleep. How had it happened? Where had Phelps sprung from? Why had he interfered? Why couldn't life be simple and good? Was it the difference in age? George touching fifty, and Katie so young, so very young. Why, why?

The scene was unforgettably vivid. Leonard Phelps and Katherine in a green park beyond the city. George himself appearing on a path only in time to see the kissing of their mouths.

The rage. The struggle. The attempt to kill Leonard Phelps.

More days, more nightmares.

George Hill awoke, weeping.

"Mr. Hill, we're ready for you now."

Hill arose clumsily. He saw himself in the high and now-silent mirrors, and he looked every one of his years. It had been a wretched error. Better men than he had taken young wives only to have them dissolve away in their hands like sugar crystals under water. He eyed himself, monstrously. A little too much stomach. A little too much chin. Somewhat too much pepper in the hair and not enough in the limbs . . .

The dark man led him to a room.

George Hill gasped. "This is *Katie's* room!"

"We try to have everything perfect."

"It *is*, to the last detail!"

George Hill drew forth a signed check for ten thousand dollars. The man departed with it.

The room was silent and warm.

George sat and felt for the gun in his pocket. A lot of money. But rich men can afford the luxury of cathartic murder. The violent unviolence. The death without death. The murder without murdering. He felt better. He was suddenly calm. He watched the door. This was a thing he had anticipated for six months and now it was to be ended. In a moment the beautiful robot, the stringless marionette, would appear, and . . .

"Hello, George."

"Katie!"

He whirled.

"Katie." He let his breath out.

She stood in the doorway behind him. She was dressed in a feather-soft green gown. On her feet were woven gold-twine sandals. Her hair was bright about her throat and her eyes were blue and clear.

He did not speak for a long while. "You're beautiful," he said at last, shocked.

"How else could I be?"

His voice was slow and unreal. "Let me look at you."

He put out his vague hands like a sleepwalker. His heart pounded sluggishly. He moved forward as if walking under a deep pressure of water. He walked around and around her, touching her.

"Haven't you seen enough of me in all these years?"

"Never enough," he said, and his eyes were filled with tears.

"What did you want to talk to me about?"

"Give me time, please, a little time." He sat down weakly and put his trembling hands to his chest. He blinked. "It's incredible. Another nightmare. How did they *make* you?"

"We're not allowed to talk of that; it spoils the illusion."

"It's magic!"

"Science."

Her touch was warm. Her fingernails were perfect as seashells. There was no seam, no flaw. He looked upon her. He remembered again the words they had read so often in the good days. *Thou art fair, my love. Behold, thou art fair; thou hast doves' eyes within thy locks. Thy lips are like a thread of scarlet. And thy speech is comedy. Thy two breasts are like two young roes that are twins, which feed among the lilies. There is no spot in thee.*

"George?"

"What?" His eyes were cold glass.

He wanted to kiss her lips.

*Honey and milk are under thy tongue.*

*And the smell of thy garments is like the smell of Lebanon.*

"George."

A vast humming. The room began to whirl.

"Yes, yes, a moment, a moment." He shook his humming head.

*How beautiful are thy feet with shoes, O prince's daughter! The joints of thy thighs are like jewels, the work of the hands of a cunning workman. . . .*

"How did they do it?" he cried. In so short a time. Nine hours, while he slept. Had they melted gold, fixed delicate watch springs, diamonds, glitter, confetti, rich rubies, liquid silver, copper thread? Had metal insects spun her hair? Had they poured yellow fire in molds and set it to freeze?

"No," she said. "If you talk that way, I'll go."

"Don't!"

"Come to business, then," she said, coldly. "You want to talk to me about Leonard."

"Give me time, I'll get to it."

"Now," she insisted.

He knew no anger. It had washed out of him at her appearance. He felt childishly dirty.

"Why did you come to see me?" She was not smiling.

"Please."

"I insist. Wasn't it about Leonard? You know I love him, don't you?"

"Stop it!" He puts his hands to his ears.

She kept at him. "You know, I spend all of my time with him now. Where you and I used to go, now Leonard and I stay. Remember the picnic green on Mount Verde? We were there last week. We flew to Athens a month ago, with a case of champagne."

He licked his lips. "You're not guilty, you're *not*." He rose and held her wrists. "You're fresh, you're not her. She's guilty, not you. You're different!"

"On the contrary," said the woman. "I *am* her. I can

act only as she acts. No part of me is alien to her. For all intents and purposes we are one."

"But you did not do what she has done!"

"I did all those things. I kissed him."

"You can't have, you're just born!"

"Out of her past and from your mind."

"Look," he pleaded, shaking her to gain her attention. "Isn't there some way, can't I—pay more money? Take you away with me? We'll go to Paris or Stockholm or any place you like!"

She laughed. "The marionettes only rent. They never sell."

"But I've money!"

"It was tried, long ago. It leads to insanity. It's not possible. Even this much is illegal, you *know* that. We exist only through governmental sufferance."

"All I want is to live with you, Katie."

"That can never be, because I am Katie, every bit of me is her. We do not want competition. Marionettes can't leave the premises; dissection might reveal our secrets. Enough of this. I warned you, we mustn't speak of these things. You'll spoil the illusion. You'll feel frustrated when you leave. You paid your money, now do what you came to do."

"I don't want to kill you."

"One part of you does. You're walling it in, you're trying not to let it out."

He took the gun from his pocket. "I'm an old fool, I should never have come. You're so beautiful."

"I'm going to see Leonard tonight."

"Don't talk."

"We're flying to Paris in the morning."

"You heard what I said!"

"And then to Stockholm." She laughed sweetly and caressed his chin. "My little fat man."

Something began to stir in him. His face grew pale. He knew what was happening. The hidden anger and revulsion and hatred in him were sending out faint pulses of thought. And the delicate telepathic web in her wondrous head was receiving the death impulse. The marionette. The invisible strings. He himself manipulating her body.

"Plump, odd little man, who once was so fair."

"Don't," he said.

"Old while I am only thirty-one, ah, George, you were blind, working years to give me time to fall in love again. Don't you think Leonard is lovely?"

He raised the gun blindly.

"Katie."

"*His head is as the most fine gold—*" she whispered.

"Katie, don't!" he screamed.

"*His locks are bushy and black as a raven, his hands are as gold rings set with the beryl!*"

How could she speak those words! It was in *his* mind, how could *she* mouth it!

"Katie, don't make me do this!"

"*His cheeks are as a bed of spices,*" she murmured, eyes closed, moving about the room softly. "*His belly is as bright ivory overlaid with sapphires; his legs are as pillars of marble—*"

"Katie!" he shrieked.

"*His mouth is most sweet—*"

One shot.

"*—this is my beloved—*"

Another shot.

She fell.

"Katie, Katie, Katie!"

Four more times he pumped bullets into her body.

She lay shuddering. Her senseless mouth clicked wide and some insanely warped mechanism had caused her to repeat again and again, "Beloved, beloved, beloved, beloved, beloved . . ."

George Hill fainted.

He awakened to a cool cloth on his brow.

"It's all over," said the dark man.

"Over?" George Hill whispered.

The dark man nodded.

George Hill looked weakly down at his hands. They had been covered with blood. When he fainted he had dropped to the floor. The last thing he remembered was the feeling of the real blood pouring upon his hands in a freshet.

His hands were now clean washed.

"I've got to leave," said George Hill.

"If you feel capable."

"I'm all right." He got up. "I'll go to Paris now, start over. I'm not to try to phone Katie or anything, am I?"

"Katie is dead."

"Yes. I killed her, didn't I? God, the blood, it was *real!*"

"We are proud of that touch."

He went down in the elevator to the street. It was raining, and he wanted to walk for hours. The anger and destruction were purged away. The memory was so terrible that he would never wish to kill again. Even if the real Katie were to appear before him now, he would only thank God, and fall senselessly to his knees. She was dead now. He had had his way. He had broken the law and no one would know.

The rain fell cool on his face. He must leave immediately, while the purge was in effect. After all, what was the use of such purges if one took up the old threads? The marionettes' function was primarily to prevent actual crime. If you wanted to kill, hit, or torture someone, you took it out on one of those unstringed automatons. It wouldn't do to return to the apartment now. Katie might be there. He wanted only to think of her as dead, a thing attended to in deserving fashion.

He stopped at the curb and watched the traffic flash by. He took deep breaths of the good air and began to relax.

"Mr. Hill?" said a voice at his elbow.

"Yes?"

A manacle was snapped to Hill's wrist. "You're under arrest."

"But—"

"Come along. Smith, take the other men upstairs, make the arrests!"

"You can't do this to me," said George Hill.

"For murder, yes, we can."

Thunder sounded in the sky.

It was eight-fifteen at night. It had been raining for ten days. It rained now on the prison walls. He put his hands out to feel the drops gather in pools on his trembling palms.

A door clanged and he did not move but stood with his hands in the rain. His lawyer looked up at him on his chair and said, "It's all over. You'll be executed tonight."

George Hill listened to the rain.

"She wasn't real. I didn't kill her."

"It's the law, anyhow. You remember. The others are sentenced, too. The president of Marionettes, Incorporated, will die at midnight. His three assistants will die at one. You'll go about one-thirty."

"Thanks," said George. "You did all you could. I guess it was murder, no matter how you look at it, image or not. The idea was there, the plot and the plan were there. It lacked only the real Katie herself."

"It's a matter of timing, too," said the lawyer. "Ten years ago you wouldn't have got the death penalty. Ten years from now you wouldn't, either. But they had to have an object case, a whipping boy. The use of marionettes has grown so in the last year it's fantastic. The public must be scared out of it, and scared badly. God knows where it would all wind up if it went on. There's the spiritual side of it, too, where does life begin or end? are the robots alive or dead? More than one church has been split up the seams on the question. If they aren't alive, they're the next thing to it; they react, they even think. You know the 'live robot' law that was passed two months ago; you come under that. Just bad timing, is all, bad timing."

"The government's right. I see that now," said George Hill.

"I'm glad you understand the attitude of the law."

"Yes. After all, they can't let murder be legal. Even if it's done with machines and telepathy and wax. They'd be hypocrites to let me get away with my crime. For it *was* a crime. I've felt guilty about it ever since. I've felt the need of punishment. Isn't that odd? That's how society gets to you. It makes you feel guilty even when you see no reason to be. . . ."

"I have to go now. Is there anything you want?"

"Nothing, thanks."

"Good-bye then, Mr. Hill."

The door shut.

George Hill stood up on the chair, his hands twisting together, wet, outside the windows bars. A red light burned in the wall suddenly. A voice came over the audio: "Mr. Hill, your wife is here to see you."

He gripped the bars.

She's dead, he thought.

"Mr. Hill?" asked the voice.

"She's dead. I killed her."

"Your wife is waiting in the anteroom, will you see her?"

"I saw her fall, I shot her, I saw her fall dead!"

"Mr. Hill, do you hear me?"

"Yes!" he shouted, pounding at the wall with his fists. "I hear you. I hear you! She's dead, she's dead, can't she let me be! I killed her, I won't see her, she's dead!"

A pause. "Very well, Mr. Hill," murmured the voice.

The red light winked off.

Lightning flashed through the sky and lit his face. He pressed his hot cheeks to the cold bars and waited, while the rain fell. After a long time, a door opened somewhere onto the street and he saw two caped figures emerge from the prison office below. They paused under an arc light and glanced up.

It was Katie. And beside her, Leonard Phelps.

"Katie!"

Her face turned away. The man took her arm. They hurried across the avenue in the black rain and got into a low car.

"Katie!" He wrenched at the bars. He screamed and beat and pulled at the concrete ledge. "She's alive! Guard! Guard! I saw her! She's not dead, I didn't kill her, now you can let me out! I didn't murder anyone, it's all a joke, a mistake, I saw her, I saw her! Katie, come back, tell them, Katie, say you're alive! Katie!"

The guards came running.

"You can't kill me! I didn't do anything! Katie's alive, I saw her!"

"We saw her, too, sir."

"But let me free, then! Let me free!" It was insane. He choked and almost fell.

"We've been through all that, sir, at the trial."

"It's not fair!" He leaped up and clawed at the window, bellowing.

The car drove away, Katie and Leonard inside it. Drove away to Paris and Athens and Venice and London next spring and Stockholm next summer and Vienna in the fall.

"Katie, come back, you can't *do* this to me!"

The red taillight of the car dwindled in the cold rain. Behind him, the guards moved forward to take hold of him while he screamed.

# Getting Through Sunday Somehow

Sunday in Dublin.

The words are Doom itself.

Sunday in Dublin.

Drop such words from a cliff and they never strike bottom. They just fall through emptiness toward five in the gray afternoon.

Sunday in Dublin. How to get through it somehow.

Sound the funeral bells. Yank the covers up over your ears. Hear the hiss of the black feathered wreath as it rustles, hung on your silent door. Listen to those empty streets below your hotel room waiting to gulp you if you venture forth before noon. Feel the mist sliding its wet flannel tongue under the window ledges, licking hotel roofs, its great bulk dripping of ennui.

Sunday, I thought. Dublin. The pubs shut tight save for a fleeting hour. The cinemas sold out two or three weeks in advance. Nothing to do but perhaps go stare at the uriny lions at the Phoenix Park Zoo, at the vultures looking like they'd fallen, covered with glue, into the rag-pickers' bin. Wander by the River Liffey, see the fog-colored waters. Wander in the alleys, see the Liffey-colored skies.

No, I thought wildly, stay in bed, wake me at sunset, feed me high tea, tuck me in again, good night, all!

But I staggered up, a hero, under the crashing blow of Sunday, shaved, and in a faint panic at noon considered the day ahead from the corner of my eye. There it lay, a deserted corridor of hours, colored like the upper side of my tongue on a dim morn. Even God must be bored with days like this, in northern lands. I could not resist thinking of Sicily, where any Sunday is a fete in regalia, a celebratory fireworks parade as springtime flocks of chickens and humans strut and pringle the warm pancake-batter alleys, waving their combs, their hands, their feet, tilting their sun-blazed eyes, while music in free gifts leaps or is thrown from each never-shut window.

But Dublin! Dublin! Ah, you great dead brute of a city! I thought, peering from my window at the snowed-on, sooted-over corpse. Here are two coins for your eyes!

Then I opened the door and stepped out into all of that criminal Sunday which awaited only me.

I shut another door. I stood in the deep silence of a Sabbath pub. I moved noiselessly to whisper for the best drink and stood a long while nursing my soul. Nearby, an old man was similarly engaged in finding the pattern of his life in the depths of his glass. Ten minutes must have passed, when, very slowly, the old man raised his head to stare deep beyond the fly specks on the mirror, beyond me, beyond himself.

"What have I done," he mourned, "for a single mortal soul this day? Nothing! And that's why I feel so terrible destroyed."

I waited.

"The older I get," said the man, "the less I do for

people. The less I do, the more I feel a prisoner at the bar. Smash and grab, that's me!"

"Well—" said I.

"No!" cried the old man. "It's an awesome responsibility when the world runs to hand you things. For an instance: sunsets. Everything pink and gold, looking like those melons they ship up from Spain. That's a gift, ain't it?"

"It is."

"Well, who do you thank for sunsets? And don't drag the Lord in the bar, now! Any remarks to Him are too quiet. I mean someone to grab and slap their back and say thanks for the fine early light this morn, boyo, or, much obliged for the look of them damn wee flowers by the road this day, and the grass laying about in the wind. Those are gifts, too, who'll deny it?"

"Not me," I said.

"Have you ever waked middle of the night and felt summer coming on for the first time, through the window, after the long cold? Did you shake your wife and tell her your gratitude? No, you lay there, a clod, chortling to yourself alone, you and the new weather! Do you see the pattern I'm at, now?"

"Clearly," I said.

"Then ain't you horribly guilty, yourself? Don't the burden make you hunchback? All the lovely things you got from life and no penny down? Ain't they hid in your dark flesh somewhere, lighting up your soul, them fine summers and easy falls, or maybe just the clean taste of stout here, all gifts, and you feeling the fool to go thank any mortal man for your fortune. What befalls chaps like us, I ask, who coin up all their gratitude for a lifetime, and spend none of it, misers that we be? One day, don't we crack down the beam and show the dry rot? Some night, don't we smother?"

"I never thought . . ."

"Think, man!" he cried. "Before it's too late. You're American, ain't you, and young? Got the same natural gifts as me? But for lack of humbly thanking someone somewhere somehow you're getting round in the shoulder and short in the breath. Act, man, before you're the walking dead!"

With this he lapsed quietly into the final half of his reverie, with the Guinness lapping a soft lace mustache slowly along his upper lip.

I walked from the pub into the Sunday weather.

I stood looking at the gray stone streets and the gray stone clouds, watching the frozen people trudge by exhaling gray funeral plumes from their wintry mouths, dressed in their smoke-colored suits and soot-black coats, and I felt the white grow out in my hair.

Days like this, I thought, all the things you never did catch up with you, unravel your laces, itch your beard. God help any man who hasn't paid his debts this day.

Drearily, I turned like a weathercock in a slow wind, started my remote feet back toward the hotel.

Right then, it happened.

I stopped. I stood very still. I listened.

For it seemed the wind had shifted and now blew from the west country and brought with it a prickling and tingling: the strum of a harp.

"Well," I whispered.

As if a cork had been pulled, all the heavy gray sea waters vanished roaring down a hole in my shoe; I felt my sadness go.

And around the corner I went.

And there sat a little woman, not half so big as her harp, her hands held out in the shivering strings like a child feeling a fine clear rain.

The harp threads flurried; the sounds dissolved like shudders of disturbed water nudging a shore. "Danny Boy" leaped out of the harp. "Wearin' of the Green" sprang after, full-clothed. Then "Limerick Is My Town, Sean Liam Is My Name" and "The Loudest Wake That Ever Was." The harp sound was the kind of thing you feel when champagne, poured in a full big glass, prickles your eyelids, sprays soft on your cheeks.

My mouth was pinned high at both corners. Spanish oranges bloomed in my cheeks. My breath fifed my nostrils. My feet minced, hidden, a secret dancing in my motionless shoes.

The harp played "Yankee Doodle."

Had the lady seen me stand near with my idiot fever? No, I thought, coincidence.

And then I turned sad again.

For look, I thought, she doesn't see her harp. She doesn't hear her music!

True. Her hands, all alone, jumped and frolicked on the air, picked and pringled the strings, two ancient spiders busy at webs quickly built, then, torn by wind, rebuilt. She let her fingers play abandoned, to themselves, while her face turned this way and that, as if she lived in a nearby house and need only glance out on occasion to see her hands had come to no harm.

"Ah . . ." My soul sighed in me.

Then:

Here's your chance! I almost shouted. Good God, of course!

But I held to myself and let her reap out the last full falling sheaves of "Yankee Doodle."

Then, heartbeat in throat, I said:

"You play beautifully."

One hundred pounds melted from my body.

The woman nodded and began "Summer on the Shore," her fingers weaving mantillas from mere breath.

"You play very beautifully indeed," I said.

Another seventy pounds fell from my limbs.

"When you play forty years," she said, "you don't notice."

"You play well enough to be in a theater."

"Be off with you!" Two sparrows pecked in the shuttling loom. "Why should I think of orchestras and bands?"

"It's indoors work," I said.

"My father," she said, while her hands went away and returned, "made this harp, played it fine, taught me how. God's sake, he said, keep out from under roofs!"

The old woman blinked, remembering. "Play out back, in front, around the sides of theaters, Da said, but don't play in where the music gets snuffed. Might as well harp in a coffin!"

"Doesn't this rain hurt your instrument?"

"It's inside places hurt harps with heat and steam, Da said. Keep it out, let it breathe, take fine tones and timbres from the air. Besides, Da said, when people buy tickets, each thinks it's in him to yell if you don't play up, down, sideways, for him alone. Shy off from that, Da said; they'll call you handsome one year, brute the next. Get where they'll pass on by; if they like your song—hurrah! Those that don't will run from your life. That way, girl, you'll meet just those who lean from natural bent in your direction. Why closet yourself with demon fiends when you can live in the streets' fresh wind with abiding angels? But I *do* go on. Ah, now, why?"

She peered at me for the first time, like someone come from a dark room, squinting.

"Who are you?" she asked. "You set my tongue loose! What're you up to?"

"Up to no good until a minute ago when I came around this corner," I said. "Ready to knock over Nelson's pillar. Ready to pick a theater queue and brawl along it, half weeping and half blasphemous . . ."

"I don't see you doing it." Her hands wove out another yard of song. "What changed your mind?"

"You," I said.

I might have fired a cannon in her face.

"Me?" she said.

"You picked the day up off the stones, gave it a whack, set it running with a yell again."

"I did that?"

For the first time, I heard a few notes missing from the tune.

"Or, if you like, those hands of yours that go about their work without your knowing."

"The clothes must be washed, so you wash them."

I felt the iron weights gather in my limbs.

"Don't!" I said. "Why should we, coming by, be happy with this thing, and not you?"

She cocked her head; her hands moved slower still.

"And why should you bother with the likes of *me*?"

I stood before her, and could I tell what the man told me in the lulling quiet of Dooley's Pub? Could I mention the hill of beauty that had risen to fill my soul through a lifetime, and myself with a toy sand-shovel doling it back to the world in dribs and drabs? Should I list all my debts to people on stages and silver screens who made me laugh or cry or just come alive, but no one in the dark theater to turn to and dare shout, "If you ever need help, I'm your friend!" Should I recall for her the man on a bus ten years before who chuckled so easy and light from the last seat that the sound of him melted everyone else to laughing warm and rollicking off out the doors, but with no one brave enough to pause and touch the man's arm and say, "Oh, man, you've favored us this night; Lord bless you!" Could I tell how she was just one part of a great account long owed and due? No, none of this could I tell. So I put it this way:

"Imagine something."

"I'm ready," she said.

"Imagine you're an American article writer, looking for material, far from home, wife, children, friends, in a hard winter, in a cheerless hotel, on a bad gray day with naught but broken glass, chewed tobacco, and sooty snow in your soul. Imagine you're walking in the damned winter streets and turn a corner, and there's this little woman with a golden harp and everything she plays is another season, autumn, spring, summer, coming, going in a free-for-all. And the ice melts, the fog lifts, the wind burns with June, and ten years shuck off your life. Imagine, if you please."

She stopped her tune.

She was shocked at the sudden silence.

"You *are* daft," she said.

"Imagine you're me," I said. "Going back to my hotel now. And on my way I'd like to hear anything, anything at all. Play. And when you play, walk off around the corner and listen."

She put her hands to the strings and paused, working her mouth. I waited. At last she sighed, she moaned. Then suddenly she cried:

"Go on!"

"What . . . ?"

"You've made me all thumbs! Look! You've spoilt it!"

"I just wanted to thank—"

"—me behind!" she cried. "What a clod, what a brute! Mind your business! Do your work! Let be, man! Ah, these poor fingers, ruint, ruint!"

She stared at them and at me with a terrible glaring fixity.

"Get!" she shouted.

I ran around the corner in despair.

There! I thought, you've done it! really done it! By thanks destroyed, that's her story. And yours, too, you must live with it! Fool, why didn't you keep your mouth shut?

I sank, I leaned, against a building. A minute must have ticked by.

Please, woman, I thought, come on. Play. Not for me. Play for yourself. Forget what I said! *Please.*

I heard a few faint, tentative harp whispers.

Another pause.

Then, when the wind blew again, it brought the sound of her very slow playing.

The song was an old one, and I knew the words. I said them to myself.

*Tread lightly to the music,*
*Nor bruise the tender grass,*

*Life passes in the weather*
*As the sand storms down the glass.*

Yes, I thought, go *on.*

*Drift easy in the shadows,*
*Bask lazy in the sun,*
*Give thanks for thirsts and quenches,*
*For dines and wines and wenches,*
*Give thought to life soon over,*
*Tread softly on the clover,*
*So bruise not any lover.*
*So exist from the living,*
*Salute and make thanksgiving,*
*Then sleep when all is done,*
*That sleep so dearly won.*

Why, I thought, how wise the old woman is.

*Tread lightly to the music.*

And I'd almost squashed her with praise.

*So bruise not any lover.*

And she was covered with bruises from my kind thoughtlessness.

But now with a song that taught more than I could say, she was soothing herself.

I waited until she was well into the third chorus before I walked by again, tipping my hat.

But her eyes were shut and she was listening to what her hands were up to, moving in the strings like the fresh hands of a very young girl who has first known rain and washes her palms in its clear waterfalls.

She had gone through caring not at all, and then caring too much, and was now busy caring just the right way.

The corners of her mouth were pinned up, gently.

A close call, I thought. Very close.

I left them like two friends met in the street, the harp and herself.

I ran for the hotel to thank her the only way I knew how: to do my own work and do it well.

But on the way I stopped at Dooley's.

The music was still being treaded lightly and the clover was still being treaded softly, and no lover at all was being bruised as I let the pub door hush and looked all around for the man whose hand I most wanted to shake.

# Drink Entire: Against the Madness of Crowds

It was one of those night that are so damned hot you lie flat out lost until 2:00 A.M., then sway upright, baste yourself with your own sour brine, and stagger down into the great bake-oven subway where the lost trains shriek in.

"Hell," whispered Will Morgan.

And hell it was, with a lost army of beast people wandering the night from the Bronx on out to Coney and back, hour on hour, searching for sudden inhalations of salt ocean wind that might make you gasp with Thanksgiving.

Somewhere, God, somewhere in Manhattan or beyond was a cool wind. By dawn, it *must* be found. . . .

"Damn!"

Stunned, he saw maniac tides of advertisements squirt by with toothpaste smiles, his own advertising ideas pursuing him the whole length of the hot night island.

The train groaned and stopped.

Another train stood on the opposite track.

Incredible. There in the open train window across the way sat Old Ned Amminger. Old? They were the same age, forty, but . . .

Will Morgan threw his window up.

"Ned, you son of a bitch!"

"Will, you bastard. You ride late like this often?"

"Every damn hot night since 1946!"

"Me, too! Glad to see you!"

"Liar!"

Each vanished in a shriek of steel.

God, thought Will Morgan, two men who hate each other, who work not ten feet apart grinding their teeth over the next step up the ladder, knock together in Dante's Inferno here under a melting city at 3:00 A.M. Hear our voices echo, fading:

"Liar . . . !"

Half an hour later, in Washington Square, a cool wind touched his brow. He followed it into an alley where . . .

The temperature dropped ten degrees.

"Hold on," he whispered.

The wind smelled of the Ice House when he was a boy and stole cold crystals to rub on his cheeks and stab inside his shirt with shrieks to kill the heat.

The cool wind led him down the alley to a small shop where a sign read:

MELISSA TOAD, WITCH
LAUNDRY SERVICE:
CHECK YOUR PROBLEMS HERE BY NINE A.M.
PICK THEM UP, FRESH-CLEANED, AT DUSK

There was a smaller sign:

SPELLS, PHILTRES AGAINST DREAD CLIMATES, HOT OR COLD. POTIONS TO INSPIRE EMPLOYERS AND ASSURE

PROMOTIONS. SALVES, UNGUENTS & MUMMY-DUSTS RENDERED DOWN FROM ANCIENT CORPORATION HEADS. REMEDIES FOR NOISE. EMOLLIENTS FOR GASEOUS OR POLLUTED AIRS. LOTIONS FOR PARANOID TRUCK DRIVERS. MEDICINES TO BE TAKEN BEFORE TRYING TO SWIM OFF THE NEW YORK DOCKS.

A few bottles were strewn in the display window, labeled:

PERFECT MEMORY.
BREATH OF SWEET APRIL WIND.
SILENCE AND THE TREMOR OF FINE BIRDSONG.

He laughed and stopped.

For the wind blew cool and creaked a door. And again there was the memory of frost from the white Ice House grottoes of childhood, a world cut from winter dreams and saved on into August.

"Come in," a voice whispered.

The door glided back.

Inside, a cold funeral awaited him.

A six-foot-long block of clear dripping ice rested like a giant February remembrance upon three sawhorses.

"Yes," he murmured. In his hometown-hardware-store window, a magician's wife, MISS I. SICKLE, had been stashed in an immense rectangle of ice melted to fit her calligraphy. There she slept the nights away, a Princess of Snow. Midnights, he and other boys snuck out to see her smile in her cold crystal sleep. They stood half the summer nights staring, four or five fiery-furnace boys of some fourteen years, hoping their red-hot gaze might melt the ice. . . .

The ice had never melted.

"Wait," he whispered. "Look . . ."

He took one more step within this dark night shop.

Lord, yes. There, in *this* ice! Weren't those the outlines where, only moments ago, a woman of snow napped away in cool night dreams? Yes. The ice was hollow and curved and lovely. But . . . the woman was gone. Where?

"Here," whispered the voice.

Beyond the bright cold funeral, shadows moved in a far corner.

"Welcome. Shut the door."

He sensed that she stood not far away in shadows. Her flesh, if you could touch it, would be cool, still fresh from her time within the dripping tomb of snow. If he just reached out his hand—

"What are you doing here?" her voice asked, gently.

"Hot night. Walking. Riding. Looking for a cool wind. I think I need help."

"You've come to the right place."

"But this is *mad!* I don't believe in psychiatrists. My friends hate me because I say Tinkerbell *and* Freud died twenty years back, with the circus. I don't believe in astrologers, numerologists, or palmistry quacks—"

"I don't read palms. But . . . give me your hand."

He put his hand out into the soft darkness.

Her fingers tapped his. It felt like the hand of a small girl who had just rummaged an icebox. He said:

"Your sign reads MELISSA TOAD, WITCH. What would a Witch be doing in New York in the summer of 1974?"

"You ever know a city needed a Witch more than New York does this year?"

"Yes. We've gone mad. But, *you?*"

"A Witch is born out of the true hungers of her time," she said. "I was born out of New York. The things that are most wrong here summoned me. Now you come, not knowing, to find me. Give me you other hand."

Though her face was only a ghost of cool flesh in the shadows, he felt her eyes move over his trembling palm.

"Oh, why did you wait so *long?*" she mourned. "It's almost too late."

"Too late for what?"

"To be saved. To take the gift that I can give."

His heart pounded. "*What* can you give me?"

"Peace," she said. "Serenity. Quietness in the midst of bedlam. I am a child of the poisonous wind that copulated with the East River on an oil-slick, garbage-infested midnight. I turn about on my own parentage. I inoculate against those very biles that brought me to light. I am a serum born of venoms. I am the antibody of all Time. I am the Cure. You die of the City, do you not? Manhattan is your punisher. Let me be your shield."

"How?"

"You would be my pupil. My protection could encircle you, like an invisible pack of hounds. The subway train would never violate your ear. Smog would never blight your lung or nostril or fever your vision. I could teach your tongue, at lunch, to taste the rich fields of Eden in the merest cut-rate too-ripe frankfurter. Water, sipped from your office cooler, would be a rare wine of a fine family. Cops, when you called, would answer. Taxis, off-duty rushing nowhere, would stop if you so much as blinked one eye. Theater tickets would appear if you stepped to a theater window. Traffic signals would change, at high noon, mind you! if you dared to drive your car from Fifty-eighth down to the Square, and not one light red. Green all the way, if you go with me.

"If you go with me, our apartment will be a shadowed jungle glade full of bird cries and love calls from the first hot sour day of June till the last hour after Labor Day when the living dead, heat-beat, go mad on stopped trains coming back from the sea. Our rooms will be filled with crystal chimes. Our kitchen an Eskimo hut in July where we might share out a provender of Popsicles made of Mumm's and Château Lafite Rothschild. Our larder?—fresh apricots in August or February. Fresh orange juice each morning, cold milk at breakfast, cool kisses at four in the afternoon, my mouth always the flavor of chilled peaches, my body the taste of rimed plums. The flavor begins at the elbow, as Edith Wharton said.

"Any time you want to come home from the office the middle of a dreadful day, I will call your boss and it will be so. Soon after, you will be the boss and come home, anyway, for cold chicken, fruit wine punch, and me. Summer in the Virgin Isles. Autumns so ripe with promise you will indeed go lunatic in the right way. Winters, of course, will be the reverse. I will be your hearth. Sweet dog, lie there. I will fall upon you like snowflakes.

"In sum, everything will be given you. I ask little in return. Only your soul."

He stiffened and almost let go of her hand.

"Well, isn't that what you *expected* me to demand?" She laughed. "But souls can't be sold. They can only be lost and never found again. Shall I tell you what I really want from you?"

"Tell."

"Marry me," she said.

Sell me your soul, he thought, and did not say it.

But she read his eyes. "Oh, dear," she said. "Is that *so* much to ask? For all I give?"

"I've got to think it over!"

Without noticing, he had moved back one step.

Her voice was very sad. "If you have to think a thing over, it will never be. When you finish a book you know if you like it, yes? At the end of a play you are awake or asleep, yes? Well, a beautiful woman is a beautiful woman, isn't she, and a good life a good life?"

"Why won't you come out in the light? How do I know you're beautiful?"

"You can't know unless you step into the dark. Can't you tell by my voice? No? Poor man. If you don't trust me now, you can't have me, ever."

"I need time to think! I'll come back tomorrow night! What can twenty-four hours mean?"

"To someone your age, everything."

"I'm only forty!"

"I speak of your soul, and *that* is late."

"Give me one more night!"

"You'll take it, anyway, at your own risk."

"Oh, God, oh, God, oh, God, God," he said, shutting his eyes.

"I wish He could help you right now. You'd better go. You're an ancient child. Pity. Pity. Is your mother alive?"

"Dead ten years."

"No, alive," she said. He backed off toward the door and stopped, trying to still his confused heart, trying to move his leaden tongue:

"How long have you been in this place?"

She laughed, with the faintest touch of bitterness.

"Three summers now. And, in those three years, only six men have come into my shop. Two ran immediately. Two stayed awhile but left. One came back a second time, and vanished. The sixth man finally had to admit, after three visits, he didn't Believe. You see, no one Believes a really all-encompassing and protective love when they see it clear. A farmboy might have stayed forever, in his simplicity, which is rain and wind and seed. A New Yorker? Suspects everything.

"Whoever, whatever, you are, O good sir, stay and milk the cow and put the fresh milk in the dim cooling shed under the shade of the oak tree which grows in my attic. Stay and pick the watercress to clean your teeth. Stay in the North Pantry with the scent of persimmons and kumquats and grapes. Stay and stop my tongue so I can cease talking this way. Stay and stop my mouth so I can't breathe. Stay, for I am weary of speech and must need love. Stay. Stay."

So ardent was her voice, so tremulous, so gentle, so sweet, that he knew he was lost if he did not run.

"Tomorrow night!" he cried.

His shoe struck something. There on the floor lay a sharp icicle fallen from the long block of ice.

He bent, seized the icicle, and ran.

The door *slammed*. The lights blinked out. Rushing, he could not see the sign: MELISSA TOAD, WITCH.

Ugly, he thought, running. A beast, he thought, she *must* be a beast and ugly. Yes, that's it! Lies! All of it, lies! She—

He collided with someone.

In the midst of the street, they gripped, they held, they stared.

Ned Amminger! My God, it was Old Ned!

It was four in the morning, the air still white-hot. And here was Ned Amminger sleepwalking after cool winds, his clothes scrolled on his hot flesh in rosettes, his face dripping sweat, his eyes dead, his feet creaking in their hot baked leather shoes.

They swayed in the moment of collision.

A spasm of malice shook Will Morgan. He seized Old Ned Amminger, spun him about, and pointed him into the dark alley. Far off deep in there, had that shop-window light blinked *on* again? Yes!

"Ned! *That* way! Go *there!*"

Heat-blinded, dead-weary Old Ned Amminger stumbled off down the alley.

"Wait!" cried Will Morgan, regretting his malice.

But Amminger was gone.

In the subway, Will Morgan tasted the icicle.

It was Love. It was Delight. It was Woman.

By the time his train roared in, his hands were empty, his body rusted with perspiration. And the sweet taste in his mouth? Dust.

Seven A.M. and no sleep.

Somewhere a huge blast furnace opened its door and burned New York to ruins.

Get up, thought Will Morgan. Quick! Run to the Village!

For he remembered that sign:

LAUNDRY SERVICE: CHECK YOUR PROBLEMS
HERE BY NINE A.M.
PICK THEM UP, FRESH-CLEANED, AT NIGHT

He did not go to the Village. He rose, showered, and went off into the furnace to lose his job forever.

He knew this as he rode up in the raving-hot elevator with Mr. Binns, the sunburned and furious personnel manager. Binns's eyebrows were jumping, his mouth worked over his teeth with unspoken curses. Beneath his suit, you could feel porcupines of boiled hair needling to the surface. By the time they reached the fortieth floor, Binns was anthropoid.

Around them, employees wandered like an Italian army coming to attend a lost war.

"Where's Old Amminger?" asked Will Morgan, staring at an empty desk.

"Called in sick. Heat prostration. Be here at noon," someone said.

Long before noon the water cooler was empty, and the air-conditioning system?—committed suicide at 11:32. Two hundred people became raw beasts chained to desks by windows which had been invented not to open.

At one minute to twelve, Mr. Binns, over the intercom, told them to line up by their desks. They lined up. They waited, swaying. The temperature stood at ninety-seven. Slowly, Binns began to stalk down the long line. A white-hot sizzle of invisible flies hung about him.

"All right, ladies and gentlemen," he said. "You all know there is a recession, no matter how happily the President of the United States put it. I would rather knife you in the stomach than stab you in the back. Now, as I move down the line, I will nod and whisper, 'You.' To those of you who hear this single word, turn, clean out your desks, and be gone. Four weeks' severance pay awaits you on the way out. Hold on! Someone's missing!"

"Old Ned Amminger," said Will Morgan, and bit his tongue.

"*Old* Ned?" said Mr. Binns, glaring. "Old? *Old?*"

Mr. Binns and Ned Amminger were exactly the same age.

Mr. Binns waited, ticking.

"Ned," said Will Morgan, strangling on self-curses, "should be here—"

"Now," said a voice.

They all turned.

At the far end of the line, in the door, stood Old Ned or Ned Amminger. He looked at the assembly of lost souls, read destruction in Binns's face, flinched, but then slunk into line next to Will Morgan.

"All right," said Binns. "Here goes."

He began to move, whisper, move, whisper. Two people, four, then six turned to clean out their desks.

Will Morgan took a deep breath, held it, waited.

Binns came to a full stop in front of him.

Don't say it? thought Morgan. Don't!

"You," whispered Binns.

Morgan spun about and caught hold of his heaving desk. *You,* the word cracked in his head, *you!*

Binns stepped to confront Ned Amminger.

"Well, *old* Ned," he said.

Morgan, eyes shut, thought: Say it, say it to him, you're fired, Ned, *fired!*

"Old Ned," said Binns, lovingly.

Morgan shrank at the strange, the friendly, the sweet sound of Binns's voice.

An idle South Seas wind passed softly on the air. Morgan blinked and stood up, sniffing. The sun-blasted room was filled with scent of surf and cool white sand.

"Ned, why dear old Ned," said Mr. Binns, gently.

Stunned, Will Morgan waited. I am mad, he thought.

"Ned," said Mr. Binns, gently. "Stay with us. Stay on."

Then, swiftly: "That's all, everyone. Lunch!"

And Binns was gone and the wounded and dying were leaving the field. And Will Morgan turned at last to look full at Old Ned Amminger, thinking, Why, God, *why?*

And got his answer . . .

Ned Amminger stood there, not old, not young, but somehow in-between. And he was not the Ned Amminger who had leaned crazily out a hot train window last midnight or shambled in Washington Square at four in the morning.

This Ned Amminger stood quietly, as if hearing far green country sounds, wind and leaves and an amiable time which wandered in a fresh lake breeze.

The perspiration had dried on his fresh pink face. His eyes were not bloodshot but steady, blue and quiet. He was an island oasis in this dead and unmoving sea of desks and typewriters which might start up and scream like electric insects. He stood watching the walking-dead depart. And he cared not. He was kept in a splendid and beautiful isolation within his own calm cool beautiful skin.

"No!" cried Will Morgan, and fled.

He didn't know where he was going until he found himself in the men's room frantically digging in the wastebasket.

He found what he knew he would find, a small bottle with the label:

DRINK ENTIRE: AGAINST THE MADNESS OF CROWDS.

Trembling, he uncorked it. There was the merest cold blue drop left inside. Swaying by the shut hot window, he tapped it to his tongue.

In the instant, his body felt as if he had leaped into a tidal wave of coolness. His breath gusted out in a fount of crushed and savored clover.

He gripped the bottle so hard it broke. He gasped, watching the blood.

The door opened. Ned Amminger stood there, looking in. He stayed only a moment, then turned and went out. The door shut.

A few moments later, Morgan, with the junk from his desk rattling in his briefcase, went down in the elevator.

Stepping out, he turned to thank the operator.

His breath must have touched the operator's face.

The operator smiled.

A wild, an incomprehensible, a loving, a *beautiful* smile!

The lights were out at midnight in the little alley, in the little shop. There was no sign in the window which said MELISSA TOAD, WITCH. There were no bottles.

He beat on the door for a full five minutes, to no answer. He kicked the door for another two minutes.

And at last, with a sigh, not wanting to, the door opened.

A very tired voice said: "Come in."

Inside he found the air only slightly cool. The huge ice slab, in which he had seen the phantom shape of a lovely woman, had dwindled, had lost a good half of its weight, and now was dripping steadily to ruin.

Somewhere in the darkness, the woman waited for him. But he sensed that she was clothed now, dressed and packed, ready to leave. He opened his mouth to cry out, to reach, but her voice stopped him:

"I warned you. You're too late."

"It's never too late!" he said.

"Last night it wouldn't have been. But in the last twenty hours, the last little thread snapped in you. I feel. I know. I tell. It's gone, gone, gone."

"What's gone, God damn it?"

"Why, your soul, of course. Gone. Eaten up. Digested. Vanished. You're empty. Nothing there."

He saw her hand reach out of darkness. It touched at his chest. Perhaps he imagined that her fingers passed through his ribs to probe about his lights, his lungs, his beating and pitiful heart.

"Oh, yes, gone," she mourned. "How sad. The city unwrapped you like a candy bar and ate you all up. You're nothing but a dusty milk bottle left on a tenement porch, a spider building a nest across the top. Traffic din pounded your marrow to dust. Subway sucked your breath like a cat sucks the soul of a babe. Vacuum cleaners got your brain. Alcohol dissolved the rest. Typewriters and computers took your final dregs in and out their tripes, printed you on paper, punched you in confettis, threw you down a sewer vent. TV scribbled you in nervous tics on old ghost screens. Your final bones will be carried off by a big angry bulldog crosstown bus holding you munched in its big rubber-lipped mouth door."

"No!" he cried. "I've changed my mind! Marry me! Marry—"

His voice cracked the ice tomb. It shattered on the floor behind him. The shape of the beautiful woman melted into the floor. Spinning about, he plunged into darkness.

He fell against the wall just as a panel slammed shut and locked.

It was no use screaming. He was alone.

At dusk in July, a year later, in the subway, he saw Ned Amminger for the first time in 365 days.

In all the grind and ricochet and pour of fiery lava as trains banged through, taking a billion souls to hell, Amminger stood as cool as mint leaves in green rain. Around him wax people melted. He waded in his own private trout stream.

"Ned!" cried Will Morgan, running up to seize his hand and pump it. "Ned, Ned! The best friend I ever had!"

"Yes, that's true, isn't it?" said young Ned, smiling.

And oh God, how true it was! Dear Ned, fine Ned,

friend of a lifetime! Breathe upon me, Ned! Give me your life's breath!

"You're president of the company, Ned! I heard!"

"Yes. Come along home for a drink?"

In the raging heat, a vapor of iced lemonade rose from his creamy fresh suit as they looked for a cab. In all the curses, yells, horns, Ned raised his hand.

A cab pulled up. They drove in serenity.

At the apartment house, in the dusk, a man with a gun stepped from the shadows.

"Give me everything," he said.

"Later," said Ned, smiling, breathing a scent of fresh summer apples upon the man.

"Later." The man stepped back to let them pass. "Later."

On the way up in the elevator, Ned said, "Did you know I'm married? Almost a year. Fine wife."

"Is she," said Will Morgan, and stopped, ". . . beautiful?"

"Oh, yes. You'll love her. You'll love the apartment."

Yes, thought Morgan; a green glade, crystal chimes, cool grass for a carpet. I know, I know.

They stepped out into an apartment that was indeed a tropic isle. Young Ned poured huge goblets of iced champagne.

"What shall we drink to?"

"To you, Ned. To your wife. To me. To midnight, tonight."

"Why midnight?"

"When I go back down to that man who is waiting downstairs with his gun. That man you said 'later' to. And he agreed 'later.' I'll be there alone with him. Funny, ridiculous, funny. And *my* breath just ordinary breath, not smelling of melons or pears. And him waiting all those long hours with his sweaty gun, irritable with heat. What a grand joke. Well . . . a toast?"

"A toast!"

They drank.

At which moment, the wife entered. She heard each

of them laughing in a different way, and joined in their laughter.

But her eyes, when she looked at Will Morgan, suddenly filled with tears.

And he knew whom she was weeping for.

# Interval in Sunlight

They moved into the Hotel de Las Flores on a hot green afternoon in late October. The inner patio was blazing with red and yellow and white flowers, like flames, which lit their small room. The husband was tall and black-haired and pale and looked as if he had driven ten thousand miles in his sleep; he walked through the tile patio, carrying a few blankets, he threw himself on the small bed of the small room with an exhausted sigh and lay there. While he closed his eyes, his wife, about twenty-four, with yellow hair and horn-rim glasses, smiling at the manager, Mr. Gonzales, hurried in and out from the room to the car. First she carried two suitcases, then a typewriter, thanking Mr. Gonzales, but steadily refusing his help. And then she carried in a huge packet of Mexican masks they had picked up in the lake town of Patzcuaro, and then out to the car again and again for more small cases and packages, and even an extra tire which they were afraid some native might roll off down the cobbled street during the night. Her face pink from the exertion, she hummed as she locked the car, checked the windows, and ran back to the room where her husband lay, eyes closed, on one of the twin beds.

"Good God," he said, without opening his eyes, "this is one hell of a bed. Feel it. I told you to pick one with a Simmons mattress." He gave the bed a weary slap. "It's as hard as a rock."

"I don't speak Spanish," said the wife, standing there, beginning to look bewildered. "You should have come in and talked to the landlord yourself."

"Look," he said, opening his gray eyes just a little and turning his head, "I've done all the driving on this trip. You just sit there and look at the scenery. You're supposed to handle the money, the lodgings, the gas and oil, and all that. This is the second place we've hit where you got hard beds."

"I'm sorry," she said, still standing, beginning to fidget.

"I like to at least sleep nights, that's all I ask."

"I said I was sorry."

"Didn't you even *feel* the beds?"

"They looked all right."

"You've got to feel them." He slapped the bed and punched it at his side.

The woman turned to her own bed and sat on it, experimentally. "It feels all right to me."

"Well, it isn't."

"Maybe my bed is softer."

He rolled over tiredly and reached out to punch the other bed. "You can have this one if you want," she said, trying to smile.

"That's hard, too," he said, sighing, and fell back and closed his eyes again.

No one spoke, but the room was turning cold, while outside the flowers blazed in the green shrubs and the sky was immensely blue. Finally, she rose and grabbed the typewriter and suitcase and turned toward the door.

"Where're you going?" he said.

"Back out to the car," she said. "We're going to find another place."

"Put it down," said the man. "I'm tired."

"We'll find another place."

"Sit down, we'll stay here tonight, my God, and move tomorrow."

She looked at all the boxes and crates and luggage, the clothes, and the tire, her eyes flickering. She put the typewriter down.

"Damn it!" she cried, suddenly. "You can have the mattress off my bed. I'll sleep on the springs."

He said nothing.

"You can have the mattress off my bed," she said. "Only don't talk about it. Here!" She pulled the blanket off and yanked at the mattress.

"That might be better," he said, opening his eyes, seriously.

"You can have both mattresses, my God, I can sleep on a bed of nails!" she cried. "Only stop yapping."

"I'll manage." He turned his head away. "It wouldn't be fair to you."

"It'd be plenty fair just for you to keep quiet about the bed; it's not that hard, good God, you'll sleep if you're tired. Jesus God, Joseph!"

"Keep your voice down," said Joseph. "Why don't you go find out about Paricutin volcano?"

"I'll go in a minute." She stood there, her face red.

"Find out what the rates are for a taxi out there and a horse up the mountain to see it, and look at the sky; if the sky's blue that means the volcano isn't erupting today, and don't let them gyp you."

"I guess I can do that."

She opened the door and stepped out and shut the door and *Señor* Gonzales was there. Was everything all right? he wished to know.

She walked past the town windows, and smelled the soft charcoal air. Beyond the town all of the sky was blue except north (or east or west, she couldn't be certain) where the huge broiling black cloud rose up from the terrible volcano. She looked at it with a small tremoring inside. Then she sought out a large fat taxi driver and the arguments began. The price started at sixty pesos and dwindled rapidly, with expressions of mournful defeat upon the buck-toothed fat man's face, to thirty-seven pesos. So! He was to come at three tomorrow afternoon, did he understand? That would give them time to drive out through the gray snows of land where the flaking lava ash had fallen to make a great dusty winter for mile after mile, and arrive at the volcano as the sun was setting. Was this very clear?

"*¡Sí, señora, esta es muy claro, sí!*"

"*Bueno.*" She gave him their hotel room number and bade him good-bye.

She idled into little lacquer shops, alone; she opened the little lacquer boxes and sniffed the sharp scent of camphor wood and cedar and cinnamon. She watched the craftsmen, enchanted, razor blades flashing in the sun, cutting the flowery scrolls and filling these patterns with red and blue color. The town flowed about her like a silent slow river and she immersed herself in it, smiling all of the time, and not even knowing she smiled.

Suddenly she looked at her watch. She'd been gone half an hour. A look of panic crossed her face. She ran a few steps and then slowed to a walk again, shrugging.

As she walked in through the tiled cool corridors, under the silvery tin candelabra on the adobe walls, a caged bird fluted high and sweet, and a girl with long soft dark hair sat at a piano painted sky blue and played a Chopin nocturne.

She looked at the windows of their room, the shades pulled down. Three o'clock of a fresh afternoon. She saw a soft-drinks box at the end of the patio and bought four bottles of Coke. Smiling, she opened the door to their room.

"It certainly took you long enough," he said, turned on his side toward the wall.

"We leave tomorrow afternoon at three," she said.

"How much?"

She smiled at his back, the bottles cold in her arms. "Only thirty-seven pesos."

"Twenty pesos would have done it. You can't let these Mexicans take advantage of you."

"I'm richer than they are; if anyones *deserves* being taken advantage of, it's us."

"That's not the idea. They *like* to bargain."

"I feel like a bitch, doing it."

"The guide book says they double their price and expect you to halve it."

"Let's not quibble over a dollar."

"A dollar is a dollar."

"I'll pay the dollar from my own money," she said. "I brought some cold drinks—do you want one?"

"What've you got?" He sat up in bed.

"Cokes."

"Well, you know I don't like Cokes much; take two of those back, will you, and get some Orange Crush?"

"Please?" she said, standing there.

"Please," he said, looking at her. "Is the volcano active?"

"Yes."

"Did you ask?"

"No, I looked at the sky. Plenty of smoke."

"You should have asked."

"The damn sky is just exploding with it."

"But how do we know it's good tomorrow?"

"We don't know. If it's not, we put it off."

"I guess that's right." He lay down again.

She brought back two bottles of Orange Crush.

"It's not very cold," he said, drinking it.

They had supper in the patio: sizzling steak, green peas, a plate of Spanish rice, a little wine, and spiced peaches for dessert.

As he napkined his mouth, he said, casually, "Oh, I meant to tell you. I've checked your figures on what I owe you for the last six days, from Mexico City to here.

You say I owe you one hundred twenty-five pesos, or about twenty-five American dollars, right?"

"Yes."

"I make it I owe you only twenty-two."

"I don't think that's possible," she said, still working on her spiced peaches with a spoon.

"I added the figures twice."

"So did I."

"I think you added them wrong."

"Perhaps I did." She jarred the chair back suddenly. "Let's go check."

In the room, the notebook lay open under the lighted lamp. They checked the figures together. "You see," said he, quietly. "You're three dollars off. How did that happen?"

"It just happened. I'm sorry."

You're one hell of a bookkeeper."

"I do my best."

"Which isn't very good. I thought you could take a little responsibility."

"I try damned hard."

"You forgot to check the air in the tires, you get hard beds, you lose things, you lost a key in Acapulco, to the car trunk, you lost the air-pressure gauge, and you can't keep books. I have to drive—"

"I know, I know, you have to drive all day, and you're tired, and you just got over a strep infection in Mexico City, and you're afraid it'll come back and you want to take it easy on your heart, and the least I could do is to keep my nose clean and the arithmetic neat. I know it all by heart. I'm only a writer, and I admit I've got big feet."

"You won't make a very good writer this way," he said. "It's such a simple thing, addition."

"I didn't do it on purpose!" she cried, throwing the pencil down. "Hell! I wish I *had* cheated you now. I wish I'd done a lot of things now. I wish I'd lost that air-pressure gauge on purpose, I'd have some pleasure in thinking about it and knowing I did it to spite you, anyway. I wish I'd picked these beds for their hard mattresses, then I could laugh in my sleep tonight, thinking how hard they are for you to sleep on, I wish I'd done *that* on purpose. And now I wish I'd thought to fix the books. I could enjoy laughing about that, too."

"Keep your voice down," he said, as to a child.

"I'll be god-damned if I'll keep my voice down."

"All I want to know now is how much money you have in the kitty."

She put her trembling hands in her purse and brought out all the money. When he counted it, there was five dollars missing.

"Not only do you keep poor books, overcharging me on some item or other, but now there's five dollars gone from the kitty," he said. "Where'd it go?"

"I don't know. I must have forgotten to put it down, or if I did, I didn't say what for. Good God, I don't want to add this damned list again. I'll pay what's missing out of my own allowance to keep everyone happy. Here's five dollars! Now, let's go out for some air, it's hot in here."

She jerked the door wide and she trembled with a rage all out of proportion to the facts. She was hot and shaking and stiff and she knew her face was very red and her eyes bright, and when *Señor* Gonzales bowed to them and wished them a good evening, she had to smile stiffly in return.

"Here," said her husband, handing her the room key. "And don't, for God's sake, lose it."

The band was playing in the green zocalo. It hooted and blared and tooted and screamed up on the bronze-scrolled bandstand. The square was bloomed full with people and color, men and boys walking one way around the block, on the pink and blue tiles, women and girls walking the other way, flirting their dark olive eyes at one another, men holding each other's elbows and talking earnestly between meetings, women and girls twined like ropes of flowers, sweetly scented, blowing in a summer night wind over the cooling tile designs, whispering, past the vendors of cold drinks and tamales and enchiladas. The band precipitated "Yankee Doodle" once, to the delight of the blonde woman with the horn-rim glasses, who smiled wildly and turned to her husband. Then the band hooted "*La Cumparsita*" and "*La Paloma Azul*," and she felt a good warmth and began to sing a little, under her breath.

"Don't act like a tourist," said her husband.

"I'm just enjoying myself."

"Don't be a damned fool, is all I ask."

A vendor of silver trinkets shuffled by. "*¿Señor?*"

Joseph looked them over, while the band played, and held up one bracelet, very intricate, very exquisite. "How much?"

"*Veinte pesos, señor.*"

"Ho ho," said the husband, smiling. "I'll give you five for it," in Spanish.

"Five," replied the man in Spanish. "I would starve."

"Don't bargain with him," said the wife.

"Keep out of this," said the husband, smiling. To the vendor, "Five pesos, *señor*."

"No, no, I would lose money. My last price is ten pesos."

"Perhaps I could give you six," said the husband. "No more than that."

The vendor hesitated in a kind of numbed panic as the husband tossed the bracelet back on the red velvet tray and turned away. "I am no longer interested. Good night."

"*¡Señor!* Six pesos, it is yours!"

The husband laughed. "Give him six pesos, darling."

She stiffly drew forth her wallet and gave the vendor some peso bills. The man went away. "I hope you're satisfied," she said.

"Satisfied?" Smiling, he flipped the bracelet in the

palm of his pale hand. "For a dollar and twenty-five cents I buy a bracelet that sells for thirty dollars in the States!"

"I have something to confess," she said. "I gave that man ten pesos."

"What!" The husband stopped laughing.

"I put a five-peso note in with those one-peso bills. Don't worry, I'll take it out of my own money. It won't go on the bill I present you at the end of the week."

He said nothing, but dropped the bracelet in his pocket. He looked at the band thundering into the last bars of "*Ay, Jalisco.*" Then he said, "You're a fool. You'd let these people take all your money."

It was her turn to step away a bit and not reply. She felt rather good. She listened to the music.

"I'm going back to the room," he said. "I'm tired."

"We only drove a hundred miles from Patzcuaro."

"My throat is a little raw again. Come on."

They moved away from the music and the walking, whispering, laughing people. The band played the "Toreador Song." The drums thumped like great dull hearts in the summery night. There was a smell of papaya in the air, and green thicknesses of jungle and waters.

"I'll walk you back to the room and come back myself," she said. "I want to hear the music."

"Don't be naïve."

"I like it, damn it, I like it, it's good music. It's not fake, it's real, or as real as anything ever gets in this world, that's why I like it."

"When I don't feel well, I don't expect to have you out running around the town alone. It isn't fair you see things I don't."

They turned in at the hotel and the music was still fairly loud. "If you want to walk by yourself, go off on a trip by yourself and go back to the United States by yourself," he said. "Where's the key?"

"Maybe I lost it."

They let themselves into the room and undressed. He

sat on the edge of the bed looking into the night patio. At last he shook his head, rubbed his eyes, and sighed. "I'm tired. I've been terrible today." He looked at her where she sat, next to him, and he put out his hand to take her arm. "I'm sorry. I get all riled up, driving, and then us not talking the language too well. By evening I'm a mess of nerves."

"Yes," she said.

Quite suddenly he moved over beside her. He took hold of her and held her tightly, his head over her shoulder, eyes shut, talking into her ear with a quiet, whispering fervency. "You know, we *must* stay together. There's only us, really, no matter what happens, no matter what trouble we have. I do love you so much, you know that. Forgive me if I'm difficult. We've got to make it go."

She stared over his shoulder at the blank wall and the wall was like her life in this moment, a wide expanse of nothingness with hardly a bump, a contour, or a feeling to it. She didn't know what to say or do. Another time, she would have melted. But there was such a thing as firing metal too often, bringing it to a glow, shaping it. At last the metal refuses to glow or shape; it is nothing but a weight. She was a weight now, moving mechanically in his arms, hearing but not hearing, understanding but not understanding, replying but not replying. "Yes, we'll stay together." She felt her lips move. "We love each other." The lips said what they must say, while her mind was in her eyes and her eyes bored deep into the vacuum of the wall. "Yes." Holding but not holding him. "Yes."

The room was dim. Outside, someone walked in a corridor, perhaps glancing at this locked door, perhaps hearing their vital whispering as no more than something falling drop by drop from a loose faucet, a running drain perhaps, or a turned bookleaf under a solitary bulb. Let the doors whisper, the people of the world walked down tile corridors and did not hear.

"Only you and I know the things." His breath was

fresh. She felt very sorry for him and herself and the world, suddenly. Everyone was infernally alone. He was like a man clawing at a statue. She did not feel herself move. Only her mind, which was a lightless, dim fluorescent vapor, shifted. "Only you and I remember," he said, "and if one of us should leave, then half the memories are gone. So we must stay together because if one forgets the other remembers."

Remembers what? she asked herself. But she remembered instantly, in a linked series, those parts of incidents in their life together that perhaps he might not recall; the night at the beach, five years ago, one of the first fine nights beneath the canvas with the secret touchings, the days at Sunland sprawled together, taking the sun until twilight. Wandering in an abandoned silver mine, oh, a million things, one touched on and revealed another in an instant!

He held her tight back against the bed now. "Do you know how lonely I am? Do you know how lonely I make myself with these arguments and fights and all of it, when I'm tired?" He waited for her to answer, but she said nothing. She felt his eyelid flutter on her neck. Faintly, she remembered when he had first flicked his eyelid near her ear. "Spider-eye," she had said, laughing, then. "It feels like a small spider in my ear." And now this small lost spider climbed with insane humor upon her neck. There was something in his voice which made her feel she was a woman on a train going away and he was standing in the station saying, "Don't go." And her appalled voice silently cried, "But *you're* the one on a train! *I'm* not going *anywhere!*"

She lay back, bewildered. It was the first time in two weeks he had touched her. And the touching had such an immediacy that she knew the wrong word would send him very far away again.

She lay and said nothing.

Finally, after a long while, she heard him get up, sighing, and move off. He got into his own bed and drew the covers up, silently. She moved at last, arranged herself on her bed, and lay listening to her watch tick in the small hot darkness. "My God," she whispered, finally, "it's only eight-thirty."

"Go to sleep," he said.

She lay in the dark, perspiring, naked, on her own bed, and in the distance, sweetly, faintly, so that it made her soul and heart ache to hear it, she heard the band thumping and brassing out its melodies. She wanted to walk among the dark moving people and sing with them and smell the soft charcoal air of October in a small summery town deep in the tropics of Mexico, a million miles lost from civilization, listening to the good music, tapping her foot and humming. But now she lay with her eyes wide, in bed. In the next hour, the band played "*La Golondrina*," "*Marimba*," "*Los Viejitos*," "*Michoacan la Verde*," "*Barcarolle*," and "*Luna Lunera*."

At three in the morning she awoke for no reason and lay, her sleep done and finished with, feeling the coolness that came with deep night. She listened to his breathing and she felt away and separate from the world. She thought of the long trip from Los Angeles to Laredo, Texas, like a silver-white boiling nightmare. And then the green technicolor, red and yellow and blue and purple, dream of Mexico arising like a flood about them to engulf their car with color and smell of rain forest and deserted town. She thought of all the small towns, the shops, the walking people, the burros, and all the arguments and near-fights. She thought of the five years she had been married. A long, long time. There had been no day in all that time that they had not seen each other; there had been no day when she had seen friends, separately; *he* was always there to see and criticize. There had been no day when she was allowed to be gone for more than an hour or so without a full explanation. Sometimes, feeling infinitely evil, she would sneak to a midnight show, telling no one, and sit, feeling free, breathing deeply of the air of freedom, watching the people, far realer than she, upon the screen, motioning and moving.

And now here they were, after five years. She looked over at his sleeping form. One thousand eight hundred and twenty-five days with you, she thought, my husband. A few hours each day at my typewriter, and then all the rest of each day and night with you. I feel quite like that man walled up in a vault in *The Cask of Amontillado*. I scream but no one hears.

There was a shift of footsteps outside, a knock on their door. "*Señora*," called a soft voice, in Spanish. "It is three o'clock."

Oh, my God, thought the wife. "Sh!" she hissed, leaping up to the door. But her husband was awake. "What *is* it?" he cried.

She opened the door the slightest crack. "You've come at the wrong time," she said to the man in the darkness.

"Three o'clock, *señora*."

"No, no," she hissed, her face wrenching with the agony of the moment. "I meant tomorrow afternoon."

"What is it?" demanded her husband, switching on a light. "Christ, it's only three in the morning. What does the fool want?"

She turned, shutting her eyes. "He's here to take us to Paricutin."

"My God, you can't speak Spanish at all!"

"Go away," she said to the guide.

"But I arose for this hour," said the guide.

The husband swore and got up. "I won't be able to sleep now, anyway. Tell the idiot we'll be dressed in ten minutes and go with him and get it over, my God!"

She did this and the guide slipped away into the darkness and out into the street where the cool moon burnished the fenders of his taxi.

"You *are* incompetent," snapped the husband, pulling on two pairs of pants, two T-shirts, a sport shirt, and a wool shirt over that. "Jesus, this'll fix my throat, all right. If I come down with another strep infection—"

"Get back into bed, damn you."

"I couldn't sleep now, anyway."

"Well, we've had six hours' sleep already, and you had at least three hours' this afternoon; that should be enough."

"Spoiling our trip," he said, putting on two sweaters and two pairs of socks. "It's cold up there on the mountain; dress warm, hurry up." He put on a jacket and a muffler and looked enormous in the heap of clothing he wore. "Get me my pills. Where's some water?"

"Get back to bed," she said. "I won't have you sick and whining." She found his medicine and poured some water.

"The least thing you could do was get the hour right."

"Shut up!" She held the glass.

"Just another of your thick-headed blunders."

She threw the water in his face. "Let me alone, damn you, let me alone. I didn't mean to do that!"

"You!" he shouted, face dripping. He ripped off his jacket. "You'll chill me, I'll catch cold!"

"I don't give a damn, let me alone!" She raised her hands into fists, and her face was terrible and red, and she looked like some animal in a maze who has steadily sought exit from an impossible chaos and has been constantly fooled, turned back, rerouted, led on, tempted, whispered to, lied to, led further, and at last reached a blank wall.

"Put your hands down!" he shouted.

"I'll kill you, by God, I'll kill you!" she screamed, her face contorted and ugly. "Leave me alone! I've tried my damnedest—beds, language, time, my God, the mistakes, you think I don't *know* it? You think I'm not *sorry?*"

"I'll catch cold, I'll catch cold." He was staring at the wet floor. He sat down with water on his face.

"Here. Wipe your face off!" She flung him a towel. He began to shake violently. "I'm cold!"

"Get a chill, damn it, and die, but leave me alone!"

"I'm cold, I'm cold." His teeth chattered, he wiped

his face with trembling hands. "I'll have another infection."

"Take off that coat! It's wet."

He stopped shaking after a minute and stood up to take off the soggy coat. She handed him a leather jacket. "Come on, he's waiting for us."

He began to shiver again. "I'm not going anywhere, to hell with you," he said, sitting down. "You owe me fifty dollars now."

"What for?"

"You remember, you promised."

And she remembered. They had had a fight about some silly thing, in California, the first day of the trip, yes, by God, the very first day out. And she for the first time in her life had lifted her hand to slap him. Then, appalled, she had dropped her hand, staring at her traitorous fingers. "You were going to slap me!" he had cried. "Yes," she replied. "Well," he said quietly, "the next time you do a thing like that, you'll hand over fifty dollars of your money." That's how life was, full of little tributes and ransoms and blackmails. She paid for all her errors, unmotivated or not. A dollar here, a dollar there. If she spoiled an evening, she paid the dinner bill from her clothing money. If she criticized a play they had just seen and he had liked it, he flew into a rage, and, to quiet him, she paid for the theater tickets. On and on it had gone, swifter and swifter over the years. If they bought a book together and she didn't like it but he did and she dared speak out, there was a fight, sometimes a small thing which grew for days, and ended with her buying the book plus another and perhaps a set of cufflinks or some other silly thing to calm the storm. Jesus!

"Fifty dollars. You promised if you acted up again with these tantrums and slappings."

"It was only water. I didn't hit you. All right, shut up, I'll pay the money, I'll pay anything just to be let alone; it's worth it, and five hundred dollars more, more than worth it. I'll pay."

She turned away. When you're sick for a number of years, when you're an *only* child, the *only* boy, all of your life, you get the way he is, she thought. Then you find yourself thirty-five years old and still undecided as to what you're to be—a ceramist, a social worker, a businessman. And your wife has always known what she would be—a writer. And it must be maddening to live with a woman with a single knowledge of herself, so sure of what she would do with her writing. And selling stories, at last, not many, no, but just enough to cause the seams of the marriage to rip. And so how natural that he must convince her that she was wrong and he was right, that she was an uncontrollable child and must forfeit money. Money was to be the weapon he held over her. When she had been a fool she would give up some of the precious gain—the product of her writing.

"Do you know," she said, suddenly, aloud, "since I made that big sale to the magazine, you seem to pick more fights and I seem to pay more money?"

"What do you mean by that?" he said.

It seemed to her to be true. Since the big sale he had put his special logic to work on situations, a logic of such a sort that she had no way to combat it. Reasoning with him was impossible. You were finally cornered, your explanations exhausted, your alibis depleted, your pride in tatters. So you struck out. You slapped at him or broke something, and then, there you were again, paying off, and he had won. And he was taking your success away from you, your single purpose, or he thought he was, anyway. But strangely enough, though she had never told him, she didn't care about forfeiting the money. If it made peace, if it made him happy, if it made him think he was causing her to suffer, that was all right. He had exaggerated ideas as to the value of money; it hurt him to lose it or spend it, therefore he thought it would hurt her as much. But I'm feeling no pain, she thought, I'd like to give him all of the money, for that's not why I write at all, I write to say what I have to say, and he doesn't understand that.

He was quieted now. "You'll pay?"

"Yes." She was dressing quickly now, in slacks and jacket. "In fact, I've been meaning to bring this up for some time. I'm giving all the money to you from now on. There's no need of my keeping my profits separate from yours, as it has been. I'll turn it over to you tomorrow."

"I don't ask that," he said, quickly.

"I insist. It all goes to you."

What I'm doing, of course, is unloading your gun, she thought. Taking your weapon away from you. Now you won't be able to extract the money from me, piece by piece, bit by painful bit. You'll have to find another way to bother me.

"I—" he said.

"No, let's not talk about it. It's yours."

"It's only to teach you a lesson. You've a bad temper," he said. "I thought you'd control it if you had to forfeit something."

"Oh, I just *live* for money," she said.

"I don't want all of it."

"Come on now." She was weary. She opened the door and listened. The neighbors hadn't heard, or if they had, they paid no attention. The lights of the waiting taxi illuminated the front patio.

They walked out through the cool moonlit night. She walked ahead of him for the first time in years.

Paricutin was a river of gold that night. A distant murmuring river of molten ore going down to some dead lava sea, to some volcanic black shore. Time and again if you held your breath, stilled your heart within you, you could hear the lava pushing rocks down the mountain in tumblings and roarings, faintly, faintly. Above the crater were red vapors and red light. Gentle brown and gray clouds arose suddenly as coronets or halos or puffs from the interior, their undersides washed in pink, their tops dark and ominous, without a sound.

The husband and the wife stood on the opposite mountain, in the sharp cold, the horses behind them. In a wooden hut nearby, the scientific observers were lighting oil lamps, cooking their evening meal, boiling rich coffee, talking in whispers because of the clear, night-explosive air. It was very far away from everything else in the world.

On the way up the mountain, after the long taxi drive from Uruapan, over moon-dreaming hills of ashen snow, through dry stick villages, under the cold clear stars, jounced in the taxi like dice in a gambling-tumbler, both of them had tried to make a better thing of it. They had arrived at a campfire on a sort of sea bottom. About the campfire were solemn men and small dark boys, and a company of seven other Americans, all men, in riding breeches, talking in loud voices under the soundless sky. The horses were brought forth and mounted. They proceeded across the lava river. She talked to the other Yankees and they responded. They joked together. After a while of this, the husband rode on ahead.

Now, they stood together, watching the lava wash down the dark cone summit.

He wouldn't speak.

"What's wrong now?" she asked.

He looked straight ahead, the lava glow reflected in his eyes. "You could have ridden with me. I thought we came to Mexico to see things together. And now you talk to those damned Texans."

"I felt lonely. We haven't seen any people from the States for eight weeks. I like the days in Mexico, but I don't like the nights. I just wanted someone to talk to."

"You wanted to tell them you're a writer."

"That's unfair."

"You're always telling people you're a writer, and how good you are, and you've just sold a story to a large-circulation magazine and that's how you got the money to come here to Mexico.

"One of them asked me what I did, and I told him.

Damn right I'm proud of my work. I've waited ten years to sell some damn thing."

He studied her in the light from the fire mountain and at last he said, "You know, before coming up here tonight, I thought about that damned typewriter of yours and almost tossed it into the river."

"You didn't!"

"No, but I locked it in the car. I'm tired of it and the way you've ruined the whole trip. You're not with me, you're with yourself, you're the one who counts, you and that damned machine, you and Mexico, you and your reactions, you and your inspiration, you and your nervous sensitivity, and you and your aloneness. I knew you'd act this way tonight, just as sure as there was a First Coming! I'm tired of your running back from every excursion we make to sit at that machine and bang away at all hours. This is a vacation."

"I haven't touched the typewriter in a week, because it bothered you."

"Well, don't touch it for another week or a month, don't touch it until we get home. Your damned inspiration can wait!"

I should never have said I'd give him all the money, she thought. I should never have taken that weapon from him, it kept him away from my real life, the writing and the machine. And now I've thrown off the protective cloak of money and he's searched for a new weapon and he's gotten to the true thing—to the *machine!* Oh Christ!

Suddenly, without thinking, with the rage in her again, she pushed him ahead of her. She didn't do it violently. She just gave him a push. Once, twice, three times. She didn't hurt him. It was just a gesture of pushing away. She wanted to strike him, throw him off a cliff, perhaps, but instead she gave these three pushes, to indicate her hostility and the end of talking. Then they stood separately, while behind them the horses moved their hooves softly, and the night air grew colder and their breath hissed in white plumes on the air, and in the scientists' cabin the coffee bubbled on the blue gas jet and the rich fumes permeated the moonlit heights.

After an hour, as the first dim furnacings of the sun came in the cold East, they mounted their horses for the trip down through growing light, toward the buried city and the buried church under the lava flow. Crossing the flow, she thought, Why doesn't his horse fall, why isn't he thrown onto those jagged lava rocks, why? But nothing happened. They rode on. The sun rose red.

They slept until one in the afternoon. She was dressed and sitting on the bed waiting for him to waken for half an hour before he stirred and rolled over, needing a shave, very pale with tiredness.

"I've got a sore throat," was the first thing he said.

She didn't speak.

"You shouldn't have thrown water on me," he said.

She got up and walked to the door and put her hand on the knob.

"I want you to stay here," he said. "We're going to stay here in Uruapan three or four more days."

At last she said, "I thought we were going on to Guadalajara."

"Don't be a tourist. You ruined that trip to the volcano for us. I want to go back up tomorrow or the next day. Go look at the sky."

She went out to look at the sky. It was clear and blue. She reported this. "The volcano dies down, sometimes for a week. We can't afford to wait a week for it to boom again."

"Yes, we can. We will. And you'll pay for the taxi to take us up there and do the trip over and do it right and enjoy it."

"Do you think we can ever enjoy it now?" she asked.

"If it's the last thing we do, we'll enjoy it."

"You insist, do you?"

"We'll wait until the sky is full of smoke and go back up."

"I'm going out to buy a paper." She shut the door and walked into the town.

She walked down the fresh-washed streets and looked in the shining windows and smelled that amazingly clear air and felt very good, except for the tremoring, the continual tremoring in her stomach. At last, with a hollowness roaring in her chest, she went to a man standing beside a taxi.

"*Señor,*" she said.

"Yes?" said the man.

She felt her heart stop beating. Then it began to thump again and she went on: "How much would you charge to drive me to Morelia?"

"Ninety pesos, *señora.*"

"And I can get the train in Morelia?"

"There is a train *here, señora.*"

"Yes, but there are reasons why I don't want to *wait* for it here."

"I will drive you, then, to Morelia."

"Come along, there are a few things I must do."

The taxi was left in front of the Hotel de Las Flores. She walked in, alone, and once more looked at the lovely garden with its many flowers, and listened to the girl playing the strange blue-colored piano, and this time the song was the "Moonlight Sonata." She smelled the sharp crystalline air and shook her head, eyes closed, hands at her sides. She put her hand to the door, opened it softly.

Why today? she wondered. Why not some other day in the last five years? Why have I waited, why have I hung around? Because. A thousand becauses. Because you always hoped things would start again the way they were the first year. Because there were times, less frequent now, when he was splendid for days, even weeks, when you were both feeling well and the world was green and bright blue. There were times, like yesterday, for a moment, when he opened the armor-plate and showed her the fear beneath it and the small loneliness of himself and said, "I need and love you, don't ever go away, I'm afraid without you." Because sometimes it had seemed good to cry together, to make up, and the inevitable goodness of the night and the day following their making up. Because he was handsome. Because she had been alone all year every year until she met him. Because she didn't want to be alone again, but now knew that it would be better to be alone than be this way because only last night he destroyed the typewriter; not physically, no, but with thoughts and words. And he might as well have picked her up bodily and thrown her from the river bridge.

She could not feel her hand on the door. It was as if ten thousand volts of electricity had numbed all of her body. She could not feel her feet on the tiled floor. Her face was gone, her mind was gone.

He lay asleep, his back turned. The room was greenly dim. Quickly, soundlessly, she put on her coat and checked her purse. The clothes and typewriter were of no importance now. Everything was a hollowing roar. Everything was like a waterfall leaping into clear emptiness. There was no striking, no impact, just a clear water falling into a hollow and then another hollow, followed by an emptiness.

She stood by the bed and looked at the man there, the familar black hair on the nape of his neck, the sleeping profile. The form stirred. "What?" he asked, still asleep.

"Nothing," she said. "Nothing. And nothing."

She went out and shut the door.

The taxi sped out of town at an incredible rate, making a great noise, and all the pink walls and blue walls fled past and people jumped out of the way and there were some few cars which almost exploded upon them, and there went most of the town and there went the hotel and that man sleeping in the hotel and there went—

Nothing.

The taxi motor died.

No, no, thought Marie, oh God, no, no, no.

The car must start again.

The taxi driver leaped out, glaring at God in his Heaven, and ripped open the hood and looked as if he might strangle the iron guts of the car with his clawing hands, his face smiling a pure sweet smile of incredible hatred, and then he turned to Marie and forced himself to shrug, putting away his hate and accepting the Will of God.

"I will walk you to the bus station," he said.

No, her eyes said. No, her mouth almost said. Joseph will wake and run and find me still here and drag me back. No.

"I will carry your bags, *señora*," the taxi driver said, and walked off with them, and had to come back and find her still there, motionless, saying no, no, to no one, and helped her out and showed her where to walk.

The bus was in the square and the Indians were getting into it, some silently and with a slow, certain dignity, and some chattering like birds and shoving bundles, children, chickens' baskets, and pigs in ahead of them. The driver wore a uniform that had not been pressed or laundered in twenty years, and he was leaning out the window shouting and laughing with people outside, as Marie stepped up into the interior of hot smoke and burning grease from the engine, the smell of gasoline and oil, the smell of wet chickens, wet children, sweating men and damp women, old upholstery which was down to the skeleton, and oily leather. She found a seat in the rear and felt the eyes follow her and her suitcase, and she was thinking: I'm going away, at last I'm going away, I'm free, I'll never see him again in my life, I'm free, I'm free.

She almost laughed.

The bus started and all of the people in it shook and swayed and cried out and smiled, and the land of Mexico seemed to whirl about outside the window, like a dream undecided whether to stay or go, and then the greenness passed away, and the town, and there was the

Hotel de Las Flores with its open patio, and there, incredibly, hands in pockets, standing in the open door but looking at the sky and the volcano smoke, was Joseph, paying no attention to the bus or her and she was going away from him, he was growing remote already, his figure was dwindling like someone falling down a mine shaft, silently, without a scream. Now, before she had even the decency or inclination to wave, he was no larger than a boy, then a child, then a baby, in distance, in size, then gone around a corner, with the engine thundering, someone playing upon a guitar up front in the bus, and Marie, straining to look back, as if she might penetrate walls, trees, and distances, for another view of the man standing so quietly watching the blue sky.

At last, her neck tired, she turned and folded her hands and examined what she had won for herself. A whole lifetime loomed suddenly ahead, as quickly as the turns and whirls of the highway brought her suddenly to edges of cliffs, and each bend of the road, even as the years, could not be seen ahead. For a moment it was simply good to lie back here, head upon jouncing seat rest, and contemplate quietness. To know nothing, to think nothing, to feel nothing, to be as nearly dead for a moment as one could be, with the eyes closed, the heart unheard, no special temperature to the body, to wait for life to come get her rather than to seek, at least for an hour. Let the bus take her to the train, the train to the plane, the plane to the city, and the city to her friends, and then, like a stone dropped into a cement mixer, let that life in the city do with her as it would, she flowing along in the mix and solidifying in any new pattern that seemed best.

The bus rushed on with a plummeting and swerving in the sweet green air of the afternoon, between the mountains baked like lion pelts, past rivers as sweet as wine and as clear as vermouth, over stone bridges, under aqueducts where water ran like clear wind in the ancient channels, past churches, through dust, and suddenly, quite suddenly the speedometer in Marie's mind said, A million miles, Joseph is back a million miles and I'll never see him again. The thought stood up in her mind and covered the sky with a blurred darkness. Never, never again until the day I die or after that will I see him again, not for an hour or a minute or a second, not at all will I see him.

The numbness started in her fingertips. She felt it flow up through her hands, into her wrists and on along the arms to her shoulders and through her shoulders to her heart and up her neck to her head. She was a numbness, a thing of nettles and ice and prickles and a hollow thundering nothingness. Her lips were dry petals, her eyelids were a thousand pounds heavier than iron, and each part of her body was now iron and lead and copper and platinum. Her body weighed ten tons, each part of it was so incredibly heavy, and, in that heaviness, crushed and beating to survive, was her crippled heart, throbbing and tearing about like a headless chicken. And buried in the limestone and steel of her robot body was her terror and crying out, walled in, with someone tapping the trowel on the exterior wall, the job finished, and, ironically, it was her own hand she saw before her that had wielded the trowel, set the final brick in place, frothed on the thick slush of mortar and pushed everything into a tightness and a self-finished prison.

Her mouth was cotton. Her eyes were flaming with a dark flame the color of raven wings, the sound of vulture wings, and her head was so heavy with terror, so full of an iron weight, while her mouth was stuffed with invisible hot cotton, that she felt her head sag down into her immensely fat, but she could not see the fat, hands. Her hands were pillows of lead to lie upon, her hands were cement sacks crushing down upon her senseless lap, her ears, faucets in which ran cold winds, and all about her, not looking at her, not noticing, was the bus on its way through towns and fields, over hills and into corn valleys at a great racketing speed, taking her each and every instant one million miles and ten million years away from the familiar.

I must *not* cry out, she thought. No! No!

The dizziness was so complete, and the colors of the bus and her hands and skirt were now so blued over and sooted with lack of blood that in a moment she would be collapsed upon the floor, she would hear the surprise and shock of the riders bending over her. But she put her head far down and sucked the chicken air, the sweating air, the leather air, the carbon monoxide air, the incense air, the air of lonely death, and drew it back through the copper nostrils, down the aching throat, into her lungs which blazed as if she swallowed neon light. Joseph, Joseph, Joseph, Joseph.

It was a simple thing. All terror is a simplicity.

I cannot live without him, she thought. I have been lying to myself. I need him, oh Christ, I, I . . .

"Stop the bus! Stop it!"

The bus stopped at her scream, everyone was thrown forward. Somehow she was stumbling forward over the children, the dogs barking, her hands flailing heavily, falling; she heard her dress rip, she screamed again, the door was opening, the driver was appalled at the woman coming at him in a wild stumbling, and she fell out upon the gravel, tore her stockings, and lay while someone bent to her; then she was vomiting on the ground, a steady sickness; they were bringing her bags out of the bus to her, she was telling them in chokes and sobs that she wanted to go that way; she pointed back at the city a million years ago, a million miles ago, and the bus driver was shaking his head. She half sat, half lay there, her arms about the suitcase, sobbing, and the bus stood in the hot sunlight over her and she waved it on; go on, go on; they're all staring at me, I'll get a ride back, don't worry, leave me here, go on, and at last, like an accordion, the door folded shut, the Indian copper-mask faces were transported on away, and the bus dwindled from consciousness. She lay on the suitcase and cried, for a number of minutes, and she was not as heavy or sick, but her heart was fluttering wildly, and she was cold as someone fresh from a winter lake. She arose and dragged the suitcase in little moves across the highway and swayed there, waiting, while six cars hummed by, and at last a seventh car pulled up with a Mexican gentleman in the front seat, a rich car from Mexico City.

"You are going to Uruapan?" he asked politely, looking only at her eyes.

"Yes," she said at last, "I am going to Uruapan."

And as she rode in this car, her mind began a private dialogue:

"What is it to be insane?"

"I don't know."

"Do you know what insanity is?"

"I don't know."

"Can one tell? The coldness, was that the start?"

"No."

"The heaviness, wasn't that a part?"

"Shut up."

"Is insanity screaming?"

"I didn't mean to."

"But that came later. First there was the heaviness, and the silence, and the blankness. That terrible void, that space, that silence, that aloneness, that backing away from life, that being in upon oneself and not wishing to look at or speak to the world. Don't tell me that wasn't the start of insanity."

"Yes."

"You were ready to fall over the edge."

"I stopped the bus just short of the cliff."

"And what if you hadn't stopped the bus? Would they have driven into a little town or Mexico City and the driver turned and said to you through the empty bus, 'All right, *señora*, all out.' Silence. 'All right, *señora*, all out.' Silence. '*Señora?*' A stare into space. '*Señora!*' A rigid stare into the sky of life, empty, empty, oh, empty. '*Señora!*' No move. '*Señora*.' Hardly a breath.

You sit there, you sit there, you sit there, you sit there, you sit there.

"You would not even hear. '*Señora*,' he would cry, and tug at you, but you wouldn't feel his hand. And the police would be summoned beyond your circle of comprehension, beyond your eyes or ears or body. You could not even hear the heavy boots in the car. '*Señora*, you must leave the bus.' You do not hear. '*Señora*, what is your name?' Your mouth is shut. '*Señora*, you must come with us.' You sit like a stone idol. 'Let us see her passport.' They fumble with your purse which lies untended in your stone lap. '*Señora* Marie Elliott, from California. *Señora* Elliott?' You stare at the empty sky. 'Where are you coming from? Where is your husband?' You were never married. 'Where are you going?' Nowhere. 'It says she was born in Illinois.' You were never born. '*Señora, señora*.' They have to carry you, like a stone, from the bus. You will talk to no one. No, no, no one. 'Marie, this is me, Joseph.' No, too late. 'Marie!' Too late. 'Don't you recognize me?' Too late. Joseph. No, Joseph, no nothing, too late, too late."

"That is what would have happened, is it not?"

"Yes." She trembled.

"If you had not stopped the bus, you would have been heavier and heavier, true? And silenter and silenter and more made up of nothing and nothing and nothing."

"Yes."

"*Señora*," said the Spanish gentleman driving, breaking in on her thoughts. "It is a nice day, isn't it?"

"Yes," she said, both to him and the thoughts in her mind.

The old Spanish gentleman drove her directly to her hotel and let her out and doffed his hat and bowed to her.

She nodded and felt her mouth move with thanks, but she did not see him. She wandered into the hotel and found herself with her suitcase back in her room, that room she had left a thousand years ago. Her husband was there.

He lay in the dim light of late afternoon with his back turned, seeming not to have moved in the hours since she had left. He had not even known that she was gone, and had been to the ends of the earth and had returned. He did not even know.

She stood looking at his neck and the dark hairs curling there like ash fallen from the sky.

She found herself on the tiled patio in the hot light. A bird rustled in a bamboo cage. In the cool darkness somewhere, the girl was playing a waltz on the piano.

She saw but did not see two butterflies which darted and jumped and lit upon a bush near her hand, to seal themselves together. She felt her gaze move to see the two bright things, all gold and yellow on the green leaf, their wings beating in slow pulses as they were joined. Her mouth moved and her hand swung like a pendulum, senselessly.

She watched her fingers tumble on the air and close on the two butterflies, tight, tighter, tightest. A scream was coming up into her mouth. She pressed it back. Tight, tighter, tightest.

She felt her hand open all to herself. Two lumps of bright powder fell to the shiny patio tiles. She looked down at the small ruins, then snapped her gaze up.

The girl who played the piano was standing in the middle of the garden, regarding her with appalled and startled eyes.

The wife put out her hand, to touch the distance, to say something, to explain, to apologize to the girl, this place, the world, everyone. But the girl went away.

The sky was full of smoke which went straight up and veered away south toward Mexico City.

She wiped the wing-pollen from her numb fingers and talked over her shoulder, not knowing if that man inside heard, her eyes on the smoke and the sky.

"You know . . . we might try the volcano tonight. It looks good. I bet there'll be lots of fire."

Yes, she thought, and it will fill the air and fall all around us, and take hold of us tight, tighter, tightest, and then let go and let us fall and we'll be ashes blowing south, all fire.

"Did you hear me?"

She stood over the bed and raised a fist high but *never* brought it down to strike him in the face.

# A Story of Love

That was the week Ann Taylor came to teach summer school at Green Town Central. It was the summer of her twenty-fourth birthday, and it was the summer when Bob Spaulding was just fourteen.

Everyone remembered Ann Taylor, for she was that teacher for whom all the children wanted to bring huge oranges or pink flowers, and for whom they rolled up the rustling green and yellow maps of the world without being asked. She was that woman who always seemed to be passing by on days when the shade was green under the tunnels of oaks and elms in the old town, her face shifting with the bright shadows as she walked, until it was all things to all people. She was the fine peaches of summer in the snow of winter, and she was cool milk for cereal on a hot early-June morning. Whenever you needed an opposite, Ann Taylor was there. And those rare few days in the world when the climate was balanced as fine as a maple leaf between winds that blew just right, those were the days like Ann Taylor, and should have been so named on the calendar.

As for Bob Spaulding, he was the cousin who walked alone through town on any October evening with a pack of leaves after him like a horde of Hallowe'en mice, or you would see him, like a slow white fish in spring in the tart waters of the Fox Hill Creek, baking brown with the shine of a chestnut to his face by autumn. Or you might hear his voice in those treetops where the wind entertained; dropping down hand by hand, there would come Bob Spaulding to sit alone and look at the world, and later you might see him on the lawn with the ants crawling over his books as he read through the long afternoons alone, or played himself a game of chess on Grandmother's porch, or picked out a solitary tune upon the black piano in the bay window. You never saw him with any other child.

That first morning, Miss Ann Taylor entered through the side door of the schoolroom and all of the children sat still in their seats as they saw her write her name on the board in a nice round lettering.

"My name is Ann Taylor," she said, quietly. "And I'm your new teacher."

The room seemed suddenly flooded with illumination, as if the roof had moved back; and the trees were full of singing birds. Bob Spaulding sat with a spitball he had just made, hidden in his hand. After a half-hour of listening to Miss Taylor, he quietly let the spitball drop to the floor.

That day, after class, he brought in a bucket of water and a rag and began to wash the boards.

"What's this?" She turned to him from her desk, where she had been correcting spelling papers.

"The boards are kind of dirty," said Bob, at work.

"Yes, I know. Are you sure you want to clean them?"

"I suppose I should have asked permission," he said, halting uneasily.

"I think we can pretend you did," she replied, smiling, and at this smile he finished the boards in an amazing burst of speed and pounded the erasers so furiously that the air was full of snow, it seemed, outside the open window.

"Let's see," said Miss Taylor. "You're Bob Spaulding, aren't you?"

"Yes'm."

"Well, thank you, Bob."

"Could I do them every day?" he asked.

"Don't you think you should let the others try?"

"I'd like to do them," he said. "Every day."

"We'll try it for a while and see," she said.

He lingered.

"I think you'd better run on home," she said, finally.

"Good night." He walked slowly and was gone.

The next morning he happened by the place where she took board and room just as she was coming out to walk to school.

"Well, here I am," he said.

"And do you know," she said, "I'm not surprised."

They walked together.

"May I carry your books?" he asked.

"Why, thank you, Bob."

"It's nothing," he said, taking them.

They walked for a few minutes and he did not say a word. She glanced over and slightly down at him and saw how at ease he was and how happy he seemed, and she decided to let him break the silence, but he never did. When they reached the edge of the school ground he gave the books back to her. "I guess I better leave you here," he said. "The other kids wouldn't understand."

"I'm not sure I do, either, Bob," said Miss Taylor.

"Why we're friends," said Bob earnestly and with a great natural honesty.

"Bob—" she started to say.

"Yes'm?"

"Never mind." She walked away.

"I'll be in class," he said.

And he was in class, and he was there after school every night for the next two weeks, never saying a word, quietly washing the boards and cleaning the erasers and rolling up the maps while she worked at her papers, and there was the clock silence of four o'clock, the silence of the sun going down in the slow sky, the silence with the catlike sound of erasers patted together, and the drip of water from a moving sponge, and the rustle and turn of papers and the scratch of a pen, and perhaps the buzz of a fly banging with a tiny high anger against the tallest clear pane of window in the room. Sometimes the silence would go on this way until almost five, when Miss Taylor would find Bob Spaulding in the last seat of the room, sitting and looking at her silently, waiting for further orders.

"Well, it's time to go home," Miss Taylor would say, getting up.

"Yes'm."

And he would run to fetch her hat and coat. He would also lock the schoolroom door for her unless the janitor was coming in later. Then they would walk out of the school and across the yard, which was empty, the janitor taking down the chain swings slowly on his stepladder, the sun behind the umbrella trees. They talked of all sorts of various things.

"And what are you going to be, Bob, when you grow up?"

"A writer," he said.

"Oh, that's a big ambition; it takes a lot of work."

"I know, but I'm going to try," he said. "I've read a lot."

"Bob, haven't you anything to do after school?"

"How do you mean?"

"I mean, I hate to see you kept in so much, washing the boards."

"I like it," he said. "I never do what I don't like."

"But nevertheless."

"No, I've got to do that," he said. He thought for a while and said, "Do me a favor, Miss Taylor?"

"It all depends."

"I walk every Saturday from out around Buetrick Street along the creek to Lake Michigan. They're a lot of butterflies and crayfish and birds. Maybe you'd like to walk, too."

"Thank you," she said.

"Then you'll come?"

"I'm afraid not."

"Don't you think it'd be fun?"

"Yes, I'm sure of that, but I'm going to be busy."

He started to ask doing what, but stopped.

"I take along sandwiches," he said. "Ham-and-pickle ones. And orange pop and just walk along, taking my time. I get down to the lake about noon and walk back and get home about three o'clock. It makes a real fine day, and I wish you'd come. Do you collect butterflies? I have a big collection. We could start one for you."

"Thanks, Bob, but no, perhaps some other time."

He looked at her and said, "I shouldn't have asked you, should I?"

"You have every right to ask anything you want to," she said.

A few days later she found an old copy of *Great Expectations*, which she no longer wanted, and gave it to Bob. He was very grateful and took it home and stayed up that night and read it through and talked about it next morning. Each day now he met her just beyond sight of her boarding house and many days she would start to say, "Bob—" and tell him not to come to meet her anymore, but she never finished saying it, and he talked with her about Dickens and Kipling and Poe and others, coming and going to school. She found a butterfly on her desk on Friday morning. She almost waved it away before she found it was dead and had been placed there while she was out of the room. She glanced at Bob over the head of her other students, but he was looking at his book! not reading, just looking at it.

It was about this time that she found it impossible to call on Bob to recite in class. She would hover her pencil about his name and then call the next person up or down the list. Nor would she look at him while they were walking to or from school. But on several late afternoons as he moved his arm high on the blackboard, sponging away the arithmetic symbols, she found herself glancing over at him for seconds at a time before she returned to her papers.

And then on Saturday morning he was standing in the middle of the creek with his overall rolled up to his knees, kneeling down to catch a crayfish under a rock, when he looked up and there on the edge of the running stream was Miss Ann Taylor.

"Well, here I am," she said, laughing.

"And do you know," he said, "I'm not surprised."

"Show me the crayfish and the butterflies," she said.

They walked down to the lake and sat on the sand with a warm wind blowing softly about them, fluttering her hair and the ruffle on her blouse, and he sat a few yards back from her and they ate the ham-and-pickle sandwiches and drank the orange pop solemnly.

"Gee, this is swell," he said. "This is the swellest time ever in my life."

"I didn't think I would ever come on a picnic like this," she said.

"With some kid," he said.

"I'm comfortable, however," she said.

"That's good news."

They said little else during the afternoon.

"This is all wrong," he said, later. "And I can't figure why it should be. Just walking along and catching old butterflies and crayfish and eating sandwiches. But Mom and Dad'd rib the heck out of me if they knew, and the kids would, too. And the other teachers, I suppose, would laugh at you, wouldn't they?"

"I'm afraid so."

"I guess we better not do any more butterfly catching, then."

"I don't exactly understand how I came here at all," she said.

And the day was over.

That was about all there was to the meeting of Ann Taylor and Bob Spaulding, two or three monarch butterflies, a copy of Dickens, a dozen crayfish, four sandwiches, and two bottles of Orange Crush. The next Monday, quite unexpectedly, though he waited a long time, Bob did not see Miss Taylor come out to walk to school. But discovered later that she had left earlier and was already at school. Also, Monday night, she left early, with a headache, and another teacher finished her last class. He walked by her boarding house but did not see her anywhere, and he was afraid to ring the bell and inquire.

On Tuesday night after school they were both in the silent room again, he sponging the board contentedly, as if this time might go on forever, and she seated, working on her papers as if she, too, would be in this room and this particular peace and happiness forever, when suddenly the courthouse clock struck. It was a block away and its great bronze boom shuddered one's body and made the ash of time shake away off your bones and slide through your blood, making you seem older by the minute. Stunned by that clock, you could not but sense the crashing flow of time, and as the clock said five o'clock, Miss Taylor suddenly looked up at it for a long time, and then she put down her pen.

"Bob," she said.

He turned, startled. Neither of them had spoken in the peaceful and good hour before.

"Will you come here?" she asked.

He put down the sponge slowly.

"Yes," he said.

"Bob, I want you to sit down."

"Yes'm."

She looked at him intently for a moment until he looked away. "Bob, I wonder if you know what I'm going to talk to you about. Do you know?"

"Yes."

"Maybe it'd be a good idea if you told me, first."

"About us," he said, at last.

"How old are you, Bob?"

"Going on fourteen."

"You're thirteen years old."

He winced. "Yes'm."

"And do you know how old I am?"

"Yes'm. I heard. Twenty-four."

"Twenty-four."

"I'll be twenty-four in ten years, almost," he said.

"But unfortunately you're not twenty-four now."

"No, but sometimes I feel twenty-four."

"Yes, and sometimes you almost act it."

"Do I, really!"

"Now sit still there; don't bound around, we've a lot to discuss. It's very important that we understand what is happening, don't you agree?"

"Yes, I guess so."

"First, let's admit we are the greatest and best friends in the world. Let's admit I have never had a student like you, nor have I had as much affection for any boy I've ever known." He flushed at this. She went on. "And let me speak for you—you've found me to be the nicest teacher of all the teachers you've ever known."

"Oh, more than that," he said.

"Perhaps more than that, but there are facts to be faced and an entire way of life to be examined, and a town and its people, and you and me to be considered. I've thought this over for a good many days, Bob. Don't think I've missed anything, or been unaware of my own feelings in the matter. Under some circumstances our friendship would be odd indeed. But then you are no ordinary boy. I know myself pretty well, I think, and I know I'm not sick, either mentally or physically, and that whatever has evolved here has been a true regard for your character and goodness, Bob; but those are not the things we consider in this world, Bob, unless they occur in a man of a certain age. I don't know if I'm saying this right."

"It's all right," he said. "It's just if I was ten years older and about fifteen inches taller it'd make all the difference, and that's silly," he said, "to go by how tall a person is."

"The world hasn't found it so."

"I'm not the world," he protested.

"I know it seems foolish," she said. "When you feel very grown up and right and have nothing to be ashamed of. You have nothing at all to be ashamed of, Bob, remember that. You have been very honest and good, and I hope I have been, too."

"You have," he said.

"In an ideal climate, Bob, maybe someday they will be able to judge the oldness of a person's mind so accurately that they can say, This is a man, though his body is only thirteen; by some miracle of circumstance and fortune, this is a man, with a man's recognition of responsibility and position and duty; but until that day, Bob, I'm afraid we're going to have to go by ages and heights in the ordinary way in an ordinary world."

"I don't like that," he said.

"Perhaps I don't like it, either, but do you want to end up far unhappier than you are now? Do you want both of us to be unhappy? Which we would certainly be. There really is no way to do anything about us—it is so strange even to try to talk about us."

"Yes'm."

"But at least we know all about us and the fact that we have been right and fair and good and there is nothing wrong with our knowing each other, nor did we ever intend that it should be, for we both understand how impossible it is, don't we?"

"Yes, I know. But I can't help it."

"Now we must decide what to do about it," she said. "Now only you and I know about this. Later, others might know. I can secure a transfer from this school to another one—"

"No!"

"Or I can have you transferred to another school."

"You don't have to do that," he said.

"Why?"

"We're moving. My folks and I, we're going to live in Madison. We're leaving next week."

"It has nothing to do with all this, has it?"

"No, no, everything's all right. It's just that my father has a new job there. It's only fifty miles away. I can see you, can't I, when I come to town?"

"Do you think that would be a good idea?"

"No, I guess not."

They sat awhile in the silent schoolroom.

"When did all of this happen?" he said, helplessly.

"I don't know," she said. "Nobody ever knows. They haven't known for thousands of years, and I don't think they ever will. People like each other or don't, and sometimes two people like each other who shouldn't. I can't explain myself, and certainly you can't explain you."

"I guess I'd better get home." he said.

"You're not mad at me, are you?"

"Oh, gosh no, I could never be mad at you."

"There's one more thing. I want you to remember, there are compensations in life. There always are, or we wouldn't go on living. You don't feel well, now; neither do I. But something will happen to fix that. Do you believe that?"

"I'd like to."

"Well, it's true."

"If only," he said.

"What?"

"If only you'd wait for me," he blurted.

"Ten years?"

"I'd be twenty-four then."

"But I'd be thirty-four and another person entirely, perhaps. No, I don't think it can be done."

"Wouldn't you like it to be done?" he cried.

"Yes," she said quietly. "It's silly and it wouldn't work, but I would like it very much."

He sat there for a long time.

"I'll never forget you," he said.

"It's nice for you to say that, even though it can't be true, because life isn't that way. You'll forget."

"I'll never forget. I'll find a way of never forgetting you," he said.

She got up and went to erase the boards.

"I'll help you," he said.

"No, no," she said hastily. "You go on now, get home, and no more tending to the boards after school. I'll assign Helen Stevens to do it."

He left the school. Looking back, outside, he saw Miss Ann Taylor, for the last time, at the board, slowly washing out the chalked words, her hand moving up and down.

He moved away from the town the next week and was gone for sixteen years. Though he was only fifty miles away, he never got down to Green Town again until he was almost thirty and married, and then one spring they were driving through on their way to Chicago and stopped off for a day.

Bob left his wife at the hotel and walked around town and finally asked about Miss Ann Taylor, but no one remembered at first, and then one of them remembered.

"Oh, yes, the pretty teacher. She died in 1936, not long after you left."

Had she ever married? No, come to think of it, she never had.

He walked out to the cemetery in the afternoon and found her stone, which said, "Ann Taylor, born 1910, died 1936." And he thought, Twenty-six years old. Why, I'm three years older than you are now, Miss Taylor.

Later in the day the people in the town saw Bob Spaulding's wife strolling to meet him under the elm trees and the oak trees, and they all turned to watch her pass, for her face shifted with bright shadows as she walked; she was the fine peaches of summer in the snow of winter, and she was cool milk for cereal on a hot early-summer morning. And this was one of those rare few days in time when the climate was balanced like a maple leaf between winds that blow just right, one of those days that should have been named, everyone agreed, after Robert Spaulding's wife.

# The Wish

A whisper of snow touched the cold window.

The vast house creaked in a wind from nowhere.

"What?" I said.

"I didn't say anything." Charlie Simmons, behind me at the fireplace, shook popcorn quietly in a vast metal sieve. "Not a word."

"Damn it, Charlie, I *heard* you. . . ."

Stunned, I watched the snow fall on far streets and empty fields. It was a proper night for ghosts of whiteness to visit windows and wander off.

"You're imagining things," said Charlie.

Am I? I thought. Does the weather have voices? Is there a language of night and time and snow? What goes on between that dark out there and my soul in here?

For there in the shadows, a whole civilization of doves seemed to be landing unseen, without benefit of moon or lamp.

And was it the snow softly whispering out there, or was it the past, accumulations of old time and need, despairs mounding themselves to panics and at last finding tongue?

"God, Charles. Just now, I could have sworn I heard you say—"

"Say what?"

"You said: 'Make a wish.' "

"*I* did?"

His laughter behind me did not make me turn; I kept on watching the snow fall and I told him what I must tell—

"You said. 'It's a special, fine, strange night. So make the finest, dearest, strangest wish ever in your life, deep from your heart. It will be yours.' That's what I heard you say."

"No." I saw his image in the glass shake its head. "But, Tom, you've stood there hypnotized by the snowfall for half an hour. The fire on the hearth talked. Wishes don't come true, Tom. But—" and here he stopped and added with some surprise, "by God, you *did* hear something, didn't you? Well, here. Drink."

The popcorn was done popping. He poured wine which I did not touch. The snow was falling steadily along the dark window in pale breaths.

"Why?" I asked. "Why would this *wish* jump into my head? If you didn't say it, what did?"

What indeed, I thought; what's out there, and who are we? Two writers late, alone, my friend invited for the night, two old companions used to much talk and gossip about ghosts, who've tried their hands at all the usual psychic stuffs, Ouija boards, tarot cards, telepathies, the junk of amiable friendship over years, but always full of taunts and jokes and idle fooleries.

But this out there tonight, I though, ends the jokes, erases smiles. The snow—why, look! It's burying our laughter. . . .

"Why?" said Charlie at my elbow, drinking wine, gazing at the red-green-blue Yule-tree lights and now at the back of my neck. "Why a *wish* on a night like this? Well, it is the night before Christmas, right? Five minutes from now, Christ is born. Christ and the winter solstice all in one week. This week, this night, proves that Earth won't die. The winter has touched bottom and now starts upward toward the light. That's special. That's incredible."

"Yes," I murmured, and thought of the old days when cavemen died in their hearts when autumn came and the sun went away and the ape-men cried until the world shifted in its white sleep and the sun rose earlier one fine morning and the universe was saved once more, for a little while. "Yes."

"So—" Charlie read my thoughts and sipped his wine. "Christ always was the promise of spring, wasn't he? In the midst of the longest night of the year, Time shook, Earth shuddered and calved a myth. And what did the myth yell? Happy New Year! God, yes, January first isn't New Year's Day. Christ's birthday is. His breath, sweet as clover, touches our nostrils, promises spring, this very moment before midnight. Take a deep breath, Thomas."

"Shut up!"

"Why? Do you hear voices again?"

Yes! I turned to the window. In sixty seconds, it would be the morn of His birth. What purer, rarer hour was there, I thought wildly, for wishes.

"Tom—" Charlie seized my elbow. But I was gone deep and very wild indeed. Is this a special time? I thought. Do holy ghosts wander on nights of falling snow to do us favors in this strange-held hour? If I make a wish in secret, will that perambulating night, strange sleeps, old blizzards give back my wish tenfold?

I shut my eyes. My throat convulsed.

"Don't," said Charlie.

But it trembled on my lips. I could not wait. Now, now, I thought, a strange star burns at Bethlehem.

"Tom," gasped Charlie, "for Christ's sake!"

Christ, yes, I thought, and said:

"My wish is, for one hour tonight—"

"No!" Charlie struck me, once, to shut my mouth.

"—please, make my father alive again."

The mantel clock struck twelve times to midnight.

"Oh, Thomas . . ." Charlie grieved. His hand fell away from my arm. "Oh, Tom."

A gust of snow rattled the window, clung like a shroud, unraveled away.

The front door exploded wide.

Snow sprang over us in a shower.

"What a sad wish. And . . . it has just come true."

"True?" I whirled to stare at that open door which beckoned like a tomb.

"Don't go, Tom," said Charlie.

The door slammed. Outside, I ran; oh, God, how I ran.

"Tom, come back!" The voice faded far behind me in the whirling fall of white. "Oh, God, *don't!*"

But in this minute after midnight I ran and ran, mindless, gibbering, yelling my heart on to beat, blood to move, legs to run and keep running, and I thought: Him! Him! I know where *he* is! If the gift is mine! If the wish comes true! I know his *place!* And all about in the night-snowing town the bells of Christmas began to clang and chant and clamor. They circled and paced and drew me on as I shouted and mouthed snow and knew maniac desire.

Fool! I thought. He's dead! Go back!

But what if he is alive, one hour tonight, and I *didn't* go to find him?

I was outside town, with no hat or coat, but so warm from running, a salty mask froze my face and flaked away with the jolt of each stride down the middle of an empty road, with the sound of joyous bells blown away and gone.

A wind took me around a final corner of wilderness where a dark wall waited for me.

The cemetery.

I stood by the heavy iron gates, looking numbly in.

The graveyard resembled the scattered ruins of an ancient fort, blown up lifetimes ago, its monuments buried deep in some new Ice Age.

Suddenly, miracles were not possible.

Suddenly the night was just so much wine and talk and dumb enchantments and I running for no reason save I believed, I truly believed, I had felt something *happen* out here in this snow-dead world.

Now I was so burdened at the blind sight of those untouched graves and printless snow, I would gladly have sunk and died there myself. I could not go back to town to face Charlie. I began to think this was all some brutal humor and awful trick of his, his insane ability to guess someone's terrible need and toy with it. *Had* he whispered behind my back, made promises, nudged me toward this wish? Christ!

I touched the padlocked gate.

What was here? Only a flat stone with a name and BORN 1888, DIED 1957, an inscription that even on summer days was hard to find, for the grass grew thick and the leaves gathered in mounds.

I let go of the iron gate and turned. Then, in an instant, I gasped. An unbelieving shout tore from my throat.

For I had sensed something beyond the wall, near the small boarded-up gatekeeper's lodge.

Was there some faint breathing there? A muted cry?

Or just a hint of warmth on the wind?

I clenched the iron gate and stared beyond.

Yes, there! The faintest track, as if a bird had landed to run along between the buried stones. Another moment, and I would have missed it forever!

I yelled, I ran, I leaped.

I have never, oh, God, in all my life, leaped so high. I cleared the wall and fell down on the other side, a last shout bloodying my mouth. I scrambled around to the far side of the gatehouse.

There in shadows, hidden away from the wind, leaning against a wall, was a man, eyes shut, his hands crossed over his chest.

I stared at him, wildly. I leaned insanely close to peer, to find.

I did not know this man.

He was old, old, very old.

I must have groaned with fresh despair.

For now the old man opened his trembling eyes.

It was his eyes, looking at me, that made me shout:

"Dad!"

I lurched to seize him into dim lamplight and the falling snows of after-midnight.

Charlie's voice, a long way off in the snowy town, echoed and pleaded: No, don't, go, run. Nightmare. Stop.

The man who stood before me did not know me.

Like a scarecrow held up against the wind, this strange but familiar shape tried to make me out with his white-blind and cobwebbed eyes. Who? he seemed to be thinking.

Then an answering cry burst from his mouth:

"—om! —om!"

He could not pronounce the *T*.

But it was my name.

Like a man on a cliff edge, terrified that the earth might fall and drop him back to night and soil, he shuddered, grappled me.

"—om!"

I held him tight. He could not fall.

Riveted in a fierce embrace, not able to let go, we

stood and rocked gently, strangely, two men made one, in a wilderness of shredding snow.

Tom, O Tom, he grieved brokenly, over and over.

Father, O dear Pa, Dad, I thought, I said.

The old man stiffened, for over my shoulder he must have truly seen for the first time the stones, the empty fields of death. He gasped as if to cry: What *is* this place?

Old as his face was, in the instant of recognition and remembrance, his eyes, his cheeks, his mouth withered and grew yet older, saying No.

He turned to me as if seeking answers, some guardian of his rights, some protector who might say No with him. But the cold truth was in my eyes.

We were both staring now at the dim path his feet had made blundering across the land from the place where he had been buried for many years.

No, no, no, no, no, no, *no!*

The words fired from his mouth.

But he could not pronounce the *n*.

So it was a wild explosion of: ". . . o . . . o . . . o . . . o . . . o . . . *o!*"

A forlorn, dismayed, child-whistling cry.

Then, another question shadowed his face.

I know this place. But *why* am I here?

He clawed his arms. He stared down at his withered chest.

God gives us dreadful gifts. The most dreadful of all is memory.

He remembered.

And he began to melt away. He recalled his body shriveling, his dim heart gone to stillness; the slam of some eternal door of night.

He stood very still in my arms, his eyelids flickering over the stuffs that shifted grotesque furnitures within his head. He must have asked himself the most terrible question of all:

*Who* has done this thing to me?

He opened his eyes. His gaze beat at me.

*You?* it said.

Yes, I thought. *I* wished you alive this night.

*You!* his face and body cried.

And then, half-aloud, the final inquisition:

"Why . . . ?"

Now it was my turn to be blasted and riven.

Why, indeed, had I done this to him?

How had I dared to wish for this awful, this harrowing, confrontation?

What was I to do now with this man, this stranger, this old, bewildered, and frightened child? Why had I summoned him, just to send him back to soils and graves and dreadful sleeps?

Had I even bothered to think of the consequences? No. Raw impulse had shot me from home to this burial field like a mindless stone to a mindless goal. Why? Why?

My father, this old man, stood in the snow now, trembling, waiting for my pitiful answer.

A child again, I could not speak. Some part of me knew a truth I could not say. Inarticulate with him in life, I found myself yet more mute in his waking death.

The truth raved inside my head, cried along the fibers of my spirit and being, but could not break forth from my tongue. I felt my own shouts locked inside.

The moment was passing. This hour would soon be gone. I would lose the chance to say what must be said, what should have been said when he was warm and above the earth so many years ago.

Somewhere far off across country, the bells sounded twelve-thirty on this Christmas morn. Christ ticked in the wind. Snow flaked away at my face with time and cold, cold and time.

Why? my father's eyes asked me; why have you brought me here?

"I—" and then I stopped.

For his hand had tightened on my arm. His face had found its own reason.

This was his chance, too, *his* final hour to say what he should have said when I was twelve or fourteen or twenty-six. No matter if *I* stood mute. Here in the falling snow, he could make his peace and go his way.

His mouth opened. It was hard, so dreadfully hard, for him to force the old words out. Only the ghost within the withered shell could dare to agonize and gasp. He whispered three words, lost in the wind.

"Yes?" I urged.

He held me tight and tried to keep his eyes open in the blizzard-night. He wanted to sleep, but first his mouth gaped and whistled again and again:

". . . I......uvv.........yuuuuuuuu . . . . . . .!"

He stopped, trembled, wracked his body, and tried to shout it again, failing:

". . . I......vvv.........yyy.........u . . . !"

"Oh, Dad!" I cried. "Let me say it *for* you!"

He stood very still and waited.

"Were you trying to say I . . . love . . . you?"

"Esssss!" he cried. And burst out, very clearly, at long last: "Oh, *yes!*"

"Oh, Dad," I said, wild with miserable happiness, all gain and loss. "Oh, and Pa, dear Pa, I love *you.*"

We fell together. We held.

I wept.

And from some strange dry well within his terrible flesh I saw my father squeeze forth tears which trembled and flashed on his eyelids.

And the final question was thus asked and answered.

Why have you brought me here?

Why the wish, why the gifts, and why this snowing night?

Because we had had to say, before the doors were shut and sealed forever, what we never had said in life.

And now it had been said and we stood holding each

other in the wilderness, father and son, son and father, the parts of the whole suddenly interchangeable with joy.

The tears turned to ice upon my cheeks.

We stood in the cold wind and falling snow for a long while until we heard the sound of the bells at twelve forty-five, and still we stood in the snowing night saying no more—no more ever need be said—until at last our hour was done.

All over the white world the clocks of one A.M. on Christmas morn, with Christ new in the fresh straw, sounded the end of that gift which had passed so briefly into and now out of our numb hands.

My father held me in his arms.

The last sound of the one-o'clock bells faded.

I felt my father step back, at ease now.

His fingers touched my cheek.

I heard him walking in the snow.

The sound of his walking faded even as the last of the crying faded within myself.

I opened my eyes only in time to see him, a hundred yards off, walking. He turned and waved, once, at me.

The snow came down in a curtain.

How brave, I thought, to go where you go now, old man, and no complaint.

I walked back into town.

I had a drink with Charles by the fire. He looked in my face and drank a silent toast to what he saw there.

Upstairs, my bed waited for me like a great fold of white snow.

The snow was falling beyond my window for a thousand miles to the north, five hundred miles to the east, two hundred miles west, a hundred miles to the south. The snow fell on everything, everywhere. It fell on two sets of footprints beyond the town: one set coming out and the other going back to be lost among the graves.

I lay on my bed of snow. I remembered my father's face as he waved and turned and went away.

It was the face of the youngest, happiest man I had ever seen.

With that I slept, and gave up weeping.

# Forever and the Earth

After seventy years of writing short stories that never sold, Mr. Henry William Field arose one night at eleven-thirty and burned ten million words. He carried the manuscripts downstairs through his dark old mansion and threw them into the furnace.

"That's that," he said, and thinking about his lost art and his misspent life, he put himself to bed, among his rich antiques. "My mistake was in ever trying to picture this wild world of A.D. 2257. The rockets, the atom wonders, the travels to planets and double suns. Nobody can do it. Everyone's tried. All of our modern authors have failed."

Space was too big for them, and rockets too swift, and atomic science too instantaneous, he thought. But at least the other writers, while failing, had been published, while he, in his idle wealth, had used the years of his life for nothing.

After an hour of feeling this way, he fumbled through the night rooms to his library and switched on a green hurricane lamp. At random, from a collection untouched in fifty years, he selected a book. It was a book three centuries yellow and three centuries brittle, but he settled into it and read hungrily until dawn. . . .

At nine the next morning, Henry William Field staggered from his library, called his servants, televised lawyers, scientists, literateurs.

"Come at once!" he cried.

By noon, a dozen people had stepped into the study where Henry William Field sat, very disreputable and hysterical with an odd, feeding joy, unshaven and feverish. He clutched a thick book in his brittle arms and laughed if anyone even said good morning.

"Here you see a book," he said at last, holding it out, "written by a giant, a man born in Asheville, North Carolina, in the year 1900. Long gone to dust, he published four huge novels. He was a whirlwind. He lifted up mountains and collected winds. He left a trunk of penciled manuscripts behind when he lay in bed at Johns Hopkins Hospital in Baltimore in the year 1938, on September fifteenth, and died of pneumonia, an ancient and awful disease."

They looked at the book.

*Look Homeward, Angel.*

He drew forth three more. *Of Time and the River. The Web and the Rock. You Can't Go Home Again.*

"By Thomas Wolfe," said the old man. "Three centuries cold in the North Carolina earth."

"You mean you've called us simply to see four books by a dead man?" his friends protested.

"More than that! I've called you because I feel Tom Wolfe's the man, the necessary man, to write of space, of time, huge things like nebulae and galactic war, meteors and planets, all the dark things he loved and put on paper were like this. He was born out of his time. He needed really *big* things to play with and never found them on Earth. He should have been born this afternoon instead of one hundred thousand mornings ago."

"I'm afraid you're a bit late," said Professor Bolton.

"I don't intend to be late!" snapped the old man. "I will *not* be frustrated by reality. You, professor, have experimented with time-travel. I expect you to finish your time machine as soon as possible. Here's a check, a blank check, fill it in. If you need more money, ask for it. You've done *some* traveling already, haven't you?"

"A few years, yes, but nothing like centuries—"

"We'll *make* it centuries! You others"—he swept them with a fierce and shining glance—"will work with Bolton. I *must* have Thomas Wolfe."

"What!" They fell back before him.

"Yes," he said. "That's the plan. Wolfe is to be brought to me. We will collaborate in the task of describing the flight from Earth to Mars, as only he could describe it!"

They left him in his library with his books, turning the dry pages, nodding to himself. "Yes. Oh, dear Lord yes, Tom's the boy, Tom is the *very* boy for this."

The months passed slowly. Days showed a maddening reluctance to leave the calendar, and weeks lingered on until Mr. Henry William Field began to scream silently.

At the end of four months, Mr. Field awoke one midnight. The phone was ringing. He put his hand out in the darkness.

"Yes?"

"This is Professor Bolton calling."

"Yes, Bolton?"

"I'll be leaving in an hour," said the voice.

"Leaving? Leaving where? Are you quitting? You can't do that!"

"Please, Mr. Field, leaving means *leaving*."

"You mean, you're actually going?"

"Within the hour."

"To 1938? To September fifteenth?"

"Yes!"

"You're sure you've the date fixed correctly? You'll arrive before he dies? Be sure of it! Good Lord, you'd better get there a good hour before his death, don't you think?"

"*Two* hours. On the way back, we'll mark time in Bermuda, borrow ten days of free floating continuum, inject him, tan him, swim him, vitaminize him, make him well."

"I'm so excited I can't hold the phone. Good luck, Bolton. Bring him through safely!"

"Thank you, sir. Good-bye."

The phone clicked.

Mr. Henry William Field lay through the ticking night. He thought of Tom Wolfe as a lost brother to be lifted intact from under a cold, chiseled stone, to be restored to blood and fire and speaking. He trembled each time he thought of Bolton whirling on the time wind back to other calendars and other days, bearing medicines to change flesh and save souls.

Tom, he thought, faintly, in the half-awake warmth of an old man calling after his favorite and long-gone child, Tom, where are you tonight, Tom? Come along now, we'll help you through, you've got to come, there's need for you. I couldn't do it, Tom, none of us here can. So the next best thing to doing it myself, Tom, is helping you to do it. You can play with rockets like jackstraws, Tom, and you can have the stars, like a handful of crystals. Anything your heart asks, it's here. You'd like the fire and the travel, Tom, it was made for you. Oh, we've a pale lot of writers today, I've read them all, Tom, and they're not like you. I've waded in libraries of their stuff and they've never touched space, Tom; we need *you* for that! Give an old man his wish then, for God knows I've waited all my life for myself or some other to write the really great book about the stars, and I've waited in vain. So, wherever you are tonight, Tom Wolfe, make yourself tall. It's that book you were going to write. It's that good book the critics said was in you when you stopped breathing.

Here's your chance, will you do it, Tom? Will you listen and come through to us, will you do that tonight, and be here in the morning when I wake? Will you, Tom?

His eyelids closed down over the fever and the demand. His tongue stopped quivering in his sleeping mouth.

The clock struck four.

Awakening to the white coolness of morning, he felt the excitement rising and welling in himself. He did not wish to blink, for fear that the thing which awaited him somewhere in the house might run off and slam a door, gone forever. His hands reached up to clutch his thin chest.

Far away . . . footsteps . . .

A series of doors opened and shut. Two men entered the bedroom.

Field could hear them breathe. Their footsteps took on identities. The first steps were those of a spider, small and precise: Bolton. The second steps were those of a big man, a large man, a heavy man.

"Tom?" cried the old man. He did not open his eyes.

"Yes," said a voice, at last.

Tom Wolfe burst the seams of Field's imagination, as a huge child bursts the lining of a too-small coat.

"Tom Wolfe, let me look at you!" If Field said it once he said it a dozen times as he fumbled from bed, shaking violently. "Put up the blinds, for God's sake, I want to see this! Tom Wolfe, is that *you?*"

Tom Wolfe looked down from his tall thick body, with big hands out to balance himself in a world that was strange. He looked at the old man and the room and his mouth was trembling.

"You're just as they said you were, Tom!"

Thomas Wolfe began to laugh and the laughing was huge, for he must have thought himself insane or in a nightmare, and he came to the old man and touched him and he looked at Professor Bolton and felt of himself, his arms and legs, he coughed experimentally and touched his own brow. "My fever's gone," he said. "I'm not sick anymore."

"Of course not, Tom."

"What a night," said Tom Wolfe. "It hasn't been easy. I thought I was sicker than any man ever was. I felt myself floating and I thought, This is fever. I felt myself traveling, and thought, I'm dying fast. A man came to me. I thought, This is the Lord's messenger. He took my hands. I smelled electricity. I flew up and over, and I saw a brass city. I thought, I've arrived. This is the city of heaven, there is the Gate! I'm numb from head to toe, like someone left in the snow to freeze. I've got to laugh and do things or I might think myself insane. You're not God, are you? You don't look like Him."

The old man laughed. "No, no, Tom, not God, but playing at it. I'm Field." He laughed again. "Lord, listen to me. I said it as if you should know who Field is. Field, the financier, Tom, bow low, kiss my ring finger. I'm Henry Field. I like your work, I brought you here. Come along."

The old man drew him to an immense crystal window.

"Do you see those lights in the sky, Tom?"

"Yes, sir."

"Those fireworks?"

"Yes."

"They're not what you think, son. It's not July Fourth, Tom. Not in the usual way. Every day's Independence Day now. Man has declared his Freedom from Earth. Gravitation without representation has been overthrown. The Revolt has long since been successful. That green Roman Candle's going to Mars. That red fire, that's the Venus rocket. And the others, you see the yellow and the blue? Rockets, all of them!"

Thomas Wolfe gazed up like an immense child caught amid the colorized glories of a July evening when the set-pieces are awhirl with phosphorus and glitter and barking explosion.

"What years is this?"

"The year of the rocket. Look here." And the old man touched some flowers that bloomed at his touch. The blossoms were like blue and white fire. They burned and sparkled their cold, long petals. The blooms were two feet wide, and they were the color of an autumn moon. "Moon-flowers," said the old man. "From the other side of the moon." He brushed them and they dripped away into a silver rain, a shower of white sparks on the air. "The year of the rocket. That's a title for you, Tom. That's why we brought you here, we've need of you. You're the only man could handle the sun without being burnt to a ridiculous cinder. We want you to juggle the sun, Tom, and the stars, and whatever else you see on your trip to Mars."

"Mars?" Thomas Wolfe turned to seize the old man's arm, bending down at him, searching his face in unbelief.

"Tonight. You leave at six o'clock."

The old man held a fluttering pink ticket on the air, waiting for Tom to think to take it.

It was five in the afternoon. "Of course, of course I appreciate what you've done," cried Thomas Wolfe.

"Sit down, Tom. Stop walking around."

"Let me finish, Mr. Field, let me get through with this, I've got to say it."

"We've been arguing for hours," pleaded Mr. Field, exhaustedly.

They had talked from breakfast until lunch until tea, they had wandered through a dozen rooms and ten dozen arguments, they had perspired and grown cold and perspired again.

"It all comes down to this," said Thomas Wolfe, at last. "I can't stay here, Mr. Field. I've got to go back. This isn't my time. You've no right to interfere—"

"But, I—"

"I was deep in my work, my best yet to come, and now you run me off three centuries. Mr. Field, I want you to call Mr. Bolton back. I want you to have him put me in his machine, whatever it is, and return me to 1938, my rightful place and year. That's all I ask of you."

"But, don't you *want* to see Mars?"

"With all my heart. But I know it isn't for me. It would throw my writing off. I'd have a huge handful of experience that I couldn't fit into my other writing when I went home."

"You don't understand, Tom, you don't understand at all."

"I understand that you're selfish."

"Selfish? Yes," said the old man. "For myself, and for others, very selfish."

"I want to go home."

"Listen to me, Tom."

"Call Mr. Bolton."

"Tom, I don't want to have to tell you this. I thought I wouldn't have to, that it wouldn't be necessary. Now, you leave me only this alternative." The old man's right hand fetched hold of a curtained wall, swept back the drapes, revealing a large white screen, and dialem a number, a series of numbers. The screen flickered into vivid color, the lights of the room darkened, darkened, and a graveyard took line before their eyes.

"What are you doing?" demanded Wolfe, striding forward, staring at the screen.

"I don't like this at all," said the old man. "Look there."

The graveyard lay in midafternoon light, the light of summer. From the screen drifted the smell of summer earth, granite, and the odor of a nearby creek. From the trees, a bird called. Red and yellow flowers nodded among the stones, and the screen moved, the sky rotated, the old man twisted a dial for emphasis, and in the center of the screen, growing large, coming closer, yet larger, and now filling their senses, was a dark granite mass; and Thomas Wolfe, looking up in the dim room, ran his eyes over the chiseled words, once, twice, three times, gasped, and read again, for there was his name:

THOMAS WOLFE.

And the date of his birth and the date of his death, and the flowers and green ferns smelling sweetly on the air of the cold room.

"Turn it off," he said.

"I'm sorry, Tom."

"Turn it off, turn it off! I don't believe it."

"It's there."

The screen went black and now the entire room was a midnight vault, a tomb, with the last faint odor of flowers.

"I didn't wake up again," said Thomas Wolfe.

"No. You died that September of 1938. So, you see. O God, the ironies, it's like the title of your book. Tom, you *can't* go home again."

"I never finished my book."

"It was edited for you, by others who went over it, carefully."

"I didn't finish my work, I didn't finish my work."

"Don't take it so badly, Tom."

"How else can I take it?"

The old man didn't turn on the lights. He didn't want to see Tom there. "Sit down, boy." No reply. "Tom?" No answer. "Sit down, son; will you have something to drink?" For answer there was only a sigh and a kind of brutal moaning.

"Good Lord," said Tom, "it's not fair. I had so much left to do, it's not fair." He began to weep quietly.

"Don't do that," said the old man. "Listen. Listen to me. You're still alive, aren't you? Here? Now? You still *feel*, don't *you?*"

Thomas Wolfe waited for a minute and then he said, "Yes."

"All right, then." The old man pressed forward on

the dark air. "I've brought you here, I've given you another chance, Tom. An extra month or so. Do you think *I* haven't grieved for you? When I read your books and saw your gravestone there, three centuries worn by rains and wind, boy, don't you imagine how it killed me to think of your talent gone away? Well, it did! It killed me, Tom. And I spent my money to find a way to you. You've a respite, not long, not long at all. Professor Bolton says that, with luck, he can hold the channels open through time for eight weeks. He can keep you here that long, and only that long. In that interval, Tom, you must write the book you've wanted to write—no, not the book you were working on for them, son, no, for they're dead and gone and it can't be changed. No, this time it's a book for us, Tom, for us the living, that's the book we want. A book you can leave with us, for you, a book bigger and better in every way than anything you ever wrote; say you'll *do* it, Tom, say you'll forget about that stone and that hospital for eight weeks and start to work for us, will you, Tom, will you?"

The lights came slowly on. Tom Wolfe stood tall at the window, looking out, his face huge and tired and pale. He watched the rockets on the sky of early evening. "I imagine I don't realize what you've done for me," he said. "You've given me a little more time, and time is the thing I love most and need, the thing I always hated and fought against, and the only way I can show my appreciation is by doing as you say." He hesitated. "And when I'm finished, then what?"

"Back to your hospital in 1938, Tom."

"Must I?"

"We can't change time. We borrowed you for five minutes. We'll return you to your hospital cot five minutes after you left it. That way, we upset nothing. It's all been written. You can't hurt us in the future by living here now with us, but, if you refused to go back, you could hurt the past, and resultantly, the future, make it into some sort of chaos."

"Eight weeks," said Thomas Wolfe.

"Eight weeks."

"And the Mars rocket leaves in an hour?"

"Yes."

"I'll need pencils and paper."

"Here they are."

"I'd better go get ready. Good-bye, Mr. Field."

"Good luck, Tom."

Six o'clock. The sun setting. The sky turning to wine. The big house quiet. The old man shivering in the heat until Professor Bolton entered. "Bolton, how is he getting on, how was he at the port; tell me?"

Bolton smiled. "What a monster he is, so big they had to make a special uniform for him! You should've seen him, walking around, lifting up everything, sniffing like a great hound, talking, his eyes looking at everyone, excited as a ten-year-old!"

"God bless him, oh, God bless him! Bolton, can you keep him here as long as you say?"

Bolton frowned. "He doesn't belong here, you know. If our power should falter, he'd be snapped back to his own time, like a puppet on a rubber band. We'll try and keep him, I assure you."

"You've got to, you understand, you can't let him go back until he's finished with his book. You've—"

"Look," said Bolton. He pointed to the sky. On it was a silver rocket.

"Is that him?" asked the old man.

"That's Tom Wolfe," replied Bolton. "Going to Mars."

"Give 'em hell, Tom, give 'em hell!" shouted the old man, lifting both fists.

They watched the rocket fire into space.

By midnight, the story was coming through.

Henry William Field sat in his library. On his desk was a machine that hummed. It repeated words that were being written out beyond the moon. It scrawled them in black pencil, in facsimile of Tom Wolfe's fevered hand a million miles away. The old man waited for a pile of them to collect and then he seized them and read them aloud to the room where Bolton and the servants stood listening. He read the words about space and time and travel, about a large man and a large journey and how it was in the long midnight and coldness of space, and how a man could be hungry enough to take all of it and ask for more. He read the words that were full of fire and thunder and mystery.

Space was like October, wrote Thomas Wolfe. He said things about its darkness and its loneliness and a man so small in it. The eternal and timeless October, was one of the things he said. And then he told of the rocket itself, the smell and the feel of the metal of the rocket, and the sense of destiny and wild exultancy to at last leave Earth behind, all problems and all sadnesses, and go seeking a bigger problem and a bigger sadness. Oh, it was fine writing, and it said what had to be said about space and man and his small rockets out there alone.

The old man read until he was hoarse, and then Bolton read, and then the others, far into the night, when the machine stopped transcribing words and they knew that Tom Wolfe was in bed, then, on the rocket, flying to Mars, probably not asleep, no, he wouldn't sleep for hours yet, no, lying awake, like a boy the night before a circus, not believing the big jeweled black tent is up and the circus is on, with ten billion blazing performers on the high wires and the invisible trapezes of space.

"There," breathed the old man, gentling aside the last pages of the first chapter. "What do you think of that, Bolton?"

"It's good."

"Good hell!" shouted Field. "It's wonderful! Read it again, sit down, read it again, damn you!"

It kept coming through, one day following another, for ten hours at a time. The stack of yellow papers on the floor, scribbled on, grew immense in a week, unbelievable in two weeks, absolutely impossible in a month.

"Listen to this!" cried the old man, and read.

"And this!" he said.

"And this chapter here, and this little novel here, it just came through, Bolton, titled 'The Space War,' a complete novel on how it feels to fight a space war. Tom's been talking to people, soldiers, officers, men, veterans of space. He's got it all here. And here's a chapter called 'The Long Midnight,' and here's one on the Negro colonization of Mars, and here's a character sketch of a Martian, absolutely priceless!"

Bolton cleared his throat. "Mr. Field?"

"Yes, yes, don't bother me."

"I've some bad news, sir."

Field jerked his gray head up. "What? The time element?"

"You'd better tell Wolfe to hurry his work. The connection may break sometime this week," said Bolton, softly.

"I'll give you anything, anything if you keep it going!"

"It's not money, Mr. Field. It's just plain physics right now. I'll do everything I can. But you'd better warn him."

The old man shriveled in his chair and was small. "But you can't take him away from me now, not when he's doing so well. You should see the outline he sent through an hour ago, the stories, the sketches. Here, here's one on spatial tides, another on meteors. Here's a short novel begun, called 'Thistledown and Fire'—"

"I'm sorry."

"If we lose him now, can we get him again?"

"I'd be afraid to tamper too much."

The old man was frozen. "Only one thing to do then. Arrange to have Wolfe type his work, if possible, or dictate it, to save time; rather than have him use pencil and paper, he's got to use a machine of some sort. See to it!"

The machine ticked away by the hour into the night

and into the dawn and through the day. The old man slept only in faint dozes, blinking awake when the machine stuttered to life, and all of space and travel and existence came to him through the mind of another:

"*. . . the great starred meadows of space . . .*"

The machine jumped.

"Keep at it, Tom show them!" The old man waited.

The phone rang.

It was Bolton.

"We can't keep it up, Mr. Field. The continuum device will absolute out within the hour."

"Do something!"

"I can't."

The teletype chattered. In a cold fascination, in a horror, the old man watched the black lines form.

"*. . . the Martian cities, immense and unbelievable, as numerous as stones thrown from some great mountain in a rushing and incredible avalanche, resting at last in shining mounds . . .*"

"Tom!" cried the old man.

"Now," said Bolton, on the phone.

The teletype hesitated, typed a word, and fell silent.

"Tom!" screamed the old man.

He shook the teletype.

"It's no use," said the telephone voice. "He's gone. I'm shutting off the time machine."

"No! Leave it on!"

"But—"

"You heard me—leave it! We're not sure he's gone."

"He is. It's no use, we're wasting energy."

"Waste it, then!"

He slammed the phone down.

He turned to the teletype, to the unfinished sentence.

"Come on, Tom, they can't get rid of you that way, you won't let them, will you, boy, come on. Tom, show them, you're big, you're bigger than time or space or their damned machines, you're strong and you've a will like iron, Tom, show them, don't let them send you back!"

The teletype snapped one key.

The old man bleated. "Tom! You *are* there, aren't you? Can you still write? Write, Tom, keep it coming, as long as you keep it rolling, Tom, they *can't* send you back!"

"*The*," typed the machine.

"More, Tom, more!"

*Odors of*, clacked the machine.

"Yes?"

*Mars*, typed the machine, and paused. A minute's silence. The machine spaced, skipped a paragraph, and began:

*The odors of Mars, the cinnamons and cold spice winds, the winds of cloudy dust and winds of powerful bone and ancient pollen—*

"Tom, your're still alive!"

For answer the machine, in the next ten hours, slammed out six chapters of "Flight Before Fury" in a series of fevered explosions.

"Today makes six weeks, Bolton, six whole weeks, Tom gone, on Mars, through the Asteroids. Look here, the manuscripts. Ten thousand words a day, he's driving himself, I don't know when he sleeps, or if he eats, I don't care, he doesn't either, he only wants to get it done, because he knows the time is short."

"I can't understand it," said Bolton. "The power failed because our relays wore out. It took us three days to manufacture and replace the particular channel relays necessary to keep the Time Element steady, and yet Wolfe hung on. There's a personal factor here, Lord knows what, we didn't take into account. Wolfe lives here, in this time, when he *is* here, and can't be snapped back, after all. Time isn't as flexible as we imagined. We used the wrong simile. It's not like a rubber band. More like osmosis; the penetration of membranes by liquids, from Past to Present, but we've got to send him back, can't keep him here, there'd be a void there, a derangement. The one thing that really keeps him here now is himself, his drive, his desire, his work. After it's over he'll go back as naturally as pouring water from a glass."

"I don't care about reasons, all I know is Tom is finishing it. He has the old fire and description, and something else, something more, a searching of values that supersede time and space. He's done a study of a woman left behind on Earth while the damn rocket heroes leap into space that's beautiful, objective, and subtle; he calls it 'Day of the Rocket,' and it is nothing more than an afternoon of a typical suburban housewife who lives as her ancestral mothers lived, in a house, raising her children, her life not much different from a cavewoman's, in the midst of the splendor of science and the trumpetings of space projectiles; a true and steady and subtle study of her wishes and frustrations. Here's another manuscript, called 'The Indians,' in which he refers to the Martians as Cherokees and Iroquois and Blackfoots, the Indian nations of space, destroyed and driven back. Have a drink, Bolton, have a drink!"

Tom Wolfe returned to Earth at the end of eight weeks.

He arrived in fire as he had left in fire, and his huge steps were burned across space, and in the library of Henry William Field's house were towers of yellow paper, with lines of black scribble and type on them, and these were to be separated out into the six sections of a masterwork that, through endurance, and a knowing that the sands were dwindling from the glass, had mushroomed day after day.

Tom Wolfe came back to Earth and stood in the library of Henry William Field's house and looked at the massive outpourings of his heart and his hand and when the old man said, "Do you want to read it, Tom?" he shook his great head and replied, putting back his thick mane of dark hair with his big pale hand, "No. I don't dare start on it. If I did, I'd want to take it home with me. And I can't do that, can I?"

"No, Tom, you can't."

"No matter *how* much I wanted to?"

"No, that's the way it is. You never wrote another novel in that year, Tom. What was written here must stay here, what was written there must stay there. There's no touching it."

"I see." Tom sank down into a chair with a great sigh. "I'm tired. I'm mightily tired. It's been hard, but it's been good. What day is it?"

"This is the fifty-sixth day."

"The *last* day?"

The old man nodded and they were both silent awhile.

"Back to 1938 in the stone cemetery," said Tom Wolfe, eyes shut. "I don't like that. I wish I didn't know about that, it's a horrible thing to know." His voice faded and he put his big hands over his face and held them tightly there.

The door opened. Bolton let himself in and stood behind Tom Wolfe's chair, a small phial in his hand.

"What's that?" asked the old man.

"An extinct virus. Pneumonia. Very ancient and very evil," said Bolton. "When Mr. Wolfe came through, I had to cure him of his illness, of course, which was immensely easy with the techniques we know today, in order to put him in working condition for his job, Mr. Field. I kept this pneumonia culture. Now that he's going back, he'll have to be reinoculated with the disease."

"Otherwise?"

"Otherwise, he'd get well, in 1938."

Tom Wolfe arose from his chair. "You mean, get well, walk around, back there, be well, and cheat the mortician?"

"That's what I mean."

Tom Wolfe stared at the phial and one of his hands

twitched. "What if I destroyed the virus and refused to let you inoculate me?"

"You can't do that!"

"But—supposing?"

"You'd ruin things."

"What things?"

"The pattern, life, the ways things are and were, the things that can't be changed. You can't disrupt it. There's only one sure thing, you're to die, and I'm to see to it."

Wolfe looked at the door. "I could run off."

"We control the machine. You wouldn't get out of the house. I'd have you back here, by force, and inoculated. I anticipated some such trouble when the time came; there are five men waiting down below. One shout from me—you see, it's useless. There, that's better. Here now."

Wolfe had moved back and now had turned to look at the old man and the window and this huge house. "I'm afraid I must apologize. I don't want to die. So very much I don't want to die."

The old man came to him and took his hand. "Think of it this way: you've had two more months than anyone could expect from life, and you've turned out another book, a last book, a fine book, think of that."

"I want to thank you for this," said Thomas Wolfe, gravely. "I want to thank both of you. I'm ready." He rolled up his sleeve. "The inoculation."

And while Bolton bent to his task, with his free hand Thomas Wolfe penciled two black lines across the top of the first manuscript and went on talking:

"There's a passage from one of my old books," he said, scowling to remember it. ". . . *of wandering forever and the Earth . . . Who owns the Earth? Did we want the Earth? That we should wander on it? Did we need the Earth that we were never still upon it? Whoever needs the Earth shall have the Earth; he shall be upon it, he shall rest within a little place, he shall dwell in one small room forever . . .*"

Wolfe was finished with the remembering.

"Here's my last book," he said, and on the empty yellow paper facing the manuscript he blocked out vigorous huge black letters with pressures of the pencil: FOREVER AND THE EARTH, by Thomas Wolfe.

He picked up a ream of it and held it tightly in his hands, against his chest, for a moment. "I wish I could take it back with me. It's like parting with my son." He gave it a slap and put it aside and immediately thereafter gave his quick hand into that of his employer, and strode across the room, Bolton after him, until he reached the door where he stood framed in the late-afternoon light, huge and magnificent. "Good-bye, good-bye!" he cried.

The door slammed. Tom Wolfe was gone.

They found him wandering in the hospital corridor.

"Mr. Wolfe!"

"What?"

"Mr. Wolfe, you gave us a scare, we thought you were gone!"

"Gone?"

"Where did you go?"

"Where? Where?" He let himself be led through the midnight corridors. "Where? Oh, if I *told* you where, you'd never believe."

"Here's your bed, you shouldn't have left it."

Deep into the white death bed, which smelled of pale, clean mortality awaiting him, a mortality which had the hospital odor in it; the bed which, as he touched it, folded him into fumes and white starched coldness.

"Mars, Mars," whispered the huge man, late at night. "My best, my very best, my really fine book, yet to be written, yet to be printed, in another year, three centuries away . . ."

"You're tired."

"Do you really think so?" murmured Thomas Wolfe. "Was it a dream? Perhaps. A good dream."

His breathing faltered. Thomas Wolfe was dead.

In the passing years, flowers are found on Tom Wolfe's grave. And this is not unusual, for many people travel there. But these flowers appear each night. They seem to drop from the sky. They are the color of an autumn moon, their blossoms are immense, and they burn and sparkle their cold, long petals in a blue and white fire. And when the dawn wind blows they drip away into a silver rain, a shower of white sparks on the air. Tom Wolfe has been dead many, many years, but these flowers never cease. . . .

# The Better Part of Wisdom

The room was like a great warm hearth, lit by an unseen fire, gone comfortable. The fireplace itself struggled to keep a small blaze going on a few wet logs and some turf, which was no more than smoke and several lazy orange eyes of charcoal. The place was slowly filling, draining, and refilling with music. A single lemon lamp was lit in a far corner, illumining walls painted a summer color of yellow. The hardwood floor was polished so severely it glowed like a dark river upon which floated throw-rugs whose plummage resembled South American wild birds, flashing electric blues, whites, and jungle greens. White porcelain vases, brimming with fresh-cut hothouse flowers, kept their serene fires burning on four small tables about the room. Above the fireplace, a serious portrait of a young man gazed out with eyes the same color as the ceramics, a deep blue, raw with intelligence and vitality.

Entering the room quietly, one might not have noticed the two men, they were so still.

One sat reclining back upon the pure white couch, eyes closed. The second lay upon the couch so his head was pillowed in the lap of the other. His eyes were shut, too, listening. Rain touched the windows. The music ended.

Instantly there was a soft scratching at the door.

Both men blinked as if to say: people don't *scratch*, they *knock*.

The man who had been lying down leaped to the door and called: "Someone there?"

"By God, there is," said an old voice with a faint brogue.

"Grandfather!"

With the door flung wide, the young man pulled a small round old man into the warm-lit room.

"Tom, boy, ah Tom, and glad I am to see you!"

They fell together in bear-hugs, pawing. Then the old man felt the other person in the room and moved back.

Tom spun around, pointing. "Grandpa, this is Frank. Frank, this is Grandpa, I mean—oh, hell—"

The old man saved the moment by trotting forward to seize and pull Frank to his feet, where he towered high above this small intruder from the night.

"Frank, is it?" the old man yelled up the heights.

"Yes, sir," Frank called back down.

"I—" said the grandfather, "have been standing outside that door for five minutes—"

"Five minutes?" cried both young men, alarmed.

"—debating whether to knock. I heard the music, you see, and finally I said, damn, if there's a girl with him he can either shove her out the window in the rain or show the lovely likes of her to the old man. Hell, I said, and knocked, and"—he slung down his battered old valise—"there *is* no young girl here, I see—or, by God, you've *smothered* her in the closet, eh!"

"There is no young girl, Grandfather." Tom turned in a circle, his hands out to show.

"But—" The grandfather eyed the polished floor, the white throw-rugs, the bright flowers, the watchful portraits on the walls. "You've *borrowed* her place, then?"

"Borrowed?"

"I mean, by the look of the room, there's a woman's touch. It looks like them steamship posters I seen in the travel windows half my life."

"Well," said Frank. "We—"

"The fact is, Grandfather," said Tom, clearing his throat, "*we* did this place over. Redecorated."

"Redecorated?" The old man's jaws dropped. His eyes toured the four walls, stunned. "The *two* of you are responsible? Jesus!"

The old man touched a blue and white ceramic ashtray, and bent to stroke a bright cockatoo throw-rug.

"Which of you did *what?*" he asked, suddenly, squinting one eye at them.

Tom flushed and stammered, "Well, we—"

"Ah, God, no, no, stop!" cried the old man, lifting one hand. "Here I am, fresh *in* the place, and sniffing about like a crazy hound and no fox. Shut that damn door. Ask me where *I'm* going, what am *I* up to, eh, *eh?* And, while you're at it, do you have a touch of the Beast in this art gallery?"

"The Beast it is!" Tom slammed the door, hustled his grandfather out of his greatcoat, and brought forth three tumblers and a bottle of Irish whiskey, which the old man touched as if it were a newborn babe.

"Well, that's more like it. What do we drink to?"

"Why, you, Grandpa!"

"No, no." The old man gazed at Tom and then at his friend, Frank. "Christ," he sighed, "you're so damn young it breaks my bones in the ache. Come now, let's drink to fresh hearts and apple cheeks and all life up ahead and happiness somewhere for the taking. Yes?"

"Yes!" said both, and drank.

And drinking watched each other merrily or warily, half one, half the other. And the young saw in the old bright pink face, lined as it was, cuffed as it was by circumstantial life, the echo of Tom's face itself peering out through the years. In the old blue eyes, especially, was the sharp bright intelligence that sprang from the old portrait on the wall, that would be young until coins weighted them shut. And around the edges of the old mouth was the smile that blinked and went in Tom's face, and in the old hands was the quick, surprising action of Tom's, as if both old man and you, had hands that lived to themselves and did sly things by impulse.

So they drank and leaned and smiled and drank again, each a mirror for the other, each delighting in the fact that an ancient man and a raw youth with the same eyes and hands and blood were met on this raining night, and the whiskey was good.

"Ah, Tom, Tom, it's a loving sight you are!" said the grandfather. "Dublin's been sore without you these four years. But, hell, I'm dying. No, don't ask me how or why. The doctor has the news, damn him, and shot me between the eyes with it. So I said instead of relatives shelling out their cash to come say good-bye to the old horse, why not make the farewell tour yourself and shake hands and drink drinks. So here I am this night and tomorrow beyond London to see Lucie and then Glasgow to see Dick. I'll stay no more than a day each place, so as not to overload anyone. Now shut that mouth, which is hanging open. I am not out collecting sympathies. I am eighty, and it's time for a damn fine wake, which I have saved money for, so not a word. I have come to see everyone and make sure they are in a fit state of half-graceful joy so I can kick up my heels and fall dead with a good heart, if that's possible. I—"

"Grandfather!" cried Tom, suddenly, and seized the old man's hands and then his shoulders.

"Why, bless you, boy, thanks," said the old man, seeing the tears in the young man's eyes. "But just what I find in your gaze is enough." He set the boy gently back. "Tell me about London, your work, this place. You too, Frank, a friend of Tom's is as good as my son's son! Tell everything, Tom!"

"Excuse me." Frank darted toward the door. "You both have much to talk about. There's shopping I must do—"

"Wait!"

Frank stopped.

For the old man had really seen the portrait over the fireplace now and walked to it to put out his hand, to squint and read the signed name at the bottom.

"Frank Davis. Is that you, boy? *You* did this picture?"

"Yes, sir," said Frank, at the door.

"How long ago?"

"Three years ago, I think. Yes, three."

The old man nodded slowly, as if this information added to the great puzzle, a continuing bafflement.

"Tom, do you know who that *looks* like?"

"Yes, Grand-da. You. A long time ago."

"So you see it, too, eh? Christ in heaven, yes. That's me on my eighteenth birthday and all Ireland and its grasses and tender maids good for the chewing ahead and not behind me. That's me, that's me. Jesus I was handsome, and Jesus, Tom, so are you. And Jesus, Frank, you *are* uncanny. You are a *fine* artist, boy."

"You do what you can do." Frank had come back to the middle of the room, quietly. "You do what you *know*."

"And you *know* Tom, to the hair and eyelash." The old man turned and smiled. "How does it feel, Tom, to look out of that borrowed face? Do you feel great, is the world your Dublin prawn and oyster?"

Tom laughed. Grandfather laughed. Frank joined them.

"One more drink." The old man poured. "And we'll let you slip diplomatically out, Frank. But come back. I must talk with you."

"What about?" said Frank.

"Ah, the Mysteries. Of Life, of Time, of Existence. What else did *you* have in mind, Frank?"

"Those will do, Grandfather—" said Frank, and stopped, amazed at the word come out of his mouth. "I mean, Mr. Kelly—"

"Grandfather will do."

"I must run." Frank doused his drink. "Phone you later, Tom."

The door shut. Frank was gone.

"You'll sleep here tonight of course, Grandpa?" Tom seized the one valise. "Frank won't be back. You'll have his bed." Tom was busy arranging the sheets on one of the two couches against the far wall. "Now, it's early. Let's drink some more, Grandfather, and talk."

But the old man, stunned, was silent, eyeing each picture in turn upon the wall. "Grand painting, that."

"Frank did them."

"That's a fine lamp there."

"Frank made it."

"The rug on the floor here now—?"

"Frank."

"Jesus," whispered the old man, "he's a maniac for work, is he not?"

Quietly, he shuffled about the room like one visiting a gallery.

"It seems," he said, "the place is absolutely blowing apart with fine artistic talent. You turned your hand to nothing like this, in Dublin."

"You learn a lot, away from home," said Tom, uneasily.

The old man shut his eyes and drank his drink.

"Is anything wrong, Grandfather?"

"It will hit me in the middle of the night," said the old man. "I will probably stand up in bed with a hell of a yell. But right now it is just a thing in the pit of my stomach and the back of my head. Let's talk, boy, let's talk."

And they talked and drank until midnight and then

the old man got put to bed and Tom went to bed himself and after a long while both slept.

About two in the morning, the old man woke suddenly.

He peered around in the dark, wondering where he was, then saw the paintings, the upholstered chairs, and the lamp and rugs Frank had made, and sat up. He clenched his fists. Then, rising, he threw on his clothes, and staggered toward the door as if fearful that he might not make it before something terrible happened.

When the door slammed, Tom jerked his eyes wide. Somewhere off in the dark there was a sound of someone calling, shouting, defying the elements, someone at the top of his lungs crying blasphemies, saying God and Jesus and Jesus and God, and finally blows struck, wild blows, as if someone were hitting a wall or a person.

After a long while, his grandfather shuffled back into the room, soaked to the skin.

Weaving, muttering, whispering, the old man peeled off his wet clothes before the fireless fire, then threw a newspaper on the coals, which blazed up briefly to show a face relaxing out of fury into numbness. The old man found and put on Tom's discarded robe. Tom kept his eyes tight as the old man held his hands out toward the dwindling blaze, streaked with blood.

"Damn, damn, damn. *There!*" He poured whiskey and gulped it down. He blinked at Tom and the paintings on the wall and looked at Tom and the flowers in the vases and then drank again. After a long while, Tom pretended to wake up.

"It's after two. You need your rest, Grand-da."

"I'll rest when I'm done drinking. And *thinking!*"

"Thinking what, Grandpa?"

"Right now," said the old man, seated in the dim room with the tumbler in his two hands, and the fire gone to ghost on the hearth, "remembering your dear grandmother in June of the year 1902. And there is the thought of your father born, which is fine, and you born after him, which is fine. And there is the thought of your father dying when you were young and the hard life of your mother and her holding you too close, maybe, in the cold beggar life of flinty Dublin. And me out in the meadows with my working life, and us together only once a month. The being born of people and the going away of people. These turn round in an old man's night. I think of you born, Tom, a happy day. Then I see you here now. That's it."

The old man grew silent and drank his drink.

"Grand-da," said Tom, at last, almost like a child crept in for penalties and forgiveness of a sin as yet unnamed, "do I *worry* you?"

"No." Then the old man added, "But what life will *do* with you, how you may be treated, good or ill—I sit up late with *that*."

The old man sat. The young man lay wide-eyed watching him and later said, as if reading thoughts:

"Grandfather, I *am* happy."

The old man leaned forward.

"*Are* you, boy?"

"I have never been so happy in my life, sir."

"Yes?" The old man looked through the dim air of the room, at the young face. "I see that. But will you *stay* happy, Tom?"

"Does anyone ever *stay* happy, Grandfather? Nothing lasts, *does* it?"

"Shut up! Your grandma and me, *that* lasted!"

"No. It wasn't *all* the same, was it? The first years were one thing, the last years another."

The old man put his hand over his own mouth and then massaged his face, closing his eyes.

"God, yes, you're right. There are two, no, three, no, four lives, for each of us. Not one of them lasts, it's sure. But the *thought* of them does. And out of the four or five or a dozen lives you live, one is special. I remember, once . . ."

The old man's voice faltered.

The young man said, "*Once*, Grandpa?"

The old man's eyes fixed somewhere to a horizon of the Past. He did not speak to the room or to Tom or to anyone. He didn't even seem to be speaking to himself.

"Oh, it was a long time ago. When I first came in this room tonight, for no reason, strange, the memory was there. I ran back down along the shoreline of Galway to that week . . ."

"What week, when?' '

"My twelfth birthday fell that week in summer, think of it! Victoria still queen and me in a turf-hut out by Galway strolling the shore for food to be picked up from the tides, and the weather so sweet you almost turned sad with the taste of it, for you knew it would soon go away.

"And in the middle of the great fair weather along the road by the shore one noon came this tinker's caravan carrying their dark gypsy people to set up camp by the sea.

"There was a mother, a father, and a girl in that caravan, and this boy who came running down by the sea alone, perhaps in need of company, for there I was with nothing to do, and in need of strangers myself.

"Here he came running. And I shall not forget my first sight of him from that day till they drop me in the earth. He—

"Ah God, I'm a failure with words! Stop everything. I must go further back.

"A circus came to Dublin. I visited the sideshows of pinheads and dwarfs and terrible small midgets and fat women and skeleton men. Seeing a crowd about one last exhibit, I thought this must be the most horrible of all. I edged over to look at this final terror! And what did I see? The crowd was drawn to nothing more nor less than: a little girl of some six years, so fair, so beautiful, so cream-white of cheek, so blue of eye, so golden of hair, so quiet in her manner that in the midst of this fleshy holocaust she called attention. By saying nothing her shout of beauty stopped the show. All *had* to come to her to get well again. For it was a sick menagerie and she the only sweet lovely Doc about to give us back life.

"Well, that girl in the sideshow was as wonderful a surprise as this boy come running down the beach like a young horse.

"He was not dark like his parents.

"His hair was all gold curls and bits of sun. He was cut out of bronze by the light, and what wasn't bronze was copper. Impossible, but it seemed that this boy of twelve, like myself, had been born on that very day, he looked that new and fresh. And in his face were these bright brown eyes, the eyes of an animal that has run a long way, pursued, along the shorelines of the world.

"He pulled up and the first thing he said to me was laughter. He was glad to be alive, and announced that by the sound he made. I must have laughed in turn, for his spirit was catching. He shoved out his brown hand. I hesitated. He gestured impatiently and grabbed my hand.

"My God, after all these years I remembered what we said: 'Isn't it funny?' he said.

"I didn't ask *what* was funny. I *knew*. He said his name was Jo. I said my name was Tim. And there we were, two boys on the beach and the universe a good rare joke between us.

"He looked at me with his great round full copper eyes, and laughed out his breath and I thought: He has chewed hay! his breath smells of grass; and suddenly I was giddy. The smell stunned me. Jesus God, I thought, reeling, I'm drunk, and *why?* I've nipped Dad's booze, but God, what's *this?* Drunk by noon, hit by the sun, giddy from what? the sweet mash caught in a strange boy's teeth? No, no!

"Then Jo looked straight at me and said, 'There isn't much time.'

" 'Much time?' I asked.

" 'Why,' said Jo, 'for us to be friends. We are, *aren't* we?'

"He breathed the smell of mown fields upon me.

"Jesus God, I wanted to cry, Yes! And almost fell down, but staggered back as if he had hit me a friend's hit. And my mouth opened and shut and I said, 'Why is there so little time?'

" 'Because,' said Jo, 'we'll only be here six days, seven at the most, then on down and around Eire. I'll never see you again in my life. So we'll just have to pack a lot of things in a few days, won't we, Tim?'

" 'Six days? That's no time at all!' I protested, and wondered why I found myself suddenly destroyed, left destitute on the shore. A thing had not begun, but already I sorrowed after its death.

" 'A day here, a week there, a month somewhere else,' said Jo. 'I must live very quickly, Tim. I have no friends that last. Only what I remember. So, wherever I go, I say to my new friends, quick, do this, do that, let us make many happenings, a long list, so you will remember me when I am gone, and I you, and say: that was a friend. So, let's begin. There!'

"And Jo tagged me and ran.

"I ran after him, laughing, for wasn't it silly, me headlong after a stranger boy unknown five minutes before? We must've run a mile down that long summer beach before he let me catch him. I thought I might pummel him for making me run so far for nothing, for something, for God knew what! But when we tumbled to earth and I pinned him down, all he did was spring his breath in one gasp up at me, one breath, and I leaped back and shook my head and sat staring at him, as if I'd plunged wet hands in an open electric socket. He laughed to see me fall away, to see me scurry and sit in wonder. 'O, Tim,' he said, 'we *shall* be friends.'

"You know the dread long cold weather, most months, of Ireland? Well, this week of my twelfth birthday, it was summer each day and every day for the seven days named by Jo as the limit which would be no more days. We walked the shore, and that's all there was, the simple thing of us upon the shore, and building castles or climbing hills to fight wars among the mounds. We found an old round tower and yelled up and down from it. But mostly it was walking, our arms around each other like twins born in a triangle, never cut free by knife or lightning. I inhaled, he exhaled. Then he breathed and I was the sweet chorus. We talked, far through the nights on the sand, until our parents came seeking the lost who had found they knew not what. Lured home, I slept beside him, or him me, and talked and laughed, Jesus, laughed, till dawn. Then out again we roared until the earth swung up to hit our backs. We found ourselves laid out with sweet hilarity, eyes tight, gripped to each other's shaking, and the laugh jumped free like one silver trout following another. God, I bathed in his laughter as he bathed in mine, until we were weak as if love had put us to the slaughter and exhaustions. We panted then like pups in hot summer, empty of laughing, and sleepy with friendship. And the weather for that week was blue and gold, no clouds, no rain, and a wind that smelled of apples, but no, only that boy's wild breath.

"It crossed my mind, long after, if ever an old man could bathe again in that summer fount, the wild spout of breathing that sprang from his nostrils and gasped from his mouth, why one might peel off a score of years, one would be young, how might the flesh resist?

"But the laughter is gone and the boy gone into a man lost somewhere in the world, and here I am two lifetimes later, speaking of it for the first time. For who was there to tell? From my twelfth birthday week, and the gift of friendship, to this, who might I tell of that shore and that summer and the two of us walking all tangled in our arms and lives and life as perfect as the letter *o*, a damned great circle of rare weather, lovely talk, and us certain we'd live forever, never die, and be good friends.

"And at the end of the week, he left.

"He was wise for his years. He didn't say good-bye. All of a sudden, the tinker's cart was gone.

"I shouted along the shore. A long way off, I saw the caravan go over a hill. But then his wisdom spoke to me. Don't catch. Let go. Weep now, my own wisdom said. And I wept.

"I wept for three days and on the fourth grew very still. I did not go down to the shore again for many months. And in all the years that have passed, never have I known such a thing again. I have had a good life, a fine wife, good children, and you, boy, Tom, you. But as sure as I sit here, never after that was I so agonized, mad, and crazy wild. Never did drink make me as drunk. Never did I cry so hard again. Why, Tom? Why do I say this, and what was it? Back so far in innocence, back in the time when I had nobody, and knew nothing. How is it I remember him when all else slips away? When often I cannot remember your dear grandmother's face, God forgive me, why does his face come back on the shore by the sea? Why do I see us fall again and the earth reach up to take the wild young horses driven mad by too much sweet grass in a line of days that never end?"

The old man grew silent. After a moment, he added, "The better part of wisdom, they say, is what's left unsaid. I'll say no more. I don't even know why I've said all *this*."

Tom lay in the dark. "*I* know."

"Do you, lad?" asked the old man. "Well, tell me. Someday."

"Someday," said Tom. "I will."

They listened to the rain touch at the windows.

"Are you happy, Tom?"

"You asked that before, sir."

"I ask again. Are you happy?"

"Yes."

Silence.

"Is it summertime on the shore, Tom? Is it the magic seven days? Are you drunk?"

Tom did not answer for a long while, and then said nothing but, "Grand-da," and then moved his head once in a nod.

The old man lay in the chair. He might have said, this will pass. He might have said, it will not last. He might have said many things. Instead he said, "Tom?"

"Sir?"

"Ah Jesus!" shouted the old man suddenly. "Christ, God Almighty! Damn it to hell!" Then the old man stopped and his breathing grew quiet. "There. It's a maniac night. I had to let out one last yell. I just had to, boy."

And at last they slept, with the rain falling fast.

With the first light of dawn, the old man dressed with careful quietness, picked up his valise, and bent to touch the sleeping young man's cheek with the palm of one hand.

"Tom, good-bye," he whispered.

Moving down the dim stairwell toward the steadily beating rain, he found Tom's friend waiting at the foot of the stairs.

"Frank! You haven't been down here *all night?*"

"No, no, Mr. Kelly," said Frank, quickly. "I stayed at a friend's."

The old man turned to look up the dark stairwell as if he could see the room and Tom in it warm asleep.

"Gah . . . !" Something almost a growl stirred in his throat and subsided. He shifted uneasily and looked back down at the dawn kindled on this young man's face, this one who had painted a picture that hung above the fireplace in the room above.

"The damn night is over," said the old man. "So if you'll just stand aside—"

"Sir."

The old man took one step down and burst out:

"Listen! If you hurt Tom, in any way ever, why, Jesus, I'll break you across my knee! You *hear?*"

Frank held out his hand. "Don't worry."

The old man looked at the hand as if he had never seen one before. He sighed.

"Ah, damn it to hell, Frank, Tom's friend, so young you're destruction to the eyes. Get away!"

They shook hands.

"Jesus, that's a hard grip," said the old man, surprised.

Then he was gone, as if the rain had hustled him off in its own multitudinous running.

The young man shut the upstairs door and stood for a moment looking at the figure on the bed and at last went over and as if by instinct put his hand down to the exact same spot where the old man had printed his hand in farewell not five minutes before. He touched the summer cheek.

In his sleep, Tom smiled the smile of his father's father, and called the old man, deep in a dream, by name.

He called him twice.

And then he slept quietly.

# Darling Adolf

They were waiting for him to come out. He was sitting inside the little Bavarian café with a view of the mountains, drinking beer, and he had been in there since noon and it was now two-thirty, a long lunch, and much beer, and they could see by the way he held his head and laughed and lifted one more stein with the suds fluffing in the spring breeze that he was in a grand humor now, and at the table with him the two other men were doing their best to keep up, but had fallen long behind.

On occasion their voices drifted on the wind, and then the small crowd waiting out in the parking lot leaned to hear. What was he saying? and now what?

"He just said the shooting was going well."

"What, where?!"

"Fool. The film, the film is shooting well."

"Is that the director sitting with him?"

"Yes. And the other unhappy one is the producer."

"He doesn't look like a producer."

"No wonder! He's had his nose changed."

"And him, doesn't he look *real?*"

"To the hair and the teeth."

And again everyone leaned to look in at the three men, at the man who didn't look like a producer, at the sheepish director who kept glancing out at the crowd and slouching down with his head between his shoulders, shutting his eyes, and the man between them, the man in the uniform with the swastika on his arm, and the fine military cap put on the table beside the almost-untouched food, for he was talking, no, making a speech.

"That's the Führer, all right!"

"God in heaven, it's as if no time had passed. I don't believe this is 1973. Suddenly it's 1934 again, when first I saw him."

"Where?"

"The Nuremberg Rally, the stadium, that was the autumn, yes, and I was thirteen and part of the Youth and one hundred thousand soldiers and young men in that big place that late afternoon before the torches were lit. So many bands, so many flags, so much heart-beat, yes, I tell you, I could hear one hundred thousand hearts banging away, we were all so in love, he had come down out of the clouds. The gods had sent him, we knew, and the time of waiting was over, from here on we could *act*, there was nothing he couldn't *help* us to do."

"I wonder how that actor in there feels, playing him?"

"Sh, he hears you. Look, he waves. Wave back."

"Shut up," said someone else. "They're talking again. I want to hear—"

The crowd shut up. The men and women leaned into the soft spring wind. The voices drifted from the café table.

Beer was being poured by a maiden waitress with flushed cheeks and eyes as bright as fire.

"More beer!" said the man with the toothbrush mustache and the hair combed forward on the left side of his brow.

"No, thanks," said the director.

"No, no," said the producer.

"More beer! It's a splendid day," said Adolf. "A toast to the film, to us, to me. Drink!"

The other two men put their hands on their glasses of beer.

"To the film," said the producer.

"To darling Adolf." The director's voice was flat.

The man in the uniform stiffened.

"I do not look upon myself—" he hesitated, "upon *him* as darling."

"He was darling, all right, and you're a doll." The director gulped his drink. "Does anyone mind if I get drunk?"

"To be drunk is not permitted," said Der Führer.

"Where does it say that in the script?"

The producer kicked the director under the table.

"How many more weeks' work do you figure we have?" asked the producer, with great politeness.

"I figure we should finish the film," said the director, taking huge swigs, "around about the death of Hindenburg, or the *Hindenburg* gasbag going down in flames at Lakehurst, New Jersey, which ever comes first."

Adolf Hitler bent to his plate and began to eat rapidly, snapping at his meat and potatoes in silence.

The producer sighed heavily. The director, nudged by this, calmed the waters. "Another three weeks should see the masterwork in the can, and us sailing home on the *Titanic*, there to collide with the Jewish critics and go down bravely singing '*Deutschland Uber Alles*.'"

Suddenly all three were voracious and snapping and biting and chewing their food, and the spring breeze blew softly, and the crowd waited outside.

At last, Der Führer stopped, had another sip of beer, and lay back in his chair, touching his mustache with his little finger.

"Nothing can provoke me on a day like this. The rushes last night were so beautiful. The casting for this film, ah! I find Göring to be incredible. Goebbels? Perfection!" Sunlight dazzled out of Der Führer's face. "So. So, I was thinking just last night, here I am in Bavaria, me, a pure Aryan—"

Both men flinched slightly, and waited.

"—making a film," Hitler went on, laughing softly, "with a Jew from New York and a Jew from Hollywood. So amusing."

"I am not amused," said the director, lightly.

The producer shot him a glance which said: the film is not finished yet. Careful.

"And I was thinking, wouldn't it be fun . . ." Here Der Führer stopped to take a big drink, ". . . to have another . . . ah . . . Nuremberg Rally?"

"You mean for the *film*, of course?"

The director stared at Hitler. Hitler examined the texture of the suds in his beer.

"My God," said the producer, "do you know how much it would cost to reproduce the Nuremberg Rally? How much did it cost Hitler for the original, Marc?"

He blinked at his director, who said, "A bundle. But he had a lot of free extras, of course."

"Of course! The Army, the Hitler Youth."

"Yes, yes," said Hitler. "But think of the publicity, all over the world? Let us go to Nuremberg, eh, and film my plane, eh, and me coming down out of the clouds? I heard those people out there, just now: Nuremberg and plane and torches. *They* remember. *I* remember. I held a torch in that stadium. My God, it was beautiful. And now, now I am exactly the age Hitler was when he was at his prime."

"He was never at his prime," said the director. "Unless you mean hung-meat."

Hitler put down his glass. His cheeks grew very red. Then he forced a smile to widen his lips and change the color of his face. "That is a joke, of course."

"A joke," said the producer, playing ventriloquist to his friend.

"I was thinking," Hitler went on, his eyes on the clouds again, seeing it all, back in another year. "If we shot it next month, with the weather good. Think of all the tourists who would come to watch the filming!"

"Yeah. Bormann might even come back from Argentina."

The producer shot his director another glare.

Hitler cleared his throat and forced the words out: "As for expense, if you took one small ad, *one* mind you! in the Nuremberg papers one week before, why, you would have an army of people there as extras at fifty cents a day, no, a quarter, no, *free!*"

Der Führer emptied his stein, ordered another. The waitress dashed off to refill. Hitler studied his two friends.

"You know," said the director, sitting up, his own eyes taking a kind of vicious fire, his teeth showing as he leaned forward, "there is a kind of idiot grace to you, a kind of murderous wit, a sort of half-ass style. Every once in a while you come dripping up with some sensational slime that gleams and stinks in the sun, buster. Archie, *listen* to him. Der Führer just had a great bowel movement. Drag in the astrologers! Slit the pigeons and filch their guts. Read me the casting sheets."

The director leaped to his feet and began to pace.

"That *one* ad in the paper, and all the trunks in Nuremberg get flung wide! Old uniforms come out to cover fat bellies! Old armbands come out to fit flabby arms! Old military caps with skull-eagles on them fly out to fit on fat-heads!"

"I will not sit here—" cried Hitler.

He started to get up but the producer was tugging his arm and the director had a knife at his heart: his forefinger, stabbing hard.

"Sit."

The director's face hovered two inches from Hitler's nose. Hitler slowly sank back, his cheeks perspiring.

"God, you *are* a genius," said the director. "Jesus, your people *would* show up. Not the young, no, but the old. All the Hitler youth, your age now, those senile bags of tripe yelling '*Sieg Heil*,' saluting, lighting torches at sunset, marching around the stadium crying themselves blind."

The director swerved to his producer.

"I tell you, Arch, this Hitler here has bilge brains but this time he's on target! If we don't shove the Nuremberg Rally *up* this film, I quit. I mean it. I will simply walk out and let Adolf here take over and direct the damned thing himself! Speech over."

He sat down.

Both the producer and Der Führer appeared to be in a state of shock.

"Order me another goddamn beer," snapped the director.

Hitler gasped in a huge breath, tossed down his knife and fork, and shoved back his chair.

"I do not break bread with such as you!"

"Why, you bootlicking lapdog son of a bitch," said the director. "I'll hold the mug and you'll do the licking. Here." The director grabbed the beer and shoved it under Der Führer's nose. The crowd, out beyond, gasped and almost surged. Hitler's eyes rolled, for the director had seized him by the front of his tunic and was yanking him forward.

"Lick! Drink the German filth! Drink, you scum!"

"Boys, boys," said the producer.

"Boys, crud! You know what this swill-hole, this chamberpot Nazi, has been thinking, sitting here, Archibald, and drinking your beer? Today Europe, tomorrow the world!"

"No, no, Marc!"

"No, no," said Hitler, staring down at the fist which clenched the material of his uniform. "The buttons, the buttons—"

"Are loose on your tunic and inside your head, worm. Arch, look at him pour! Look at the grease roll off his forehead, look at his stinking armpits. He's a sea of sweat because I've read his mind! Tomorrow the world! Get this film set up, him cast in the lead. Bring him down out of the clouds, a month from now. Brass bands. Torchlight. Bring back Leni Reifenstahl to show us how she shot the Rally in '34. Hitler's lady-director friend. Fifty cameras she used, fifty she used, by God, to get all the German crumbs lined up and vomiting lies, and Hitler in his creaking leather and Göring awash in his blubber, and Goebbels doing his wounded-monkey walk, the three superfags of history aswank in the stadium at dusk, make it all happen again, with this bastard up front, and do you know what's going through his little graveyard mind behind his bloater eyes at this very moment?"

"Marc, Marc," whispered the producer, eyes shut, grinding his teeth. "Sit down. Everyone sees."

"Let them see! Wake up, you! Don't you shut your eyes on me, too! I've shut my eyes on you for days, filth. Now I want some attention. Here."

He sloshed beer on Hitler's face, which caused his eyes to snap wide and his eyes to roll yet again, as apoplexy burned his cheeks.

The crowd, out beyond, hissed in their breath.

The director, hearing, leered at them.

"Boy, is this funny. They don't know whether to come in or not, don't know if you're real or not, and neither do I. Tomorrow, you bilgy bastard, you really dream of becoming Der Führer."

He bathed the man's face with more beer.

The producer had turned away in his chair now and was frantically dabbing at some imaginary breadcrumbs on his tie. "Marc, for God's sake—"

"No, no, seriously, Archibald. This guy thinks because he puts on a ten-cent uniform and plays Hitler for four weeks at good pay that if we actually put together the Rally, why Christ, History would turn back, oh turn back, Time, Time in thy flight, make me a stupid Jew-baking Nazi again for tonight. Can you see it, Arch, this lice walking up to the microphones and shouting and the crowd shouting back, and him *really* trying to take over, as if Roosevelt still lived and Churchill wasn't six feet deep, and it was all to be lost or won again, but mainly won, because *this* time they wouldn't stop at the Channel but just cross on over, give or take a million German boys dead, and stomp England and stomp America, isn't *that* what's going on inside your little Aryan skull, Adolf? *Isn't* it!"

Hitler gagged and hissed. His tongue stuck out. At last he jerked free and exploded:

"Yes! Yes, goddamn you! Damn and bake and burn you! You dare to lay hands on Der Führer! The Rally! Yes! It must be in the film! We must make it again! The plane! The landing! The long drive through streets. The blonde girls. The lovely blond boys. The stadium. Leni Reifenstahl! And from all the trunks, in all the attics, a black plague of armbands winging on the dusk, flying to assault, battering to take the victory. Yes, yes, I, Der Führer, I will stand at that Rally and dictate terms! I—I—"

He was on his feet now.

The crowd, out beyond in the parking lot, shouted.

Hitler turned and gave them a salute.

The director took careful aim and shot a blow of his fist to the German's nose.

After that the crowd arrived, shrieking, yelling, pushing, shoving, falling.

They drove to the hospital at four the next afternoon.

Slumped, the old producer sighed, his hands over his eyes. "Why, why, why are we going to the hospital? To visit that—monster?"

The director nodded.

The old man groaned. "Crazy world. Mad people. I never saw such biting, kicking, biting. That mob almost killed you."

The director licked his swollen lips and touched his half-shut left eye with a probing finger. "I'm okay. The important thing is I hit Adolf, oh, how I hit him. And now—" He stared calmly ahead. "I think I am going to the hospital to finish the job."

"Finish, *finish*?" The old man stared at him.

"Finish." The director wheeled the car slowly around a corner. "Remember the twenties, Arch, when Hitler got shot at in the street and not hit, or beaten in the streets, and nobody socked him away forever, or he left a beer hall ten minutes before a bomb went off, or was in that officers' hut in 1944 and the briefcase bomb exploded and *that* didn't get him. Always the charmed life. Always he got out from under the rock. Well, Archie, no more charms, no more escapes. I'm walking in that hospital to make sure that when that half-ass extra comes out and there's a mob of krauts to greet him, he's walking wounded, a permanent soprano. Don't try to stop me, Arch."

"Who's stopping? Belt him one for me."

They stopped in front of the hospital just in time to see one of the studio production assistants run down the steps, his hair wild, his eyes wilder, shouting.

"Christ," said the director. "Bet you forty to one, our luck's run out again. Bet you that guy running toward us says—"

"Kidnaped! Gone!" the man cried. "Adolf's been taken away!"

"Son of a bitch."

They circled the empty hospital bed; they *touched* it.

A nurse stood in one corner wringing her hands. The production assistant babbled.

"Three men it was, three men, three men."

"Shut up." The director was snowblind from simply looking at the white sheets. "Did they force him or did he go along quietly?"

"I don't know, I can't say, yes, he was making speeches, making speeches as they took him out."

"Making speeches?" cried the old producer, slapping his bald pate. "Christ, with the restaurant suing us for broken tables, and Hitler maybe suing us for—"

"Hold on." The director stepped over and fixed the production assistant with a steady gaze. "*Three* men, you say?"

"Three, yes, three, three, three, oh, three men."

A small forty-watt lightbulb flashed on in the director's head.

"Did, ah, did one man have a square face, a good jaw, bushy eyebrows?"

"Why . . . yes!"

"Was one man short and skinny like a chimpanzee?"

"Yes!"

"Was one man big, I mean, slobby fat?"

"How did you *know?*"

The producer blinked at both of them. "What goes on? What—"

"Stupid attracts stupid. Animal cunning calls to laughing jackass cunning. Come on, Arch!"

"Where?" The old man stared at the empty bed as if Adolf might materialize there any moment now.

"The back of my car, quick!"

From the back of the car, on the street, the director pulled a German cinema directory. He leafed through the character actors. "Here."

The old man looked. A forty-watt bulb went on in his head.

The director riffled more pages. "And here. And, finally, here."

They stood now in the cold wind outside the hospital and let the breeze turn the pages as they read the captions under the photographs.

"Goebbels," whispered the old man.

"An actor named Rudy Steihl."

"Göring."

"A hambone named Grofe."

"Hess."

"Fritz Dingle."

The old man shut the book and cried to the echoes.

"Son of a bitch!"

"Louder and funnier, Arch. Funnier and louder."

"You mean right now out there somewhere in the city three dumbkopf out-of-work actors have Adolf in hiding, held maybe for ransom? And do we *pay* it?"

"Do we want to finish the film, Arch?"

"God, I don't know, so much money already, time, and—" The old man shivered and rolled his eyes. "What if—I mean—what if they don't *want* ransom?"

The director nodded and grinned. "You mean, what if this is the true start of the Fourth Reich?"

"All the peanut brittle in Germany might put itself in sacks and show up if they knew that—"

"Steihl, Grofe, and Dingle, which is to say, Goebbels, Göring, and Hess, were back in the saddle with dumbass Adolf?"

"Crazy, awful, mad! It couldn't happen!"

"Nobody was ever going to clog the Suez Canal. Nobody was ever going to land on the Moon. Nobody."

"What do we do? This waiting is horrible. Think of something, Marc, think, think!"

"I'm thinking."

"And—"

This time a hundred-watt bulb flashed on in the director's face. He sucked air and let out a great braying laugh.

"I'm going to help them organize and speak up, Arch! I'm a genius. Shake my hand!"

He seized the old man's hand and pumped it, crying with hilarity, tears running down his cheeks.

"You, Marc, on their side, helping from the Fourth Reich!?"

The old man backed away.

"Don't hit me, help me. Think, Arch, think. What was it Darling Adolf said at lunch, and damn the expense! What, what?"

The old man took a breath, held it, exploded it out, with a final light blazing in his face.

"Nuremberg?" he asked.

"Nuremberg! What month is this, Arch?"

"October!"

"October! October, forty years ago, October, the big, big Nuremberg Rally. And this coming Friday, Arch, an Anniversary Rally. We shove an ad in the international edition of *Variety*: RALLY AT NUREMBERG. TORCHES. BANDS. FLAGS. Christ, he won't be able to stay away. He'd shoot his kidnapers to be there and play the greatest role in his life!"

"Marc, we can't afford—"

"Five hundred and forty-eight bucks? For the ad plus the torches plus a full military band on a phonograph record? Hell, Arch, hand me that phone."

The old man pulled a telephone out of the front seat of his limousine.

"Son of a bitch," he whispered.

"Yeah." The director grinned, and ticked the phone. "Son of a bitch."

The sun was going down beyond the rim of Nuremberg Stadium. The sky was bloodied all across the western horizon. In another half-hour it would be completely dark and you wouldn't be able to see the small platform down in the center of the arena, or the few dark flags with the swastikas put up on temporary poles here or there making a path from one side of the stadium to the other. There was a sound of a crowd gathering, but the place was empty. There was a faint drum of band music but there was no band.

Sitting in the front row on the eastern side of the stadium, the director waited, his hands on the controls of a sound unit. He had been waiting for two hours and was getting tired and feeling foolish. He could hear the old man saying:

"Let's go home. Idiotic. He won't come."

And himself saying, "He will. He must," but not believing it.

He had the records waiting on his lap. Now and again he tested one, quietly, on the turntable, and then the crowd noises came from lilyhorns stuck up at both ends of the arena, murmuring, or the band played, not loudly, no, that would be later, but very softly. Then he waited again.

The sun sank lower. Blood ran crimson in the clouds. The director tried not to notice. He hated nature's blatant ironies.

The old man stirred feebly at last and looked around.

"So this was the place. It was really *it*, back in 1934."

"This was it. Yeah."

"I remember the films. Yes, yes. Hitler stood—what? Over there?"

"That was it."

"And all the kids and men down there and the girls there, and fifty cameras."

"Fifty, count 'em, fifty. Jesus, I would have liked to have been here with the torches and flags and people and cameras."

"Marc, Marc, you don't *mean* it?"

"Yes, Arch, sure! So I could have run up to Darling Adolf and done what I did to that pig-swine half-ass actor. Hit him in the nose, then hit him in the teeth, then hit him in the *blinis!* You *got* it, Leni? Action! *Swot!* Camera! *Bam!* Here's one for Izzie. Here's one for Ike. Cameras running, Leni? Okay. *Zot!* Print!"

They stood looking down into the empty stadium where the wind prowled a few newspapers like ghosts on the vast concrete floor.

Then, suddenly, they gasped.

Far up at the very top of the stadium a small figure had appeared.

The director quickened, half rose, then forced himself to sit back down.

The small figure, against the last light of the day, seemed to be having difficulty walking. It leaned to one side, and held one arm up against its side, like a wounded bird.

The figure hesitated, waited.

"Come on," whispered the director.

The figure turned and was about to flee.

"Adolf, no!" hissed the director.

Instinctively, he snapped one of his hands to the sound-effects tape deck, his other hand to the music.

The military band began to play softly.

The "crowd" began to murmur and stir.

Adolf, far above, froze.

The music played higher. The director touched a control knob. The crowd mumbled louder.

Adolf turned back to squint down into the half-seen stadium. Now he must be seeing the flags. And now the few torches. And now the waiting platform with the microphones, two *dozen* of them! *one* of them real.

The band came up in full brass.

Adolf took one step forward.

The crowd roared.

Christ, thought the director, looking at his hands, which were now suddenly hard fists and now again just fingers leaping on the controls, all to themselves. Christ, what do I do with him when I get him down here? What, *what?*

And then, just as insanely, the thought came. Crud. You're a director. And that's *him*. And this *is* Nuremberg.

So . . . ?

Adolf took a second step down. Slowly his hand came up in a stiff salute.

The crowd went wild.

Adolf never stopped after that. He limped, he tried to march with pomp, but the fact was he limped down the hundreds of steps until he reached the floor of the stadium. There he straightened his cap, brushed his tunic, resaluted the roaring emptiness, and came gimping across two hundred yards of empty ground toward the waiting platform.

The crowd kept up its tumult. The band responded with a vast heartbeat of brass and drum.

Darling Adolf passed within twenty feet of the lower stands where the director sat fiddling with the tape-deck dials. The director crouched down. But there was no need. Summoned by the "*Sieg Heils*" and the fanfare of trumpets and brass, Der Führer was drawn inevitably toward that dais where destiny awaited him. He was walking taller now and though his uniform was rumpled and the swastika emblem torn, and his mustache moth-eaten and his hair wild, it was the old Leader all right, it was him.

The old producer sat up straight and watched. He whispered. He pointed.

Far above, at the top of the stadium, three more men had stepepd into view.

My God, thought the director, that's the team. The men who grabbed Adolf.

A man with bushy eyebrows, a fat man, and a man like a wounded chimpanzee.

Jesus. The director blinked. Goebbels. Göring. Hess. Three actors at liberty. Three half-ass kidnapers staring down at . . .

Adolf Hitler climbing up on the small podium by the fake microphones and the real one under the blowing torches which bloomed and blossomed and guttered and smoked on the cold October wind under the sprig of lilyhorns which lifted in four directions.

Adolf lifted his chin. That did it. The crowd went absolutely mad. Which is to say, the director's hand, sensing the hunger, went mad, twitched the volume high so the air was riven and torn and shattered again and again and again with "*Sieg Heil, Sieg Heil, Sieg Heil!*"

Above, high on the stadium rim, the three watching figures lifted their arms in salute to their Führer.

Adolf lowered his chin. The sounds of the crowd faded. Only the torch flames whispered.

Adolf made his speech.

He must have yelled and chanted and brayed and sputtered and whispered hoarsely and wrung his hands and beat the podium with his fist and plunged his fist at the sky and shut his eyes and shrieked like a disemboweled trumpet for ten miuntés, twenty minutes, half an hour as the sun vanished beyond the earth and the three other men up on the stadium rim watched and listened and the producer and the director waited and watched. He shouted things about the whole world and he yelled things about Germany and he shrieked things about himself and he damned this and blamed that and praised yet a third, until at last he began to repeat, and repaat the same words over and over as if he had reached the end of a record inside himself and the needle was fastened to a circle track which hissed and hiccuped, hiccuped and hissed, and then faded away at last into a silence where you could only hear his heavy breathing, which broke at last into a sob and he stood with his head bent while the others now could not look at him but looked only at their shoes or the sky or the way the wind blew dust across the field. The flags fluttered. The single torch bent and lifted and twisted itself again and talked under its breath.

At last, Adolf raised his head to finish his speech.

"Now I must speak of them."

He nodded up to the top of the stadium where the three men stood against the sky.

"They are nuts. I am nuts, too. But at least I know I am nuts. I told them: crazy, you are crazy. Mad, you arc mad. And now, my own craziness, my own madness, well, it has run itself down. I am tired.

"So now, what? I give the world back to you. I had it for a small while here today. But now you must keep it and keep it better than I would. To each of you I give the world, but you must promise, each of you to keep your own part and work with it. So there. Take it."

He made a motion with his free hand to the empty seats, as if all the world were in his fingers and at last he were letting it go.

The crowd murmured, stirred, but said nothing loud.

The flags softly tongued the air. The flames squatted on themselves and smoked.

Adolf pressed his fingers onto his eyeballs as if suddenly seized with a blinding headache. Without looking over at the director or the producer, he said, quietly:

"Time to go?"

The director nodded.

Adolf limped off the podium and came to stand below where the old man and the younger director sat.

"Go ahead, if you want, again, hit me."

The director sat and looked at him. At last he shook his head.

"Do we finish the film?" asked Adolf.

The director looked at the producer. The old man shrugged and could find nothing to say.

"Ah, well," said the actor. "Anyway, the madness is over, the fever has dropped. I have *made* my speech at Nuremberg. God, look at those idiots up there. Idiots!" he called suddenly at the stands. Then back to the director, "Can you think? They wanted to hold me for ransom. I told them what fools they were. Now I'll go tell them again. I had to get away from them. I couldn't stand their stupid talk. I had to come here and be my own fool in my own way for the last time. Well . . ."

He limped off across the empty field, calling back quietly:

"I'll be in your car outside, waiting. If you want, I am yours for the final scenes. If not, no, and that ends it."

The director and the producer waited until Adolf had climbed to the top of the stadium. They could hear his voice drift down, cursing those other three, the man with the bushy eyebrows, the fat man, and the ugly chimpanzee, calling them many things, waving his hands. The three backed off and went away, gone.

Adolf stood alone high in the cold October air.

The director gave him a final lift of the sound volume. The crowd, obedient, banged out a last "*Sieg Heil.*"

Adolf lifted his free hand, not into a salute, but some sort of old, easy, half-collapsed mid-Atlantic wave. Then he was gone, too.

The sunlight went with him. The sky was no longer blood-colored. The wind blew dust and want-ads from a German paper across the stadium floor.

"Son of a bitch," muttered the old man. "Let's get out of here."

They left the torches to burn and the flags to blow, but shut off the sound equipment.

"Wish I'd brought a record of *Yankee Doodle* to march us out of here," said the director.

"Who needs records. We'll whistle. Why not?"

"Why not!"

He held the old man's elbow going up the stairs in the dusk, but it was only halfway up, they had the guts to try to whistle.

And then it was suddenly so funny they couldn't finish the tune.

# The Miracles of Jamie

Jamie Winters worked his first miracle in the morning. The second, third, and various other miracles came later in the day. But the first miracle was always the most important.

It was always the same: "Make Mother well. Put color in her cheeks. Don't let Mom be sick too much longer."

It was Mom's illncss that had first made him think about himself and miracles. And because of her he kept on, learning how to be good at them so that he could keep her well and could make life jump through a hoop.

It was not the first day that he had worked miracles. He had done them in the past, but always hesitantly, since sometimes he did not say them right, or Ma and Pa interrupted, or the other kids in the seventh grade at school made noise. They spoiled things.

But in the past month he had felt his power flow over him like cool, certain water; he bathed in it, basked in it, had come from the shower of it beaded with glory water and with a halo of wonder about his dark-haired head.

Five days ago he'd taken down the family Bible, with real color pictures of Jesus as a boy in it, and had compared them with his own face in the bathroom mirror, gasping. He shook all over. There it *was*.

And wasn't Ma getting better every day now? Well—*there!*

Now, on Monday morning, following the first miracle at home, he worked a second one at school. He wanted to lead the Arizona State Day parade as head of his class battalion. And the principal, naturally, selected Jamie to lead. Jamie felt fine. The girls looked up to him, bumping him with their soft, thin little elbows, especially one named Ingrid, whose golden hair rustled in Jamie's face as they all hurried out of the cloakroom.

Jamie Winters held his head so high, and when he drank from the chromium fountain he bent so carefully and twisted the shining handle so exactly, so precisely—so godlike and indomitable.

Jamie knew it would be useless to tell his friends. They'd laugh. After all, Jesus was pounded nail through palm and ankle to a Calvary Hill cross because he told on himself. This time, it would be wise to wait. At least until he was sixteen and grew a beard, thus establishing once and for all the incredible proof of his identity!

Sixteen was somewhat young for a beard, but Jamie felt that he could exert the effort to force one if the time came and necessity demanded.

The children poured from the schoolhouse into the hot spring light. In the distance were the mountains, the foothills spread green with cactus, and overhead was a vast Arizona sky of very fine blue. The children donned paper hats and crepe-paper Sam Browne belts in blue and red. Flags burst open upon the wind; everybody yelled and formed into groups, glad to escape the schoolrooms for one day.

Jamie stood at the head of the line, very calm and quiet. Someone said something, and Jamie realized that it was young Huff who was talking.

"I hope we win the parade prize," said Huff worriedly.

Jamie looked at him. "Oh, we'll win all right. I know we'll win. I'll guarantee it! Heck, yes!"

Huff was brightened by such steadfast faith. "You think so?"

"I *know* so! Leave it to me!"

"What do you mean, Jamie?"

"Nothing. Just watch and see, that's all. Just watch!"

"Now, children!" Mr. Palmborg, the principal, clapped hands; the sun shone on his glasses. Silence came quickly. "Now, children," he said, nodding, "remember what we taught you yesterday about marching. Remember how you pivot to turn a corner, and remember those special routines we practiced, will you?"

"Sure!" everybody said at once.

The principal concluded his brief address and the parade began, Jamie heading it with his hundreds of following disciples.

The feet bent up and straightened down, and the street went under them. The yellow sun warmed Jamie and he, in turn, bade it shine the whole day to make things perfect.

When the parade edged onto Main Street, and the high-school band began pulsing its brass heart and rattling its wooden bones on the drums, Jamie wished they would play "Stars and Stripes Forever."

Later, when they played "Columbia, Gem of the Ocean," Jamie thought quickly, oh, yeah, that's what he'd meant—"Columbia," not "Stars and Stripes Forever"—and was satisfied that his wish had been obeyed.

The street was lined with people, as it was on the Arizona rodeo days in February. People sweated in intent layers, five deep for over a mile; the rhythm of feet came back in reflected cadence from two-story frame fronts. There were occasional glimpses of mirrored armies marching in the tall windows of the J. C. Penney Store or of the Morble Company. Each cadence was like a whip thud on the dusty asphalt, sharp and true, and the band music shot blood through Jamie's miraculous veins.

He concentrated, scowling fiercely. Let us win, he thought. Let everyone march perfectly: chins up, shoulders back, knees high, down, high again, sun upon denimed knees rising in a blue tide, sun upon tanned girl-knees like small, round faces upping and falling. Perfect, perfect, perfect. Perfection surged confidently through Jamie, extending into an encompassing aura that held his own group intact. As he moved, so moved the nation. As his fingers snapped in a brisk pendulum at his sides, so did their fingers, their arms cutting an orbit. And as his shoes trod asphalt, so theirs followed in obedient imitation.

As they reached the reviewing stand, Jamie cued them; they coiled back upon their own lines like bright garlands twining to return again, marching in the original direction, without chaos.

Oh, so darn perfect! cried Jamie to himself.

It was hot. Holy sweat poured out of Jamie, and the world sagged from side to side. Presently the drums were exhausted and the children melted away. Lapping an ice-cream cone, Jamie was relieved that it was all over.

Mr. Palmborg came rushing up, all heated and sweating.

"Children, children, I have an announcement to make!" he cried.

Jamie looked at young Huff, who stood beside him, also with an ice-cream cone. The children shrilled, and Mr. Palmborg patted the noise into a ball which he made vanish like a magician.

"We've won the competition! Our school marched finest of all the schools!"

In the clamor and noise and jumping up and down and hitting one another on the arm muscles in celebration, Jamie nodded quietly over his ice-cream cone, looked at young Huff, and said, "See? I told you so. Now, will you believe in me!"

Jamie continued licking his cold cone with a great, golden peace in him.

Jamie did not immediately tell his friends why they had won the marching competition. He had observed a tendency in them to be suspicious and to ridicule anyone who told them that they were not as good as they thought they were, that their talent had been derived from an outside source.

No, it was enough for Jamie to savor his minor and major victories; he enjoyed his little secret, he enjoyed the things that happened. Such things as getting high marks in arithmetic or winning a basketball game were ample reward. There was always some byproduct of his miracles to satisfy his as-yet-small hunger.

He paid attention to blonde young Ingrid with the placid gray-blue eyes. She, in turn, favored him with her attentions, and he knew then that his ability was well rooted, established.

Aside from Ingrid, there were other good things. Friendships with several boys came about in wondrous fashion. One case, though, required some little thought and care. The boy's name was Cunningham. He was big and fat and bald because some fever had necessitated shaving his skull. The kids called him Billiard; he thanked them by kicking them in the shins, knocking them down, and sitting on them while he performed quick dentistry with his knuckles.

It was upon this Billiard Cunningham that Jamie hoped to apply his greatest ecclesiastical power. Walking through the rough paths of the desert toward his home, Jamie often conjured up visions of himself picking up Billiard by his left foot and cracking him like a whip so as to shock him senseless. Dad had once done that to a rattlesnake. Of course, Billiard was too heavy for this neat trick. Besides, it might hurt him, and

Jamie didn't really want him killed or anything, just dusted off a little to show him where he belonged in the world.

But when he chinned up to Billiard, Jamie got cold feet and decided to wait a day or two longer for meditation. There was no use rushing things, so he let Billiard go free. Boy, Billiard didn't know how lucky he was at such times, Jamie clucked to himself.

One Tuesday, Jamie carried Ingrid's books home. She lived in a small cottage not far from the Santa Catalina foothills. Together they walked in peaceful content, needing no words. They even held hands for a while.

Turning about a clump of prickly pears, they came face to face with Billiard Cunningham.

He stood with his big feet planted across the path, plump fists on his hips, staring at Ingrid with appreciative eyes. Everybody stood still, and Billiard said:

"I'll carry your books, Ingrid. Here."

He reached to take them from Jamie.

Jamie fell back a step. "Oh, no, you don't," he said.

"Oh, yes, I do," retorted Billiard.

"Like heck you do," said Jamie.

"Like heck I don't," exclaimed Billiard, and snatched again, knocking the books into the dust.

Ingrid yelled, then said, "Look here, you can both carry my books. Half and half. That'll settle it."

Billiard shook his head.

"All or nothing," he leered.

Jamie looked back at him.

"Nothing, then!" he shouted.

He summoned up his powers like wrathful storm clouds; lightning crackled hot in each fist. What matter if Billiard loomed four inches taller and some several broader? The fury-wrath lived in Jamie; he would knock Billiard senseless with one clean bolt—maybe two.

There was no room for stuttering fear now; Jamie was cauterized clean of it by a great rage. He pulled away back and let Billiard have it on the chin.

"Jamie!" screamed Ingrid.

The only miracle after that was how Jamie got out of it with his life.

Dad poured Epsom salts into a dishpan of hot water, stirred it firmly, and said, "You oughta known better, darn your hide. Your mother sick an' you comin' home all banged up this way."

Dad made a leathery motion of one brown hand. His eyes were bedded in crinkles and lines, and his mustache was pepper-gray and sparse, as was his hair.

"I didn't know Ma was very sick anymore," said Jamie.

"Women don't talk much," said Dad, dryly. He soaked a towel in steaming Epsom salts and wrung it out. He held Jamie's beaten profile and swabbed it. Jamie whimpered. "Hold still," said Dad. "How you expect me to fix that cut if you don't hold still, darn it."

"What's going on out there?" Mother's voice asked from the bedroom, real tired and soft.

"Nothing," said Dad, wringing out the towel again. "Don't you fret. Jamie just fell and cut his lip, that's all."

"Oh, Jamie," said Mother.

"I'm okay, Ma," said Jamie. The warm towel helped to normalize things. He tried not to think of the fight. It made bad thinking. There were memories of flailing arms, himself pinned down, Billiard whooping with delight and beating downward while Ingrid, crying real tears, threw her books, screaming, at his back.

And then Jamie staggered home alone, sobbing bitterly.

"Oh, Dad," he said now. "It didn't work." He meant his physical miracle on Billiard. "It didn't work."

"What didn't work?" said Dad, applying liniment to bruises.

"Oh, nothing. Nothing." Jamie licked his swollen lip and began to calm down. After all, you can't have a perfect batting average. Even the Lord made mistakes. And—Jamie grinned suddenly—yes, yes, he had *meant* to lose the fight! Yes, he had. Wouldn't Ingrid love him all the more for having fought and lost just for her?

Sure. That was the answer. It was just a reversed miracle, that was all!

"Jamie," Mother called him.

He went in to see her.

With one thing and another, including Epsom salts and a great resurgence of faith in himself because Ingrid loved him now more than ever, Jamie went through the rest of the week without much pain.

He walked Ingrid home, and Billiard didn't bother him again. Billiard played after-school baseball, which was a greater attraction than Ingrid—the sudden sport interest being induced indirectly by telepathy via Jamie, Jamie decided.

Thursday, Ma looked worse. She bleached out to a pallid trembling and a pale coughing. Dad looked scared. Jamie spent less time trying to make things come out wonderful in school and thought more and more of curing Ma.

Friday night, walking alone from Ingrid's house, Jamie watched telegraph poles swing by him very slowly. He thought, If I get to the next telegraph pole before that car behind me reaches me, Mama will be all well.

Jamie walked casually, not looking back, ears itching, legs wanting to run to make the wish come true.

The telegraph pole approached. So did the car behind.

Jamie whistled cautiously. The car was coming too fast!

Jamie pumped past the pole just in time; the car roared by.

There now. Mama would be all well again.

He walked along some more.

Forget about her. Forget about wishes and things, he told himself. But it was tempting, like a hot pie on a windowsill. He had to touch it. He couldn't leave it be, oh, no. He looked ahead on the road and behind on the road.

"I bet I can get down to Schabold's ranch gate before another car comes and do it walking easy," he declared to the sky. "And that will make Mama well all the quicker."

At this moment, in a traitorous, mechanical action, a car jumped over the low hill behind him and roared forward.

Jamie walked fast, then began to run.

I bet I can get down to Schabold's gate, I bet I can—

Feet up, feet down.

He stumbled.

He fell into the ditch, his books fluttering about like dry, white birds. When he got up, sucking his lips, the gate was only twenty yards further on.

The car motored by him in a large cloud of dust.

"I take it back, I take it back," cried Jamie. "I take it back, what I said, I didn't mean it."

With a sudden bleat of terror, he ran for home. It was all his fault, *all* his fault!

The doctor's car stood in front of the house.

Throught the window, Mama looked sicker. The doctor closed up his little black bag and looked at Dad a long time with strange lights in his little black eyes.

Jamie ran out onto the desert to walk alone. He did not cry. He was paralyzed, and he walked like an iron child, hating himself, blundering into the dry riverbed, kicking at prickly pears and stumbling again and again.

Hours later, with the first stars, he came home to find Dad standing beside Mama's bed and Mama not saying much—just lying there like fallen snow, so quiet. Dad tightened his jaw, screwed up his eyes, caved in his chest, and put his head down.

Jamie took up a station at the end of the bed and stared at Mama, shouting instructions in his mind to her.

Get well, get well, Ma, get well, you'll be all right, sure you'll be fine, I command it, you'll be fine, you'll be swell, you just get up and dance around, we need you, Dad and I do, wouldn't be good without you, get well, Ma, get well, Ma. Get well!

The fierce energy lashed out from him silently, wrapping, cuddling her and beating into her sickness, tendering her heart. Jamie felt glorified in his warm power.

She *would* get well. She *must!* Why, it was silly to think any other way. Ma just wasn't the dying sort.

Dad moved suddenly. It was a stiff movement with a jerking of breath. He held Mama's wrists so hard he might have broken them. He lay against her breasts sounding the heart and Jamie screamed inside.

Ma, don't, Ma, don't, oh, Ma, please don't give up.

Dad got up, swaying.

She was dead.

Inside the walls of Jericho that was Jamie's mind, a thought went screaming about in one last drive of power: Yes, she's dead, all right, so she is dead, so what if she is dead? Bring her back to life again, yes, make her live again, Lazarus, come forth, Lazarus, Lazarus, come forth from the tomb, Lazarus, come forth.

He must have been babbling aloud, for Dad turned and glared at him in old, ancient horror and struck him bluntly across the mouth to shut him up.

Jamie sank against the bed, mouthing into the cold blankets, and the walls of Jericho crumbled and fell down about him.

Jamie returned to school a week later. He did not stride into the schoolyard with his old assurance; he did not bend imperiously at the fountain; nor did he pass his tests with anything more than a grade of seventy-five.

The children wondered what had happened to him. He was never quite the same.

They did not know that Jamie had given up his role. He could not tell them. They did not know what they had lost.

# The October Game

He put the gun back into the bureau drawer and shut the drawer.

No, not that way. Louise wouldn't suffer that way. She would be dead and it would be over and she wouldn't suffer. It was very important that this thing have, above all, duration. Duration through imagination. How to prolong the suffering? How, first of all, to bring it about? Well.

The man standing before the bedroom mirror carefully fitted his cuff links together. He paused long enough to hear the children run by swiftly on the street below, outside this warm two-story house; like so many gray mice the children, like so many leaves.

By the sound of the children you knew the calendar day. By their screams you knew what evening it was. You knew it was very late in the year. October. The last day of October, with white bone masks and cut pumpkins and the smell of dropped candle fat.

No. Things hadn't been right for some time. October

didn't help any. If anything it made things worse. He adjusted his black bow-tie. If this were spring, he nodded slowly, quietly, emotionlessly, at his image in the mirror, then there might be a chance. But tonight all the world was burning down into ruin. There was no green of spring, none of the freshness, none of the promise.

There was a soft running in the hall. "That's Marion," he told himself. "My little one. All eight quiet years of her. Never a word. Just her luminous gray eyes and her wondering little mouth." His daughter had been in and out all evening, trying on various masks, asking him which was most terrifying, most horrible. They had both finally decided on the skeleton mask. It was "just awful!" It would "scare the beans" from people!

Again he caught the long look of thought and deliberation he gave himself in the mirror. He had never liked October. Ever since he first lay in the autumn leaves before his grandmother's house many years ago and heard the wind and saw the empty trees. It had made him cry, without a reason. And a little of that sadness returned each year to him. It always went away with spring.

But, it was different tonight. There was a feeling of autumn coming to last a million years.

There would be no spring.

He had been crying quietly all evening. It did not show, not a vestige of it, on his face. It was all hidden somewhere and it wouldn't stop.

A rich syrupy smell of candy filled the bustling house. Louise had laid out apples in new skins of caramel; there were vast bowls of punch fresh-mixed, stringed apples in each door, scooped, vented pumpkins peering triangularly from each cold window. There was a water tub in the center of the living room, waiting, with a sack of apples nearby, for dunking to begin. All that was needed was the catalyst, the inpouring of children, to start the apples bobbling, the stringed apples to penduluming in the crowded doors, the candy to vanish, the halls to echo with fright or delight, it was all the same.

Now, the house was silent with preparation. And just a little more than that.

Louise had managed to be in every other room save the room he was in today. It was her very fine way of intimating, Oh look, Mich, see how busy I am! So busy that when you walk into a room *I'm* in there's always something I need to do in *another* room! Just see how I dash about!

For a while he had played a little game with her, a nasty childish game. When she was in the kitchen then he came to the kitchen saying, "I need a glass of water." After a moment, he standing, drinking water, she like a crystal witch over the caramel brew bubbling like a prehistoric mudpot on the stove, she said, "Oh, I must light the pumpkins!" and she rushed to the living room to make the pumpkins smile with light. He came after her, smiling, "I must get my pipe." "Oh, the cider!" she had cried, running to the dining room. "I'll check the cider," he had said. But when he tried following she ran to the bathroom and locked the door.

He stood outside the bathroom door, laughing strangely and senselessly, his pipe gone cold in his mouth, and then, tired of the game, but stubborn, he waited another five minutes. There was not a sound from the bath. And lest she enjoy in any way knowing that he waited outside, irritated, he suddenly jerked about and walked upstairs, whistling merrily.

At the top of the stairs he had waited. Finally he had heard the bathroom door unlatch and she had come out and life below-stairs had resumed, as life in a jungle must resume once a terror has passed on away and the antelope return to their spring.

Now, as he finished his bow-tie and put on his dark coat there was a mouse-rustle in the hall. Marion appeared in the door, all skeletonous in her disguise.

"How do I look, Papa?"

"Fine!"

From under the mask, blonde hair showed. From the skull sockets small blue eyes smiled. He sighed. Marion and Louise, the two silent denouncers of his virility, his dark power. What alchemy had there been in Louise that took the dark of a dark man and bleached and bleached the dark brown eyes and black hair and washed and bleached the ingrown baby all during the period before birth until the child was born, Marion, blonde, blue-eyed, ruddy-cheeked? Sometimes he suspected that Louise had conceived the child as an idea, completely asexual, an immaculate conception of contemptuous mind and cell. As a firm rebuke to him she had produced a child in her *own* image, and, to top it, she had somehow *fixed* the doctor so he shook his head and said, "Sorry, Mr. Wilder, your wife will never have another child. This is the *last* one."

"And I wanted a boy," Mich had said, eight years ago.

He almost bent to take hold of Marion now, in her skull mask. He felt an inexplicable rush of pity for her, because she had never had a father's love, only the crushing, holding love of a loveless mother. But most of all he pitied himself, that somehow he had not made the most of a bad birth, enjoyed his daughter for herself, regardless of her not being dark and a son and like himself. Somewhere he had missed out. Other things being equal, he would have loved the child. But Louise hadn't wanted a child, anyway, in the first place. She had been frightened of the idea of birth. He had forced the child on her, and from that night, all through the year until the agony of the birth itself, Louise had lived in another part of the house. She had expected to die with the forced child. It had been very easy for Louise to hate this husband who so wanted a son that he gave his only wife over to the mortuary.

But—Louise had lived. And in triumph! Her eyes, the day he came to the hospital, were cold. I'm alive, they said. And I have a *blonde* daughter! Just look! And when he had put out a hand to touch, the mother had turned away to conspire with her new pink daughter-child—away from that dark forcing murderer. It had all been so beautifully ironic. His selfishness deserved it.

But now it was October again. There had been other Octobers and when he thought of the long winter he had been filled with horror year after year to think of the endless months mortared into the house by an insane fall of snow, trapped with a woman and child, neither of whom loved him, for months on end. During the eight years there had been respites. In spring and summer you got out, walked, picnicked; these were desperate solutions to the desperate problem of a hated man.

But, in winter, the hikes and picnics and escapes fell away with the leaves. Life, like a tree, stood empty, the fruit picked, the sap run to earth. Yes, you invited people in, but people were hard to get in winter with blizzards and all. Once he had been clever enough to save for a Florida trip. They had gone south. He had walked in the open.

But now, the eighth winter coming, he knew things were finally at an end. He simply could not wear this one through. There was an acid walled off in him that slowly had eaten through tissue and bone over the years, and now, tonight, it would reach the wild explosive in him and all would be over!

There was a mad ringing of the bell below. In the hall, Louise went to see. Marion, without a word, ran down to greet the first arrivals. There were shouts and hilarity.

He walked to the top of the stairs.

Louise was below, taking wraps. She was tall and slender and blonde to the point of whiteness, laughing down upon the new children.

He hesitated. What was all this? The years? The boredom of living? Where had it gone wrong? Certainly not with the birth of the child alone. But it had been a symbol of all their tensions, he imagined. His jealousies and his business failures and all the rotten rest of it. Why didn't he just turn, pack a suitcase, and leave? No. Not without hurting Louise as much as she had hurt him. It was simple as that. Divorce wouldn't hurt her at all. It would simply be an end to numb indecision. If he thought divorce would give her pleasure in any way he would stay married the rest of his life to her, for damned spite. No, he must hurt her. Figure some way, perhaps, to take Marion away from her, legally. Yes. That was it. That would hurt most of all. To take Marion away.

"Hello down there!" He descended the stairs, beaming.

Louise didn't look up.

"Hi, Mr. Wilder!"

The children shouted, waved, as he came down.

By ten o'clock the doorbell had stopped ringing, the apples were bitten from stringed doors, the pink child faces were wiped dry from the apple bobbing, napkins were smeared with caramel and punch, and he, the husband, with pleasant efficiency had taken over. He took the party right out of Louise's hands. He ran about talking to the twenty children and the twelve parents who had come and were happy with the special spiked cider he had fixed them. He supervised pin the tail on the donkey, spin the bottle, musical chairs, and all the rest, amid fits of shouting laughter. Then, in the triangular-eyed pumpkin shine, all house lights out, he cried, "Hush! Follow me!" toptoeing toward the cellar.

The parents, on the outer periphery of the costumed riot, commented to each other, nodding at the clever husband, speaking to the lucky wife. How *well* he got on with children, they said.

The children crowded after the husband, squealing.

"The cellar!" he cried. "The tomb of the witch!"

More squealing. He made a mock shiver. "Abandon hope all ye who enter here!"

The parents chuckled.

One by one the children slid down a slide which Mich had fixed up from lengths of table-section, into the dark cellar. He hissed and shouted ghastly utterances after them. A wonderful wailing filled the dark pumpkin-lighted house. Everybody talked at once. Everybody but Marion. She had gone through all the party with a minimum of sound or talk; it was all inside her, all the excitement and joy. What a little troll, he thought. With a shut mouth and shiny eyes she had watched her own party, like so many serpentines thrown before her.

Now, the parents. With laughing reluctance they slid down the short incline, uproarious, while little Marion stood by, always wanting to see it all, to be last. Louise went down without help. He moved to aid her, but she was gone even before he bent.

The upper house was empty and silent in the candleshine.

Marion stood by the slide. "Here we go," he said, and picked her up.

They sat in a vast circle in the cellar. Warmth came from the distant bulk of the furnace. The chairs stood in a long line along each wall, twenty squealing children, twelve rustling relatives, alternately spaced, with Louise down at the far end, Mich up at this end, near the stairs. He peered but saw nothing. They had all grouped to their chairs, catch-as-you-can in the blackness. The entire program from here on was to be enacted in the dark, he as Mr. Interlocutor. There was a child scampering, a smell of damp cement, and the sound of the wind out in the October stars.

"Now!" cried the husband in the dark cellar. "Quiet!"

Everybody settled.

The room was black black. Not a light, not a shine, not a glint of an eye.

A scraping of crockery, a metal rattle.

"The witch is dead," intoned the husband.

"Eeeeeeeeeeee," said the children.

"The witch is dead, she has been killed, and here is the knife she was killed with."

He handed over the knife. It was passed from hand to hand, down and around the circle, with chuckles and little odd cries and comments from the adults.

"The witch is dead, and this is her head," whispered the husband, and handed an item to the nearest person.

"Oh, I know how this game is played," some child cried, happily, in the dark. "He gets some old chicken innards from the icebox and hands them around and says, 'These are her innards!' And he makes a clay head and passes it for her head, and passes a soup bone for her arm. And he take a marble and says, 'This is her eye!' And he takes some corn and says, 'This is her teeth!' And he takes a sack of plum pudding and gives that and says, 'This is her stomach!' I know how *this* is played!"

"Hush, you'll spoil everything," some girl said.

"The witch came to harm, and this is her arm," said Mich.

"Eeeee!"

The items were passed and passed, like hot potatoes, around the circle. Some children screamed, wouldn't touch them. Some ran from their chairs to stand in the center of the cellar until the grisly items had passed.

"Aw, it's only chicken insides," scoffed a boy. "Come back, Helen!"

Shot from hand to hand, with small scream after scream, the items went down, down, to be followed by another and another.

"The witch cut apart, and this is her heart," said the husband.

Six or seven items moving at once through the laughing, trembling dark.

Louise spoke up. "Marion, don't be afraid; it's only play."

Marion didn't say anything.

"Marion?" asked Louise. "Are you afraid?"

Marion didn't speak.

"She's all right," said the husband. "She's not afraid."

On and on the passing, the screams, the hilarity.

The autumn wind sighed about the house. And he, the husband, stood at the head of the dark cellar, intoning the words, handing out the items.

"Marion?" asked Louise again, from far across the cellar.

Everybody was talking.

"Marion?" called Louise.

Everybody quieted.

"Marion, answer me, are you afraid?"

Marion didn't answer.

The husband stood there, at the bottom of the cellar steps.

Louise called, "Marion, are you there?"

No answer. The room was silent.

"Where's Marion?" called Louise.

"She was here," said a boy.

"Maybe she's upstairs."

"Marion!"

No answer. It was quiet.

Louise cried out, "Marion, Marion!"

"Turn on the lights," said one of the adults.

The items stopped passing. The children and adults sat with the witch's items in their hands.

"No." Louise gasped. There was a scraping of her chair, wildly, in the dark. "No. Don't turn on the lights, oh, God, God, God, don't turn them on, please, please *don't* turn on the lights, *don't!*" Louise was shrieking now. The entire cellar froze with the scream.

Nobody moved.

Everyone sat in the dark cellar, suspended in the suddenly frozen task of this October game; the wind blew outside, banging the house, the smell of pumpkins and apples filled the room with the smell of the objects in their fingers while one boy cried, "I'll go upstairs and look!" and he ran upstairs hopefully and out around the house, four times around the house, calling, "Marion, Marion, Marion!" over and over and at last coming slowly down the stairs into the waiting breathing cellar and saying to the darkness, "I can't find her."

Then . . . some idiot turned on the lights.

# The Pumpernickel

Mr. and Mrs. Welles walked away from the movie theater late at night and went into the quiet little store, a combination restaurant and delicatessen. They settled in a booth, and Mrs. Welles said, "Baked ham on pumpernickel." Mr. Welles glanced toward the counter, and there lay a loaf of pumpernickel.

"Why," he murmured, "pumpernickel . . . Druce's Lake . . ."

The night, the late hour, the empty restaurant—by now the pattern was familiar. Anything could set him off on a tide of reminiscences. The scent of autumn leaves, or midnight winds blowing, could stir him from himself, and memories would pour around him. Now in the unreal hour after the theater, in this lonely store, he saw a loaf of pumpernickel bread and, as on a thousand other nights, he found himself moved into the past.

"Druce's Lake," he said again.

"What?" His wife glanced up.

"Something I'd almost forgotten," said Mr. Welles. "In 1910, when I was twenty, I nailed a loaf of pumpernickel to the top of my bureau mirror. . . ."

In the hard, shiny crust of the bread, the boys at Druce's Lake had cut their names: *Tom, Nick, Bill, Alec, Paul, Jack*. The finest picnic in history! Their faces tanned as they rattled down the dusty roads. Those were the days when roads were *really* dusty; a fine brown talcum floured up after your car. And the lake was always twice as good to reach as it would be later in life when you arrived immaculate, clean, and unrumpled.

"That was the last time the old gang got together," Mr. Welles said.

After that, college, work, and marriage separated you. Suddenly you found yourself with some other group. And you never felt as comfortable or as much as ease again in all your life.

"I wonder," said Mr. Welles. "I like to think maybe we all *knew*, somehow, that this picnic might be the last we'd have. You first get that empty feeling the day after high-school graduation. Then, when a little time passes and no one vanishes immediately, you relax. But after a year you realize the old world is changing. And you want to do some one last thing before you lose one another. While you're all still friends, home from college for the summer, this side of marriage, you've got to have something like a last ride and a swim in the cool lake."

Mr. Welles remembered that rare summer morning, he and Tom lying under his father's Ford, reaching up their hands to adjust this or that, talking about machines and women and the future. While they worked, the day got warm. At last Tom said, "Why don't we drive out to Druce's Lake?"

As simple as that.

Yet, forty years later, you remember every detail of picking up the other fellows, everyone yelling under the green trees.

"Hey!" Alec beating everyone's head with the pumpernickel and laughing. "This is for extra sandwiches, later."

Nick had made the sandwiches that were already in the hamper—the garlic kind they would eat less of as the years passed and the girls moved in.

Then, squeezing three in the front, three in the rear, with their arms across one another's shoulders, they drove through the boiling, dusty countryside, with a cake of ice in a tin washtub to cool the beer they'd buy.

What was the special quality of that day that it should focus like a stereoscopic image, fresh and clear, forty years later? Pcrhaps each of them had had an experience like his own. A few days before the picnic, he had found a photograph of his father twenty-five years younger, standing with a group of friends at college. The photograph had disturbed him, made him aware as he had not been before of the passing of time, the swift flow of the years away from youth. A picture taken of him as he was now would, in twenty-five years, look as strange to his own children as his father's picture did to him—unbelievably young, a stranger out of a strange, never-returning time.

Was that how the final picnic had come about—with each of them knowing that in a few short years they would be crossing streets to avoid one another, or, if they met, saying, "We've *got* to have lunch sometime!" but never doing it? Whatever the reason, Mr. Welles could still hear the splashes as they'd plunged off the pier under a yellow sun. And then the beer and sandwiches underneath the shady trees.

We never ate that pumpernickel, Mr. Welles thought. Funny, if we'd been a bit hungrier, we'd have cut it up, and I wouldn't have been reminded of it by the loaf there on the counter.

Lying under the trees in a golden peace that came from beer and sun and male companionship, they promised that in ten years they would meet at the courthouse on New Year's Day, 1920, to see what they had done with their lives. Talking their rough easy talk, they carved their names in the pumpernickel.

"Driving home," Mr. Welles said, "we sang 'Moonlight Bay'."

He remembered motoring along in the hot, dry night with their swimsuits damp on the jolting floorboards. It was a ride of many detours taken just for the hell of it, which was the best reason in the world.

"Good night." "So long." "Good night."

Then Welles was driving alone, at midnight, home to bed.

He nailed the pumpernickel to his bureau the next day.

"I almost cried when, two years later, my mother threw it in the incinerator while I was off at college."

"What happened in 1920?" asked his wife. "On New Year's Day?"

"Oh," said Mr. Welles. "I was walking by the courthouse, by accident, at noon. It was snowing. I heard the clock strike. Lord, I thought, we were supposed to meet here today! I waited five minutes. Not right in front of the courthouse, no. I waited across the street." He paused. "Nobody showed up."

He got up from the table and paid the bill. "And I'll take that loaf of unsliced pumpernickel there," he said.

When he and his wife were walking home, he said, "I've got a crazy idea. I often wondered what happened to everyone."

"Nick's still in town with his café."

"But what about the others?" Mr. Welles's face was getting pink and he was smiling and waving his hands. "They moved away. I think Tom's in Cincinnati." He looked quickly at his wife. "Just for the heck of it, I'll send him this pumpernickel!"

"Oh, but—"

"Sure!" He laughed, walking faster, slapping the bread with the palm of his hand. "Have him carve his name on it and mail it on to the others if he knows their addresses. And finally back to me, with all their names on it!"

"But," she said, taking his arm, "it'll only make you unhappy. You've done things like this so many times before and . . ."

He wasn't listening. Why do I never get these ideas by day? he thought. Why do I always get them after the sun goes down?

In the morning, first thing, he thought, I'll mail this pumpernickel off, by God, to Tom and the others. And when it comes back I'll have the loaf just as it was when it got thrown out and burned! Why not?

"Let's see," he said, as his wife opened the screen door and let him walk into the stuffy-smelling house to be greeted by silence and warm emptiness. "Let's see. We also sang 'Row Row Row Your Boat,' didn't we?"

In the morning, he came down the hall stairs and paused a moment in the strong full sunlight, his face shaved, his teeth freshly brushed. Sunlight brightened every room. He looked in at the breakfast table.

His wife was busy there. Slowly, calmly, she was slicing the pumpernickel.

He sat down at the table in the warm sunlight, and reached for the newspaper.

She picked up a slice of the newly cut bread, and kissed him on the cheek. He patted her arm.

"One or two slices of toast, dear?" she asked gently.

"Two, I think," he replied.

# Long After Midnight

The police ambulance went up into the palisades at the wrong hour. It is always the wrong hour when the police ambulance goes anywhere, but this was especially wrong, for it was long after midnight and nobody imagined it would ever be day again, because the sea coming in on the lightless shore below said as much, and the wind blowing salt cold in from the Pacific reaffirmed this, and the fog muffling the sky and putting out the stars struck the final, unfelt-but-disabling blow. The weather said it had been here forever, man was hardly here at all, and would soon be gone. Under the circumstances it was hard for the men gathered on the cliff, with several cars, the headlights on, and flashlights bobbing, to feel real, trapped as they were between a sunset they hardly remembered and a sunrise that would not be imagined.

The slender weight hanging from the tree, turning in the cold salt wind, did not diminish this feeling in any way.

The slender weight was a girl, no more than nineteen, in a light green gossamer party frock, coat and shoes lost somewhere in the cool night, who had brought a rope up to these cliffs and found a tree with a branch half out over the cliff and tied the rope in place and made a loop for her neck and let herself out on the wind to hang there swinging. The rope made a dry scraping whine on the branch, until the police came, and the ambulance, to take her down out of space and place her on the ground.

A single phone call had come in about midnight telling what they might find out here on the edge of the cliff and whoever it was hung up swiftly and did not call again, and now the hours had passed and all that could be done was done and over, the police were finished and leaving, and there was just the ambulance now and the men with the ambulance to load the quiet burden and head for the morgue.

Of the three men remaining around the sheeted form there were Carlson, who had been at this sort of thing for thirty years, and Moreno, who had been at it for ten, and Latting, who was new to the job a few weeks back. Of the three it was Latting now who stood on the edge of the cliff looking at that empty tree limb, the rope in his hand, not able to take his eyes away. Carlson came up behind him. Hearing him, Latting said, "What a place, what an awful place to die."

"Any place is awful, if you decide you want to go bad enough," said Carlson. "Come on, kid."

Latting did not move. He put out his hand to touch the tree. Carlson grunted and shook his head. "Go ahead. Try to remember it all."

"Any reason why I shouldn't?" Latting turned quickly to look at that emotionless gray face of the older man. "You got any objections?"

"No objections. I was the same way once. But after a while you learn it's best not to see. You eat better. You sleep better. After a while you learn to forget."

"I don't want to forget," said Latting. "Good God,

somebody died up here just a few hours ago. She deserves—"

"She *deserved*, kid, past tense, not present. She deserved a better shake and didn't get it. Now she deserves a decent burial. That's all we can do for her. It's late and cold. You can tell us all about it on the way."

"That could be your daughter there."

"You won't get to me that way, kid. It's not my daughter, that's what counts. And it's not yours, though you make it sound like it was. It's a nineteen-year-old girl, no name, no purse, nothing. I'm sorry she's dead. There, does that help?"

"It could if you said it right."

"I'm sorry, now pick up the other end of the stretcher."

Latting picked up one end of the stretcher but did not walk with it and only looked at the figure beneath the sheet.

"It's awful being the young and deciding to just quit."

"Sometimes," said Carlson, at the other end of the stretcher, "I get tired, too."

"Sure, but you're—" Latting stopped.

"Go ahead, say it, I'm old. Somebody fifty, sixty, it's okay, who gives a damn, somebody nineteen, everybody cries. So don't come to my funeral, kid, and no flowers."

"I didn't mean . . ." said Latting.

"Nobody means, but everybody says, and luckily I got the hide of an iguana. March."

They moved with the stretcher toward the ambulance where Moreno was opening the doors wider.

"Boy," said Latting, "she's light. She doesn't weigh anything."

"That's the wild life for you, you punks, you kids." Carlson was getting into the back of the ambulance now and they were sliding the stretcher in. "I smell whiskey. You young ones think you can drink like college fullbacks and keep your weight. Hell, she don't even weigh ninety pounds, if that."

Latting put the rope in on the floor of the ambulance. "I wonder where she got this?"

"It's not like poison," said Moreno. "Anyone can buy rope and not sign. This looks like block-and-tackle rope. She was at a beach party maybe and got mad at her boyfriend and took this from his car and picked herself a spot. . . ."

They took a last look at the tree out over the cliff, the empty branch, the wind rustling in the leaves, then Carlson got out and walked around to the front seat with Moreno, and Latting got in the back and slammed the doors.

They drove away down the dim incline toward the shore where the ocean laid itself, card after white card, in thunders, upon the dark sand. They drove in silence for a while, letting their headlights, like ghosts, move on out ahead. Then Latting said, "I'm getting myself a new job."

Moreno laughed. "Boy, you didn't last long. I had bets you wouldn't last. Tell you what, you'll be back. No other job like this. All the other jobs are dull. Sure, you get sick once in a while. I do. I think: I'm going to quit. I almost do. Then I stick with it. And here I am."

"Well, you can stay," said Latting. "But I'm full up. I'm not curious anymore. I seen a lot the last few weeks, but this is the last straw. I'm sick of being sick. Or worse, I'm sick of your not caring."

"Who doesn't care?"

"Both of you!"

Moreno snorted. "Light us a couple, huh, Carlie?" Carlson lit two cigarettes and passed one to Moreno, who puffed on it, blinking his eyes, driving along by the loud strokes of the sea. "Just because we don't scream and yell and throw fits—"

"I don't want fits," said Latting, in the back, crouched by the sheeted figure. "I just want a little human talk, I just want you to look different than you would walking through a butcher's shop. If I ever get like you two, not worrying, not bothering, all thick skin and tough—"

"We're not tough," said Carlson, quietly, thinking about it, "we're acclimated."

"Acclimated, hell, when you should be *numb*?"

"Kid, don't tell us what we should be when you don't even know what we *are*. Any doctor is a lousy doctor who jumps down in the grave with every patient. All doctors did that, there'd be no one to help the live and kicking. Get out of the grave, boy, you can't see nothing from there."

There was a long silence from the back, and at last Latting started talking, mainly to himself:

"I wonder how long she was up there alone on the cliff, an hour, two? It must have been funny up there looking down at all the campfires, knowing you were going to wipe the whole business clean off. I suppose she was to a dance, or a beach party, and she and her boyfriend broke up. The boyfriend will be down at the station tomorrow to identify her. I'd hate to be him. How he'll *feel*—"

"He won't feel anything. He won't even show up," said Carlson, steadily, mashing out his cigarette in the front-seat tray. "He was probably the one found her and made the call and ran. Two bits will buy you a nickel he's not worth the polish on her little fingernail. Some slobby lout of a guy with pimples and bad breath. Christ, why don't these girls learn to wait until morning."

"Yeah," said Moreno. "Everything's better in the morning."

"Try telling that to a girl in love," said Latting.

"Now a man," said Carlson, lighting a fresh cigarette, "he just gets himself drunk, says to hell with it, no use killing yourself for no woman."

They drove in silence awhile past all the small dark beach houses with only a light here or there, it was so late.

"Maybe," said Latting, "she was going to have a baby."

"It happens."

"And then the boyfriend runs off with someone and this one just borrows his rope and walks up on the cliff," said Latting. "Answer me, now, *is* that or *isn't* it love?"

"It," said Carlson, squinting, searching the dark, "is a kind of love. I give up on what kind."

"Well, sure," said Moreno, driving. "I'll go along with you, kid. I mean, it's nice to know somebody in this world can love that hard."

They all thought for a while, as the ambulance purred between quiet palisades and now quiet sea and maybe two of them thought fleetingly of their wives and tract houses and sleeping children and all the times years ago when they had driven to the beach and broken out the beer and necked up in the rocks and lay around on the blankets with guitars, singing and feeling like life would go on just as far as the ocean went, which was very far, and maybe they didn't think that at all. Latting, looking up at the backs of the two older men's necks, hoped or perhaps only nebulously wondered if these men remembered any first kisses, the taste of salt on the lips. Had there ever been a time when they had stomped the sand like mad bulls and yelled out of sheer joy and dared the universe to put them down?

And by their silence, Latting knew that yes, with all his talking, and the night, and the wind, and the cliff and the tree and the rope, he had gotten through to them; it, the event, had gotten through to them. Right now, they had to be thinking of their wives in their warm beds, long dark miles away, unbelievable, suddenly unattainable while here they were driving along a salt-layered road at a dumb hour half between certainties, bearing with them a strange thing on a cot and a used length of rope.

"Her boyfriend," said Latting, "will be out dancing

tomorrow night with somebody else. That gripes my gut."

"I wouldn't mind," said Carlson, "beating the hell out of him."

Latting moved the sheet. "They sure wear their hair crazy and short, some of them. All curls, but short. Too much makeup. Too—" He stopped.

"You were saying?" asked Moreno.

Latting moved the sheet some more. He said nothing. In the next minute there was a rustling sound of the sheet, moved now here, now there. Latting's face was pale.

"Hey," he murmured, at last. "Hey."

Instinctively, Moreno slowed the ambulance.

"Yeah, kid?"

"I just found out something," said Latting. "I had this feeling all along, she's wearing too much make-up, and the hair, and—"

"So?"

"Well, for God's sake," said Latting, his lips hardly moving, one hand up to feel his own face to see what its expression was. "You want to know something funny?"

"Make us laugh," said Carlson.

The ambulance slowed even more as Latting said, "It's not a woman. I mean, it's not a girl. I mean, well, it's not a female. *Understand?*"

The ambulance slowed to a crawl.

The wind blew in off the vague morning sea through the window as the two up front turned and stared into the back of the ambulance at the shape there on the cot.

"Somebody tell me," said Latting, so quietly they almost could not hear the words. "Do we stop feeling bad now? Or do we feel worse?"

Nobody answered.

A wave, and then another, and then another, moved in and fell upon the mindless shore.

# Have I Got a Chocolate Bar for You!

It all began with the smell of chocolate.

On a steaming late afternoon of June rain, Father Malley drowsed in his confessional, waiting for penitents.

Where in all the world were they? he wondered. Immense traffics of sin lurked beyond in the warm rains. Then why not immense traffics of confession here?

Father Malley stirred and blinked.

Today's sinners moved so fast in their cars that this old church was an ecclesiastical blur. And himself? An ancient watercolor priest, tints fading fast, trapped inside.

Let's give it another five minutes and stop, he thought, not in panic but in the kind of quiet shame and desperation that neglect shoulders on a man.

There was a rustle from beyond the confessional grate next door.

Father Malley sat up, quickly.

A smell of chocolate sifted through the grille.

Ah, God, thought the priest, it's a lad with his small basket of sins soon laid to rest and him gone. Well . . .

The old priest leaned to the grate where the candy essence lingered and where the words must come.

But, no words. No "Bless me, Father, for I have sinned . . ."

Only strange small mouse-sounds of . . . *chewing!*

The sinner in the next booth, God sew up his mouth, was actually sitting in there devouring a candy bar!

"No!" whispered the priest, to himself.

His stomach, gathering data, rumbled, reminding him that he had not eaten since breakfast. For some sin of pride which he could not now recall, he had nailed himself to a sain't diet all day, and now—*this!*

Next door, the chewing continued.

Father Malley's stomach growled. He leaned hard against the grille, shut his eyes, and cried:

"Stop that!"

The mouse-nibbling stopped.

The smell of chocolate faded.

A young man's voice said, "That's exactly why I've come, Father."

The priest opened one eye to examine the shadow behind the screen.

"*What's* exactly why you've come?"

"The chocolate, Father."

"The *what?*"

"Don't be angry, Father."

"Angry, hell, who's angry?"

"You are, Father. I'm damned and burnt before I start, by the sound of your voice."

The priest sank back in the creaking leather and mopped his face and shook his senses.

"Yes, yes. The day's hot. I'm out of temper. But then, I never had much."

"It will cool off later in the day, Father. You'll be fine."

The old priest eyed the screen. "Who's taking and who's *giving* confession here?"

"Why, you are, Father."

"Then, get *on* with it!"

The voice hastened forth the facts:

"You have smelled the chocolate, Father?"

The priest's stomach answered for him, faintly.

Both listened to the sad sound. Then:

"Well, Father, to hit it on the head, I was and still am a . . . chocolate junkie."

Old fires stirred in the priest's eyes. Curiosity became humor, then laughed itself back to curiosity again.

"And *that's* why you've come to confession this day?"

"That's it, sir, or, Father."

"You haven't come about sweating over your sister or blueprints for fornication or self-battles with the grand war of masturbation?"

"I have not, Father," said the voice in remorse.

The priest caught the tone and said, "Tut, tut, it's all right. You'll get around to it. For now, you're a grand relief. I'm full-up with wandering males and lonely females and all the junk they read in books and try in waterbeds and sink from sight with suffocating cries as the damn things spring leaks and all is lost. Get on. You have bruised my antennae alert. Say more."

"Well, Father, I have eaten, every day of my life now for ten or twelve years, one or two pounds of chocolate. I cannot leave it alone, Father. It is the end-all and be-all of my life."

"Sounds like a fearful affliction of lumps, acne, carbuncles, and pimples."

"It was. It *is*."

"And not exactly contributing to a lean figure."

"If I leaned, Father, the confessional would fall over."

The cabinet around them creaked and groaned as the hidden figure beyond demonstrated.

"Sit still!" cried the priest.

The groaning stopped.

The priest was wide awake now and feeling splendid.

Never in years had he felt so alive and aware of his happily curious and beating heart and fine blood that sought and found, sought and found the far corners of his cloth and body.

The heat of the day was gone.

He felt immensely cool. A kind of excitement pulsed his wrists and lingered in his throat. He leaned almost like a lover to the grille and prompted more spillage.

"Oh, lad, you're rare."

"And sad, Father, and twenty-two years old and put upon, and hate myself for eating, and need to do something about it."

"Have you tried chewing more and swallowing less?"

"Oh, each night I go to bed saying: Lord, put off the crunch-bars and the milk-chocolate kisses and the Hershey's. Each morning I rave out of bed and run to the liquor store not for liquor but for eight Nestle's in a row! I'm in sugar-shock by noon."

"That's not so much confession as medical fact, I can see."

"My doctor yells at me, Father."

"He should."

"I don't listen, Father."

"*You* should."

"My mother's no help, she's hog-fat and candy-wild."

"I hope you're not one of those who live at home still?"

"I loiter about, Father."

"God, there should be laws against boys loitering in the round shade of their ma's. Is your father surviving the two of you?"

"Somehow."

"And *his* weight?"

"Irving Gross, he calls himself. Which is a joke about size and weight and not his name."

"With the three of you, the sidewalk's full?"

"No bike can pass, Father."

"Christ in the wilderness," murmured the priest, "starving for forty days."

"Sounds like a terrible diet, Father."

"If I knew the proper wilderness, I'd boot you there."

"Boot away, Father. With no help from my mom and dad, a doctor and skinny friends who snort at me, I'm out of pocket from eating and out of mind from the same. I never dreamed I'd wind up with *you*. Beg pardon, Father, but it took a lot to drive me here. If my friends knew, if my mom, my dad, my crazy doctor knew I was here with *you* at this minute, oh what the hell!"

There was a fearful stampede of feet, a careening of flesh.

"Wait!"

But the weight blundered out of the next-door cubby.

With an elephant trample, the young man was gone.

The smell of chocolate alone stayed behind and told all by saying nought.

The heat of the day swarmed in to stifle and depress the old priest.

He had to climb out of the confessional because he knew if he stayed he would begin to curse under his breath and have to run off to have *his* sins forgiven at some other parish.

I suffer from Peevish, O Lord, he thought. How many Hail Marys for *that*?

Come to think of it, how many for a thousand tons, give or take a ton, of chocolate?

Come back! he cried silently at the empty church aisle.

No, he won't, not ever now, he thought, I pressed too hard.

And with that as supreme depression, he went to the parish house to tub himself cool and towel himself to distemper.

A day, two days, a week passed.

The sweltering noons dissolved the old priest back into a stupor of sweat and vinegar-gnat mean. He snoozed in his cubby, or shuffled papers in the unlined library, looked out at the untended lawn and reminded himself to caper with the mower one day soon. But most of all he found himself brambling with irritability. Fornication was the minted coin of the land, and masturbation its handmaiden. Or so it seemed from the few whispers that slid through the confessional grille during the long afternoons.

On the fifteenth day of July, he found himself staring at some boys idling by on their bicycles, mouths full of Hershey bars that they were gulping and chewing.

That night he awoke thinking Power House and Baby Ruth and Love Nest and Crunch.

He stood it as long as he could and then got up, tried to read, tossed the book down, paced the dark night church, and at last, spluttering mildly, went up to the altar and asked one of his rare favors of God.

The next afternoon, the young man who loved chocolate at last came back.

"Thank you, Lord," murmured the priest, as he felt the vast weight creak the other half of the confessional like a ship foundered with wild freight.

"What?" whispered the young voice from the far side.

"Sorry, I wasn't addressing you," said the priest.

He shut his eyes and inhaled.

The gates of the chocolate factory stood wide somewhere and its mild spice moved forth to change the land.

Then, an incredible thing happened.

Sharp words burst from Father Malley's mouth:

"You shouldn't be *coming* here!"

"What, what, Father?"

"Go somewhere else! I can't help. You need special work. No, no."

The old priest was stunned to feel his own mind jump out his tongue this way. Was it the heat, the long days and weeks kept waiting by this fiend, what, *what?* But still his mouth leaped on:

"No help here! No, no. *Go* for help—"

"To the shrinks, you mean?" the voice cut in, amazingly calm, considering the explosion.

"Yes, yes, Lord save us, to those people. The—the psychiatrists."

This last word was even more incredible. He had rarely heard himself say it.

"Oh, God, Father, what do *they* know?" said the young man.

What indeed, thought Father Malley, for he had long been put off by their carnival talk and to-the-rear-march chat and clamor. Good grief, why don't I turn in my collar and buy me a beard! he thought, but went on more calmly:

"What do they know, my son? Why, they claim to know everything."

"Just like the Church *used* to claim, Father?"

Silence. Then:

"There's a difference between claiming and knowing," the old priest replied, as calmly as his beating heart would allow.

"And the Church *knows*, is that it, Father?"

"And if it doesn't, *I* do!"

"Don't get mad again, Father." The young man paused and sighed. "I didn't come to dance angels on the head of a pin with you. Shall I start confession, Father?"

"It's about time!" The priest caught himself, settled back, shut his eyes sweetly, and added, "Well?"

And the voice on the other side, with the tongue and the breath of a child, tinctured with silver-foiled kisses, flavored with honeycomb, moved by recent sugars and memories or more immediate Cadbury fetes and galas, began to describe its life of getting up and living with and going to bed with Swiss delights and temptations out of Hershey, Pennsylvania, or how to chew the dark skin off the exterior of a Clark Bar and keep the caramel and textured interior for special shocks and celebrations.

Of how the soul asked and the tongue demanded and the stomach accepted and the blood danced to the drive of Power House, the promise of Love Nest, the delivery of Butterfinger, but most of all the sweet African murmuring of dark chocolate between the teeth, tinting the gums, flavoring the palate so you muttered, whispered, murmured pure Congo, Zambesi, Chad in your sleep.

And the more the voice talked, as the days passed and the weeks, and the old priest listened, the lighter became the burden on the other side of the grille. Father Malley knew, without looking, that the flesh enclosing that voice was raining and falling away. The tread was less heavy. The confessional did not cry out in such huge alarms when the body entered next door.

For even with the young voice there and the young man, the smell of chocolate was truly fading and almost gone.

And it was the loveliest summer the old priest had ever known.

Once, years before, when he was a very young priest, a thing had happened that was much like this, in its strange and special way.

A girl, no more than sixteen by her voice, had come to whisper each day from the time school let out to the time autumn school renewed.

For all of that long summer he had come as close as a priest might to an alert affection for that whisper and that dear voice. He had heard her through her July attraction, her August madness, and her September disillusion, and as she went away forever in October, in tears, he wanted to cry out: Oh, stay, stay! Marry me!

But I am the groom to the brides of Christ, another voice whispered.

And he had *not* run forth, that very young priest, into the traffics of the world.

Now, nearing sixty, the young soul within him sighed, stirred, recalled, compared that old and shopworn memory with this new, somehow funny yet withal sad encounter with a lost soul whose love was not summer madness for girls in dire swimsuits, but chocolate unwrapped in secret and devoured in stealth.

"Father," said the voice, late one afternoon. "It has been a fine summer."

"Strange you would say that," said the priest. "I have thought so myself."

"Father, I have something really awful to confess to you."

"I'm beyond shocking, I think."

"Father, I am not from your diocese."

"That's all right."

"And, Father, forgive me, but, I—"

"Go on."

"I'm not even Catholic."

"You're *what!*" cried the old man.

"I'm not even Catholic, Father. Isn't that awful?"

"Awful?"

"I mean, I'm sorry, truly I am. I'll join the church, if you want, Father, to make up."

"Join the church, you idiot?" shouted the old man. "It's too late for that! Do you know what you've done? Do you know the depths of depravity you've plumbed? You've taken my time, bent my ear, driven me wild, asked advice, needed a psychiatrist, argued religion, criticized the Pope, if I remember correctly, and I *do* remember, used up three months, eighty or ninety days, and now, now, *now* you want to join the church and 'make up'?"

"If you don't mind, Father."

"Mind! Mind!" yelled the priest, and lapsed into a ten-second apoplexy.

He almost tore the door wide to run around and seize the culprit out into the light. But then:

"It was not all for nothing, Father," said the voice from beyond the grille.

The priest grew quiet.

"For you see, Father, God bless you, you have helped me."

The priest grew very quiet.

"Yes, Father, oh bless you indeed, you have helped me so very much, and I am beholden," whispered the voice. "You haven't asked, but don't you guess? I have lost weight. You wouldn't believe the weight I have lost. Eighty, eighty-five, ninety pounds. Because of you, Father. I gave it up. I gave it up. Take a deep breath. Inhale."

The priest, against his wish, did so.

"What do you smell?"

"Nothing."

"Nothing, Father, nothing! It's gone. The smell of chocolate and the chocolate with it. Gone. Gone. I'm free."

The old priest sat, knowing not what to say, and a peculiar itching came about his eyelids.

"You have done Christ's work, Father, as you yourself must know. He walked through the world and helped. You walk through the world and help. When I was falling, you put out your hand, Father, and saved me."

Then a most peculiar thing happened.

Father Malley felt tears burst from his eyes. They brimmed over. They streaked along his cheeks. They gathered at his tight lips and he untightened them and the tears fell from his chin. He could not stop them. They came, O Lord, they came like a shower of spring rain after the seven lean years and the drought over and himself alone, dancing about, thankful, in the pour.

He heard sounds from the other booth and could not be sure but somehow felt that the other one was crying, too.

So here they sat, while the sinful world rushed by on streets, here in the sweet incense gloom, two men on opposite sides of some fragile board slattings, on a late afternoon at the end of summer, weeping.

And at last they grew very quiet indeed and the voice asked, anxiously, "Are you all right, Father?"

The priest replied at last, eyes shut, "Fine. Thanks."

"Anything I can do, Father?"

"You have already done it, my son."

"About . . . my joining the church. I meant it."

"No matter."

"But it does matter. I'll join. Even though I'm Jewish."

Father Malley snorted half a laugh. "Wha-what?"

"Jewish, Father, but an Irish Jew, if that helps."

"Oh, yes!" roared the old priest. "It helps, it helps!"

"What's so funny, Father?"

"I don't know but it is, it is, funny, funny!"

And here he burst into such paroxysms of laughter as made him cry and such floodings of tears as made him laugh again until all mingled in a grand outrush and uproar. The church slammed back echoes of cleansing laughter. In the midst of it all he knew that, telling all this to Bishop Kelley, his confessor, tomorrow he would be let off easy. A church is washed well and good and fine not only by the tears of sorrow but by the clean fresh-cut meadowbrooms of that self-forgiveness and other-forgiveness which God gave only to man and called it laughter.

It took a long while for their mutual shouts to subside, for now the young man had given up weeping and taken on hilarity, too, and the church rocked with the sounds of two men who one minute had done a sad thing and now did a happy one. The sniffle was gone. Joy banged the walls like wild birds flying to be free.

At last, the sounds weakened. The two men sat, wiping their faces, unseen to each other.

Then, as if the world knew there must be a shift of mood and scene, a wind blew in the church doors far away. Leaves drifted from trees and fell into the aisles. A smell of autumn filled the dusky air. Summer was truly over.

Father Malley looked beyond to that door and the wind and the leaves moving off and gone, and suddenly, as in spring, wanted to go with them. His blood demanded a way out, but there was no way.

"I'm leaving, Father."

The old priest sat up.

"For the time being, you mean."

"No, I'm going away, Father. This is my last time with you."

You can't do that! thought the priest, and almost said it.

But instead he said, as calmly as he could:

"Where are you off to, son?"

"Oh, around the world, Father. Many places. I was always afraid, before. I never went anywhere. But now, with my weight gone, I'm heading out. A new job and so many places to be."

"How long will you be gone, lad?"

"A year, five years, ten. Will you be here ten years from now, Father.

"God willing."

"Well, somewhere along the way I'll be in Rome and buy something small but have it blessed by the Pope and when I come back I'll bring it here and look you up."

"Will you do that?"

"I will. Do you forgive me, Father?"

"For what?"

"For everything."

"We have forgiven each other, dear boy, which is the finest thing that men can do."

There was the merest stir of feet from the other side.

"I'm going now, Father. Is it true that good-bye means God Be With You?"

"That's what it means."

"Well then, oh truly, good-bye, Father."

"And good-bye in all its original meaning to you, lad."

And the booth next to his elbow was suddenly empty.

And the young man gone.

Many years later, when Father Malley was a very old man indeed and full of sleep, a final thing happened to fill out his life. Late one afternoon, dozing in the confessional, listening to rain fall out beyond the church, he smelled a strange and familiar smell and opened his eyes.

Gently, from the other side of the grille, the faintest odor of chocolate seeped through.

The confessional creaked. On the other side, someone was trying to find words.

The old priest leaned forward, his heart beating quickly, wild with amazement and surprise. "Yes?" he urged.

"Thank you," said a whisper, at last.

"Beg pardon . . . ?"

"A long time ago," said the whisper. "You helped. Been long away. In town only for today. Saw the church. Thanks. That's all. Your gift is in the poor-box. Thanks."

Feet ran swiftly.

The priest, for the first time in his life, leaped from the confessional.

"Wait!"

But the man, unseen, was gone. Short or tall, fat or thin, there was no telling. The church was empty.

At the poor-box, in the dusk, he hesitated, then reached in. There he found a large eighty-nine-cent economy-size bar of chocolate.

*Someday, Father,* he heard a long-gone voice whisper, *I'll bring you a gift blessed by the Pope.*

This? *This?* The old priest turned the bar in his trembling hands. But why not? What could be more perfect?

He saw it all. At Castel Gandolfo on a summer noon with five thousand tourists jammed in a sweating pack below in the dust and the Pope high up on his balcony there waving out the rare blessings, suddenly among all the tumult, in all the sea of arms and hands, one lone brave hand held high . . .

And in that hand a silver-wrapped and glorious candy bar.

The old priest nodded, not surprised.

He locked the chocolate bar in a special drawer in his study and sometimes, behind the altar, years later, when the weather smothered the windows and despair leaked in the door hinges, he would fetch the chocolate out and take the smallest nibble.

It was not the Host, no, it was not the flesh of Christ. But it was a life. And the life was his. And on those occasions, not often but often enough, when he took a bite, it tasted (O thank you, God) it tasted incredibly sweet.

## ABOUT THE AUTHOR

RAY DOUGLAS BRADBURY was born in Waukegan, Illinois, in 1920. He graduated from a Los Angeles high school in 1938. His formal education ended there, but he furthered it by himself—at night in the library and by day at his typewriter. He sold newspapers on Los Angeles street corners from 1938 to 1942—a modest beginning for a man whose name would one day be synonymous with the best in science fiction! Ray Bradbury sold his first science fiction short story in 1941, and his early reputation is based on stories published in the budding science fiction magazines of that time. His work was chosen for best American short story collections in 1946, 1948 and 1952. His awards include: The O. Henry Memorial Award, The Benjamin Franklin Award in 1954 and The Aviation-Space Writer's Association Award for best space article in an American magazine in 1967. Mr. Bradbury has written for television, radio, the theater and film, and he has been published in every major American magazine. Editions of his novels and shorter fiction span several continents and languages, and he has gained worldwide acceptance for his work. His titles include: *The Martian Chronicles, Dandelion Wine, I Sing the Body Electric!, The Golden Apples of the Sun, A Medicine for Melancholy* and *The Illustrated Man.*